Saris and the City

Rekha Waheed

little
black
dress

First published in 2010
by LITTLE BLACK DRESS
An imprint of HEADLINE PUBLISHING GROUP

A LITTLE BLACK DRESS paperback

1

Cataloguing in Publication Data is available from the British Library

ISBN 978 0 7553 5613 3

Typeset in Transit511BT by Avon DataSet Ltd,
Bidford-on-Avon, Warwickshire

Printed and bound in Great Britain by
Clays Ltd, St Ives plc

Headline's policy is to use papers that are natural, renewable and
recyclable products and made from wood grown in sustainable forests.
The logging and manufacturing processes are expected to conform to the
environmental regulations of the country of origin.

HEADLINE PUBLISHING GROUP
An Hachette UK Company
338 Euston Road
London NW1 3BH

www.littleblackdressbooks.com
www.headline.co.uk
www.hachette.co.uk

Acknowledgements

First of all, I have to thank the Almighty for all that I have been blessed with.

For bringing this novel to life, I thank Nazim, Mum & Dad, and my dearest brothers and sisters.

My sincere gratitude extends to Laura Longrigg, Claire Baldwin and Charles Beckitt for their invaluable guidance. I would also like to thank the Arts Council for their support.

Danyal, Alayna, Suhailah – every day you light up my world. Shabab, Lamisha, Armaan, and Liyana, keep laughing!

Finally, I would like to dedicate this book to Nazim, for making me smile through tears; and for Adam, my most wonderful reminder that every eventuality is a blessing.

Lesson One:
If he's the bad boy and you're the good girl, you will get burnt

Somewhere amongst a world population of 6.7 billion people, smart single savvy women expect to find The One. Even if you discounted the vast majority of that population as ineligible, you would soon figure out that the odds were stacked against us women. And yet for some reason we refuse to settle for Mr Nice or Mr Dependable or Mr He Doesn't Make My Heart Race and My Knees Go Weak, because despite the odds, we are programmed to believe that nothing less than The One will do. We ignore the mathematics in the hope that one day Mr Right will turn up and become The One.

As implausible as this sounds, somehow I had defied the odds and found The One. And tonight . . . well, it was *the* night, the night I'd dreamt of, even craved for, since I understood the mathematics of actually finding The One. I had imagined the moment a hundred times over. That moment where, perfectly composed, I would raise my gaze to lock with his, and then curb a slow sexy smile just before my One asked me that question: *Will you marry me?* And then he would open up the small iconic mint green ring box before me, and I would freeze and catch my breath, because it was the Tiffany's Jean Schlumberger sixteen-stone ring. The sparkling diamond would mesmerise me and I would simply whisper: *Yes*.

You see, tonight was that night for me. I'm Yasmin Yusuf, and I'm a thirty-year-old Deshi girl, a Bengali babe with a career. For far too long I'd immersed myself in chasing a cosmopolitan City career instead of that one-carat diamond ring that pledged marital bliss. I'd learnt too late that happiness for me was not promised by politically navigated promotions, but was in fact found in the arms of The One. And tonight, my One was going to commit to me. I held out my ring-free left hand and stared down at it.

'Yes!' I whispered, smiling at the thought of wearing the Schlumberger.

'Good.' I jumped at the heavy document that fell on to my desk. 'Eight p.m.'

'What?'

'You said yes.' The deep, rich tone was patronising. 'You're the market analyst; do your job and get me the information before eight p.m.' I turned and found Zachary Khan walking away. I looked back at the thick document and stared at it. Then it dawned on me. Day end clashed with dinner: *the* dinner, *my* dinner. Grabbing the document, I raced after him.

'Wait, wait . . . does it have to be day end?' I called out, stopping sharp to avoid bumping into him. 'Would first thing tomorrow morning do?'

'I've got a conference call scheduled with our guys in New York tonight, so no, tomorrow morning won't do.'

I stared at the banker in front of me. Zach was disarmingly handsome and lethally driven, a combination that most women found intoxicating. It was inevitable that I couldn't maintain the intense stare.

'Anything else?'

I wanted to say yes but my brain refused to respond. As hard as I tried not to notice how handsome he was or how his hazel eyes pierced through me, I couldn't speak. He frowned at my silence and then turned to walk away. I hit my forehead in frustration and looked up at his disappearing form.

'I'm getting married,' I announced. My colleagues stilled around me and watched as Zach slowly turned around. I cringed at my desperate outburst and waited as the awkward silence continued around us.

'I take it you're not getting married tonight?' The question was crisp and yet underlined with contained humour.

'No, no I'm not,' I answered. 'I . . . I mean, I'm getting engaged. Tonight. At seven thirty.'

'Congratulations.' His salutation lacked any enthusiasm. 'Make sure you leave the findings with my PA on your way out.' And he walked away, leaving me stunned by his lack of consideration. My colleagues busied themselves to fill the humiliating silence. Phone calls were made. Keyboards were frantically tapped upon. Conversations were started without purpose. I raised an eyebrow and counted to ten before I followed Zach.

'Zach, I'm trying to manage your expectations—'

'Good, I want to be well briefed before my meeting,' he cut in.

'I don't think I'll have enough time to review—'

'Then make time.' I stopped at Zach's tone and looked at him directly. He was testing me, and my commitment to Abraham & Co., the private bank I had worked for for more than two years, as well as my commitment to my career. I looked down at the heavy document I had to review for his meeting and shook my head. I paused and chose my words carefully.

'I don't think you understand—'

'No, I don't think *you* understand how important this meeting is,' Zach stated. 'How many clients do I have, Yasmin?'

'Eleven.'

'What's the size of the portfolio I manage?' I looked at him and knew he was going to make me spell out why I would end up working late for him.

'Roughly six hundred and fifty million . . .'

'More like one point three billion, making each client worth about a hundred million. So when I ask for information on a new prospect, you understand how important it is for the firm to win?'

Zach stared at me and waited for an answer. I cleared my throat and looked away from him. There was no point in appealing to his human side. He was one of those people where no one could tell what his background was. His lifestyle was that of the high-flying, jet-setting and hard-partying. One fact everyone knew was that his sharp, sophisticated, ruthless style left many of the female executives at work burnt. Now, though, with my engagement dinner at risk, his pushiness served to evoke anger in me.

Yes, but unlike you, I have a life to build, I wanted to say. Instead I nodded reluctantly.

'Why don't you brief me about the prospect at seven?'

I held his hazel eyes as he forced me to make the decision to put his needs before my life.

'OK.' I accepted without any emotion. He smiled.

'Good, I'll see you at seven then.'

I frowned at his amused tone. It sounded like he was asking me out on a date. The light in his eyes told me he enjoyed provoking me.

'Fine,' I stated, refusing to break the contact.

'I look forward to it.' He actually looked like he was

stopping himself from grinning. I turned on my heel to walk away without another word. 'Make sure you're wearing the right lingerie.' I froze in disbelief, my cheeks burning at what he was implying. Slowly I looked back at him, mortified, and watched him cock a brow. He read my shock and grinned. 'For your dinner tonight. You know us guys don't care how late you run, as long as the lingerie makes it worth the wait.'

The penny dropped and I was lost for words.

'I need to . . . uh . . . I should get started . . .' I stopped, cleared my throat and patted the document. Unable to think of one single half-decent reply to put him in his place, I turned around to walk back to my desk. I felt his eyes piercing into my back and concentrated on not tripping on my ridiculously high heels. Each step took effort as my knees felt weak and for some stupid reason my heart was pounding away. I fell into my chair, placed the document on my desk and leaned forward to type. All the while, I daren't look back.

'You need a coffee.' Mia appeared at my side in an instant.

'Is he still standing there?' I whispered, unable to move. Mia was more than my work buddy; she was my confidante. We met on my first day at Abraham & Co., and as fellow analysts we hit it off from the get-go. Perfectly groomed, a model for the latest design trends and totally driven, Mia took no prisoners and afforded a level of honesty that was alien to most City girls. Trust me, every girl needs a Mia.

'He's long gone. You've been tangoed by Zach and you need a coffee,' Mia told me as she grabbed the pitch document and led me by my arm to the coffee break-out area. 'Did you have to announce your unconfirmed engagement to the entire office?'

'There isn't anything unconfirmed about it,' I

corrected as Mia collected two cappuccinos from the vending machine. 'Zach Khan's going to ruin my life.'

'First up, Miss Exaggeration, many girls here have said that. Only he did far worse than drop a pitch document with an impossible deadline on their desk,' Mia said as I sank on to a leather couch and took the coffee from her. 'Secondly, he got to you.'

'He did not.'

'Sure he did!' Mia sat down beside me and crossed her long lithe legs. She was a striking woman with long black curly hair, glowing caramel complexion and the most dangerously disarming smile. And right at this time, I couldn't avoid her interrogating dark brown eyes or her cheeky wide grin.

'He did not!'

'If you say so . . .'

'He's an arrogant, patronising, egotistical banker who uses his good looks to disarm women,' I threw back as Mia raised a brow and took a sip of coffee. 'He walks around here like he's a God-given gift to womankind. He also hides his background and pretends to be something he's not. You know how I hate that.'

'He's the fourth-largest fee-earner for the firm, Yasmin; he manages over a billion dollars in the Wealth Management Group, so it's a fact that he's going to have a God mentality,' Mia pointed out. 'And there's nothing wrong with admitting that you fancy him. He's drop-dead gorgeous. *I* fancy him and I have a man. Trust me, Yasmin, it's easier if you admit it.'

'I don't fancy him,' I stated. And then I looked at Mia. 'I can't fancy Zachary Khan, I'm getting engaged tonight.'

'I get it.' Mia laughed as she sat forward to look at me.

'What?' I leaned back from her. 'What do you get?'

'You feel guilty for fancying Zach.'

'He asked me if I had the right lingerie on. If he asked *you* that, he'd distract you.'

'He what?' Mia whispered in disbelief.

'Can I sue him for sexual harassment?' I asked as Mia waited for an explanation.

'He hit on you!'

'Sssshhhh!' I breathed out as Kevin, the office gossip, wandered into the break-out area.

'He hit on you!' Mia repeated, loud enough to make Kevin stop and stare at us. 'Zachary Khan asked you about your panties.'

'He did not ask about my panties,' I corrected, turning to smile at Kevin, who busied himself by the vending machine. 'Would you lower your voice!'

'Yasmin Yusuf, that man asked you about your panties and you're telling me to be quiet. Are you insane, girl?' Mia had grown up with a Jamaican father and a Filipino mother in the wrong part of Hackney. Every so often her roots shone through like a brilliant sun on a gloomy miserable winter day. Only sometimes, much like a brilliant sun, you often felt burnt by her energy.

'Mia, I'm so not his type. I'm the complete opposite to the haughty, stick-thin, moody types we always see him with.' Kevin stood by the fruit basket and inspected the range in a way that told you he had time to waste. 'Anyhow, why are we talking about Zach when I'm getting engaged tonight?'

'You mean you're not the slightest bit interested?'

I shook my head at her question. There was no hesitation in my heart or mind that Samuel was the only man for me. 'Zach may be handsome and disarming, but I already have the most wonderful man.'

'Yeah, he's a right Prince Charming,' Mia muttered, making no apologies for disliking Samuel.

'He's going to do right by me, Mia. He's going to do the honourable thing tonight.'

'So, you've told your family about him?'

I stared at my friend and she knew that I hadn't. With no more gossip to gain, Kevin chose an orange and headed back to his desk.

'We have to decide on the details before . . .' I stopped at Mia's smirk. 'Be happy for me, Mia.'

'Yasmin, you know—'

'Mia, thirty-plus Bengali girls like me don't get proposals from my community, those are given to girls ten years younger than me, and yet somehow I've managed to find someone who's right for me.'

'But *is* he right for you?' I looked away. 'Yasmin, I know you were up at the crack of dawn trying on a million different outfits, changing hairstyles, and he won't so much as notice it, let alone give you a compliment.'

'I should get started—'

'Yasmin, I don't mean to bring you down.' Mia grabbed my arm to stop me from leaving.

'So please don't,' I said as I sat back down on the couch. 'Tell me where I'm going to find an educated savvy Bengali guy who's as refined as Sam is?'

'Mr Right doesn't have to be Bengali . . .'

'For me he does. I know you don't get it, but it's important for me to build a life with a shared culture.' I put my hand over hers and she looked away, knowing what I was going to say. 'I love him, Mia.'

'You know he's a player . . .'

'. . . who's changing his ways. For starters, he stopped clubbing.'

'He's a bad boy and you're a good girl. You will get burnt.'

'He's changed, Mia, he's going to do the right thing tonight.' I shook her hand until she looked at me.

'You better text me later and tell me that he's proposed.'

'I promise,' I said with a wide smile. 'So tell me, do I look gorgeous enough to be proposed to?'

Mia laughed as I struck a pose. 'Gorgeous enough for Zachary Khan to hit on you.'

At the mention of his name, I froze. 'Oh my God, I got to get his prospect brief ready for seven p.m.'

'Tonight?' I nodded at Mia's question. 'Who's the prospect?'

I opened up the pitch document and read from the summary page.

'Arun Jayachand, youngest brother of the Indian Jayachand family. He has a personal fortune of eight hundred and ninety million made from distribution, precious jewels and retail.' Mia whistled at the opportunity. 'Zach wants personal information, investment trends, portfolio breakdown, who we're competing against . . . I'm never going to make my dinner. Never. I hate this job. I hate it.'

'No you don't. You love the adrenalin rush of doing the impossible, and this sounds impossible.'

'Exactly! How am I going to find information on a private Indian tycoon *and* make my dinner?' I moaned.

'Come on, Cinders, we'll get you to the ball.'

Slowly I looked across the thick folder at Mia and curbed a smile at her offer to help.

'You sure?'

She nodded with a reluctant grin. 'Don't get happy. I got two hours free and I'm billing them to this project . . .'

'Fine, but you got two hours, right?' I grabbed her hands to pull her to her feet. 'You are a godsend, Mia. Have I ever told you that?'

Mia walked over to the vending machine for another coffee and looked across at me.

'Does that mean I get to sit in on the debrief with the gorgeous Zach?'

'Let it go, Mia!' I returned, ignoring her cheeky laughter as I led her back to my desk.

Five hours and fifteen minutes later, I was waiting outside Zach Khan's office. Zach was late. I leaned back against his door, tapping my pen against my notepad whilst avoiding the watching eyes of Ingrid, his faithful PA. I looked at my mobile for the hundredth time hoping that there would be a text from Samuel telling me that he couldn't wait to see me. The inbox was empty; there were no new messages. I slipped my phone into my pocket and shook my head. Why don't men get that one text is important to a woman. Just one simple text, ten words, not even that, to make a woman feel beautiful inside. I released a deep sigh and looked at my watch.

'Is he on his way?' I asked, looking at the cold indifferent blonde.

'If I knew that I would've told you.' I dropped my smile and looked away from her condescending sneer. I paced before her desk just to annoy her whilst reciting the key findings in my head.

'You're new to working with Zach.' I nodded at her statement. 'He's always late. Always. There's a chair over there.' I stopped at the suggestion and looked over to the empty chair.

'I'm good, thanks,' I refused, curbing a smile at her unimpressed sigh. 'How come you're working late?' Ingrid's cold look told me she didn't want to engage in conversation. 'He's a hard taskmaster, right?' She continued staring at me without a word.

'I take it you're talking about me.' I spun around and spotted Zach. The PA raised an amused overplucked brow and I wanted to disappear. 'The meeting's been brought forward and you need to sit in.' I froze at his comment, holding the summary findings against me, unprepared to provide a formal briefing to the heavyweight partners in our New York office. I had enough to brief Zach, but certainly not enough to field questions to the dozen from the powerbrokers. I looked up with dread as Zach walked out of his office. 'I'm kidding. Come in.'

I breathed out in relief and followed him in. His office was plush, filled with state-of-the-art technology and wide flat screens mounted on to every wall to track his investments.

'Grab a seat.' I walked up to his desk as he shrugged off his jacket and took off his tie. He was broad, lithe and perfectly formed. 'Yasmin.' I looked up at him and met his eyes. 'Do we have any chance of stealing Arun Jayachand from Schwarz Investments?'

'We do,' I replied. He seemed surprised by my confidence. I smiled and handed him my findings. He didn't look at the document but stared at me.

'We do, huh?' he muttered, forcing himself to look down at the document. 'What makes you so sure?'

'First of all, you would never have looked at Arun Jayachand if you didn't believe you could win him for this firm.' He raised a brow at my cocky answer. 'More importantly, Schwarz Investments have made serious bad investment calls over the last two years which resulted in Arun Jayachand's portfolio growth trailing behind his brothers'.'

'And you know this because?'

'Because it's my job to talk to the our finance guys, and the finance guys tell me that Arun Jayachand's accountant has been talking to Black Rock, Henderson's and Masser Klein.'

Zach looked impressed. He worked through my findings, debating key points until we verged on arguing.

I had his undivided attention, and that told me that I was arming him with what he needed.

'His Baby O for Oshanti retail arm is really struggling . . .'

'His daughter, Rania Jayachand, has school-girl aspirations of inheriting it as a designer trophy,' Zach cut in dismissively. I paused at his impatience and waited until he acquiesced to allowing me to make my point.

I went on, 'We have a private equity opportunity there. If we can't win the wealth management option, we could take a stake in Oshanti through our sister company Namhar Capital. It's a two hundred and fifty million pound lingerie boutique, losing huge market share year on year due to operational inefficiencies. This is a turnaround team's dream job.'

'You think you could help turn it around?' His amused tone caught my attention.

'You think I can't because I'm just some analyst who crunches through information all day?'

His grin dropped. 'I didn't say that . . .'

'Knowledge is power, Zach. We arm you with the power to broker and win deals!' I told him with half a smile.

'But turnaround jobs are different.'

'Turnaround jobs are textbook. You buy an ailing company at cost price, fix the leaks, sell off the property assets, dispose of the weakest links and build up the label as a luxury brand that you sell in thirty-six months at a premium. Why would you think I couldn't be on the turnaround team?'

'My mistake.' The glimmer in his eyes told me that he had been testing me. I held his eyes, read his humour and smiled reluctantly before looking down at my document.

'Yasmin . . .'

'One sec. If you refer to page ten, you'll find a portfolio breakdown for the Jayachand family and Oshanti's performance.'

'Yasmin, it's ten to eight and you have a dinner to attend.' I froze at Zach's comment and closed my eyes. 'Ingrid's got a cab waiting for you outside.'

'Thanks, but I'm meeting Sam downstairs.' I had planned the briefing to last fifteen minutes; it had overrun by half an hour. I gathered my notes together and pulled out my mobile. There were two messages from Sam, both asking me where I was. I stopped and looked at Zach. 'Do I need to finish up?'

'Go.' He indicated towards the door.

'Thanks,' I threw behind me as I rushed to leave, calling Sam at the same time. 'Hey you, I'm sorry I'm late—'

'Yasmin.' I stopped at Zach's call and turned around to look at him. 'You're a good analyst.' I smiled at his appreciation.

'Who are you with?' My smile dropped at Sam's demand. I waved at Zach before striding back to my desk. 'Where've you been?'

'I'm sorry, my meeting dragged on. I'm on my way down . . .'

'I'm freezing my butt off out here, so don't take hours dolling yourself up, OK?'

I stopped at his attitude and stared at the phone.

'I've had a long day, so do not tell me you're going to ruin our special dinner by being crabby . . .'

'I'm freezing, gorgeous, and you know I hate having to hang around.'

He called me gorgeous, so instantly I melted and felt bad for keeping him waiting in the cold.

'I'll be down in two minutes, OK?'

'Tell me what you're wearing.' I smiled slowly at his suggestive question. 'It'll help me spot you.' My smile disappeared at the thought that he still needed help to recognise me.

'I'll see you downstairs,' I told him before ending the call.

Shaking my head, I put my documents away and shut down my computer. I decided I would keep him waiting so that there was no way of missing me. I walked through the nearly empty office, passing by those with imminent deadlines or clients to please. Inside the ladies', I stood beneath the harsh light and stared at myself. I saw a woman with her hair pulled back into a bun and dressed in a fitted black suit, a pink tailored shirt and high heels. I looked tired, old and unprepared for the evening with Sam. Closing my eyes, I tried to shrug off Mia's words and the feeling that no matter what I did, however good I tried to make myself look, it would go totally unnoticed by Sam. I paused and whispered a quick prayer. I had to believe that he would do right by me tonight. He had to.

Once I had composed myself, I slipped out of my fitted shirt and pulled on a blood-red polo neck that moulded to every curve. I released the bun and brushed my ironed-straight hair into a shiny mane, reapplied barely there make-up that illuminated my tanned skin and lined my wide brown eyes. The slim, lithe woman staring back would now turn heads. Feeling my confidence return, I folded my clothes away in the lockers that work provided and pulled on my long fitted winter coat. As I headed for the lifts, I held out my hand and stared down at my ringless fingers. I couldn't help but smile. Tonight was going to be my night.

I walked amidst the towering financial buildings and huge Christmas trees that lit up Broadgate Circus in the bitterly cold London evening. Pulling my pashmina around me to keep the cold out, I stopped at the heart of the circus and looked at the ice rink intended for City executives who barely noticed it as they rushed home. I came to a stop outside the Barclays building and watched a half-hearted game of ice hockey being played by overeager City types. I couldn't spot Sam, so I called him.

'I'm standing outside Barclays and looking down at the match,' I told him.

'I'm looking at you,' he replied. I searched for him and frowned when I couldn't see him. 'I'm standing behind you.'

My heart skipped a beat as I pocketed my phone. I closed my eyes as his voice alone warmed up every cell within me. Turning around, I found him walking towards me. Sam always dressed immaculately. He was striking beyond the average Bengali man.

'Hey you.' I smiled at the sight of him and felt exhilarated just looking at him. 'You look good,' I added as he came to stand before me. He was smoking.

'You took your time.' I carried on smiling, even though he failed to return the compliment.

'I'm worth the wait,' I said.

'Really?' Sam asked with a grin. I punched him playfully on his arm. 'It sounds like you had one busy day.' I nodded and we started walking.

'You remember that private banker I told you about, the one that we couldn't figure out whether or not he was Asian?' Sam nodded. 'Well, he dropped a new bid on my desk just after lunch and said he needed the findings for a meeting this evening. He's vicious about his career, he works all the hours God sends and he expects everyone else to do the same.'

'Doesn't he have a life?' Sam mocked. I remembered how grateful Zach was for my assistance and felt bad.

'Actually, I admire his commitment. It takes a lot of

discipline to be the fourth-highest fee-earner in the firm.'

'Sounds like you more than admire him . . .'

'No! He's a total sell-out, but he did show me something new about discipline and focus today.'

'Talking about something new, what do you think of this?' I froze as he reached towards his pocket. He was going to propose, he was going to bring out my ring and I wasn't ready for it.

'You're going to do it now?' I grabbed his wrist and caught his confused expression.

'Yeah, why, don't you want to see it?' Sam asked, as I contemplated the choice between being proposed to in the middle of Broadgate Circus or over a candlelit dinner. 'Yasmin, what's wrong with seeing it now?' He didn't want to wait. He wanted to propose there and then.

'Nothing,' I answered with a deep breath and a wide expectant smile. Only Sam didn't go down on one knee. He reached into his pocket and pulled out his new iPhone. I looked down at the slick black phone that he held out to me. I took it and stared up at him, confused. There was no iconic mint-green ring box. There was no Tiffany's ring. 'This is the surprise you told me about?'

Sam nodded at my question. 'I texted you first with this phone. Isn't it great?' he asked with pride. 'I wanted you to see it as soon as I picked it up.'

I buried my disappointment deep down inside of me. Maybe this wasn't the surprise; maybe he was trying to put me off the scent.

'It's really nice. Are you going to show me how to use it?' I asked, frowning when he took it back from me with a nervous laugh.

'You can play with it over dinner. Let's get going.'

We walked side by side. I forced myself not to

dwell on whether or not he had another surprise for me.

'Where are we going?' I asked, remaining upbeat.

'Sri Triam. You been there?'

I shook my head as he led us past Liverpool Street station.

'Thai?' I asked, watching him drag on his cigarette before nodding.

'It's your favourite, right?' He'd remembered! I stopped myself from looking touched. 'I chose it because it's close by.'

'Great reason for choosing a restaurant!' I threw back, and heard him chuckle.

'It's well recommended!' he returned as I raised a brow. 'Hey, I only go to the best places . . .'

'Good, because I'm only used to the best.'

He laughed, waiting for the traffic to clear before leading me across the road. I spotted the restaurant at the junction and smiled at Sam as he held open the door for me.

'Good evening, sir, do you have a reservation?' asked a Thai maître d' as Sam pulled off his scarf and shrugged out of his coat.

'I have a reservation for two booked under Sam Gulam.' I folded up my pashmina and began unbuttoning my coat. 'We're late but I called ahead to ensure you kept our table.'

'That's right, sir, we have,' the petite lady confirmed with a little bow. 'Please, we'll take your coats and bags.' An attendant appeared to take our belongings and issued Sam with a token for collection. 'When you're ready, please head downstairs where we have your table waiting for you.'

I looked around the restaurant, impressed by the tasteful, understated, soothing ambience of the Orient.

Sam led the way down the circular marble stairway.

'Good evening. Would you like to have a drink at our bar before dinner?' asked a male waiter as we entered the dimly lit dining area.

'Sure, what'll you have?'

I froze at Sam's question. He knew I avoided bars and alcohol.

'I'll have an orange juice.' The waiter looked to Sam and Sam looked at me. 'With ice.'

Sam seemed embarrassed by my order and led me into the bar area. 'We'll have an OJ and a sparkling water,' he ordered as he pushed between two City types.

I felt awkward in the bar, out of place with all the cosmopolitan types holding Bloody Marys and Tia Marias. I caught Sam looking at a sexy Indian executive until she looked back at him. I was forgotten and felt invisible. Guys don't get it that when they take the shortest of double looks at another woman, they cheat. I peeked over at Sam and caught another glance exchanged between the two. I smarted at the disrespect and turned away, clutching my bag, unsure of what to do. I realised that the waiter had caught my discomfort.

'Ma'am, let me show you to your table and sir can join you there,' he suggested, indicating towards our reserved table.

I smiled in appreciation and followed the waiter to the table. He held out my chair and unfolded a napkin as I took my seat. I leaned back to allow him to place it on my lap and took the heavy leather-bound menu he handed to me.

'Two minutes in and you already got men tending to your needs?' Sam had arrived with our drinks.

'Sir, you have a beautiful lady. It's a pleasure to tend to her.'

I smiled at the compliment and looked to Sam with a raised brow.

'It's a dangerous precedent to set!' he countered with a wide grin.

'But a pleasure none the less,' the waiter replied as he bowed before departing.

'Gorgeous, keep an eye on my phone whilst I use the gents'.'

I nodded at Sam's request and looked at his iPhone that he left in the middle of the table. Taking a deep breath, I stared at the slim phone, resenting it for not being my Schlumberger sixteen-stone engagement ring. I took a sip of my drink and reached out for it. There was no password lock so I flicked through the applications and stared at his messaging service. I stole a quick glance up to ensure that he wasn't on his way back before selecting it. It wasn't that I was checking up on him; I was just . . . curious. Curiosity turned into intrigue when there was a message from someone signing themself 'H'.

Last night was incredible. Let's do it again and again and again . . . H xx

I could hear the slow, methodical beat of my heart and forced myself to keep breathing. I didn't want it to make sense. No matter how much I tried, the beat of my heart told me that I knew. Every woman knows when she's not The One. A moment of truth arrives which she can no longer ignore. This was my moment of truth.

'You playing with my phone, gorgeous?'

I pressed the menu button at Sam's arrival and randomly selected an application to go into.

'It's good, huh?'

I smiled as he sat down opposite me. He took the phone from me, eager to demonstrate various applications. I saw his excitement, saw his lips move but failed to hear a single word he spoke. I wanted to step back five minutes, where I would control my curiosity and choose not to pick up his iPhone. The text reverberated in my mind and my vision blurred before me. I closed my eyes and breathed deeply. Sam was cheating on me, and the saddest thing was that I didn't have to look deep within myself to know that that was the truth.

'You OK?'

I opened my eyes and looked at him. 'It's just another slick phone, right?'

His smile faltered at my indifference. Sam was a junior accountant with the ego of an executive ten years his senior. He didn't take to indifferent responses well.

'Shall we order?' I picked up the thick menu and held it before me so that I didn't have to look at him.

'What's the rush, and why are you hiding?' The irony of his question left me speechless as he pushed down the menu to look at me. I stared at his chiselled face, the heart-melting brown doe eyes and the charismatic white grin that had broken too many women's hearts.

'I'm not hiding, I'm just starving. Honestly, I could murder every item on the menu.' Ten minutes ago I would never have attested to the size of my appetite for fear of his opinion. Now it didn't matter what he thought about me.

'You OK, gorgeous? You seem . . .' I watched Sam wait for me to conveniently finish his sentence. 'Distracted?' he thought up when I remained silent.

'I'm good,' I stated with a quick smile. I avoided his searching eyes and looked back down at the menu, steeling myself to see dinner through and leave without any dramas.

'I thought you'd like it here.' I looked up at him and saw him grin slowly. Sam had had me from the moment I met him. 'So tell me, what do you fancy?' He asked that every time we went for a meal. And each and every time

I'd stupidly tell him that I fancied him. It was time for a change. I searched through the parchment pages for the most expensive item on the menu and stopped when I found it. Lobster. I curbed a smile at the three-digit price tag and looked up at his expectant face.

'Lobster.' His own smile faltered. 'I've never had lobster before. I'd like to try it tonight.'

Sam looked down at the menu and searched out the item. When he froze, I knew that he had spotted its price tag.

'OK . . . uh, wow . . .' he muttered with a nervous laugh. 'That sounds like some meal.'

I looked back down at the menu. I hadn't quite finished; in fact I had only just started.

'And I've got to have a green curry with jasmine rice along with a tom yum. As for the starters . . . how about king prawns, spring rolls, vegetable dim sum and some steamed scallops?' I bit my lip as Sam flipped between the pages to keep up with me.

'They all sound good. Which one do you want to go for?' he asked, giving up on searching out the items. I paused and slowly looked up at him.

'All of them,' I told him as if he was slow. His smile faltered again and he frowned.

'All of them?'

'Yes. All of them,' I repeated.

'Are you going to have any room for the lobster?'

'Sam, you make me laugh!' I teased as I looked back down at the menu. 'What are you having?'

'I'm happy to share . . .'

I wrinkled my nose in disapproval at his suggestion. 'I've a better idea. Why don't you choose yourself a main dish?'

Sam balked at my suggestion until he realised I was serious. I watched him peruse the menu as the text circulated in my mind. He had spent the night with another woman doing the dirty over and over again. I wondered who she was, if she was Bengali, how many times it had happened, how long it had been going on for. Her message was on his shiny new phone, unlike my simple *Hey handsome, I can't wait to see you tonight*. I had sent that first thing this morning when I still believed that we would be engaged by the end of the evening. I smirked at my naivety.

'Yasmin, you're in a really odd mood tonight. Are you OK?'

I looked down at the table to find that he had covered my hand with his. My heart was breaking and there was nothing I could do to stop it. I shook my head at the adoration I had once rained upon him.

'Have you decided?' I asked, moving my hand away from his. He caught the gesture and put the menu down.

'What's going on?'

'Are you ready to order?' The waiter arrived with a pot of green tea.

'Yes, we are!' I answered, smiling at the man for his perfect timing. I reeled out the list of items that I had chosen before Sam could speak. 'Oh, and can I also get a Virgin Pina Colada,' I finished, feeling very cosmopolitan for ordering something other than an OJ.

'Ma'am, can I say that the lobster is a fine choice,' the waiter said as he collected the menu from me.

'But he hasn't told you what he's having,' I pointed out, ignoring the waiter's surprise. 'What would you like, Sam?' I met his doe eyes and waited.

'I'll have a jungle curry,' he said, handing the menu back without breaking eye contact.

Barely an hour ago, a passing look from Sam would have left me breathless. Now he was just another tall, dark and handsome man with a killer smile.

'Let's play ten questions,' I said.

'What?' He looked confused, so I smiled.

'Ten questions,' I repeated as I poured him a cup of green tea. 'It's how we get to really, really know each other.' I poured myself a cup and waited for a response.

'I like it when you pour me tea.' His warm words hurt me. 'Not many girls know what it means to give first—'

'So, how about it?' I cut in, taking a sip of tea before looking at him over the rim. 'To be fair, you should go first. What would you like to know about me?'

'I want to know what's up with you today,' he said.

'OK, well I had a long, stressful day at work, I'm tired and I'm really hungry,' I answered clinically. 'My turn. What's your favourite colour?'

'What?' Sam sat back and shook his head. He wasn't in control and it left him at odds.

'I don't know what your favourite colour is,' I explained as the first of our starters arrived.

'It's emerald green. You happy now?'

I helped myself to the sizzling king prawns and then looked at Sam, waiting for his next question.

'What's *your* favourite colour?' he asked.

'Black. Are you going to repeat each of my questions?' I asked as several waiters arrived one after the other with the remainder of our starters.

'That's question two for you.' His quick reply made me smile. 'And the answer's no.'

'Next question,' I prompted.

'What do you love about me?'

I bit my bottom lip to stop myself from laughing at his question.

'I don't love you.' He looked startled by my admission. 'I'll only love my husband. Anyone who can't step up to that responsibility doesn't deserve my love.'

'You don't love me?' he asked with disbelief.

'Depends on whether or not you're going to be my husband.'

'I'm talking about now. This instant.'

I kept him waiting as I piled my plate with servings of dim sum and spring rolls.

'You're breaking the rules of the game, Sam. Ten questions is meant to illicit quick answers given instinctively without pressure or elaboration.' I bit into a dim sum and closed my eyes at the gentle fusion of spices. 'This is divine; taste it.' I breathed out as I held out my fork to him. He opened his mouth and closed his eyes ready to be fed. I dropped the dim sum on his plate.

'What's your favourite meal?' I continued, stealing a glance at him to find him peeking down at the half-bitten dim sum sitting in the middle of his plate.

'Rice and curry,' he muttered, unimpressed with me leaving him there with his eyes closed and his mouth open. 'What's yours?'

'Chicken jaalfrezi and rice. When we get married, we have got to have a custom-fitted kitchen. I love cooking so I need to have a good kitchen.' He froze at my presumption but I continued. 'What's your kitchen like now? Actually, when are we going to get married?'

Sam put his cutlery down and stared at me. He grinned, shook his head and then leaned forward.

'Is this why you started this game?'

'Excuse me?'

'You want to know if we've got a future . . .'

'What do you mean, "if"?' I demanded. He looked caught out.

'Listen, if you want to talk about us, you don't have to play games.'

'I don't want to talk about "us". I want to know you better. Sometimes I feel like I don't really know what makes you tick.' There was no doubt that my controlled answers had left him unnerved.

'I know you well,' he told me with a heart-melting smile. 'I'm a good judge of character.'

'Given that I've told you what I'm like, you'd have to be thick not to know my character.' The unimpressed reply made him frown. 'Are you going to answer question three or question four?'

'Neither. I don't want to play the game,' he said. I raised a brow and caught his eye.

'Spoilsport.' I lowered my gaze. His attitude didn't surprise me.

'You're going to go all moody and quiet on me?' Sam joked as he reached out to hold my wrist. 'Don't be mad, gorgeous,' he added, caressing the inside of my wrist.

'Would you pass me a couple more spring rolls?' I asked, ignoring his attempt at intimacy. Instead of releasing my wrist, he used his free hand to pierce a spring roll with a fork. I looked at the appetiser he held out for me, smiled widely and tried to pull my hand free. But he released my wrist in a move to interlock our fingers.

'I've received a proposal,' I lied. Sam drew away his hand.

'What are you going to do?' His flippant question told me that he didn't feel enough for me to tell me to turn down the marriage proposal.

'What else am I going to do?' I said. He grinned at my answer and shook his head.

'Don't be hasty. Maybe you should consider it?' I froze, stupefied by his arrogance. 'I mean, we have so many hurdles ahead of us . . .'

'I am considering it.' I beckoned the waiter to take away the starters to give Sam time to understand my position. 'I'm sorry, did you want to have any more of the starters, Sam?' He shook his head.

'You're considering it?'

I nodded and stopped the waiter from taking the plate of dim sum. Sam's ego had been dented and it actually felt good.

'Who is he?'

'Our families are just talking . . .'

'Your families are talking?' I looked at Sam and read his disapproval.

'Yup, they're talking. Can we get another plate of these?' I asked the waiter just as Sam grabbed my hand and forced me to look at him.

'You want to give me the heads up on what's going on?'

'Sam, I can't keep stalling my family whilst you try and bring your dad around to accepting me. I don't even know what your dad's issue is . . .'

'Let's not go there.'

'Why?'

'You know why.'

'Actually, what *is* your father's issue with me? I come from a well-respected, loving family. I'm accomplished, financially independent and attractive . . .'

'Your age . . .'

'Well, here's a news flash, Sam – I'm not going to get any younger,' I mocked.

'I'm not stupid, Yasmin . . .'

'I don't have time for this nonsense,' I laughed, realising just how feeble his excuses sounded.

'Nonsense?' My heart raced at his terse question. I'd never pushed him like this before.

'Yes, nonsense. My age is a fact: you either get your dad to accept it or you don't.'

'I'm the oldest son, Yasmin. This would be the first

wedding in our family. I want my dad to be happy for me, not critical.'

'Seriously, let's drop it.' I stared at him until he accepted my decision.

'Ma'am, shall we bring the main courses through with the lobster?' We both looked at the waiter, who somehow managed to appear at the perfect time.

'Yes, thank you,' I answered as Sam leaned back in his chair. 'And can I make my selection from the dessert menu so that it's served straight after our mains?' The waiter nodded and disappeared to find a menu.

'So, where did this *rishta* come from?'

I took the leather-bound menu from the waiter. 'Our fathers have mutual friends. You want the details?' I asked, looking up from the menu to watch Sam nod. 'He's a surgeon from Finchley, thirty-four, comes from a small family, has his own pad . . .'

'Have you met him? Spoken to him?' He looked like he was getting angry.

'No.' I held his eyes. 'But we're having brunch on Sunday.'

'I see,' he muttered as he brought out his cigarette pack and tapped it on the table.

'You can't light up inside.' I pointed out, but he carried on tapping away.

'When did this all happen?' he asked. I realised that it was easy to make someone feel replaceable when you stopped caring.

'It needn't happen at all if you give me a reason to stop it.'

Sam narrowed his eyes and looked at me closely before breaking out in a laugh.

'You should see him.' He was calling my bluff and I held his look.

'OK,' I accepted with a smile. In that instant I knew

that I hadn't lost Sam because he was never mine to lose. I looked down at the dessert menu. 'I'll have the ice cream with lychees in syrup.'

'I'm going to have a smoke,' Sam stated, backing his chair up before heading for the exit.

I watched him stride out and noticed that he had taken his phone with him. I held my head in my hands and closed my eyes. My head buzzed with loss, anger, fear, shame and a million other emotions that left me silent. Tears blurred my vision and I gritted my teeth, refusing to break.

'Ma'am.' I shot upright and looked at the waiter, who stood holding a large silver platter with the largest lobster I had ever seen. 'Are you ready?' He noticed my tear-filled eyes. 'I promise you, the lobster is worth crying for!' I laughed at his kindness and sniffed back my tears.

'Thank you.' I breathed out as he rearranged the table to ensure that there was space for all the mains. The table was jam-packed with sizzling, aromatic Thai food. Green curry, jungle curry, jasmine rice, sticky rice, and the huge platter of lobster that sat ready to be tucked into. I took a deep breath and cleared my thoughts. 'It looks delicious.'

'These will help you crack through the claws.' I had no idea how to use the pincers, but I nodded as he placed them by the platter before leaving.

Sam was nowhere to be seen, so I reached over and spooned green curry on to my plate with some rice. I refused to think. I refused to feel. I couldn't allow myself to look beyond the dinner as it would bring me to my knees.

'The lobster looks good,' Sam stated as he arrived back at the table.

'The green curry's great,' I added, ignoring the underlying tension between us.

'This is a first,' he said, picking up the pincers. Sam

looked at the lobster, gripped a claw between the pincers and clamped down until the claw cracked open.

'Now that's how it's done.' He laughed with achievement before scooping out the meat to place on my plate. The gesture was kind and the warm look he gave me left me short of breath. I nodded and looked down at my plate. The hollowness inside of me deepened and I picked up my fork and toyed with the meat. In an instant I had lost all my energy and appetite and I struggled to stay composed. 'Tuck in, it's delicious.'

'I'm really not hungry . . .'

'You have this glorious lobster in front of you and you tell me you're not even tempted to taste it?' I smiled at Sam's jokey comment and allowed him to ladle sauce on to my plate.

'I really can't.' I actually didn't want to. Not because I couldn't but because I didn't want to share any more new experiences with him.

'One mouthful?'

'I think I'm going to throw up,' I lied before pushing back my chair to walk swiftly towards the ladies'.

I closed the door behind me and stood in the warm, dark reception room that held the cubicles. I walked over to the mirror and stared at myself. A pretty lady with wide, thickly lashed brown eyes stared back. I had undermined her for so long that I didn't recognise myself. I held a white towel beneath the tap and then wrung it dry so that I could hold it against my neck. I felt dizzy, nauseous and weak all at once. I wasn't interested in the lobster or the dessert; I wanted to get away from Sam. I put the towel down and looked at myself in the mirror, knowing what I had to do. Finger-combing my hair back into place, I took a deep breath, composed myself and then headed back to the table.

'Hey, you OK?'

I shook my head at Sam's question and sat down before him. 'I'd like to leave.'

'What?' I watched Sam look at all the food in front of him.

'I'd like to leave . . .'

'But the lobster's just arrived,' he pointed out as he served himself another portion.

'Why don't you have it packed up as takeaway?' I suggested. Sam looked like he had been slapped.

'Yasmin, this is two hundred and fifty pounds' worth of lobster. It can't just be packaged up as takeaway.'

'You're right, I'm sorry,' I offered, looking duly regretful. 'I'm being selfish. I've just had a really stressful day and I need to get home. Why don't you finish up here?'

'What, on my own?' I nodded at his question before picking up my bag. 'You're serious?'

'Sam, I'm shattered,' I emphasised as he placed his cutlery down to stare at me. 'You carry on, I can make my way back to the station.'

He was annoyed. Very annoyed. But that only served to reinforce my resolve to end the farce otherwise known as my engagement dinner.

'Fine, let's call it a night,' Sam muttered as he leaned back on his chair.

'Do you want to have this packed up as takeaway?' I beckoned the waiter.

'Forget it,' Sam threw back, and I asked for the bill to be brought to us.

'Why don't you settle up, and I'll grab our coats upstairs?' I said. Sam was used to splitting the bill with me, and the realisation that he was picking up a £400 bill was plastered over his face. I wished I could have taken a picture of him but instead I stood up and walked away. I thanked the waiter and made my way upstairs, where

I asked the attendants for our coats. Then I texted Mia to tell her I was about to dump Sam.

'You ready?'

I hit the send button and spun around to find Sam shrugging on his coat. I nodded and he held the door open for me.

'Thanks for dinner,' I said as we made the short walk back to Liverpool Street station.

Sam didn't reply. He was still smarting from the pain of paying for an expensive uneaten meal.

'You want me to take you home?' he asked, and I smiled at his superficial kindness.

'No, thank you.' He didn't offer again. Sam and I lived at opposite ends of London. He had only ever driven me home once. On every other occasion I had insisted that he didn't put himself out for me. And he didn't. I realised that we, independent women, made life harder for ourselves. In our bid to prove our independence, we allowed men to abrogate their responsibilities all too easily.

'You'll be OK on the Central line?'

I nodded at his question and looked at my Baume & Mercier. 'It's not late. I'll be home by eleven.' I covered my watch and felt my phone vibrate with a message. I knew it would be from Mia. 'It's a weekday. It'll be pretty safe.'

We made small talk until we entered Liverpool Street station and stood before the entrance to the underground.

'Call me when you get home?' he asked. I smiled at him and he drew me close to him. I stepped forward and felt his hands slide over my lower back. I leaned up to cup his face.

'It's over,' I whispered, stopping him from leaning in closer. The words didn't register with him. His intent clouded the reality I was creating. 'It's over,' I repeated.

'What?'

My words sank in slowly, as I caressed his cheeks and smiled.

'I'm ending this,' I told him as he pulled back without releasing my hips. He didn't believe me so he leaned forward again. Once again I stopped him. 'I'm done with this.'

'Yasmin . . .'

'Check your phone.' He looked totally mystified. 'You'll understand when you check your phone . . .'

'Did you text me to tell me that you've chosen the surgeon when I was settling the bill?' I placed my hands on his. 'Have you dumped me by text?'

'Just check your texts and you'll understand,' I repeated as I pulled his hands away.

He stared at me with disbelief and I stared at him for the last time. I wanted him to be The One. I wanted him to make me The One. Make this the night. But it wasn't. I wasn't. I stepped back and turned around. I waited for him to stop me as I took the first few steps hesitantly. But he didn't. I quickened my pace. I took the stairs down to the turnstiles. I could feel his eyes piercing into my back, daring me to continue walking. So I did, I took each step faster and faster until I found myself running down the escalators and racing to catch the tube. Jumping in between the closing doors, I leaned back against them and gasped for breath as I realised what I had done. I laughed, exhilarated by the thought that I had left him dumped and stupefied. I had ended it. It was my decision and I felt liberated. Only the feeling didn't last long.

Slowly my laughter died and tears stung my eyes at the realisation that I was alone. It was an age-old truth that bad boys turned good girls into the bad girls that even good, geeky, nerdy boys avoided. I had saved myself that indignity, but was now unable to decide whether losing Sam was worse than the realisation that I had long ago lost good judgement. Somehow I had absolved myself of the responsibility for choosing badly, because I had held on to the thinnest shred of hope that he would change. That he would indeed wake up to realise that I was The One. In the meantime, I had jumped through so many hoops, put on so many faces, hid so many disappointments, that I had long lost sense of myself. At some point, every woman knows when she is not The One. I knew long before tonight, and yet I had failed to act. I had failed to say that that wasn't good enough for me. Maybe this was my turning point. Maybe this was the beginning of the end of being Miss Compromise, Miss Accommodate, Miss Pretend to be Anything but the Real Me. Whichever the case, I was hurting, and as much as I wanted to blame Sam, the undeniable truth was that I was hurting because I had failed myself.

Lesson Two:
A woman knows when her man
doesn't love her

There is no feeling like the feeling of your heart breaking. All night I had stared up at my ceiling, unchanged. My phone flashed umpteen times with calls from Sam. Left unanswered, he opted to text to tell me that I had misunderstood the message. My instincts told me he was lying, and ironically, my instincts were the only thing that I trusted at that point. At the crack of dawn, I grabbed my coat and bag and headed for the office. It was 6.30 a.m. and I walked into work ringless and single. Everything had changed but I carried on as if nothing had changed. Feeling like I was stuck in some slow silent vacuum, I stared at the screen before me, read the introduction about Oshanti. I read it over again and again, until it felt like I had read the same excerpt a hundred times or more. Yet I absorbed nothing, felt nothing.

'So, you figured out that you screwed up last night?' Zach's question behind me was too controlled, too quiet. I looked at the time. It was 7.30 and I didn't know where the last hour had gone. 'I'll see you in my office in ten minutes.' I heard him stride away.

I watched the seconds tick by and counted the minutes until ten had passed. Then I gathered my notebook and headed to Zach's office. Ingrid hadn't arrived, so I knocked on his door and entered.

'You're on notice.' It took a moment for Zach's statement to sink in. I looked at him confused. 'You've been put on notice.' I stood by the door and felt my heart stop.

'Pardon?'

'You forgot to tell me that Arun Jayachand is under investigation for fraud.' I jumped at the bellow and leaned back against the mahogany door.

'I didn't run a—'

'A fucking KYC check, a basic, routine Know Your Client check.' He hung his jacket on a suit hanger and leaned back on the edge of his desk. 'I looked like a fucking idiot in front of the managing partner. So, get back to your desk and pack your shit up, because you're done here.'

I closed my eyes and smiled.

'You think this is a joke?'

I opened my eyes and looked at Zach. 'No, Zach, I know this isn't a joke.' He paused at my tone. 'I know this isn't a joke, because no matter how hard I try, it counts for nothing. Everything I do counts for nothing.' I was trying to keep composed, but my breaking voice caught his attention.

'Be glad you got engaged yesterday. You can go home and start planning your wedding.'

A short laugh started deep within me and I bit my lip. Only I couldn't stem the laughter bubbling up inside.

'What's funny?' The terse question amused me further and I burst out laughing. 'Yasmin?' I looked at him but I couldn't stop. 'Yasmin, trust me, you do not want to be laughing right now.'

At that threat, I doubled over, shaking with pent-up

laughter. I held my side and raised a hand, asking him for some patience.

'You're holding up the wrong hand, Yasmin, your ring's on the other one.' At his comment, I looked at my ringless hand and my laughter died.

'There is no ring,' I whispered as I straightened up. 'I'm not engaged.' Zach's silence made the reality harder to bear. I looked at him through tear-filled eyes. He looked like he had misheard me and glanced to my hand again. A tear spilled over and slipped down my cheek. I brushed it away and smiled. 'I caught him cheating on me . . .' I couldn't finish. Zach looked down, as if to temper his reaction and give me time to compose myself. 'I know that's no excuse . . .'

'Yasmin, go home.'

I shook my head and bit my lip to stop myself from crying. 'I need to work,' I said, looking down. Nothing made sense beyond that one undeniable fact. Confused and lost, I looked at Zach. The anger in his eyes had been replaced by patient concern. 'Why . . . why would he do that to me?'

Zach raked a hand through his hair before gripping the back of his neck and letting out a long sigh.

'Go home, take the week off,' he advised quietly.

'It wasn't meant to . . . I didn't expect him to . . .' I stopped, losing the ability to rationalise.

'Yasmin, go home . . .'

'Please, let me put it right,' I implored, feeling I was losing everything that was precious to me. 'I know I screwed up, but I can put it right. I promise I can put it right, just give me the chance . . .'

Zach stood up to walk towards me. 'You're in no state to be at work.'

I grabbed his hand to stop him from opening the door behind me.

'Please, please don't . . .' I couldn't finish the sentence. I had lost Sam. I had lost him and everything that I had dreamt of building with him. Zach let go of the doorknob and took my hand. I gripped it tightly and leaned against him.

'Yasmin, let me arrange for you to be taken home.'

I shook my head and closed my eyes. 'He cheated on me,' I whispered as tears seeped down my cheeks. Zach slipped his arms around me and I felt sobs well within me. 'Please don't take my job from me. Please, I . . . I won't have anything, I won't be able . . .' I heard deep, heartfelt, soul-breaking crying. And slowly I realised that it came from me, that I was crying.

Zach held me silently, until I stopped and stood exhausted in his arms. I didn't want to move. It felt safe and secure in his arms.

'I can't stop the HR process. I instigated it last night.'

'No, you *can* change the decision.'

'Yasmin.' I paused at his firm tone. 'We've a small stake in Oshanti. The turnaround will get messy so they'll need more hands on deck. I'll see what I can do to get you in to Namhar Capital,' he offered. I nodded but I couldn't stop the flow of tears again. 'You better do right by me, Yasmin Yusuf.'

Zach's reluctant help made me cry even harder. He pulled me back into his arms and I held on to him as if he was the only thing I had left in the world. We have a saying that teaches you not to hate your enemy, as one day he may be your only saviour. I was now the living proof of that. I had written Zach off, judged him unfairly, and now he was the only thing I had.

I closed the door to Zach's office behind me and headed back to my desk. Ingrid had arrived, looked over her computer and arched an overplucked brow at my appearance. Ignoring her, I started what felt like a long walk back to my desk where a large brown box sat containing all my personal items. Early-start colleagues paused in surprise at my appearance and then looked towards my desk.

'We'll courier all personal items to you.' I heard a stern voice and looked towards it. A burly security guard stood waiting to escort me off the premises.

'My family pictures are in—'

'Like I said, we'll courier anything that's of personal importance to you.' I stared at the bulldog of a man, and when he showed no emotion I stared back at the box.

'There's a cab waiting for you downstairs.' I turned at horrible Ingrid's comment and saw her holding out the mobile phone that I had left in Zach's room. She looked unimpressed at the sight of my empty desk. Without a word I took the phone from her and watched her stride away. There were several more texts from Sam. I pulled on my coat and headed for the glass lifts with security following close behind. Once the steel doors slid open, I used my pass to walk through the corporate turnstiles and head for the wide reception area. I waited for an expressionless, perfectly groomed receptionist to afford me her time.

'How can I help you?' The crisp cold tone matched how I felt.

I stared at her, dropped my pass on the marble desk and walked out through the large rotating glass doors.

Corporate executives raced around me to get in on time but I stood still. I stood still and took a deep breath of air. I watched bankers, brokers, executives and administrators rush around like driver ants, busy getting somewhere to do someone else's bidding, to meet another short deadline until the bell rang to mark the end of another working day. There was a look to City folk, they looked sharp, polished, wealthy. Jermyn Street's sharpest suits, Links' finest cuffs and Tiffany's stunning jewellery were boldly modelled to prove the old adage that to act the part you had to look the part. The crisp icy winter air felt good. It felt fresh and I needed it. I needed it to feel.

I started walking. I cut through Broadgate Circus, passed the executive car waiting for me at London Wall and then headed down Old Broad Street. Tall steel towers and tough granite-faced buildings surrounded me. I didn't know where I was going, but I knew that I needed to walk through the cold, impersonal financial heart of London to find some solace. My mobile buzzed to life as I passed the Royal Exchange at Bank and I looked at the screen to scroll through Sam's continuous stream of texts.

Let me explain, don't freeze me out. Give me a chance to put it right.

Why aren't you answering your phone? Are you at work? Meet me for lunch, let me explain.

I need to see you, you don't have to say anything . . . please, just let me see you.

I felt the cold trail of tears on my cheeks as I hit the delete button over and over again. I went to pocket my phone and caught Sam's picture on the screen. He had a heart-stopping smile, a brilliant white stunning smile. I shook my head as if to erase the memory and continued walking, but it was too late. I remembered. I recalled. I recollected every moment I had with Sam. The first time we met, the first exchange we had, the first moment we shared. And it was too much. Tears welled up and spilled over. I dashed them away, wrapped my arms around myself and walked faster. Another text arrived and I again stopped to stare at it.

I'm outside your building. Come down and see me, if only to show me that you're OK.

Laughter spilled out at the thought of Sam waiting in the cold outside my firm. I covered my mouth with my hand as another laugh spilled over. Only the laughter turned into a heart-wrenching sob. It hurt. It hurt too much. I didn't want to cry, so I quickened my pace, slipped around pedestrians and passing traffic until I was sprinting down Queen Street. My coat billowed around me, my hair caught the wind and I raced into full stride towards Southwark Bridge. I laughed out loud. Nothing mattered but the feeling of running free. In that moment my breath raced away and my heart pounded because I wanted to escape from myself. Just when I felt I had fled my own misery, my heel caught on a cracked pavement and sent me crashing to the ground. I winced as I knocked my head against the hard pavement. My belongings spilled out of my bag and clattered around me. Long silent moments passed. My head throbbed with the collision and I blinked to focus on London's passing traffic.

'Are you OK?' I closed my eyes against the concerned query. A tear slipped down my face and hit the ground. Humiliation disappeared as the coarse, cold pavement matched the numbness inside me.

'Is she OK?' another passer-by asked as I felt a firm grip on my elbow.

'Can you move? Let me help you up.'

I reached behind me to push his hand away and slowly levered myself up off the ground. For a moment I just sat and held my head until the dizziness passed, before moving on to my hands and knees to gather my belongings. One by one I stuffed them back into my bag and then stared down at the broken heel caught between the pavement cracks.

'Do you understand English? Can you speak a little?'

I pushed my hair back from my face and looked up at the mature gentleman. He was a weathered City man, suave, gracious, who had stepped out of the law firm behind me.

'I've broken my heel. They were really expensive . . .'

'They can be replaced.' He smiled and then pointed to my forehead. 'You're bleeding.'

I reached up and winced as I felt the grazed skin. I looked down at the red tips of my fingers whilst he reached into his blazer to pull out a handkerchief.

'I should take you to the hospital,' he offered.

'No . . . no thank you, I'm fine.' I held his neat hankie against my head and wrenched my heel free to put it into my bag.

'You're not having a good day, are you?'

I shook my head and looked at him. 'I've lost my job and my man, scarred myself, and now, to top it all off, I've snapped the heel off a pair of Jimmy Choos, so yes, I am having a horrible day.'

'You forgot to mention that you also lost your dignity when you crashed gracelessly to the ground,' he added. I stared at his unhelpful comment, and then we both burst out laughing.

'Yes, I forgot, my dignity!' I repeated as he helped me up and steadied me.

'You know, you haven't lost anything that can't be found again.' His comment made me well up.

'I'll be fine now. Thank you. For stopping, for your hankie, for picking me up . . .'

'Not at all.' I stopped and met the warm blue eyes. 'You're going to be OK.' I closed my own eyes and nodded at him. 'I can get my driver to give you a lift home.' I shook my head and used his hankie to wipe away my tears.

'No thank you, my mother told me never to accept rides from strangers.' He laughed warmly at my reply and then patted me on my arm.

'She sounds like a very wise woman.'

I nodded as more tears spilled over my lashes.

'She was, she was a very good, wise, loving woman.' I sniffed back my tears.

'Then you'll know that you'll be fine.' His kind words made me smile tearfully. 'Now, allow me to call you a cab.'

I shook my head.

'I'm going to walk, thank you,' I whispered.

He understood, and without another word he smiled before returning to the law firm. I watched him disappear behind the glass entrance. Holding my bag beside me and the hankie against my forehead, I limped in one heel to Southwark Bridge. People stared at me, but the important thing was that I was going to be OK. Halfway across the bridge, my phone rang. And it continued ringing until I rummaged it out of my bag and stared down at it. It was Mia. There was also another text from Sam.

You left me standing there like an idiot. You're acting like a spoilt diva, so after you've calmed down, call me.

Tears dripped off my lashes to join the river below. I was tired, my head was pounding and I hurt. I let the phone slide through my fingers and down into the murky Thames below. I stared over the edge of the bridge and watched it disappear from sight. There was no going back. I turned away, hailed a black cab and told the driver to take me to Shepherd's Bush. A woman knows when her man doesn't love her. I knew that Sam didn't love me, not instinctively. It was time to go home.

Lesson Three:
If you've loved and lost, make a
clean break by losing the memories,
trinkets and token gestures

The house was empty when I let myself in. I dropped everything in the hallway and took the stairs to my bedroom to change into a Gap sweatshirt and track pants. My cure for everything in life was cooking. I cooked in good times, bad times and for every other occasion known to man. Birthdays, anniversaries, weddings, family dinners and girls' nights in: whatever the occasion, I cooked. My speciality, however, was desserts, which I cooked only when I needed to cheer myself up. Blueberry tarts, chocolate molten cakes, shortcake, cranberry scones and hot apple pie served with vanilla ice cream would appear in a flurry of non-stop activity, and things never felt so bad afterwards.

I headed down to the kitchen, where I hoisted myself up on to the black granite worktop in our black and walnut-finish Möben kitchen. This was undoubtedly the heart of our home. I pulled out my mum's recipe manual and leafed through the pages until I stopped at her favourite dessert recipe. She loved baking Abba's favourite, chocolate butter cake topped with berries and cream. I read her recipe, skimming over the ingredients and instructions, and then paused at the void she had left. I smiled sadly at the memory of baking with her. She would wrap the train of her sari around her waist to tuck in at her hip before she brought out the ingredients. She would catch me watching, give me her widest smile, a cheeky wink and then dab flour on my nose before she started. She was a devoted mum: her laughter warmed our home and her spirit challenged us to be better than we were. And yet she had a gentleness that left us cocooned in love. Mum had passed away over ten years ago, but in that moment, I missed her more than I could ever remember.

Slowly I opened my eyes and slipped off the worktop to begin cooking. In volume. I pulled out all the ingredients and tools. Flour, butter, baking powder, baking soda, sugar, eggs, milk, vanilla extract, dark chocolate, cream, berries of every shade of red lined the worktop. Bowls, spatulas, spoons, whisks, trays, shape cutters joined them. And then without a further thought, I began. I preheated the oven, melted the dark bitter chocolate and stirred it with the cocoa powder until it gleamed temptingly. I creamed the butter with a whisk, slowly added sugar until it fluffed up and then added eggs one at a time until the mixture was ready for the vanilla extract and chocolate. In a separate bowl I mixed the flour, baking powder, soda and salt and then moistened it with enough milk so that both mixtures could be gently brought together. The smooth batter looked too scrummy to resist, and I dipped a finger in, scooped out a dollop and then with a naughty smile licked it off my finger. I let the taste roll over my tongue and paused when the flavour seemed lacking. Turning around, I walked over to the double-door stainless-steel fridge and pulled out a bottle of lemonade. I added one tablespoon into the mixture and then tested it to ensure it was perfect. I split the batter between two baking pans, stuck toothpicks in the middle of both and popped them into the stainless-steel built-in oven.

'You're home!' I turned at the sound of my dad's voice. Instantly he noticed the mess on the worktop and looked to me. 'Is everything OK, Yaya?' The quiet concern of my father was enough to bring tears to my eyes.

'I've been reassigned to a new team so I've got a couple weeks off whilst the firm sorts my paperwork out,' I explained as I busied myself with cleaning up the counter.

'You're making your mother's chocolate cake,' Abba noticed, and I paused with a smile.

'It's *your* favourite cake,' I corrected as he took off his white cap and folded it to put away in his pocket. 'Are you hungry, Daddy?' He nodded at my question, washed his hands and perched himself on a stool by the island. I heated up a pan of lamb bhouna and quickly fried up ready-made parathas.

'You not joining me?' Abba asked when I set the meal before him and gave him a glass of water.

'I'm not hungry . . .'

'. . . because something has upset you,' he stated before tucking into his lunch. I looked at my father and knew that he would fail to understand how I had allowed myself to be misled for so long. I was the youngest and the only girl in the family. With three elder brothers, I was and had always been the most protected. If Daddy knew about Sam and what he had done, he'd get my three brothers with their typical Bengali rhyming names, Jamal, Zamal and Kamal, to march down to Sam's home to give him a good beating. I shook my head at the thought and started making the frosting for the cake.

'I may be a man, Yaya, but I'm also your father. It'd be good for you to talk to me.'

'It's women's stuff, Daddy; trust me, this isn't the kind of stuff daughters talk to their fathers about,' I lied, avoiding his eyes as I melted the chocolate above a saucepan of simmering water. Once it began cooling, I added milk, sugar and vanilla extract and whisked it slowly. I added knobs of soft butter and then a little more before ramping up the speed to enable the frosting to come together.

'You know your cousin Maya's getting married?'

I paused at the announcement and felt the dagger of fresh and unwanted singledom pierce through my heart. Taking a deep breath, I poured double cream into a fresh bowl and whisked it until it stiffened.

'To the American doctor she proposed to?' I asked. My father chuckled and nodded. 'That's great, when's the wedding going to take place?'

'You know that she's younger than you?'

My smile disappeared at Daddy's comment so I turned away to get him another portion of lamb bhouna. Though he was oblivious to my current pain, my father couldn't have chosen a worse moment to talk about arranging an introduction.

'Maya's mother and your Chachijhi Fauzia have suggested a young man . . .'

'Daddy . . .'

'No, Yasmin! I've listened to your protests enough. Now you must let me try to do the right thing for you . . .'

'But Daddy—'

'No, Yaya, I don't want to hear another word from you,' he said as he finished his lunch. 'You have always had your way, being the only girl; the boys and I have spoiled you, but now enough is enough. Marriage is our way and you must accept this.' He gulped down his water before washing his hands.

I didn't have the energy to fight him. In fact, I realised that I didn't want to fight him; maybe there was a reason why our traditions had stood the test of time. Maybe this was how the heart could be protected from breaking.

'OK,' I whispered.

'I'm setting the date for the introduction and you will accept to see this boy . . .'

'OK, Daddy, I'll see the boy.'

'Now, I'm going back to work. If you wait up for me, we can talk more about this and you will see that I have a point and maybe you will understand why I must do this.'

'Daddy, I said yes,' I told him calmly and then watched him stop. He looked stunned. 'It's fine, Daddy. If it makes you happy, I'll see the boy.' He didn't know how to react so he searched his pocket and pulled out his white toupee that he wore as a cap.

'That's good, Yaya, your mother would be happy with you.' He didn't look at me again. The thought that I had come to accept a proposal finally marked the beginning of the end of our father-daughter relationship. He walked out without another word.

Tears blurred my vision as I cleaned up after him. My parents had been devoted to each other until Mum passed away. And unlike most Bengali fathers, Daddy had broken with convention and refused to marry again to give his children a mother figure. Single-handedly he had raised us, and for the past five years, after the last of my brothers had moved out, it had been just the two of us. I shook my head and spotted the inhaler he had left behind, grabbed it and raced out behind him.

'Daddy.' I found him turning on to Uxbridge Road. 'Your inhaler,' I said, holding it out to him. He took it, smiled and patted my cheek.

'You're going to be OK, aren't you, Yasmin?' he asked, watching me closely.

'Yes, Daddy, I'm going to be fine,' I answered.

'You promise?'

I held the warm aged dark brown eyes and smiled. 'I promise.' He nodded at my words. 'Go or you'll miss your bus to Bayswater,' I advised and watched him continue his journey. I waited, knowing he would turn around to check on me, and waved when he did.

I returned home to my cake and stared at it through the oven window. Tears threatened to roll down my cheeks and I promised myself everything was going to be OK. Opening the door, I pressed the top of the cake gently to see it spring back. Reassured it was perfectly baked, I placed it on a wire rack to cool and then walked through to our study to stare at our computer. Contact with Sam and my emails were only a few clicks away. I sat before the monitor and looked at the blank screen. I placed my fingers on the keys and fought the urge to check my email account. He had said that the text was a mistake, that it was some schoolboy prank, and I wanted to believe him. I so badly wanted to believe him, but more than anything I wanted to protect myself. So my fingers refused to move.

When ten minutes had passed and my fingers remained still, I knew the last thing I needed was to be back in touch with Sam. I returned to the kitchen. Gently I placed one of the cakes on a serving dish before covering it with generous amounts of frosting. Once a smooth clean layer covered the cake, I placed the second tier on top and again began applying the frosting. I then took the bowl of whisked cream and with a hot ice-cream scoop gently placed dollops on top of the cake and topped it off with handfuls of berries. I stared at the finished cake and still felt restless. I popped the serving platter into the fridge and returned to my mum's recipe manual. Once again I rifled through the pages until I stopped at Mum's cupcake recipes. I tapped my fingers on the counter, and then with half a smile I started baking again.

'Scrubbed face, no make-up, and wearing sweatpants that are too small for you – yes, Daddy's right, there is something wrong,' Rita, my eldest sister-in-law, stated when I opened the front door. The Yusuf brides arrived late afternoon to find out what was wrong. I should have guessed that Daddy would call my oldest brother, who would then text the entire family to come and spend the evening with me.

'Daddy called Jamal *bhai* and he's sent you two round to cheer me up?' Both nodded at my question and I stepped back to allow them in. Of course the only thing I needed was peace and quiet, but that's not something my family understood. If there was ever a problem in the family, the unspoken rule ruled: food and company would solve everything.

'If you're on a diet, do NOT walk into the kitchen,' Rita shouted out when she entered. 'Yasmin's baked for the Third World.' I leaned back on the wall and looked at Zeena, the wife of my second brother, Zamal.

'I'm not feeling up to a girls' night in,' I whispered as she came to stand beside me.

Zeena smiled with understanding. She was close to me in age and cultural expectations. She had married Zamal last year and spent the year juggling her job as a corporate accountant and the traditional responsibilities of a new Bengali bride.

'Tell her you want to eat something and she'll spend the evening cooking instead of trying to find out what's wrong.'

I looked at Zeena and smiled sadly.

'Rita *bhabi*,' I called out, heading towards the kitchen.

'What, sweetie?' Rita was my outgoing, funny but above all opinionated sister-in-law. She had married Jamal, my oldest brother, and avoided having children by spending the past seven years managing his GP practice. 'On a baking scale of one to ten, you're at fifteen. Your brother's not going to stop eating if he sees all this.' She pointed to the array of cakes and confectionery covering the worktops.

'Maya's getting married, and with all the family she's going to have around, I thought she could do with some home-made desserts.'

'Yeah, yeah, tell it to someone who doesn't know you better,' Rita threw back as she picked up a lemon zest cupcake. 'You want to talk about it?' I shook my head, smiling at her candidness. She had met Jamal soon after my mother had passed away and became his rock; in fact she thought nothing of being there for all of us. 'What can I do?' I smiled at her question and watched her raise a brow.

'I could murder a very very spicy chicken jaalfrezi tonight—'

'Grab the ingredients, I'll start chopping,' Rita threw out before I could finish. I caught the wink she gave me and started pulling the ingredients together.

By nightfall, my friends Mia, Gemma and Bibi had arrived in tandem with my brothers. I felt like the day would never end, as their arrival only served to emphasise how badly I needed some space. So whilst the house buzzed with conversation and laughter, I busied myself in the kitchen, cleaning and washing. Every surface was wiped down, every piece of glass sparkled and every item was put back into place. The floor had been mopped, the trays and equipment put away and the cakes packed into tins, and yet I ached for more to do.

'You want to talk?' Bibi asked as she walked into the kitchen to perch on a stool.

'Not really,' I said as Gemma and Mia followed, closing the door behind them. I paused to look at my good friends. Whilst I'd met Mia at work and connected with her in an instant, Gemma, Bibi and I went back to university days and had shared the best and worst of what life had thrown at us. But I felt different. This was different; this I wanted to deal with alone.

'He was an asshole, Yasmin.' Mia put the kettle on and pulled out several mugs to make coffee. 'I'm sorry you're hurting, but I'm not sorry he's gone.'

'He was a total jerk; you deserved better,' Gemma added. 'You were chasing him too fast . . .'

'. . . and no man wants to be chased,' Bibi pointed out. 'Look at how they constantly fiddle with their bits; they want to free them. Being free is in their genetic make-up.' Her logic always left us silent and we stared at her for an explanation. 'What? I may wear the headscarf but that doesn't make me blind!'

'Holy lord, someone help this girl!' Mia muttered before looking to me. 'He would've ruined you, Yasmin, and thrown you away like a used tissue.'

'You know his type, you can't change his type,' Bibi stated as Gemma shook her head to stop her from speaking. 'He told you about the one love of his life, the rich girl who he fought for. Why do you think her dad wouldn't let her marry him? I'll tell you why, because the daddy saw what he was . . .'

'He's scum,' Gemma filled in.

'He's an idiot,' Mia added.

'He's a fool,' Bibi finished.

I stared at each of them and shook my head. Each insult against Sam still hurt, and it was raw enough to make me want to defend him.

'Say something,' Mia said quietly as she handed out coffees to Gemma and Bibi.

'What do you want me to say?' I asked with a smile.

'You look like death walking and you've baked for Britain; undoubtedly that fool has something to do with it, but you haven't anything to say?' I nodded at Gemma's question and watched her arch a brow.

'Say anything. Speak, scream, rant, rave, cry . . . just *please* talk,' Mia pleaded.

I stared at my friends and wrapped my arms around my waist.

'He cheated on me . . .'

'What?'

'He didn't?'

'He did,' Mia concluded when I nodded in silence. I waited until they went through the stages of denial, shock and then saddened disbelief before they looked at me for more detail.

'I saw a text from the woman he's sleeping with saying how great he had been in bed.'

'No . . .'

'You didn't . . .'

'You did,' Mia finished. 'And that's when you texted me last night.'

I nodded. 'I told him that we were finished and that's it.'

They looked to each other, confused by my comment. Then they turned back to me.

'That's it?' Bibi repeated as if she didn't understand English. 'What's it?'

'Didn't you crack his dinner plate over his head?' Gemma demanded.

'Why?'

Bibi's eyes were ready to pop out of their sockets at my question. Once again they looked at each other, equally concerned and confused by my logic, before turning back to face me.

'Because he cheated and lied and played you . . .'

'So, who's the fool?' I asked with half a smile.

'You are so not going to blame yourself for that idiot's behaviour.'

'He's a scumbag playboy wannabe who needs a good kicking.'

'But who's the fool?' I asked again, quietly.

'Oh no, no, no, no!' Mia asserted as she placed her hands on her hips. 'Yasmin . . .' I looked directly at Mia to stop her.

'I fell for him, and I expected him to change his ways for me. I wanted to believe that so bad, I refused to see that he had no intention of changing.'

'Yasmin . . .' Mia tried again. 'He *cheated* on you, he lied to you and led you on.'

'But I could've seen it coming had I listened. Why didn't I listen to you guys?' I asked.

'Because you fell in love. You fell for him so fast and so deep that you couldn't have seen this coming,' Bibi answered quietly. I closed my eyes to stop myself from welling up. 'This isn't your fault, Yasmin, this isn't on you.'

'Now I have to fall out of love with him,' I whispered as I frowned at the feat I had to accomplish.

'Has he been in touch?'

The question made me laugh. 'He's tried,' I giggled as the girls watched with concern.

'And . . . ?' Gemma asked frowning when I curbed a laugh.

'He kept texting me until I dropped my phone into the Thames, and I got fired so I don't know if he emailed—'

'You got fired?' Mia repeated in shock.

'Who got fired?' Zamal asked as he let himself into the

kitchen. He was a handsome, well-groomed man who attracted attention wherever he went. As expected, everyone froze at my second oldest brother's arrival and looked to me to answer his question.

'I've been deployed to another team,' I corrected as Zamal walked over to the counter.

'Is that why you're upset?'

'I'm not upset, *bhaya*, I've just had a bad day.'

'Is that why she's upset?' he asked the girls, who looked at me for approval. When I smiled, they nodded in unison. He turned back to me and pierced me with his deep green eyes. He was a corporate finance lawyer, with an instinct for spotting inconsistencies, and he had watched over me long enough to know that I was lying. 'What happened?'

'I made a stupid mistake, a mistake that cost my director a big client. He's decided to deploy me to another team to save me from getting fired.' I wanted to confide in Zamal, I wanted him to make everything OK, like he did when we were younger. But, that closeness had been replaced by overzealous protectiveness ever since Mum had passed away.

'You sure?'

I was seconds away from tearing up, so I looked at Mia and nodded. I didn't know what would be worse: losing Zamal's respect for being dumped by a secret boyfriend or hearing how Sam ended up in intensive care following a surprise visit by my brothers. As tempting as the latter sounded, I couldn't bear disappointing them by owning up to such a stupid error of judgement.

'I've lost her from my team. I can't believe she's not sitting around the corner from me! You're moving to a different building, aren't you?' I nodded at Mia's instant but over-perky explanation.

'We're coming back on Saturday for the Man U

match,' Zamal stated, not believing a word Mia said. 'You around to join us boys?' I nodded. 'We're all heading out now. You going to be OK until Dad gets back in?' I walked around the island and reached up to hug my brother, appreciating the space he was getting the family to give me. He held me warmly and then spun me around like he had since I was a child. I laughed until he put me back down on my feet and looked down at me. 'Mia, take care of my baby sister until Dad gets home,' he ordered, causing her to nod instantly. We walked to the hall, where Jamal, Kamal and my *bhabis* were waiting.

'You and I need to talk,' Kamal said as he held me and stared at me. I avoided his eyes and knew he had noticed. Kamal was the youngest of my brothers, a big burly man who was the most protective of the three. 'I'm back on Saturday, and whatever mess you're in, I'm going to sort it out, OK?' He pulled on my arm until I looked back at him and nodded. 'Patience is a blessing, Yasmin. Everything works out in time.' Kamal was the most religious of us, and his words comforted me in a way that made me want to hug him for ever. He pulled away, and I nodded and showed everyone out.

When I closed the door, I rested my head against the cold glass panel.

'It's not wrong to cry.' I heard Mia's quiet voice behind me and cleared my throat. I walked past her to enter the kitchen and found Bibi taking off her headscarf in the absence of men, whilst body-conscious gym addict Gemma smiled guiltily as she helped herself to another slice of raspberry cheesecake.

'You guys want to watch a movie?' Both stopped at my question and looked at each other. 'Movie with ice cream and an endless supply of cake?'

'So you're just going to pretend that nothing happened?' I turned to find Mia at the door, arms folded.

'You're just going to bottle it up and act like it's all good?'

'Mia . . .'

'I don't buy it. I don't buy it that less than twenty-four hours ago you were hoping to get a Tiffany's engagement ring, and now you're a cheated-on, played-up thirty-year-old with no future and you're fine with it. I don't buy it.'

'What's not to buy, Mia?' I asked as I watched her walk in and stand before me. 'I fell for a man who played me. Do you want me to crumple into some broken-hearted heroine who can't function because the man she loved didn't love her back? Would that make you feel better?'

'Yes, yes, it would.'

'But I don't want to break down. I don't want to fall apart . . . I don't want to psychoanalyse everything we spoke about and dreamed of. I don't want to remember everything that was done, the small gestures, the token gifts. Do you want to know why?' I demanded of Mia, angry for making me feel, for making my pain real and acute and breathtakingly raw. She shook her head slowly. 'Because I know, I wasn't enough for him. I know I wasn't the one for him, because if I was, he would've been faithful, he would've been a better man for me.'

'Yasmin . . .'

'I'm not that girl I once was or the woman he turned me into. I'm . . . I'm a nothing.'

Suddenly all the anger left me and I was bereft of any energy. Shaking my head, I turned around and went to the living room. The girls followed, holding cakes, muffins and mugs of coffee.

'You dumping him may wake him up . . .' Bibi trailed off, knowing how ludicrous she sounded.

'You think?' I asked with half a smile. They sat on the floor in a circle around me and I joined them, resting my head on my knees as I hugged them to my chest.

'Yasmin, I don't want you to bottle it up inside, that's all,' Mia said as she sidled up next to me.

'I need you guys to figure out how I can fall out of love with him. Will you do that?' When they all nodded at my question, I did the one thing I'd promised myself I wouldn't do: I cried. I relived every moment with Sam. How we met and where, what we did, the promises that were made, the future that we planned. Through it all, my girls provided me with a never-ending supply of tissues, nodded when needed and gasped in disgust at the right times, until I sat in silence before them.

'Let's send him some unexpected gifts,' Bibi suggested. We all looked at her like she was crazy, but she smiled at us knowingly. Switching on her iPhone, she logged on to the internet and surfed for takeaway. I gave her Sam's home address and she laughed. 'OK, there's twelve restaurants that do home delivery in his area. Let's split these up, tell them we'll pay in cash and make sure the little shit eats well tonight . . .'

'Yes, yes, yes!' Gemma laughed as she brought her phone out. Mia whooped in agreement, and I stared in silent wonder as my girls one after the other ordered Sam an assortment of Indian, Chinese, Italian and Persian takeout until he was left with another bill amounting to several hundred pounds. We fell about laughing at the small gesture until the laughter died and we were left with the undeniable fact that he had played the ultimate joke on me. Quietly the others shared stories of their heartache and broken dreams, illustrating how resilient the heart and soul were in the midst of despair.

One by one they departed and I sat alone at home. I caught sight of our framed family photo, where my mother smiled down at me, eyes sparkling, full of life. We had taken that at the height of her illness, yet no one could spot the pain she was in when that picture was taken. I felt humbled by her strength and closed my eyes. The voice I wanted to hear was the one that I wrenched out from deep down within me, the one that shouted out that Sam had made the biggest mistake of his life. That he had lost the one decent, honest, good thing in his life, and that in fact I deserved better. I had doubted my very essence around him, and that voice now told me I was and would be a better person without him. So I cleaned up all that the girls and my family had left behind, then grabbed two bin liners from the kitchen cupboard and raced up the stairs up to my room.

Closing the door behind me, I switched my CD player on full volume and walked over to my cupboard. Beyoncé belted out 'Ring the Alarm' and I stared at all that hung before me. In an instant, I began pulling out every item of clothing that I had worn with Sam. I threw them into a neat pile on the floor in the middle of my room. I took off my sweats that I had worn when we went roller-blading in the park. In my underwear, I walked over to my desk and pulled out my treasure box. It was packed with the sparkling trinkets and keepsakes that Sam had given me. I shifted through the ticket stubs and receipts for the places we had visited, plays we had watched and movies we had seen. I pushed aside cheap pieces of jewellery he had given me, which back then had made my world. I rolled my eyes at my own stupidity and walked over to the pile to upend the contents of the box. Every item cascaded down on to the pile and I returned to my dresser to pull out my diary. I shifted through all the pages of documented emotions, desires and dreams, and ripped out every page that made the briefest reference to him or us. Those pages too joined the pile.

Then I sat down and stared at myself in the mirror. I failed to recognise the woman who stared back. Shaking my head, I rummaged through my drawers until I found a pair of scissors. Pulling my hair back into a ponytail, I hacked off the length until it swung freely and unevenly against my shoulders. Turning away, I began clearing the clutter into the bin liners. I crouched down to gather the small items and stopped when I spotted the diamond earrings Sam had bought me. I picked up the delicate stud drop diamonds and stared at them, smiling slowly in spite of what I felt. He had presented them to me for my thirtieth birthday at the London Eye as the pod crept over the city sunset. He couldn't have timed it better or made me feel any more precious. In that moment, he'd become my world. Closing my eyes, I clenched the earrings until the image disappeared. Without another thought, I threw them into the bin bag, then took the bin liners downstairs to the hallway before racing back up to my room. The act of madness had left me cleansed and breathless with exhilaration. There was nothing left of him or us and I felt all the stronger for it. I had made a clean break and I knew without any doubt that there was power to the saying: throw out the old to make room for the new. I stared at myself in the mirror and smiled. I felt lighter, almost unburdened and younger.

Barely a day had passed since my world had been turned upside down, but it was enough time for me to realise it would become a better place for the change. I took my toiletries into the bathroom, turned on the shower and stepped in beneath the pouring water. The pain was still raw, but as I leaned against the cold tiles and stared ahead, one comforting thought made me smile. It was over, and *I* had made that decision.

Lesson Four:
Female instincts were created
for a reason; listen to them

In the month that followed, I worked tirelessly to become a woman I could respect. I was determined to make the best of my new job, and I lost countless hours in Waterstone's reading every private equity book available without actually buying them. I took up rollerblading, and walked, rain or shine, to Hyde Park every day to ensure I pushed my body to the limit. I hired a stylist and invested in a classic capsule wardrobe that would outlast all fashion trends. I smiled as I remembered the girlie afternoons wasted at the Westfield Centre, being made over, trying, fitting and changing my mind until I had the outfits that would forever make me feel chic, stylish and hot. The new clothes cost me a small fortune, but I was investing in me. I changed my eating habits, I played Gloria Gaynor, Aretha Franklin and Beyoncé, who reminded me how strong I was, and I watched movies about underdogs who won against all odds. I was programming my brain to believe that I was worth more, that I deserved more and that Sam had missed out on a very good, very hot and very attractive deal. In short, I promised myself that I would never allow a man to make me feel like a nothing. I promised myself that I would avoid men until one convinced me an alternative was more attractive. I promised myself that I would stop talking about men, or the lack of them, or the quality of them or anything else related to them. For now.

So when the fine day that I started my new job arrived, I woke up to Gloria blaring out 'I Will Survive'. I jumped out of bed, danced around my room in my boy shorts and tiny T knowing that today I would do more than survive. I opened both my cupboard doors and rifled through my new suits until I pulled out the fitted black trouser suit that made the most of my small waist and long legs. I held the suit against me and spun around and around.

'Yaya, what are you—'

'Daddy!' I called out, scrabbling to hold the suit against me to give me some modesty. He covered his eyes with his hand and waved at me.

'Why are you having a disco at this time in the morning?'

'I'm sorry, Daddy, I totally . . .' Paralysed with embarrassment, I reached out to turn down the iPlayer and then scrambled back when I nearly dropped my suit. 'Daddy . . .'

I heard the door slam behind him and rushed over to turn down the volume. The door opened again and I grabbed a pillow to cover me.

'Yaya . . .'

'Don't come in, Daddy . . .'

'I just want to say, leave the music on and enjoy it enough to dance through your first day in your new job.' He closed the door again and I fell back on my bed with the widest grin. I felt great. I laughed out loud. I leaned over, turned up the volume and started dancing all over again.

*

The music stayed with me as I arrived at Green Park station and headed towards Berkeley Square to Namhar Capital. I stopped off at Starbucks, picked up a full-fat macchiato with a blueberry muffin and bounced along to my new office. I took off my black slouchy beanie and pulled out my Bose earplugs as I entered the small reception area.

'Hi,' the young receptionist greeted brightly. 'You're early.'

'It's my first day,' I explained, resting the coffee, Starbucks bag and beanie on the desk to take my leather gloves off. 'Could you call down Ella Jacobs . . .'

'You must be Yasmin Yusuf.' I smiled at her friendly demeanour. 'I'm Jesse. We're a small company, everyone's on first-name terms . . . except for the directors. Avoid calling the directors by their first names, that's a big no-no. I did that and it didn't go down well.'

I held my smile in place as Jesse prattled on and showed no sign of stopping. I sneaked a peak at the clocks behind her and saw the time in London, New York, Tokyo and Dubai. All told me that I was late.

'Eh, Jesse, I'm late. Would you mind letting Ella Jacobs know that I've arrived?'

'Oh sure, I'll do that right now. You're in Hannah Gibbs-Smythson's team. Be wary, be very wary. She is one tough scary cookie. Tough, tough, tough. But she has to be, she manages the tenders and bids for the retail sector. She goes through analysts like a compulsive gambler goes through chips in a casino. A word of advice, don't make her mad. She does not like timid or opinionated people. She likes people who look like they take pride in themselves, but can't stand loose cannons. Do as she wants and she'll leave you alone. Do anything else and be prepared to pick up your P45 on your way out.' She leaned forward as if to share a secret, so I tentatively stepped closer. 'Between you and me, I think she's getting a little paranoid about hitting the big five-oh,' she whispered before leaning back to wink at me.

'Thanks for sharing that. Now would you please call Ella and let her know I'm in the building . . .'

'Sure.' I watched as she reached out to pick up the phone, and prayed for her to make the call. 'Oh, I forgot.' I grimaced as she looked up at me. 'One last thing and I promise to call Ella. Don't ever turn up early for meetings because Hannah believes that's a sign that you don't have enough work to do. But more importantly, never ever turn up late . . . for anything, and when I say anything, I mean *anything*.' Jesse spoke very slowly in case I didn't understand her. She seemed to have forgotten that I had been standing in the lobby for more than ten minutes and by all accounts had done the one thing most detested by my new manager. I was lost for words as she gave me a wide smile.

'Ella,' I reminded and watched as she finally made that long-overdue call. In an instant, I heard the clatter of heels against the wooden floorboards.

'Wo, wo, wooo!' blurted out the young woman who skidded to a stop in front of me clutching a huge mound of documents. She was the type that looked frayed and harassed and always three steps behind. 'You're late for a meeting, and she won't be impressed to see us arrive late,' Ella said as I grabbed my breakfast, gloves and hat and followed her.

'I'm so sorry, I've been—'

'We'll walk in, head right to the back, find the nearest chairs and avoid making any eye contact for at least a quarter of an hour. Don't squeak, speak or have an opinion until I get a chance to brief you. Hopefully she'll forget we're there by then.' Ella breathed out as we stepped into a small archaic lift and waited for the doors to close. She pushed the close button several times, struggling to hold the pile of documents, but still the doors refused to close.

'Can I help you?' I asked. She smiled brightly and handed me half of the documents. That was a stupid suggestion, as I struggled to balance the pile of documents along with all my belongings.

Ella's patience ran out. 'Let's walk,' she said.

I tried to stay right on her heels as she raced up two flights of stairs and waved a pass across the security tab before entering what looked like the meeting floor. I struggled to keep hold of everything, and felt my heavy tote bag about to slip off my shoulder.

'We're here,' Ella whispered, stopping at a door. 'You're to take the meeting minutes, document everything, the team's participants and Hannah's directives. Most importantly, note every single question.'

I nodded at the instruction, but kept praying my bag wouldn't drop and send all that I held crashing to the floor. I followed close behind Ella, ignoring the chill of disapproving looks, and headed towards the back of the meeting room.

'Ella, do you think there's any point in us sitting here twiddling our thumbs whilst you scuttle to the back clutching the project details?' The slow, calm question stopped us dead in our tracks.

'I'm sorry, Ms Gibbs-Smythson, I got held up by . . .' I felt my heart racing about being identified as the cause of Ella's lateness, '. . . by the printer. It managed to eat up—'

'Whilst I'm sure you have time to waste on pointless matters, I on the other hand don't.'

I looked at the infamous Hannah. She was the archetypal elder, a stunning ice queen with sharp angular features and slicked-back blonde hair, with no discernible emotion other than bored contempt.

'The . . . the reports. I have them,' Ella stuttered, her confidence shattered.

'Well, distribute them!' The bark made everyone jump. At once Ella and I took opposite sides of the large oval mahogany table to hand out the reports. I daren't lean over, praying that the executives who reached up to take a copy didn't push my bag down to my elbow and send my coffee straight into the lap of Hannah Gibbs-Smythson.

'Edward, bring the team up to speed on this excuse of a company.'

When the final copy was taken, I rushed to the back and crouched down to put all my belongings on the floor and discreetly dig out my notebook and pen.

'What are you doing?'

I cringed at the demand, knowing that I hadn't been discreet enough. Slowly I looked up over the table at the impatient Hannah. Everyone was peering round or leaning up to look down on me.

'Uh, I'm looking for my notebook . . .'

'When you're done searching through all your worldly possessions, do you think you could bring yourself to stop distracting the team?'

I felt the rush of humiliation redden my cheeks and nodded. Quickly I scrambled around my trainers, Gucci wallet, make-up, house keys and chocolate stash amongst other essential female items. As expected, I had left my impress-anyone-who-sees-it Mont Blanc pen at home. So I slipped on my dark-rimmed spectacles, pulled out my notebook and took a seat at the table with my coffee and muffin. Everyone stared at the muffin bag, and then at the small pink notebook I put on the table.

'Edward?' Instantly a faceless corporate suit stood up

to lead the meeting. Ella slid a corporate pad and pen to me and took the muffin bag off the table. I smiled at her before focusing on taking notes. Within minutes I was struggling to keep up. For one, I didn't know who anyone was, and secondly I was lost in the barrage of acronyms and terms that were being thrown around. LBOs, PIPE, financial engineering, playing the yield curve were bandied around as the team moved through the MBI and hostile takeover scenarios for Oshanti. I had no idea what some of the terms meant, things like shark repellent, poison pills and angel investor, but they made for good doodles until a stone-faced Hannah stared at me unimpressed. Covering my scribbles, I stared up at the graphs that were projected on to the screen, trying to cover my confusion at the many ratios and profit scenarios. I waited to see Oshanti discussed in layman's terms, but that never happened. Before long I had pages of notes, dotted with question marks, underlined and bolded, representing all that I had failed to understand.

'*Girlfriend, you had better answer your phone right now, and I mean right now.*' The screaming voice stopped all conversation. It was my new iphone, playing Mia's personalised ringtone, and I prayed to God that she would hang up. Every pair of eyes in the room was on me. I hadn't turned on the meeting setting on my mobile. '*Girl, answer your phone.*'

'Are you going to answer that?' At Hannah's calm, controlled question, I ducked beneath the desk and scrambled through my bag for my iPhone. Just as I found it, Mia decided to hang up. I put the mobile on silent mode, tried to ignore the silence in the room and then bumped my head as I peeked above the desk at the peering eyes.

'Do you have an important business deal that you

need to attend to?' The caustic question came from Hannah. I shook my head, avoided her wilting glare and took my seat.

'I can . . . I can return the call later,' I said.

'Right, well, what are *you* waiting for?' she demanded, turning her wrath to the suit who had been smirking at my humiliation.

'Noth . . . nothing . . .'

'Well, continue!' Once again, the bark startled everyone in the room.

As the debate about portfolios, models and ratios became one long drone, I looked around the room at what I called the corporate robots. These were the finely groomed, suited and booted, without a strand of hair out of place, personality-devoid androids that kept the world of mergers and acquisitions alive. Not one displayed a jot of emotion beyond a competitive hunger to be the best. I realised at that moment that I was the only person of colour in the room. Hannah caught me pondering and looked like she had read my mind. A perfectly plucked eyebrow arched and I busied myself with the minutes until I felt the weight of her stare move on. Hannah's presence was as terrific as it was terrifying. She drove the meeting by saying or doing very little and I admired her for it. The next time she deigned to speak, I smiled.

'Something amuse you?' She slowly turned to look at me, and my smile dropped. My heart raced as every other face turned in my direction. 'Hmmm?'

I refused to be another corporate android; I was determined to be the best on *my* terms. So in spite of the fear coursing through my heart, I looked around for inspiration and spotted my Starbucks bag.

'Blueberry muffin,' I stuttered, ignoring the muted laughs and smirks.

'Blueberry muffin?' Hannah repeated slowly. She was a disciplined woman who wasn't the type to give in to the temptations of sweet sins.

I looked around the room and realised everyone was waiting for a response. I caught Ella's look and remembered her advice never to have an opinion. But I had started, and somehow I had to finish off without being turned into human powder by Hannah's super-stare.

'Yes, blueberry muffins are like . . . like . . . lingerie,' I said as the muted laughs turned into short chortles of disbelief. Hannah remained silent. I guess she was waiting for me to hang myself. 'You see, I know those calories will take me three aerobic sessions, two sessions of aqua dance and one spin class to burn off, and then only if I pay attention to the instructor, but I know that that muffin there is worth it. Good lingerie is worth the same sacrifice. Now if you can excuse my ignorance about portfolio modelling, I haven't heard any of you speak about what Baby O for Oshanti has to offer. All you've spoken about are figures, forecasts and turnaround deadlines, with no long-term considerations. But I believe if you can tap into the blueberry muffin magic for Oshanti, no woman will be able to resist it.'

The silence that followed was deafening. I caught the look of disbelief on every android's face, and watched as they looked to Hannah to give them some direction as to how to respond. She stared at me with narrow-eyed curiosity, but I couldn't hold her look.

'Charming.' Her dry response made me smile. 'Ella, ensure HR puts our naive newbie on the dummies' guide to private equity so that . . .' She struggled to remember my name.

'Yasmin, Yasmin Yusuf,' Ella supplied.

'. . . so that Jasmine understands that there is no such

thing as long term in private equity.' I refused to look down as the room rang with laughter. 'Edward, explain to Jasmine—'

'Yasmin,' I corrected, but she continued none the less.

'. . . why figures and forecasts and turnaround timelines are all that matter—'

'I get it.' My interruption startled her. 'We buy, renovate and sell on. I get that that's a profitable formula. What I don't understand is how we're going to make the most profit if we don't know what we're selling,' I explained, refusing to be intimidated into silence.

'Uh, the company overview is provided in the report,' Ella whispered. I froze at the comment and hesitantly looked at Hannah, who I could have sworn looked vaguely amused.

'Ella, give Jasmine the turnaround case notes for Urban Lady, Secret Couture and Hargreaves Gentry. Actually, give her the retail case notes for the last two years.' And then she looked directly at me. 'If you don't walk into Namhar Capital tomorrow morning like a human calculator, I don't want to see you back here again. Do we have an understanding, Jasmine?'

I cleared my throat, shifted in my seat and then looked up at Hannah. She arched that eyebrow again. I nodded, but it wasn't enough.

'Hmmm?'

'Yes . . . yes we do.'

'Good. Ella, take over the minutes. Jasmine, get yourself down to HR, get onto the dummies' guide to everything and once you've worked through the case studies and decided you want to be a human calculator and not a glorified panty-seller, come back and see me tomorrow evening.'

Hannah had put me in my place and given me two days to prove my worth in front of the entire team. I

handed the notepad over to Ella, and picked up my bag
and pink notepad. I stared at the guilty muffin bag that
had nearly caused me to talk myself out of my job. It had
now become symbolic of the struggle between passion
and profit. I looked up at Hannah and found her waiting
for my decision. I stood up and headed for the door,
leaving the muffin behind. The fact that Hannah started
talking behind me proved that it was the right decision to
make. But as I went to open the conference-room door,
Sam's face flashed before me as if to remind me not to
doubt myself. It was wrong to stop believing that passion
drove profit. It suddenly became important that I didn't
abandon that belief. I paused, and then quickly raced
back to the desk to grab the muffin bag. Hannah stopped
talking.

'I'll see you tomorrow,' I confirmed with a broad smile
before I headed for the exit.

'She's going to fire me,' I announced when I joined Ella
for a sandwich at lunch. Grabbing my purse, I followed
her down the stairs. 'She is. There is no way I'm going to
get all this by tomorrow evening.'

'I wish I could tell you to take it easy, but there's a
reason why I'm single, and keeping up with Ms Gibbs-
Smythson has a lot to do with it,' Ella told me as I pulled
on my mac.

'Great,' I muttered, pausing when Ella turned to look
at me. 'I've got ten times as much to learn just to get on
the same page as you, which means I'll be available to
date until I'm ninety!'

'Trust me, there's nothing like making yourself a
professional success to get you through heartache,' Ella
advised with half a smile before walking on. I smiled at
her comment and warmed to her down-to-earth nature.
'You'll find at some point you forget that you're single,

because Namhar Capital becomes your demanding, uncompromising and very stubborn partner.'

'Shame about the sex appeal, right?' I asked, laughing with Ella as we passed Jesse.

'He is sexy, isn't he?' Jesse piped up, making both of us stop and look at the seating area where Zach stood. I felt my smile falter the instant he spotted me.

'It's raining, I'm going to run up for my brolly,' Ella said. As always, he looked like he had been attired by Savile Row and groomed at the Refinery.

'Yasmin?' he called.

'The sex god is talking to you!' Jesse whispered behind me unhelpfully.

'Hi, Zach.' I smiled as he contemplated my madeover appearance and nodded in appreciation.

'First day?' Zach asked. I prayed that he couldn't hear my heart pounding as I looked at his piercing eyes. I forgot how breathtakingly striking he was. I wanted to thank him for getting me into Namhar, but for some reason I was unable to string a sentence together.

'First day,' I confirmed with a nod. I struggled to think of the right thing to say. I looked down and took a deep breath. 'Zach, I wanted to thank you—'

'Oh there you are, Zachary.' I spun round to see Hannah Gibbs-Smythson striding towards Zach to exchange air kisses. 'I'm running terribly late, it doesn't help to work with imbeciles that—' she stopped when she spotted me. 'Jasmine, what are you doing out of the dummies' guide tutorials?' I couldn't drag my eyes away from her cold stare to see Zach's reaction to her question. 'Well?'

'Answer her; you don't want to see her mad—'

'Thank you, Jesse!' Hannah snapped at the receptionist behind me. 'Will you get that Selina down here immediately, otherwise we'll lose the booking at Hush.'

'I'm waiting for Ella, we're grabbing a sandwich from Starbucks,' I said, when Hannah looked back at me. She shook her head as if my existence disappointed her, and I looked away, wishing Ella would hurry up.

'Were you about to say something?' Zach asked.

'No,' I corrected quickly with a shake of my head. 'No thank you,' I murmured, wanting to avoid giving Hannah further ammunition to ridicule me.

Hannah turned away and murmured something to Zach. I heard the hushed laughter and burned with humiliation at the thought that I was the source of amusement. Turning away, I saw Jesse calling Selina, one of the senior managers, to pass on Hannah's message.

'I warned you she was something else,' Jesse whispered loudly whilst leaning forward. 'But *he* really is something else,' she murmured, staring at Zach like a lovesick puppy.

Taking a quick peek back at Zach, I could see why. He stood there immersed in conversation, oblivious to the impact he had on every red-blooded women within five metres of his presence.

'There you are!' Jesse and I turned to Selina's loud, confident greeting.

'Here comes the superbitch,' Jesse muttered as she sat back and pretended to look busy. Selina shook hands with Zach, and held his gaze with a small smile. Zach then darted his gaze across to me, and I felt my cheeks burn with the embarrassment of being caught watching. He nodded, causing Selina to look at me.

'Shall we?' Hannah muttered, stepping in front of Zach to stare at me with haughty iciness.

'Let's go,' Ella announced as she finally arrived with umbrella in hand. Her timing couldn't have been worse. We headed for the exit at the same time as Hannah, Zach and Selina, and awkwardly hesitated to allow Hannah to stride out with Selina first. Zach held the door open for Ella, and I briefly caught his eye as I passed by him.

'Zach, stop teasing the girl!' Selina taunted from the back of the waiting cab. He laughed at the comment and went to join them. We stood and watched the departing cab.

'Don't even go there,' Ella stated as she opened up her umbrella.

'He *is* something else, isn't he?' I muttered as we started walking.

'Do you know his reputation? He's a jet-setting, hard-working playboy who parties harder.'

'I know, I know, I know . . .'

'And he works with Hannah very closely, so you don't want to give her any more ammunition to come after you.'

'You're talking like I have a chance in hell with the guy!' I laughed as Ella looked at me.

'You fancy him . . .'

'No!'

'Please tell me you're not into that kind of chiselled, polished City boy!' Ella challenged.

'How can you not be?' I returned as she cried out in mock outrage.

'Precisely because they live in a boys' world packed with disposable totty, fast cars, and fat pay packets,' Ella told me with a quirky smile. 'No siree, I'll take a cultured, educated man of intelligence any day.'

'Ella, you know that means we'll never fight over the same man,' I pointed out with a wide smile.

'Well that's just grand!' she returned, looping an arm through mine. 'I think we'll get on fine!'

That evening I was late meeting Mia, Gemma and Bibi for our regular Monday evening meal at Wagamama. I hopped off the bus at the corner of Hyde Park, crossed Kensington High Street and walked into the side entrance of Habitat. The lift opened up on the second floor to the bustling, busy eatery and I spotted the girls by the window bench tucking into their meals.

'Here she is!' Mia called out as I took off my coat, folded it and placed it on the under-table panel before perching on the bench.

'I'm so sorry I'm late,' I started as they all pointed to my files.

'You look like you got some homework with you . . .'

'Don't, it's not even funny,' I said to Gemma. 'My manager hates me, and trust me, if I don't get my homework done, I'll be unemployed this time tomorrow.'

'That's funny,' Mia laughed, handing me a dish of yasai gyoza, my favourite vegetarian dumplings.

'I'm serious,' I said. She stopped laughing to stare at me.

'You're serious?' Mia breathed out in disbelief.

'Seriously, I'm serious,' I repeated as Gemma hailed a waiter over for me. She wasn't put off by the ones who always managed to look like pissed-off student designers or hairdressers.

'I'll have the amai udon; can you ask the chef to go crazy with the tofu?' I told the waiter, who had an asymmetrical blonde and purple bob.

'What do you mean, go crazy with the tofu?' The blunt question caused us to look up.

'What do you think I mean?' I returned, replicating his attitude.

'I don't know. That's why I'm asking,' he explained in a stroppy tone.

'You don't know what I mean?' He shook his head. I stared at him, prepared to carry on as long as he wanted to act like a bored, unhelpful waiter.

'She means an extra serving of tofu,' Mia explained as he stared back at me unimpressed.

'That's one amai udon with an extra serving of tofu,' he repeated slowly as he looked down to his order pod.

'And one green tea.' He looked up and shook his head. The green tea was free at Wagamama, and the Asian in me had to have anything that didn't cost me money. The stroppy waiter knew it and I knew it.

'And one green tea,' he repeated for my benefit. 'Anything else—' I shook my head before he could finish his question. We watched him slope off and then stared back at each other in amused disbelief.

'He's not worth it,' Bibi said before we all let loose. 'So, did you see the arrogant, drop-dead, make-my-knees-weak-and-lashes-flutter Zach today?'

'You mean stomach-flutter-with-a-million-butterflies knight-in-shining-armour Zach?' Gemma corrected as she fanned Bibi, who acted all flustered and bothered.

'You've never met the man, how would you know . . .?' I stopped, looking to Mia, who avoided my eyes. 'You told them about that flirty conversation and how he rescued my career, didn't you?'

'You forget to mention that he just happened to ask you about your lingerie.'

'Mia! He's the biggest playboy there is.'

'Did you see him today?' I stopped at the question and watched Mia smile a slow, naughty smile. My silence gave me away. 'Did he ask you about your lingerie again?'

'You are such a child!' I told her, trying to stem a smile.

'He makes my heart race and oh, oh the emotions . . . I feel so giddy!' Bibi whispered.

'So, did he show you the *ropes*?' Mia added before they all looked at me pointedly.

'You girls are too funny. Seriously, you should be a comedy act!'

'Seriously, did he?' Mia teased before we burst out laughing. 'So, how *was* your day?'

'It was crazy!' I told them with barely contained excitement. 'I didn't have a minute to stop and think.'

'We know you've been offline all day. Was it Zach, did he keep you busy?' Gemma asked with a naughty wink.

'Honestly, I have no idea how that man got me into private equity. I'm not a qualified accountant; no matter how many dummies' guide courses my manager puts me on, I'm not going to get it.'

'She put you on a dummies' guide course?'

'In front of the entire team, and then she told me not to return unless I'm a human calculator.' Mia stopped drinking to stare at me. I nodded to confirm her disbelief. 'Yep, in front of the whole team, before I had even been introduced to them. And you know, the worst thing is that I didn't realise just how out of my depth I was until I spent all day locked away on this idiots' course.'

'It helped, right?' I stared at Gemma blankly and shook my head. 'What about all the preparatory reading you did running up to today?' she asked.

I thanked the short squat waiter who brought me my meal and green tea.

'Putting the concepts into context real-time has thrown me. I just want the numbers to make sense. So I'm going to spend the night reading through the case notes, and pray I can become at least a basic human calculator.' None of the girls looked convinced, so I took a large mouthful of noodles.

'Why don't you call in sick tomorrow and buy yourself some time?' Bibi suggested.

'She's not going to buy it.'

'But you can't get fired!' Gemma pointed out.

'You can't, it's just not the right time to get fired,' Mia added, looking from Gemma to me.

'I have no intention of getting fired, but—'

'Surely they'll see that you're trying . . .'

'Girls, it's not my choice. I'm going to bust a gut to prove myself, but—'

'Can't you ask Zachary Khan to give you a crash course?' Bibi breathed out as if she had made some new discovery. 'And that'll give you ample room to impress him!' Mia and Gemma nodded in support. I stared at them, at a loss for words.

'Bibi's got a point. Maybe you can reach out to him and you two can . . . *you know* . . . over some coaching sessions . . .'

'Trust me, the guy won't want to have anything to do with me after today.'

'So you *did* see him today!' Mia announced with a wide grin.

'I'd rather not have.' The girls looked confused at my embarrassed mutter. 'Hannah told him about the dummies' guide thing,' I explained and watched them stare at me in silence.

'Did he say anything to you?'

'He didn't get a chance before the Ice Queen turned up!' I told them and looked on as the silence continued. Mia busied herself with the deep-fried black tiger prawns, whilst Bibi and Gemma looked at each other.

'Maybe he felt sympathy for you!' Bibi suggested, unsure of whether she was trying to convince herself or me.

'You think Mr Perfect's going to find happy-ever-after with me, the new office idiot, as if we're in some sassy chick flick?' The girls were too scared to nod, but I could see that that was exactly what they were desperately hoping to believe. 'OK, I can see that you have been plotting my happy-ever-after since I screwed up with loser of the year.'

'That's not the point . . .'

'Gemma, you have a besotted French lawyer; Bibi, you're secretly loved up with Malik, your mysterious high-flying consultant; and Mia, you're still giving Bryan the runaround,' I stated. 'So I get that you want to see me happy, but this . . . this is insane! The guy fired me. Zach Khan fired me—'

'And then he found you a job,' Mia pointed out quickly.

'After I begged him whilst having an emotional breakdown . . .'

'He looked out for you by giving you a job,' she insisted.

'A job that's way *way* out of my league, which is a classic way to set someone up for failure.'

'You're the only one he hasn't tried it on with! The playground antics tell me he's totally into you.' I stopped at Bibi's cheeky comment.

'Are you kidding me?' I asked as they all stared at me.

'You're not seeing it, are you?' Gemma asked, before she turned to Bibi. 'She can't see it from our perspective.'

'She can't, she's in the eye of the storm.'

'*Eye of the storm?*' I repeated slowly, but they carried on nonetheless.

'She's in denial,' Mia threw in as Bibi nodded and pointed at me.

'She's so in denial.'

'Denial of what?' I demanded.

'Don't be impatient, Yasmin, it's only your first day,' Gemma pointed out, like I was the one who had lost sight of the facts.

'It's unattractive to be so impatient, Yasmin. My Malik says it gives women premature wrinkles,' Bibi added. 'You don't want to age before your time.'

'No, not when you're trying to win the man over. He does not need to know you have wrinkles or that you're impatient,' Gemma concluded as she helped herself to my dish.

'You guys are insane,' I said as I collected my bag and folders. 'Insane . . .'

'Ohhhhh, we've hit a nerve, ladies!' Mia called out as I pulled on my coat.

'I can't reason with you and I have work to do . . .'

'She's running, girls, Yasmin Yusuf is running!' she added as they broke into Kylie Minogue's 'Can't Get You Out of My Head'. I left a twenty-pound note by my plate as diners around us turned to watch them carry on.

'You guys need help,' I told them, restraining a laugh when they started mimicking the dance actions. 'Yep, therapy; you all need to be in therapy.' I took my belongings and headed out.

'Give lover boy our best!' Mia's loud request left me grinning like a Cheshire cat.

I was still laughing as the lift pinged open, but my smiled disappeared as I saw my reflection and the thick folders I carried. It was going to be a long night.

When Beyoncé belted out 'Ring the Alarm', I knew it was the fifth song on her album, which meant that I was seriously late for work. I had fallen asleep amongst the endless case notes. I jumped out of bed to get ready, but knew that I would never recover the time to start the day with perfect control and composure. I left my house forty minutes late, squeezed on to the packed carriages of the Central line at Shepherd's Bush and disembarked at Marble Arch. I raced down Park Lane to get to my offices in Green Park and arrived just as Hannah Gibbs-Smythson was about to enter her executive car. She paused and noted the thick volumes of notes that I clutched against me.

'Jasmine,' she acknowledged.

'Morning,' I mumbled, waiting until she got into the car before racing up to my desk. Ella stopped to look at me as I fell into my chair. 'Typical!' I gasped.

'I take it you caught Ms Gibbs-Smythson on your way in?' Ella asked.

'She's just finished her morning briefing, hasn't she?' I asked as I took off my trainers to slip on my Nine West patent leather pumps.

'Correction, her second morning meeting, and we've got two new team members,' she explained.

'I missed the introductions, right?' Ella nodded before pointing three tables down, where I spotted a familiar face talking to a young Asian girl. 'They've seconded Randy Raj from my old team?'

'He's a maths genius, and she's stunning, smart and worst of all young,' Ella admitted as I focused on the pretty girl. With a mane of sleek black hair, a pouty white smile and dark wide exotic eyes, the new recruit could have any man of her choice. I looked at Ella and recognised the insecurities the newbie caused in us, single, cynical, thirty-something women. Ella caught my watchful eyes and grinned. We barely knew each other, but we connected with a tacit understanding of shared experience. So through no fault of her own, we took an instant dislike to the new girl.

'Who is she?' I asked Ella, who perched on my desk holding her notebook against her.

'Helen Choudhury, recent recruit from Henderson's, with a killer body, killer brain and killer smile. Life is so not fair,' she muttered as we both stared at the girl with envy. 'And she's got an engagement ring on.'

'It's from . . .'.

'Tiffany's,' Ella finished as if she had read my mind. 'She's part of a perfect couple. I've already seen the engagement picture just in case I didn't have enough reason to hate her already.' She breathed out.

'How is it possible for one woman to have everything?'

'Work is my salvation. It's where I, the cynical confirmed office spinster, find grace. So tell me, Yasmin, what's fair about placing that perfect women with her perfect ring, fiancé and future here?' Ella asked before freezing. 'She's coming over . . .'

I peeped up over my screen and saw the pretty girl heading towards us.

'Look busy . . .' I whispered. Ella opened up her notepad and pointed down to it.

'Hannah's asked you to pull together an overview of Baby O's competitive presence in the UK,' she said as I looked at her notebook, hoping the girl would be put off from interrupting us.

'Are you still pretending?' I whispered in confusion.

'No,' Ella whispered back. 'She does want you to get that information.'

'But I still haven't finished the case reviews and courses,' I reminded her.

'At this morning's briefing she said she wanted a competitor angle by this evening.' I scribbled down Ella's directions, shaking my head.

'There's no way I'm going to get this done . . .'

'Hello!' The perky, confident greeting made us stop short. Our act hadn't worked, so we both took off our spectacles and looked up. 'I'm Helen Choudhury . . .'

'Oh my God, Yasmin! When did you be joining this team?' Randy Raj cried out as he joined Helen. 'Now I have two Indian beauties at work to choose from . . .'

'Uh, Raj, I'm off the market!' Helen reminded him with a bright laugh as she flashed her Tiffany's diamond ring. 'It's nice to meet you, Yasmin.' I shook the slim hand she held out. She looked like a young corporate Deepika Padukone and I couldn't bring myself to smile.

'Welcome to the team,' I muttered before looking back at Raj. 'Raj, it's not polite to call two women beautiful when you're in the presence of three stunning girls.' I smiled when he overcompensated and kissed Ella's hand in apology, whilst Helen cleared her throat at the oversight. Ella giggled and looked like a prudish librarian who had been surprised.

'Raj and I will be working on the forecasting models for Baby O,' Helen said with a stunning smile. Ella's giggles stopped when she realised that Helen had asserted her seniority over the two of us.

'Great!' I replied. 'You'd better get to it . . .'

'Will you be in attendance for the company party?' Raj asked me with a big smile.

'Aww! My fiancé and I are going to watch *Blood Brothers*; it's our first theatre production together, so I'm so disappointed I can't make it,' Helen cried out as Ella looked as uninterested as I felt.

'I thought I be asking ahead. Before any other young gentleman gets a chance with you,' Randy Raj said as I forced myself to smile nervously.

'It's not for a while yet,' I reminded him hesitantly.

'You have a partner to be going with?' Raj pursued.

'Yes.' The short simple lie was enough to silence Raj and leave us all staring at each other in awkward silence.

'Well, maybe we can all grab lunch sometime this week . . .'

'That's a fantastic idea, Helen.' Raj laughed over-enthusiastically. 'What day shall we make the booking for?'

'Sounds good,' Ella muttered with very little enthusiasm as she headed back to her desk.

'Why don't you look at everyone's diaries and book it straight into a slot where we're all free,' I told Helen as I checked the time. 'I'm late for a training course. Nice meeting you.' And with that I grabbed my notebook, pen and mobile and left them both standing at my desk. En route, I called Mia.

'I owe you my life if you call in a favour with the research team,' I stated when she took my call.

'I'm not rollerblading through Hyde Park or jumping on this "new woman" bandwagon . . .'

'I'm serious, Mia. The director's flooding me with work and I can't keep up.'

'That bad, huh?'

'Worse, I walked in late to work to find that Ms World, engaged, younger and more talented than myself, has joined my team, so I really need you to pull this favour.'

'Spill,' Mia offered in a show of solidarity.

'I need a competitive overview of Baby O's presence in the UK by close of business. The O stands for Oshanti, that's O-S-H-A-N-T-I.' I spelt it out for Mia. 'They're in the lingerie market with an HQ in Delhi.'

'So a top level overview, right, that's it?' Mia asked as I headed for the training room.

'I promise I owe you,' I whispered before switching off my phone and taking a deep breath.

I didn't know when I had developed these female insecurities. I had always felt confident with my lot, and considered such qualities to be ugly. Helen, for all her perfection, was accomplished, and her success was something for all women to celebrate. Yet instinctively, Ella and I were threatened by her and wanted somehow to have a small fleeting moment of one-upmanship over her.

I stared at the entrance to the training room, forty-five minutes late. I knew in that moment that I felt ugly because thirty-something single women don't want to hear about women in their twenties having it all. We singletons are happier hearing about the emotional scars, relationship wars and broken hearts, because they validate us, they resonate with what we know. So when Ms Perfection enters into that utopia, we see a reflection of what we aren't, or what we've lost, or worst of all, what we could have had. I had spent the past month rebuilding myself, cell by cell, until I felt significant again. I couldn't allow myself to feel insignificant again. Ugly as it might be, insecurities were now my alarm bell. Cruel as it seems, female instincts exist for a reason, and I had to listen to mine until I believed that even in the presence of perfection, I too was equally perfect. With that thought and an ironic smile, I entered into the dummies' guide course for the second day in a row.

Lesson Five:
New beginnings are good, but you have to make time for them

Friday lunchtime used to be my favourite time of the week. The long cosmopolitan lunches at chic restaurants once marked the end of the manic week, and the beginning of a slow, relaxing weekend. Not at Namhar Capital. Now, every day was the same and Fridays just reminded me that I had more to-do items to complete by week end and not enough hours to do them in. So the closest thing I got to lunch on a Friday was a five-bean cassoulet soup from Pret mid-afternoon.

'Hannah's chasing you for the preliminary store headcount and stock figures,' Jesse called out to stop me racing for the lift.

'But I've already emailed it to her,' I said, taking the note that Jesse held out to me.

'Selina left that for you,' she said as I looked down at the message.

'You got to be kidding me!' I muttered in response to the request it contained.

'P45?' Jesse asked with a sad frown. Looking up at the nosy receptionist, I raised an eyebrow.

'No, they're not sacking me,' I said.

Jesse's frown turned into a smile. 'Well, aren't you lucky.'

Her perky voice didn't do anything to calm me down. I raced up to my desk, found Ella missing and picked up my phone.

'Selina Cruz speaking.' Hannah's mini-me protégé answered with a cut-glass English accent that had no warmth to it.

'Selina, it's Yasmin Yusuf.' I felt jealous at the background clatter of cutlery and conversation that marked glamorous Friday lunches in fine city eateries.

'Who?'

'Yasmin from the office . . .'

'Sssshhh, it's Yasmin!' The muffled whisper made me frown with suspicion. 'Yes?'

'You left a note asking me to pick up items from some of the lingerie shops. I can't see how this is going to help the project . . .'

'Do you want to ask Hannah to explain her reasons to you?' I closed my eyes at being cornered.

'No . . .'

'She's in a meeting with Richard Haverford. Do you really want to call her out from that meeting?'

'But I have the store positioning analysis as well as the headcount stats to complete.'

'That's not my problem.'

'Surely Hannah's PA could pick all this stuff up?'

'Hannah would've asked her PA if she had availability.' Selina's patronising tone was as irritating as it was blunt. 'Whatever you decide, know that Hannah expects to find the goods in the office with a product presentation for our Monday-morning meeting.'

'Presentation? What presentation?'

'The one about competitor product ranges, of course.'

'But I haven't finished—'

'Good thing you have the weekend,' Selina pointed out.

'But I have plans—'

'Yup, OK, that's very interesting but I do have to dash now.' Selina ended the call before I could finish.

'Jasmine, are you going to get me what I need?' I shot up straight at Hannah's demand as she suddenly appeared behind me.

'Yep, I'm on to it.' I answered. 'And my name's Yas—' I froze as I saw Zach stride alongside Hannah. I waited for him to turn to me, but he didn't look in my direction and instead entered her office.

'I want to see the positioning analysis at five and I need more on the stock range,' Hannah called out as she continued striding towards her office. 'More insight means more knowledge means more power.' She slammed the door shut behind her. I leaned back against my chair and closed my eyes.

'You OK?' Helen's perky question made me shoot up and compose myself. She stood perfectly poised, dressed in a tan cardigan set over a black pencil skirt and patent heels, smiling at me expectantly.

'I'm fine.' In truth, I hadn't felt closer to being frazzled, disorganised and tired than I did in that moment.

'You look stressed.'

'I'm fine,' I repeated without a smile.

'I'm happy to help with the positioning piece if you need assistance.'

I narrowed my eyes at the offer and smiled at Helen's attempt to steal my thunder. She pushed her black-rimmed glasses up her pert nose before patting her elegant bun.

'Really, I'm fine,' I said, forcing a wide smile before

returning to my documents. 'I thought you'd be out with the team for lunch.'

'I wish, if only so I could bump into that handsome Zachary Khan. I tell you, if I wasn't engaged, he'd be mine.'

I looked up slowly from my documents and glanced behind her to where Zach stood talking aggressively to Hannah. Helen giggled mischievously, oblivious to the fact that he was right behind her.

'Oh come on, tell me you don't go weak at the knees when you see him.' She caught my stare and turned around. Her eyes widened as she looked back at me and then returned to staring at Zach. 'Come on! A specimen of a man like him?'

Moments passed as we silently appreciated the well-groomed, handsome man. When Helen turned back to face me, I dragged my eyes away and cleared my throat.

'I don't go weak at the knees when I see him,' I said patiently, disliking her even more for attempting to have more than her fair share of one man per woman.

'You don't mean that . . .'

'Yes I do. I've no time for men. *I'm* the most important person in my life, and no man is worth getting all hot and bothered over,' I assured her.

'But Zachary Khan . . . He's so . . . so . . . God, he's the package: he's stunning, sculpted and he is so loaded. Why wouldn't you be interested?' Helen asked in disbelief as she pointed back towards Hannah's office.

'But how can you look at another man when you're engaged?' I asked.

Helen laughed and we both looked at Zach again. Only this time he caught us staring and frowned until Hannah turned the glass walls opaque. Helen turned to me and smiled.

'I love my fiancé, Yasmin, but trust me, he's not half as accomplished or wealthy as Zachary.'

'But you wouldn't dump your fiancé, right?' She raised a brow in challenge, and I stared at her in shock. 'Helen!'

'I know, I'm terrible, but powerful men make me weak. I can't resist them, and don't act like you're any better. I know you can't not notice Zachary Khan.'

'I'm avoiding all men, Helen, and that includes Zachary Khan.'

'Only a lesbian would want to avoid him.' Helen froze and stared at me. 'You're not . . . Oh my goodness, have I offended you? You're not . . .'

'Not that it's any of your business, but I'm not!' I refuted as Ella returned with a McD's takeout.

'You're not what?' she asked me, ignoring Helen, who giggled at my response.

'I said Zachary Khan was irresistible, and Yasmin said she didn't fancy him, and for a second I thought she might be a lesbian,' Helen explained. We watched her in silence until her giggles faded into uncertain awkwardness.

'That's just stupid,' Ella stated. 'Some men might find you sexy, Helen, and some might find your obvious prettiness superficial and unattractive, but that doesn't necessarily mean they're gay.'

I stared at Ella's calm comment and then looked to the obviously offended Helen.

'Well there is no need to be so blunt, Ella,' she retorted.

'Yes there is,' Ella returned, before drawing on her vanilla milkshake. I caught her laughing eyes and she gave me a cheeky wink.

I contained a smile, and silently counted to ten slowly. By the time I got to seven, Helen had stormed away. Ella offered me some of her fries, but I refused reluctantly.

'Come on, make me feel better. I'm premenstrual, I'm

OD-ing on junk food, and I'm feeling old, dowdy and very single.'

Laughing at her invitation, I walked over to her desk and helped myself to a chip.

'You think you have issues? Zach's in Hannah's office and he caught us both staring at him like lovesick puppies,' I told her as she chuckled at my embarrassment.

'Is that why she's turned the glass opaque?'

I nodded at Ella's question and laughed too. Then we both froze as Zach stormed out of Hannah's office and strode out. We watched him in silence until he was out of sight and then helped ourselves to more chips.

'This is ridiculous, I don't even fancy his type!' Ella threw out in disgust.

'Admit it, the Zach factor's got to you!' I teased as we caught Helen leaning forward to continue watching Zach. 'She'd cheat on her fiancé if she could have Zachary,' I stated as Ella looked up in disgust. 'And the worst thing is she could probably have both of them fighting over her . . .'

'Her fiancé's gorgeous . . . She's such a tramp,' Ella muttered as she pulled her curly hair back into a bun. 'Seriously, if I had a man like hers, I'd get him locked into marriage so fast there'd be no time to look at another man.' She leaned down on her palms and sighed in despondency.

'You've seen him?' I watched her nod and continued to help myself to her fries.

'He picks her up after work. I met him once, and even though he's an accountant, he could charm the Ice Queen into melting.' Ella's description reminded me of Sam. The fries lost their appeal and I couldn't hold my smile.

'I always found the Ice Queen more interesting when she was immune to any man.'

'That's pain talking,' Ella quipped as I returned to my desk. 'Was he a total loser?'

'No, he wasn't.' I logged on and stared at my screen. 'I was.'

A week at Namhar Capital left me exhausted and ready for bed every Friday evening. There were no more girls' nights out, family nights in or dinner parties galore; just a simple salad supper and a quick shower before heading straight for bed so that I felt human on Saturday morning. Only this week I let myself in late Friday night and found Daddy in the kitchen waiting with my dinner. He put down his paper and looked at me over the rim of his spectacles.

'Salaams, Daddy,' I said as I perched on the stool next to him, surprised to see him still up on his day off from work. I looked at the array of dishes and rice that he had laid out for me. 'How come you're up?'

'You work so hard with this new job that I hardly ever see you,' he said, pulling his spectacles off to look at me. 'I come home and you're studying, I wake up and you're jogging or already left for work . . .'

'I'm sorry.'

'You know what the worst thing is?' I shook my head and looked at him. 'You've stopped baking. Don't smile, I'm serious. I miss the smell of fresh baking and the house feels cold without it.' I leaned over to hug my father until he chuckled. I had spent the past weeks living in financial books, journals and case notes that left me neglecting my family.

'I'm just trying to prove myself, Daddy. This job doesn't put up with novices.'

'You're a smart, intelligent, educated girl. You're no novice!'

'I'm reading and studying everything under the sun to

keep the director happy; that's on top of doing every stupid mindless piece of administration for everyone else in the team, but nothing I do feels good enough. I feel like such an idiot . . .'

'Yaya, you're not an idiot, and your work should not be your life.'

I held my glass of water and peeked at him, wanting to ask him what else a girl of my age could do. I stopped myself and then it dawned on me.

'You're awake for a reason, aren't you?'

Daddy tried to look innocent.

'We have a *rishta* for you tomorrow evening . . .'

'No!'

'Before you start screaming, you said it was OK to bring you marriage proposals; remember, it was a month ago you said it was OK, that you—'

'But Saturday night . . .'

'I've been wanting to talk to you about it, but you're never around,' Daddy said. 'He's a good boy. Your Kamal *bhai*'s facilitated the *rishta* with the middleman . . .'

'Does it have to be tomorrow night? I'm just so busy . . .'

'Yaya, you have to make time.' I helped myself to dhal and rice, as I realised how unprepared I was to meet a new potential. 'New beginnings are good, but you have to make time for them.'

I looked at my father and noticed the excitement in his eyes. I wondered who the man was, what he was like and what he did, and couldn't muster any enthusiasm to meet someone who needed their parents to matchmake.

'Who are you waiting for, Yaya?' Daddy asked with his hands wide open.

'I'm not waiting for anyone.' Even as I said the words, the glimmer died in my father's eyes.

'A lovely girl like you should be excited about a *rishta*.

Why aren't you interested?' I looked down at my hands, quelling the sadness of Sam, the silly but consuming thoughts about Zach, and comparing them to the cold, calculated introduction to a stranger. 'If your mother was here, what would you say to her?' I smiled at his question and met his warm stare.

'I'd say, I don't want to leave my daddy alone for a weak man, or an unconfident man, or a deceitful man, or a hurtful, stupid or ungracious man . . .'

'OK, OK, OK, Yaya, instead of telling me what you don't want, why don't you tell me what you *do* want in a husband.'

Daddy's question floored me. I felt embarrassed and unsure, but most of all I felt scared. I looked at him as he spooned a serving of chicken bhouna on to my plate. As hard as I tried to find the words, I struggled until he looked up at me.

'I don't know, Daddy, I guess I'll know him when I see him, right?' My hesitant humorous question failed to make him smile.

'I want a good, decent, honest man for you, Yaya. A man who cherishes you and makes you feel precious.' His words made me look away so he couldn't see the tears in my eyes. '*Inshaallah*, maybe we'll find him tomorrow.'

Smiling, I laughed and nodded. 'With the help of Allah, maybe, just maybe we may find him,' I accepted as he took a deep breath and smiled widely. 'But I have some work to do . . .'

'On a Saturday?'

I nodded at his question. 'I'll be done by early afternoon,' I promised and looked at him apologetically.

'You promise . . .'

'Yes, Daddy!' I agreed as I finished off my dinner and debated whether I could do with another serving.

'Six thirty?' He chuckled as I reached out to hug him. 'Don't forget.'

'I promise,' I pledged before deciding I had worked hard enough to spoil myself with another serving.

'Yaya's finally making time for new beginnings,' Daddy muttered sleepily as he kissed the top of my head before leaving to go to bed.

I stayed on in the kitchen, and stared ahead, thinking about the *rishta* tomorrow. Age-old images of 1970s Bollywood movies ran through my mind, with actresses being chased around pretty gardens by handsome actors for stolen kisses. I smiled at the idea of awkwardly meeting this anybody, with the hope that he could turn into a somebody. Shaking my head, I washed up the dishes, dried them and then stacked them away. OK, so maybe I wouldn't meet my Mr Right at some cosmopolitan diner or suave City social. Maybe the fact that my brothers were intrinsically involved meant that this man would act honourably and appropriately. Maybe this was the better way for cynical spinsters to avoid false dreams and time-wasters. I breathed out in nervous exasperation, wondering whether anticipating for a hopeful potential was too much to ask for.

Lesson Six:
It may give you some ideas if
you pop into La Senza, La Perla or
Coco de Mer

It was a new day, and Daddy's words resonated in my
mind. I was hopeful. Moderately hopeful that maybe
today there could be a new beginning to all of my
tomorrows. But before I could lose myself in that hope, I
had to get Selina's task completed.

'I'm telling you, it's a prank and you shouldn't bother,'
Mia told me as I talked to her on my mobile and walked
towards Bond Street.

'I can't screw up, Mia. I'm chasing my tail at work, I
can't afford not to do this.'

'Your team's stitching you up,' she insisted.

'We're doing a turnaround on a lingerie shop; it makes
sense to do a product review.' I heard myself and didn't
believe a word I spoke. Mia stayed silent, waiting for me
to break. 'I can't, I can't buy this stuff. It's dirty!' I burst
out as she laughed. 'It's not funny, I don't even . . . It's just
. . . it's dirty!' The more I spoke, the more Mia laughed.

'It's just bras and knickers . . .'

'And more. If that's all it was, I'd have no problem. But I'm buying stuff from Agent Provocateur all the way to Ann Summers,' I corrected, dodging the pedestrians and traffic. 'Seriously, this is stuff that perverts use.'

'Like . . .?' Mia's audacious laughter had me smiling.

'I feel dirty even mentioning them.'

'Go on!'

'Pink fur handcuffs . . .' I cleared my voice and continued. 'Padlock collar, whip, a nurse's outfit . . .'

'Stop!' Mia still couldn't stop laughing.

'Seriously, this is meant to be a product comparison exercise . . .'

'This is a joke.'

'I wish it was.' I stopped at Starbucks to pick up a cappuccino. 'If Hannah Gibbs-Smythson wants it, trust me, it's no joke.'

'That Hannah Gibbs-Smythson has one kinky side to her!' Mia remarked. 'Seriously, do you think she's into the naughty—'

'Stop!' Taking a deep breath, I made a decision. 'I can do this. I'm just going to walk into these stores; I mean, they're there for a reason and they don't need to know who I am or what I want their products for . . .'

'Yasmin, you're as innocent as a newborn lamb.'

'I'm an adult and it's just stuff. It's stuff I have been asked to buy, it's no big deal.'

'It's kinky stuff . . .'

'I've bought bras and knickers before, so whips and collars can't be that different.' The young Starbucks attendant stared at me as he held out my coffee. I took it from him and walked out.

'Sure.' Mia's answer failed to build any confidence.

'OK, this is no big deal. I'm just going to hand the list to the assistant and tell her to go pick the items up for me,' I stated with a new-found confidence that seemed to disappear as soon I came to a stop before Ann Summers. 'I'm here.'

'Good luck,' Mia offered.

As soon as I put my mobile away, my confidence disappeared and I looked around to ensure that no one spotted me. To get caught walking into what the Bengali community considered to be a sex shop was shameful; to be caught going in as a girl outside of marriage would cause aunties to twitter until spinsterhood became an eternal fact of life. So once reassured, I took a deep breath, strode into the shop and headed straight for the counter.

'Excuse me—'

'Hold on.' I stopped at the sharp retort as the teen stood up to face me. 'Yeah?'

'I need these products.' I placed the list before her and watched her work down it.

'The bondage accessories are near the back, the sex outfits are near the front, and the sex toys are just over there.' I stared at the blonde girl when she finished.

'Could you collect each of the items for me.' She shook her head, too busy chewing gum to speak. 'Why not?'

'I can't leave the counter.'

'You have no other colleague who can cover the counter?' Once again she shook her head. 'Really?' She nodded and continued to stare at me, bored.

I took the list back from her. Turning around, I walked to the front of the store, past scantily clad mannequins with dodgy wigs to the uniforms section. The outfits ranged from saucy secretary to a French maid's outfit. I grinned at the foxy cheerleader's kit, but stopped in shock at the barely there pole-dancer's outfit. I tilted my head, confused, unable to make out which tiny cover went where, and realised a shopper was watching me. Moving on, I searched and found the nurse's outfit.

Picking it up, I headed down to the back and froze as I stared at the range of accessories, chains and gadgets that adorned the wall. Eyes wide open, jaw to the ground, I felt irreversibly corrupted. Shaking my head, I whispered 'tawbah' for forgiveness and touched both sides of my cheeks. Then I spun around, straight into a short, podgy man. Falling back on to a table, I felt a long hard object and knew intuitively what it was. I gasped, and threw it away from me, before wiping my hands vigorously. I heard the mountainous display tumble down behind me and closed my eyes until the last of the rampant rabbits clattered to the floor and buzzed to life. Shoppers who had stayed discreetely behind displays and mannequins suddenly appeared to stare at me.

'That wasn't me . . . I fell and . . . I, uh . . .'

'What are you doing?' yelled the shop girl, racing from the counter. I straightened up as the balding podgy man grinned at me with too much familiarity. 'Look at what you've done.'

'It wasn't my fault, it was that pervert who bumped into me!' I shouted as the balding man turned red and scuffled away quickly. Mortified, I stared down at the punky blonde shop assistant, and then cleared my throat.

'I'll take the red one,' I muttered and held out the basket to the shop girl. She gave me a dirty look and dumped a rabbit into it. Then I moved towards the wall and filled the basket with items. Once it was full, I walked over to the counter and waited for the shop girl to return.

'You sure you have everything on the list?' The comment was sarcastic.

'Yes,' I answered as she rang up each item. 'Eh, could you . . . do you wrap . . . could you wrap the items in a more discreet bag or something?'

She stared at me with that bored unimpressed expression that all teenagers somehow mastered and then shook her head unhelpfully. I waited until she finished before handing her my company credit card.

'Thanks.' I didn't acknowledge Shopgirl's caustic grunt as I answered my mobile.

'Yaya, it's Daddy.' I spun around the shop, terrified that he would someone know where I was.

'Daddy . . . wha . . . what do you want?' I answered as I saw Shopgirl grinning at me.

'I just wanted to remind you you're to be back here for six thirty tonight at the latest. The guests are arriving at seven . . .'

'I know, Daddy, I won't be late.' Shopgirl handed me the card terminal to type in the pin.

'Your Chachijhi Fauzia's helping tonight . . .'

'No, no, no, Daddy . . . we don't need Chachijhi Fauzia.'

'Yaya, we need a woman's guidance in matters of marriage, and she's always—'

'Daddy, not Chachijhi Fauzia, she's the biggest gossip.'

'Yaya, don't bad-mouth my sister. Her heart is in the right place and she's spending the day preparing for you. She married Leila off in the summer and we can use her experience for you.'

I took the card back and slipped in into my purse.

'Thank you for shopping at Ann Summers.' The loud, overeager comment was intended for my father to hear. And it worked.

'Yasmin, where are you?'

Wide-eyed, I glared at the shop girl, who smiled innocently at me. Spotting the display behind her, I hooked the large bags over my shoulder and swung around just as I passed the display. She read my mind.

'No . . . no . . . no . . .' The clatter of falling accessories stopped her plea.

'Ooops, sorry!' I called behind me as I headed out of the shop.

'Where are you?' The seconds of satisfaction disappeared at the sound of my father's question.

'Nowhere . . .'

'Aren't you at work?' I couldn't lie to my daddy for the world, but this was one truth that I couldn't spell out.

'I'm doing some primary research for work. I have to go now, but I promise to be on time, OK?' I flagged down a cab and then ended the call before he could ask me any further questions. I fell back on the seat, and paused as I found the cabbie starring at the large bags I carried.

'Busy weekend ahead?' he asked with a muted smile.

'Uh, no, I need them for work.' His eyebrows rose at my response, and I realised what he had assumed. 'No, no, I don't mean that I use . . . They're not for personal use . . . I'm in private equity, we're . . .' I stopped. It didn't matter what I said, I had already done the damage. 'Coco de Mer, Covent Garden,' I directed, ignoring his smile.

Digging out the list, I stared down at the remaining items that I had to collect. There was the vintage satin baby-doll dress, massage milk, Japanese bondage ropes and leather reins. Closing my eyes, I shook my head, at a loss as to what people got up to in their bedrooms.

'*Tawbah, tawbah, tawbah,*' I whispered before touching both sides of my cheeks for forgiveness.

I spotted Baby O a few blocks from Coco de Mer. My curiosity got the better of me and I asked the cabbie to drop me off in front of the small plain shop. It stood inconspicuous amongst the trendy eye-catching boutiques of Covent Garden. Once inside, I paused and frowned. The stark white store was empty, silent and crammed full of stock with large hand-written signs promising massive discounts. It felt like a walk back in time as I squeezed between the rails holding too many items. I looked at the pants on display and held up a pair. In that instant, I knew that the cheap outdated polyester cream bloomers represented all that was wrong with Baby O. I continued browsing, making mental notes of the oversized nylon pants, the crane-sized bras and the endless rows of basic white nylon nighties.

'Hi, may I help you?' I spun around at the quiet enquiry that was marked with a heavy Indian accent. I looked at the slight simple-looking Indian assistant.

'Uh, do you have anything for my age range?' My question made her nervous and she looked around uncertainly.

'Uh, sure . . .' I smiled at the embarrassed answer. 'In actuality, I'm not sure, but if you wait . . .'

'That's OK, I can browse . . .'

'I think if you look here, through these items, you'll find something for your size.' The assistant was trying hard to spot anything that could be suitable. After a few minutes she stopped and looked at me with a defeated smile.

'I'm sure between us we can find something.' I spotted a double-G-size bra, pulled it out and held it against me until she laughed.

'I tell the staff we have too much stock in the store . . .' She paused as she looked at the bags I carried. 'You must have a very happy boyfriend?' I laughed and shook my head.

'No, I'm doing some research on lingerie shops. For a report at work,' I explained.

'What are your thoughts on Baby O?'

I grimaced at the question. 'Honestly?' She nodded, but I hesitated, feeling sorry that the sales girl actually cared about the failing brand.

'Honestly,' she insisted. I looked around before facing her.

'Promise you won't take this personally?' She nodded again. 'The reality is that we're in the heart of Covent Garden with tourists, fashionistas, celebrities and every twenty/thirty-something passing by, and not one of them will step in here to buy this,' I said, holding up the double-G bra.

'M&S do regular lingerie and they're very successful . . .'

'I don't think double-G bras are their biggest seller, though I may be wrong!' I explained.

'But there is a market for low-cost simple underwear,' she stated without hesitation.

'I agree, and Primark dominates that market,' I returned as she shifted uncomfortably.

'We have a particular customer type, loyal customers . . .'

'It's a Saturday afternoon, the busiest shopping day for retailers, and I'm the only shopper in here.' I saw her look down. 'You know, it might give you some ideas if you popped into La Senza, or Coco de Mer.'

'We're so behind them,' the shop assistant said despondently.

'I'm sorry, I didn't mean to offend you.' I looked at the bra that I held and smiled. 'If it helps, I'll take this one.'

'This shop doesn't have a chance in hell competing with high-street stores or exclusive lingerie brands, does it?' My smile faltered at her question. I looked at her and she was deadly serious.

'Not unless things change fast,' I agreed. She nodded at my honesty and took the bra from me.

'What if it's too late? I mean, we're different, we're late to the trends, and things are getting worse and worse for the economy . . . What if it's too late?' I felt she was describing me: late to the game, different, and getting worse with age. I felt everything that Sam had made me feel. I closed my eyes and shook my head.

'Everyone deserves a second chance. It's never too late,' I whispered as I looked at the sales girl. A couple of seconds passed, and for the first time I believed that things were going to be OK. As I smiled, she smiled too and nodded at me.

'Do you have a business card?' She asked. I nodded and pulled out a slim card for her. 'Namhar Capital,' she read with a small smile.

'You sound like you know them,' I said, watching her shrug indifferently.

'I'd love to read your report, if that's OK?' she asked.

'Maybe you can talk to your manager and give her your ideas for how you can shake things up a little?' I suggested and watched her pocket the card.

'Sure. Now are you sure you want this monstrosity of a bra?' I laughed as she held up the offending item but nodded without any hesitation. 'Fine, let me pack it up for you.'

I weaved around the packed rails and came to stand by the counter as the girl rang up the transaction.

'I'll see you soon.' The comment made me pause, and I wondered what made her think I'd return to the store. She looked confident that I would, so I smiled and took the plain blue carrier bag from her.

I was late. I was horribly late. My buzzing phone told me that my family were trying to reach me as the cab pulled outside my house. I paid up and rushed to the front door carrying fifteen lingerie-packed bags. Using my nose to hit the doorbell, I jerked back at the speed with which the door was yanked open. Then I stared at the number of people who stood in our porch.

'Where have you . . . you've been shopping?' Daddy breathed out in disbelief.

'Uh, well, I'm so sorry . . .' I didn't know how to hide

the many bags that I carried. Few were discreet and they said all the wrong things to the *rishta*, who had obviously just arrived moments before I did. 'I got caught up . . .'

I caught the eye of the man who was to be my intended and frowned at how familiar he looked. He raised a curious brow and seemed to freeze with recognition, but I couldn't place him. He was cute and made me want to smile naughtily, but I couldn't escape the feeling that something wasn't right about him. Then I spotted the disapproving glares of his parents and dropped my smile. They looked strict and unimpressed so I shifted as many bags as I could behind me.

'Aaahhh, there she is. Here's my niece!' Chachijhi Fauzia laughed as she pushed her way past all the guests. Chachijhi was our larger-than-life gossip who always made the most of her rotund figure with her usual bright yellow sari, multicoloured cardigan and red headscarf. Zamal and Zeena followed her closely. They both froze at the sight of my bags, though Chachijhi barely paused at the fact that I was carrying so much shopping. 'And she fits in time to do my shopping, what a darling!' Chachijhi Fauzia said, trying too hard to make up for my tardiness. Zamal and a few of the guests coughed in disbelief.

'Why don't we all go into the living room?' Zamal suggested through gritted teeth as Zeena disappeared quietly to the kitchen.

'Yes, great idea, wonderful idea,' Chachijhi agreed enthusiastically. 'Yasmin, why don't you give me the treats that I asked you to pick up for me?' she said as she reached out to the take the bags.

'Uh, I'll take the bags up, OK?' I countered with a wide smile.

'Don't worry, I can do it . . .'

'Actually, I'll put it away . . .'

'I'll help you since you went to the trouble to shop for me,' Chachijhi insisted, grabbing a couple of the bags, but I held fast, refusing to let go of the Coco de Mer bag. The guests paused to watch the stand-off, and yet I couldn't give her the bag. I knew she would search through it in front of everyone to find something to brag about. With that thought, I held on even tighter.

'Chachijhi, really, I'm fine. I'll put the shopping in my room.'

'I'll help you . . .'

'I can manage.'

'Give me that bag.'

Everyone gasped as the bag gave way, causing the box to go flying and crack open at the foot of my intended's father. With a dull thud, a leather tasselled whip rolled out on to his foot. We all stood in silence, staring at the offending item. Nobody knew what to say, so we waited in silence. All I could hear was the slow but deafening thump of my heartbeat. It quickened immediately as I felt everyone look to me with a damning judgement.

'Oh my goodness, I have been after a Coco de Mer whip for months!' The excited outburst from (who I assumed was) my intended's brother elongated the shocked silence. Every pair of eyes turned to the man. 'It's a rare designer item . . . one of those antiquey treasures . . .' I caught his hazel eyes, and he suddenly looked terrified at his own admission.

'That's my niece, she will only get the best items for me. I tell her, don't spend any money on your Chachijhi, but she insists that she will give me only the best!' Chachijhi picked up the item to examine it. 'Yes, very nice duster. The leather strands get the dust from difficult places . . .' I stood mortified as she appeared to be the only one who failed to understand what the whip was.

'OK everyone, come through, you can relax in here,'

Kamal suggested quickly to break up the incredulous silence. I watched each member of the family file into the living room after my father and looked to my intended. He glanced back at me quickly and uncomfortably. Intuitively I knew he was hiding something. Then I saw Chachijhi survey the whip closely.

'Why are you still standing there?' she demanded as she handed me the whip before giving me a swift sharp slap to the back of my arm. 'Go and change. You must have something nice to wear in one of those bags.' I stared at her and wondered if I had the guts to shock her by walking downstairs in any one of the items I had been forced to buy today. The thought of facing my brothers doused me into reality and I discarded the thought instantly.

'Ten minutes, I promise,' I whispered before racing up the stairs. I didn't stop until I'd locked myself in my bedroom, dropped my bags and then leaned back against the door. 'Crap,' I whispered before bursting out in laughter.

Ten minutes later, I had hidden all the bags beneath my bed, changed into a simple black shalwaar kameez and was reapplying my make-up when Rita walked in.

'You dressing to go to a funeral?' I turned to look at her and smiled. 'I'm just warning you, your brothers want to have a word.'

'I know, but I bought all that stuff for work.' Rita frowned in shock. 'For research . . . product range reviews . . .' I stopped. No matter how I tried to explain, it didn't sound appropriate.

'OK, I'll let you do the explaining!' she said with half a smile. 'Did Chachijhi say she was going to use to the whip as a duster?'

'Please tell me she's stopped going on about it downstairs, because I don't think I can keep a straight face!' I said as I applied the last of my bronzer before reaching out for my chiffon dupatta. Throwing it over my shoulder, I stood up and caught her watching me. 'What?' I asked, looking down at what I wore.

'Nothing,' she said with a warm smile. Then she pulled me into a hug. 'He seems like a good potential, Yasmin, I hope you think so.'

My smile faded as it dawned on me that this was serious. This could be the man I had to build a future with, might have children with, might grow old with. I held on to Rita and closed my eyes as the events of the past couple of months flashed through my mind.

'Malik's never going to see you if we both start crying!' Rita laughed as she pulled back.

The name made me pause. Suddenly I recognised the man downstairs.

'Malik?' Rita nodded at my question. 'He's an IT consultant, right?' She nodded again and my heart raced ahead. 'Works for IBM . . .' She nodded once more before I could finish.

'Dad's already told you about him?' Rita stopped as I shook my head.

'I know him,' I whispered as I walked over to my desk and logged on to Facebook.

'What . . . what do you mean?' Rita asked, following me to the laptop to stand behind me.

I checked Bibi's profile and clicked through to her friends list.

'The two-timing, cheating, immoral, devious, lying, scummy—'

'Yasmin!' Rita's call made me stop and look up at her. I pointed to Malik's profile.

'I've never met him, but he's been seeing Bibi for the past eighteen months.' Rita's jaw dropped open and I nodded when she struggled to speak. 'She's been waiting for him to propose for the past two months. We've been telling her that he's been waiting for Valentine's Day.' My anger at his behaviour brimmed over and I slammed shut my laptop before storming out of the room.

'Yasmin . . . Yasmin!' Rita called. She caught me at the top of the stairs and spun me around. 'Stop! Stop and think about what you're going to say.'

'I'm going to tell his parents what he should've told them eighteen months ago when he told Bibi that he wanted to marry her!' I said clearly.

'He's here for you . . .'

'He's mistaken if he thinks this is going to end in happy-ever-after.'

'Yasmin, he's here for you.' Rita repeated herself and I realised she was asking me to keep my peace.

'You're kidding me . . .' I breathed out in disbelief. 'You're serious, aren't you?'

'If you go in there screaming and shouting, what will they think of you?'

'He is cheating on my friend, one of my best friends, who is dreaming about marrying the man who happens to be sitting in my living room, waiting to check me out for marriage.'

'Think of Dad! If you're going to walk in like this, think how it'll reflect on him.' Placing my hands on my hips, I paced on the landing until Rita stopped me. 'See the *rishta* out.'

'No!'

'See it out like a decent, well-brought-up woman.'

'I am a decent, well-brought-up woman; that's why I won't be party to this *rishta*,' I stated before I took the stairs down and entered the living room. My abrupt entrance startled everyone and I smiled broadly as I sat down next to my father.

'Oh, she's here!' Chachijhi stated as she ran in behind

me to pull my dupatta over my head. Each time she pulled it up, the chiffon material slipped down, so she perched on the arm of the sofa and held a hand against the back of my head to keep the scarf in place.

'Yaya, aren't you going to salaam everyone?' Daddy asked as Rita beckoned Jamal out of the room. 'Yasmin?'

'She's shy!' Chachijhi filled in as I stared directly at Malik.

'Judging by the shopping bags, she's so not!' A smile crept on to my face despite the fury within me, and I turned to Malik's oversize brother.

'You seem to know your dusters well,' I stated. 'How about your brother? Is he into dusting?' He seemed shocked by my forwardness and looked to Malik.

'I'd be more than happy to discuss dusting with you.' My flesh crawled at the smarmy answer. I held my smile in place as I looked at Malik.

'What is all this talk about dusting?' Chachijhi laughed nervously as we caught Rita pull an angry Jamal back out of the room. 'That's a woman's job; why are you all talking about dusting! Yasmin's good at dusting, you don't need to worry about that.'

'I hate dusting,' I corrected, and watched Chachijhi's smile falter before she burst out laughing.

'Yasmin! You're such a funny girl, teasing your Chachijhi like that!' she said as she patted the back of my head hard enough to teach me not to do that again.

'So, Yasmin, we hear that you're settling into a new job. How are you finding it?' Malik's father asked as he helped himself to a few somosas. 'Just so you know, my son's a very successful consultant, I don't think it would do him well to have an ambitious wife. He needs a strong wife who can be a good woman for him, make sure he eats well, makes his house a clean, welcoming home, good for him to sleep adequately . . .'

'Oh, I see,' Daddy murmured, looking at me hesitantly. My heart went out to him. He was lost without my mum, so I smiled at him supportively.

'Well that suits me perfectly. There's nothing I want to be more than a perfect wife slash cook slash cleaner slash masseur slash domestic servant,' I told Malik's father with a wide sincere smile. He smiled too until the meaning of my words sank in. Then his smile slowly disappeared. Once again I felt the strong tap of Chachijhi's hand against the back of my head as she burst out laughing.

'She's such a comedian! I tell you, Appa, she's the family clown. She is always making jokes . . .'

'What my husband meant to say is that we don't want a hard-nosed career woman for Malik. He needs a good wife to make life easy for him.' Malik's mother was a dragon in disguise. Correction, a designer-clad dragon who wore a cream banarasi sari with antique gold paisley motifs at the base and asol, to match the cream silk headscarf that framed her poised, haughty expression. She attempted to smile as she looked to my dad, only the smile failed to reach her eyes. 'You see, brother, we have seen plenty of girls for my Malik. Doctors, lawyers, architects, the whole range. We've seen beautiful girls who'd give me gorgeous grandchildren and ugly girls who would've given them brains, but none of them were to our standards. They all had that . . .' As she searched for the right word, she looked to me and I swear I saw her narrow her eyes into hard pearly beads. '. . . that sense of desperation about them.' Everyone sat in stunned silence as she gave a short smile and then proceeded to sip tea from her cup. I didn't know whether I hated or admired her type.

'You must be relieved to finally meet a family where your son's likely to be rejected,' I said and ignored everyone's shock as she choked on her tea.

'Yaya, stop teasing Malik's mother!' Daddy weighed in as he leaned forward to offer the dragon an almond slice. 'What Yasmin means is that we're equally happy to take our time to find the right life partner for our Yasmin.'

'It's so true, we parents only want the best for our children.' She smiled, accepting the almond slice as Jamal walked back in. But I wasn't fooled by her accommodating tone. 'The only shame is that time doesn't do daughters any favours.' With that pristine put-down, she bit into the almond slice.

'I guess it helps sons to play the field that much longer, albeit to the ignorance of Mummy and Daddy, who are busy trying to get son dearest to settle down.' I yelped as Chachijhi's pat took a forceful turn. Malik coughed and straightened up at my words.

'Why don't you give Malik some tea?' Chachijhi directed and I obeyed her request.

'So what do you do for a living, Yasmin?' Malik asked as I knelt by the coffee table to pour him a cup of tea. I held it out to him and met his eyes as he reached out to take it from me.

'You mean Bibi hasn't told you?' The cup clattered against the saucer as he started at my question.

'Who's Bibi?' his mother demanded, turning to stare at her son. 'You two know each other from before . . .'

'No, no, Ammi, we've never met,' Malik answered meekly.

'You mean you've never met Bibi?' Jamal asked. I turned to my oldest brother and gave him the widest smile for his support.

'What's Bibi got to do with this?' Daddy asked in confusion.

'Isn't that your assistant at work who keeps you on top of everything?' I didn't think my eyes could widen any more, but Malik's father proved otherwise. 'She calls him at all hours, there's nothing unusual in that . . .'

'You mean you haven't ever told them about Bibi?' I asked in disbelief.

'For the sake of my sanity, general well-being and weak bladder, would somebody in this room please tell me who this Bibi is?' Chachijhi pleaded as Malik fingered his collar before clearing his throat.

'Ammi, we should leave. Yasmin's not the type of girl we want in the family,' Malik stated as he stood up and straightened his blazer. 'I mean, you saw the places she shops at; they're not where decent girls frequent.'

'I knew it. The minute she first spoke back at me, I thought, this isn't a daughter-in-law any family would want,' his mother said as she finished her tea before standing up.

'What is going on?' Daddy asked, turning to me for answers in total bewilderment.

'Daddy, he's been promising Bibi marriage for nearly two years,' I said, reaching out to pat his arm.

'Bibi . . . as in your friend and . . .'

'. . . his make-believe assistant,' I finished with a regretful nod.

'What? You promised marriage without my permission?' the dragon demanded of her son.

'No, Ammi, she's lying.'

'She's not your assistant?'

'She is . . .'

'You've been lying!' We gasped as his mother started battering him with her handbag.

'Mother, you're embarrassing us!' cried Malik's brother as he protected his tea.

'Ammi, Ammi . . . wait . . . stop!' Malik called out, racing around the table to dodge her blows. He ran straight into his father, who tried to hold him in place for his wife's blows to land.

'Get out.' I froze at Daddy's quiet command. Malik's family, however, didn't hear it and I shook my head at that mistake. 'Get out of my house!' The bellow erupted and caused everyone to stop and stare at my father.

'*Bhai*, let's see them out . . .' Chachijhi was silenced at his glare.

'How dare you come in here looking down your haughty nose at my daughter, making demands of a wife, when your son is running around ruining another girl's reputation?'

'Listen, we do not know the details of what is going on,' Malik's father returned aggressively, shaking a finger at my dad.

'GET OUT!' he bellowed, making Malik's family race for the exit.

'We have never been treated so badly,' we heard the dragon whisper.

'What have you done to our family name?' Malik's father shouted at his son. 'Wait till you get home. Answers. I want answers!' And with that the door shut behind the departing family.

We sat in the sudden silence and waited for Daddy to say something.

'There's something wrong with that family,' Chachijhi stated. 'I could tell the minute the sons started talking about dusting. I knew then they were not right up here,' she said as she pointed to her head.

I bit my lip and stole a glance at Jamal. He was shaking to suppress his laughter. I did a double-take, and then briefly looked at Daddy, who was shaking too.

'I should've joined the mother; maybe I could've knocked some sense into the boy,' Chachijhi added. And with that, Daddy, Jamal *bhai* and I all burst out laughing.

*

A little while later, I walked into the kitchen to find my brothers freeze at my entrance. I looked to Zeena, who avoided my eyes, and I knew that they were unhappy. I wanted to turn around and leave, but I stood waiting for one of them to break the silence. They looked at each other, uncertain and unsure.

'Yasmin, come sit,' Rita *bhabhi* said as she glared at Jamal. 'Your *bhai* wants a word with you.'

Reluctantly I perched on a stool next to Zeena. All my brothers avoided looking at me. I knew it was the lingerie shopping. They had questions, lots of questions, but they didn't know where to begin or what to say about it to their baby sister.

'What's wrong?' I finally asked, unable to deal with their silence. Jamal cleared his throat, Zamal shifted in his seat and Kamal leaned down on his arms. 'Is it Malik's—'

'No,' Jamal *bhai* said quickly. He was still unable to meet my eyes. Rita *bhabhi* continued to glare at him and he cleared his throat again.

'Your brothers want to know why you were shopping at all those shops today,' Rita explained.

'I want to know why a decent girl is in those stores. Why you, Yasmin?' Jamal asked.

'Who is he?' Kamal demanded.

'What?' I asked in shock.

'Well, who is he?' Zamal added. 'The bastard who's corrupted you . . .'

'There isn't a he!' I told them in outrage. Jamal covered his face with his hands as Zamal and Kamal turned away from me. I grabbed their hands to stop them from leaving. 'It's to do with the product review strategy for work. My team asked me to pick up those items as part of the exercise.'

My words created an embarrassed silence. They had

assumed the worst. Jamal released a long and deep sigh of relief. Then he stopped smiling.

'I want you to change projects.' Stunned, I stared at my oldest brother. 'I'm serious. I want you to change projects. You shouldn't be exposed to these things.'

'I'm not a child.'

'You're a Muslim woman; you have no place being in those shops or seeing those things. No place at all.'

'I went there for work . . .'

'That's why you're to ask for a change in projects.' I stared at my stubborn brother and then turned to Kamal, who also worked in the corporate world.

'He's right, Yaya, you shouldn't be exposing yourself to—'

'I'm in private equity and we're working on the turnaround of a failing lingerie label—'

'You're a Deshi girl, Yaya; it's not proper for a Muslim woman to see that world. You're not married, you should be preserving your innocence.'

'Innocence?' I asked Kamal *bhai* with a laugh.

'This isn't funny,' he told me. Immediately, I stopped. He had always been the most observant one amongst us and his tone was serious. 'You're an unmarried woman; what would people think if they saw you frequent those places?'

'Depends on whether they're inside the store or not.' He stared at me until I looked away. 'Listen, if it makes you happy, I was uncomfortable in those places, but it's research.'

'That's why we're asking you to change projects,' Jamal repeated.

'I don't make those decisions, *bhai*. I'm not a manager or a director. I've only been in the job for just over a month,' I explained as Kamal stormed out in anger. 'I'm a researcher, that's all . . .'

'Then you should leave your job,' Jamal stated. Everyone looked shocked and then turned to me. 'You should just quit.'

'I'm not quitting,' I stated, matter-of-fact.

'Give them an option. Tell them you want to be on another project, or you leave.'

'I'm not quitting.'

'Yasmin, we're on your side.'

'Listen to me, I'm not quitting,' I told Zamal, who looked at me pointedly before following Kamal out of the room. I turned to my oldest brother.

'You can't reconcile what you did today with your faith; your job is not worth that,' Jamal stated.

'My job is the only thing I have going for me right now.'

'Your faith is worth more than that.'

'But it hasn't been compromised,' I insisted as I looked at Jamal, who shook his head.

'You don't get it, Yasmin. You're our baby sister, you're yet to be married; what business do you really have knowing what these places stock?'

'That's just it, *bhai*, it's business.'

'Quit, Yasmin, and reconcile your vocation with your faith.'

I shook my head at his advice. 'Listen, every one of us wears underwear. Sometimes it happens to be pretty, sometimes it's functional and sometimes, just sometimes, it can be a little bit more than that. My advice is to keep it simple and not sleazy,' I stated slowly. 'That I can reconcile with my faith.'

Before I had finished Jamal had stood up to leave. I watched him go and leaned my head down on my arms.

'It's not fair,' I whispered to my sisters-in-law. 'I'm just doing my job.'

'They're being protective brothers, Yasmin. You have

to choose whether you want to be their sister or a businesswoman,' Rita said before she too left. I looked up and found Zeena looking at me.

'Is that what you think?' I asked. She stood up too and headed for the door. Closing my eyes, I leaned back down on my arms.

'Yasmin.' At Zeena *bhabi*'s call, I looked up. 'It's only underwear.' With a quick wink and half a smile, she walked out.

But it was more than that. This was about the ability to take my own decision, judge a situation and make the right call. This was about living up to everybody else's expectations on everybody else's terms. Asian ways for women were different; there was a set path. So right now I was still a child in my family's eyes, an innocent, and as much as I wished that was true, I couldn't reconcile it with who I really was. I had become so much more in the last few months, but like all discreet Asian women I hid it well from the family to safeguard their reputation. Normally family protection was comforting, but it was becoming suffocating and undermining. I didn't want to go backwards, I didn't want to back down. But my judgement had been impaired, and I was left with the one question that I wasn't ready to answer: was this battle for independence worth fighting?

Lesson Seven:
When a man loves a woman, she feels it

The following morning, the sharp chimes of numerous texts woke me. I didn't have to check my iPhone to know that it was a distraught Bibi. But I was surprised at how fast the two-timing slime ball had got to her. I scrambled out from beneath my duvet, rolled over and picked up my phone to read the messages.

Is it true? Did you and your family give Malik's family a proposal?

You have a lot of explaining to do. Wagamama today at twelve. Malik told me everything, how could you? Bibi

Is it true? Did you entertain a proposal from Malik's family? Need the lowdown at lunch. Gem xx

My phone chimed to life again.

I know you wouldn't do the dirty but something's not right. You didn't tell us you had a proposal. You didn't tell us it was from Malik's family. You didn't tell us what happened. Why? M

Bibi had informed the girls, and judging by the texts, weasel Malik had weaved a fine story that made me the bad guy. The lack of faith in me displayed by my closest friends left me fuming. Falling back on to my pillows, I shut my eyes and counted to a thousand to calm myself down. Then I got up, showered and changed into my most comfortable tracks and vest before I headed down to the kitchen. Scrambled eggs, beans and toast along with coffee made for my perfect breakfast, but still I was left unsatisfied. Perching on a high stool, I stared at the fridge and once again counted to a thousand to dissuade myself from eating any more. Tapping my fingers on the granite worktop, I recited all the reasons why I shouldn't.

You want to fit into the RR jeans without a muffin overhang.

You want to be perfectly toned.

You need to have the fittest body.

It didn't work, so I breathed out.

Imagine Sam seeing you fat and flabby.

Nothing worked like a spot of anger to make your hunger disappear, so with that feat accomplished, I washed up and looked to my ringing phone.

'Mia . . .'

'Why Malik?' I started at the abrupt question. Drying my hands, I leaned back on the counter and listened. 'Bibi's sobbing her heart out and you're nowhere to be found.'

'And somehow that's my fault?' The silence that followed my reply was a shocked one.

'You serious?' The uncertainty in Mia's voice infuriated me even more.

'Why wouldn't I be? Between the three of you, you've decided that I am somehow responsible for Bibi's emotional breakdown.'

'You are serious!' Mia breathed out.

'Yes, I am serious. You do not know what I went through last night.'

'I can't believe you're being so selfish.'

'Selfish? I kicked Malik out of my house . . . You know what, I'm not doing this now. I'll face the inquisition at lunch, OK?' Furious, I hung up and looked for my cleaning materials. When you're mad, I find that there is nothing like throwing yourself into dusting, wiping, polishing and hoovering to work that anger out. So that's what I did. I switched on MTV, heard Duffy belt out 'Mercy' and then I began. I dusted each and every room. I plumped every cushion into fluffy fattiness, tidied every item back into its place and then used Mr Muscle to wipe and polish every surface until I saw my reflection gleam back at me. Finally I hoovered every floor space until I fell back on the couch shattered but content.

Running late, I dressed in a short black poloneck dress with a black grandad cardigan pulled over a pair of skinny jeans. Dropping to my knees beside my bed, I pulled out all the lingerie bags that I had hidden away the night before. I lined up the boutique bags and doubled them up where possible. Then I searched beneath my mattress for a large carrier bag. Asian girls never throw away carrier bags. As the pioneers of recycling, we keep a stash of bags of every range and size. I had my designer carrier bags, which I'd only reuse to show off; my high-street bags to take things into work in; and then the regular bags that doubled as bin liners. I found a large Abercrombie & Fitch bag to fill with all the offensive items. Ignoring my buzzing phone, I pulled on my knee-length flat boots and pinned my hair back with an alice band. Make-up free, I threw all the bags into the boot of my black Audi TT and drove down to Kensington to park at the apex of Kensington Court. Wagamama was a stone's throw away, and judging by the number of missed calls from the girls, they were already there figuring out how to get me to answer for last night's events. I spotted them at the window bench seats and walked over to join them.

'It's childish to ignore us,' Gemma stated as I pushed my leather bag into the space beneath the table.

'It's good to see you too,' I returned, seeing a pale, crushed Bibi sniffling into an overused tissue. 'Have you all ordered?' Mia nodded, and they sat there looking at me. Bibi looked how I felt when I discovered Sam's betrayal. I reached for Bibi's hand to comfort her, but she withdrew sharply and turned away.

'So, do you want to hear what actually happened, or do you want to tell me what that excuse for a man told you?'

With that, Bibi burst into what looked like her umpteenth crying fit.

'Nice one,' Gemma muttered, before consoling Bibi with a hug and a new tissue. 'Bibi said that you knew it was Malik; that's why you never told us anything about it.' I raised my eyebrow at the assumption, but stayed quiet whilst helping myself to vegetable dumplings. 'That you were only going to tell us if Malik had gone along with the proposal . . .'

'Why am I not surprised?' I asked drily. 'Let me guess. Did he tell Bibi that I was desperately flirting with him, trying to convince him that I was right for him whilst he tried to fight me off?' I said with a bemused laugh. I stopped laughing when I saw Mia's serious expression. 'He didn't?' I whispered in disbelief. I cleared my throat and paused for a while to absorb the lies that had been told. 'He did, he actually told you that . . .' Mia and Gemma both nodded, and then Bibi looked at me from red, tear-filled eyes.

'How could you!' she demanded of me.

'I didn't!' I promised, aghast that she would believe that of me. 'I wouldn't . . . What's wrong with you?'

'But you're heartbroken and single . . .'

'You think I'd do the dirty on my best friend because I was cheated on?' The silence at my question was more revealing than any answer I could've received. 'Why? Why would you think I'd do that?'

'Well, you really fell for Sam and you haven't been normal since . . .'

'What?' I demanded of Gemma, who nervously pushed her long fringe back from her eyes.

'It's true. Ever since things ended with Sam, you've been acting half human.'

'Half human? What the hell is that supposed to mean?'

'You haven't cried since that night you found out about Sam!' Bibi pointed out, waving her tissue in my direction. 'Look at me, I'm a wreck, and this is normal!'

'You just carried on as if Sam didn't exist, like you weren't affected . . .'

'. . . like he meant nothing, when all you'd done was dream of a magical future with him,' Bibi added after Gemma.

'What has that got to do with Malik?' I asked calmly as I folded my arms before me.

'You act like nothing gets you, like you're some kind of ice princess,' Mia offered reluctantly.

'And that naturally means I'd flirt with my best friend's man?' I asked, refusing to get angry.

'Yasmin—'

'You all know me better than that,' I said cutting Mia off.

'Yasmin—'

'Don't Yasmin me!' I told Mia. 'Just because I don't do public displays, or sob my heart out over ice cream and chocolate, you think I don't hurt? I have relived the moment I walked away from Sam a million times over and my heart shattered into so many pieces that I don't know if it'll ever be whole. But that means nothing to any of you,' I said as the girls shifted with discomfort. 'You would rather believe that instead of crying myself to sleep and accepting that I'm going to be single for ever, I spend my time plotting whose boyfriend I can steal because I'm so desperately single.'

'That's not what we meant . . .'

I shook my head to stop Mia from explaining.

'I miss him. Every moment, I miss him,' I whispered, looking down and then got up to go.

'Yasmin, don't run . . .'

'I'm not running, but I can't become any less of a woman. Here you are, the closest things to sisters, and you want me to bawl over a man who promised me everything, and all he delivered was a text message telling me he was screwing someone else. You're making me a weaker woman.'

'Yasmin, we just want to—'

'What?' I demanded of them, causing the diners around us to stare at us. 'Why don't you ask yourself why Malik is seeing proposals if he loves Bibi? When a man loves a woman, she knows, she feels it to her very core.'

'So do you . . . uh, still want to cancel your order?' the waiter asked nervously.

'Yes.'

'No.'

Mia and I answered at the same time and the waiter stood silently in confusion. Gemma signalled for him to leave, and as he did, Bibi's quiet sobbing melted our tense exchange. Gemma handed her another tissue.

'Daddy kicked Malik and his family out of our house.' Bibi stopped crying and turned to look at me. 'He was so disgusted by their behaviour and Malik's deceitfulness that he threw them out.'

'You mean you told them about me?' she asked quietly. I nodded. 'They don't know about me, do they?' I shook my head and smiled sadly. 'What *do* they know?'

'It doesn't matter, Bibi. He's not worth it.'

'What do they know about me?' Bibi insisted, as tears spilled down her cheeks. I wanted to protect her from the pain that came with heartbreak, but she wouldn't let me. Sometimes, a girl needs to feel her heart break to believe that Mr Right is indeed Mr Wrong. And only when the full picture, in all its ugliness, can be seen can the heart believe that Mr Wrong is undeniably, irrefutably and unconditionally Mr Wrong.

'Yasmin?'

I looked at Bibi and took a deep breath.

'They thought that you were his PA.'

Mia whistled at my quiet admission and Gemma cleared her throat.

'His PA?' We sat in silence, and in that moment we knew Bibi's heart would never be the same again. 'His PA?' she repeated quietly.

'If it helps, his mother battered him with her handbag when I told them that he had promised to marry you.' My attempt to lighten the mood failed.

Our food arrived and we tucked into our respective dishes as Bibi struggled to stifle her sobs.

'He told Bibi that you guys forced his family's hand, and that you were all over his parents trying to act like the perfect wife,' Gemma explained whilst avoiding my eyes.

'He also told Bibi that he wants her to cut all ties with you,' Mia added.

'I'm so tired,' Bibi whispered as she looked at me. 'I'm so confused. Why . . . why would he lie to me?'

Mia and I looked at her in shock. She still believed Malik. After everything that I had told her, she refused to accept him for what he was.

'Because he's a two-timing, no-good, lying con merchant.'

'But I've given him everything!' Bibi told us, as if that made any sense. 'He loves me, I know he loves me.'

'And what has he given you?' I asked.

'He told me that his parents knew about me but that they were in Bangladesh, and when they came back in February our families would meet and we'd start planning our wedding.'

'Instead they were at my house checking me out for their innocent accomplished boy.'

'Why did you even entertain the *rishta*? Maybe he didn't have a choice . . .'

'He's a thirty-six-year-old man; he had a choice,' I told her matter-of-factly.

'Maybe he forgot to mention that they came back from Bangladesh early.' Mia's look of shock at Bibi's answer mirrored mine.

'Tell me, Bibi, if Malik loved you, why did he come to see your best friend for marriage?' I asked again, and watched her flounder.

'Your family coerced his parents . . .'

'If you choose to believe that I am desperate enough to cheat on you, instead of realising that your man is a lying, two-timing gutless wonder, then you should listen to Malik and cut all ties with me.' I stood up and dropped my portion of the bill beside my unfinished meal. Shaking my head, I ignored Mia and Gemma's calls to remain. Sometimes the only way to get out of a mess is to walk.

I kept walking until I reached my car, then I drove through Knightsbridge to my offices in Green Park. I parked up, grabbed the bags from the boot and walked to Namhar Capital. Spotting the security guard, I waved my pass at him and waited for him to let me in.

'Thanks, I'm here to drop these off for my manager,' I stated, putting the bags down beside the reception desk.

'She's got you working on a Sunday?'

I nodded at his question and rolled my eyes.

'What has she got you to pick up for her?'

'Just some retail stuff for our latest project!' I said, knotting the handles together to stop him from searching through the bags.

'Well you know I have to vet everything that goes through reception . . .'

'But it's all wrapped,' I lied, dreading the idea of the guard handling the range of items I had bought.

'Then you're going to have to bring it back in tomorrow,' the portly guard told me.

'I've driven down today because I can't carry all this in on the tube . . .'

'Miss, I'm sure you understand that I can't accept unchecked packages. It's a security risk.' He wasn't shifting from his position, so I smiled at him softly.

'Honestly . . .' I looked at his name badge, 'Steve, I've had the worst couple of days ever. Please please please don't make me lug this back in on Monday morning.'

'I'd really like to help, but my hands are tied.'

'Why don't you call my manager and get her permission?'

'I can't make outgoing calls unless it's an emergency. This isn't an emergency so it's against company policy.'

I contained my frustration and put on my most charming smile.

'Why don't you just tuck it away behind the reception desk and I'll be in extra early tomorrow to take it upstairs.'

'It's still a security risk.' I dropped my smile and folded my arms. 'The simple solution is to allow me to check your bags.'

'I can't let you do that.'

'Steve, has my lunch arrived?'

I came to a sudden stop when I spotted Zachary Khan. Steve walked around the reception desk as I stared at Zach. It was the first time I had seen him dressed down. He swaggered in wearing an Abercrombie & Fitch grey hooded fleece over a pair of baggy jeans.

'Right here, sir.' Steve pulled out a large Domino's Pizza box with a bag of garlic bread and various condiments to hand them to Zach.

'Yasmin, what are you doing here?'

I gripped the bags until my knuckles gleamed white.

'Nothing.' The answer came too quickly. I looked behind him to see if Hannah or Selina was present too, and then returned my gaze to Zach.

'The young lady's dropping off a few items for her manager,' Steve explained as Zach took his lunch. I avoided his look of confusion. 'I've told her I can't allow it because she's refusing to let me check the bags. My job would be on the line, Mr Khan.'

'What's Hannah asked you to pick up?'

I avoided the hazel eyes and felt my cheeks burn with humiliation.

'Items for . . .' I cleared my throat and forced myself to speak. 'I'm writing the Baby O product review report and the team asked me to pick up a few competitor samples and—'

'Samples?' His look of incredulity made me wish the floor would swallow me up and spit me out on the other side of the world. 'Steve, I'll sign off on the packages,' he stated, leaning over to scribble his signature on the clipboard that the guard held out to him.

'I've got them,' I told him when he reached out to give me a hand as we walked to the elevator. 'Thanks for getting me past security,' I said as the elevator trundled slowly up to my floor. He stood in front of me, and I forced myself not to notice how attractive he was, or how my heart raced, or how unprepared I was to see him.

'You happy with the product review report?'

I forced myself to remember my 'no man' policy, my pledge to put myself first, my promise to never fall for a man before he fell for me.

'Yasmin?' I looked up, startled.

'Yeah?'

'Yeah, you're happy, or yeah, you have no idea what I asked?'

I didn't know what was wrong with me so I shrugged. He grinned slowly.

'What?' I asked.

'Are you tongue-tied?' I wanted to stop staring at his broad white smile, but I was fixated.

'Why would I be tongue-tied?' I asked.

'Why don't you tell me why you're lost for words?'

I felt like a sixteen-year-old. I reminded myself of Sam, of Malik, of my brothers' interrogation and my best friends' betrayal to regain full use of my faculties.

'I want to thank you for getting me into Namhar Capital,' I finally spurted out.

'You're welcome,' he replied with narrowed eyes. 'Has everything worked itself out?'

'It's working itself out,' I returned.

'Well should I congratulate you on an engagement?' Zach offered as he searched to see the ring on my hand.

'Oh no, I didn't . . . we didn't get back together. I uh . . .' I stopped and took a moment before I looked up at him. 'I made a clean break.'

'I thought only men were capable of doing that,' he said with half a smile.

'Well I guess you learn something new every day.' His smile widened at my response and I held his look. The doors pinged open. 'Excuse me,' I whispered as I lugged the bags past him and headed for Hannah's office. I stopped as Zach walked beside me in the same direction and looked towards the closed office.

'She's not in, if that's what you're worried about.' He read my mind and I looked at him.

'I'm not worried.' He didn't look convinced. 'OK, I lied, I'm worried.'

'She's not as bad or as scary as she seems . . .'

'She is when you're a nobody!' I covered my mouth and looked at him wide-eyed. 'I didn't mean that; please don't tell her I said that.' He laughed and shook his head.

'I'm using her office today, I'll be sure to leave her a message.' I looked at him with disbelief and dropped the bags by my desk. Then I read the mischief in his eyes as he leaned back on Ella's desk.

'I deserve a slice of pizza for that.' I was flirting and I couldn't help it. He looked down at his lunch order.

'You can't take food from a man,' he stated, pulling the pizza box out of my reach when I attempted to take a slice.

'Oh, it's like that, is it?' I asked, watching him nod.

'Don't you women fixate about being on some size-zero low-carb diet?' he asked.

'Oh my goodness, you're calling me fat . . .'

'Holy God, no!'

I burst out laughing at his response and we laughed until we stood there looking at each other. At that moment I knew I could seriously fall for him.

'Don't let me hold you up,' I said, returning to my desk and pulling out my notes in a modest attempt to try and look busy. He disappeared at my suggestion and I sat alone in the silence, disappointed that he had gone, and then held my head in my hands.

'Why are you working today?'

I smiled at his return and looked up to face him.

'Because I have to finish my product review report . . . and because right now this is the only thing that's right in my life.' Zach looked surprised by my reluctant candidness. 'Don't say it, I know that means I have no life.'

'Well that makes two of us,' he said, rolling Ella's chair across to my desk to offer me a slice of pizza: 'Only because we both have empty work-driven lives,' he made clear.

'Much appreciated . . .' I stopped when he pulled the slice out of my reach. Confused, I looked at him.

'First you've got to tell me what you've got in those bags for Hannah.'

I balked at the question. 'Keep the slice,' I replied.

Zach laughed and took a swig of drink before pointing at me.

'Now I gotta know what you have in those bags!' I watched the way his eyes creased at the corners and felt warmed by his deep rumbling laugh. He spotted me watching him and I looked to where the bags were. I contemplated trying to talk him out of it, but suddenly realised that I wanted to see his reaction.

'Go ahead.' He looked surprised and put his slice of pizza down. 'Really, go ahead.' Biting my bottom lip, I watched him lean over and peek into a couple of the Agent Provocateur bags. He arched a brow and cleared his throat before he looked back at me.

'You know you've been had.' That wasn't the response I expected.

'Had?' I asked reluctantly.

'Your team's pranked you.'

I shook my head at Zach and walked over to the bags. Kneeling on the ground, I opened up the Baby O bag and I pulled out the monstrosity of a bra. I laughed at the surprise on his face.

'Exactly!' I pointed out. 'This is why Baby O is failing. No boutique gaining market share is stocking this sort of thing. I sit here and stare at figures, statistics and models, and hypothesise about the company's failure, but because the team sent me out there, in one sentence I can sum up why it's struggling.'

'There's more to it . . .'

'They've got a three-floor flagship store in Covent Garden stocking underwear from the 1960s as if it's a bargain basement outlet. In Covent Garden of all places!'

'They've got a strong property portfolio . . .'

'Disposal of that in this economic climate would barely give us any margin.'

'You think?' He was testing me and I nodded before carrying on.

'Baby O has thirty-odd stores scattered around the UK; that's thirty-odd stores stocking lingerie ranges so bad our grandmothers would refuse to shop there.'

'What's the solution?' he asked.

I narrowed my eyes. I knew I had caught his attention.

'Dispose of twenty-five non-essential stores to competitors wanting to expand their reach.'

'So help the competitors?' Zach asked in total confusion.

'No, distract them with a disposal strategy and give Baby O the legs to go high-end. Turn five stores into key brand boutiques, build an online presence for volume and market an exclusive USP like mad.'

Zach paused, put his pizza slice down and considered my proposition.

'That's just clever store planning. The core range still sucks.'

'In-source a designer to get Baby O into the right fashion spreads and worn by the right celebs. Look at Serano Luigi or Zamil Hussain; they've turned around the lingerie world. Bring someone like that in and go totally go upstream.'

'Rania Jayachand's meeting Zamil Hussain in Dubai.' I stopped at his comment.

'To turn Baby O around?' He nodded and I smiled. 'But he hosts private viewings of his new range in London, not Dubai.'

'She's meeting a few designers and retailers out in Dubai.'

'To attract investment or to build a presence?' I asked with barely contained excitement.

'Both. You do know that the European Fashion and Textile Export Council state that the UAE and Saudi account for seventy-seven per cent of Europe's total lingerie exports to the Gulf.'

I shook my head at the fact. I felt embarrassed by my lack of knowledge and put the bra away before heading back to my desk.

'Rania's looking for analysts to accompany her out there,' Zach said. The offer was too good to be true and we sat there looking at each other.

'To go to Dubai?' Zach nodded at my hesitant question.

'To help her research the market and joint venture opportunities in Dubai, and with meetings with entrepreneurs out there.'

My heart raced at the thought of getting away, far from the pressures of being single, from the betrayal of friends, from the memories of my heart breaking. Then I remembered my family and shook my head.

'I can't, and in any case, Hannah would never choose me over Selina and Co.'

Zach watched me carefully. 'It never hurts to put your hand up, Yasmin.'

I avoided his eyes, and then cleared my throat.

'I've got commitments here.' My reluctant admission made him nod in acceptance.

'Such as your, uh, accessories?'

I looked at the rest of the bags and realised that it was indeed a prank. I stopped a smile and glanced at him.

'I've been had,' I accepted as he rumbled with laughter.

'Yes you have.'

I refused to smile, but I accepted the pizza he held out.

'Yes I have,' I repeated. 'How do I get myself out of it?'

'Who was responsible for it?' Zach asked, and I bit my lip, hesitating to reveal Selina's identity. 'Hey, they were going to let you present whips and all this gear at the team meeting, so I wouldn't be big on loyalty right now.'

'Selina,' I offered reluctantly. 'It was Selina with her crew of suits.'

'So you present everything you've told me backed up with statistics and anecdotes, but invoice the bill to Selina and leave all this packaged up on Hannah's desk with a note from Selina—'

'You're crazy,' I cut in.

'Because you know it's genius, right?' I grinned at his suggestion.

My mobile buzzed to life. I checked it, saw it was Chachijhi and switched it off. Zach caught my action.

'My dad set up a *rishta* for me last night and it went horribly wrong and I'm trying to avoid my auntie.' I stopped at his look of confusion. 'Do you know what a *rishta* is?'

'I'm guessing it's some kind of arranged marriage or introduction?'

'A *rishta* is a protocol where the parents seek a suitable

boy for their daughter and arrange an informal family introduction.'

'That still happens?' His condescending comment did not amuse me. 'I thought Asian kids are in such a rush to be white that that kind of stuff went out in the dark ages.'

'Being a banker doesn't give you the right to be stupid,' I told him.

'Be fair, you're not exactly the type to accept an arranged marriage.'

'Why is that?' I asked. His judgemental tone was fast eroding my patience.

'You seem tense . . .'

'I'm not tense.'

'Well, you seem irritated.'

'I'm not irritated. Why do you think an arranged marriage is a bad idea for me when I'm obviously still very single and nowhere near getting married.' I was actually very irritated indeed.

'Because you're a beautiful, spirited, feisty woman with a stunning smile and a penchant for bad timing who can find a man any day of the week on her own.'

Zach's words left me silent. I opened my mouth to say something, anything, but found myself lost for words. He seemed oblivious to the impact of what he'd said and helped himself to another slice of pizza as I searched for something smart to say.

'Oh please!' I breathed out with half a laugh. He looked up, surprised. 'That is such a line!'

'Yasmin, I can compliment you without wanting to get into your pants,' he told me.

'You don't want to get into my pants?' I asked with incredulity and then realised what I had said. 'Well, uh, that's your loss, given that they're very nice itsy-bitsy little things.' I refused to cringe at my embarrassing response.

'I take it Mr Saturday Night didn't get a chance to get into your pants?'

'You see, that's precisely what's wrong with men these days. You judge a woman by her bedability factor—'

'Bedability factor?' Zach laughed.

'*Rishtas* judge men and women alike on their merit, their combined physical, social, financial and reputational worth . . .'

'Reputational worth?'

I ignored his guffaw and carried on. 'Yes, reputational worth. So someone like you wouldn't get through my family vetting process because you have the reputation of a Casanova, which doesn't make for a good husband,' I threw at him cheekily.

'Low blow, Yasmin.' I smiled at his unamused expression. 'So some guy who has the right job, reputation and family automatically makes for a good husband?'

'He makes for a worthy candidate,' I explained. 'That's all this is. An introduction to a worthy candidate, which rules out scumbag players, gutless wonders and shameless spongers. It saves women time, money and heartache.'

'So, did Mr Saturday Night qualify as a candidate who could potentially get into your pants?'

I looked at him and narrowed my eyes. I couldn't lie.

'No, he didn't. But you don't know how much I wish he was.' We laughed together at my reluctant admission. 'He turned out to be my best friend's long-term secret boyfriend.' He didn't believe me. I nodded to assure him that I had indeed told him the truth.

'That small detail escape the vetting process?' I grinned at his question.

'We have a faction of men who have no balls. They mess around with decent girls to prove how macho they are, but when Mummy and Daddy crack the whip for a grandchild, they dump Ms Now Indecent for a purer parent-approved model.'

'That's harsh,' Zach stated, putting his lunch away.

'And we have a group of girls so eager to find Mr Right that they get played and played until the only thing we know is how to choose Mr Wrong.'

'That's worse,' Zach returned.

'That's reality,' I whispered.

'Yasmin, happy-ever-after only exists in Hollywood chick flicks. Reality bites.'

'Oh, is that how you set expectations for the women you see?'

He laughed at my question, and then sobered up. I tried to avoid his hazel eyes, but found it hard to.

'That's not my favourite line.'

'That's right; that'll come after you've spotted the next totty you want to bed, right?'

'Well, since you put it like that . . .'

'How would you put it, Zach?' I don't know why I was pushing him, but his blasé attitude to relationships angered me.

'I'm a banker, Yasmin. When you're a banker, everything and everyone has a price tag. I'm surrounded by seasoned bankers who live the happy-ever-after with their high-school sweethearts and their two point four children in some lavish country home. And all the while they have the brainless but unbelievably young and sexy secretary on their arm at every corporate do.'

'That's pathetic!'

'Pathetic?' Zach looked at me surprised. 'That's reality.'

'Only if you have such low expectations from life.'

'And having teenage pipe dreams of happy-ever-after is better? I mean, how many happy-ever-afters do you know about?'

I looked down at his words and smiled.

'My mum married Daddy on her father's recommendation. They were besotted with each other for many wonderful years. After she passed on, Daddy used to tell me she'd left him with enough love to last a lifetime.' I looked up and held Zach's hazel eyes. 'You see, I know it exists. I've seen how beautiful it can be, and—'

'You want nothing less than that,' Zach finished. I nodded. 'What if your father can't deliver Mr Right?' he asked.

'You don't have much faith, do you?' I smiled from within and shook my head. He chuckled in agreement and I felt bad for him. 'Is it easier to have low expectations of people you love?'

The amusement faded from his eyes. 'I'm guessing it's gotta be easier than having high expectations and being proven wrong.'

'Oooh, I don't know,' I said. 'You know what they say: low risk, low return. High risk . . .'

'High return,' Zach finished with half a laugh. 'You brave enough to put me in front of your father?'

I stopped laughing to stare at him. It was a question born out of amused curiosity, but there was something in his eyes that told me otherwise.

'You'd be a gamble, Zach, not a high-risk investment.'

'Really?'

'Yes, really.'

'So you don't have a high-risk appetite for—'

'I didn't say that,' I corrected. 'You have to be able to gauge the risk level before investing; you have to know the market risks, the credit risks, the security risks, and you have to run your "know your client" search.'

'It looks like private equity might be teaching you something after all!'

I laughed at his comment. 'It's quite simple really.' He

looked at me in surprise. 'It teaches you to be greedy; it teaches you to know what return you want before you make that investment.'

'Are you saying I won't give you a good enough return?' Zach asked.

'I'm saying you're one of those complex investment products where the risks are so high that the rewards are obscured.'

'It's simple, Yasmin: high risks mean high returns.'

'Or being left bankrupt.'

We stared at each other, waiting with eyes sparkling with attraction, knowing that the subtext was me negating the potential of there ever being an us. He cleared his throat and looked down.

'So, you want to tell me what you're trying to do with this report?'

'Sure,' I accepted eagerly. We were pulling back into the safety zone, and right now that was fine by me.

Zach cleared away his lunch as I searched through my files for the relevant documents. We spent the rest of the afternoon dissecting, reviewing and reworking my report. He grilled me until we argued, he questioned until I held my head in my hands and he pushed until I gave him the answers that he needed. He left me late afternoon following a call from Hannah. I stayed on to finish off the report. I couldn't have done it without Zach. I'd thought he was acting as my gatekeeper; now I knew he was enabling me to become my own gatekeeper, and that meant a lot to me. For the first time since I started at Namhar Capital I felt on top of my work. It was good to be good at something.

The feeling only got better with the start of the week. As we congregated in the meeting room for the Monday-morning briefing, we heard Hannah bellow for Selina from her office. Fifteen minutes later Selina walked out with bags loaded with lingerie products, red-faced, meek and humiliated. I sat with a small smile as everyone turned to look at me.

On Tuesday, Hannah asked me to give her a walk-through of Baby O and on Wednesday she asked me to lead the research on emerging lingerie designers. My reports had made their mark, and in spite of the pressure, I was exhilarated by the interaction I had had with Zach. I tried to avoid checking my emails, but couldn't help glancing at them in the belief that he would write, that he would say something about Sunday, but he didn't.

On Thursday Mia called, reminding me that I was using the long hard hours to hide from the conflicts in my personal life.

'You still mad at us?' I pegged the phone between my jaw and shoulder so that I could finish the yoghurt that I had grabbed for lunch.

'What's Bibi's decided?' I asked. I heard Mia sigh, and I put down the yoghurt at her silence. 'She's taken him back . . .'

'I don't want you to judge us all by Bibi's actions.'

'She's taken him back!' I breathed out in disbelief.

'That doesn't mean we can't be friends.'

'Oh my God, she's actually taken him back,' I repeated as I sat back in my chair and shook my head.

'Yes, she has. In spite of all our advice, she believes that they have a future.' I balked at the comment. 'She believes he's worth giving another chance.'

'Wow, she must really love him,' I whispered, recalling how I had cut Sam off at the first sign of infidelity.

'Yasmin, she's fighting for her man and her future.' Mia's comment caught my attention.

'Does that mean that I didn't love Sam?' The

silence that followed my question was frightening. Suddenly I doubted my decision about Sam and felt guilty for thinking about Zach. 'Did I do the wrong thing? Why can Bibi forgive where I couldn't? Did I give up too easily?'

'Stop, Yasmin. Sam was a long time ago.'

'But I loved him, Mia, and I cut him loose. I didn't give him the chance to explain, I didn't give him the benefit of the doubt. I just cut him loose.'

'I think Bibi's making a mistake she'll come to regret. You saved yourself from that,' Mia stated, but my head was reeling with self-doubt.

'But what if it's me who's made the mistake?' I whispered as I logged on to Hotmail.

'Don't do it, don't check the emails he sent you,' she said, reading my mind.

I opened up the folder that filtered his emails and looked at the ten unopened messages he had sent since that night several months ago.

'You've done it, haven't you?'

I nodded at Mia's question and read out the first of the emails.

'*Don't shut me out, Yasmin, answer your phone and give me a chance to explain.*'

'*You're making a mistake, Yasmin, don't do this to us.*'

'*You've made a mistake and you owe it to me, to us, to talk this through. Please give me a call.*'

'Please, give me a break!' Mia muttered as I opened the fourth, fifth and sixth emails that all read in the same vein. '*I can't let you do this to yourself.*'

'Listen to this, Mia, he sent this one a week after we split,' I said as I looked at the sixth email. '*I deserve more from you, Yasmin, I expected more. Your mobile line is dead, your workplace tells me you've left, and you don't*

*answer your emails. I miss you and I don't know what I
can do to make you believe me. I don't know what more
I can do to reach out to you.'*

'He hasn't explained the text, though, has he? That's
the crucial thing,' Mia stated.

I skimmed through the remaining emails and froze.

*'This is the last email I'm going to send as it appears
you're intent on putting an end to what we had. I don't
want you to think the worst of me so I want you to know
the truth. That text was a wind-up joke from my mate, a
lads' laugh, a stupid prank, and I know it must have hurt
you deeply when you read it. But if you have any feelings
left for me, come back to me.'*

'He's lying . . .'

'No, he's not,' I whispered as I read and then reread
the message over and over again.

'Yasmin . . .'

'Mia, I have to go. I promise to call you later.' I hung
up and stared at the email on my screen. A million
thoughts raced through my mind, a million more
emotions coursed through me until I faced the single
most important question about my actions: had I been
wrong? Holding my head in my hands, I tried desperately to remember the wording of the text message, but
the memory escaped me amidst the pain I had felt that
night. Doubts over my snap judgement plagued me and I
wanted to scream at the future it had cost me.

'Jasmine, have you finished that designer profile on
Bare Jyang for me?' Spinning around, I found Hannah
standing at my desk.

'Uh, I . . . let me print it off for you,' I said as she
pierced me with her electric-blue eyes.

'Your Baby O visit paid off.' I hit the print icon on the
latest profile I had completed and then waited for the
wilting criticism Hannah was renowned for. 'I've just

read your product range review. It was good. I wish more of my analysts had that instinctive nose for turnaround.'

One hour ago, the compliment would've made my week; now it rang hollow compared to the disaster I had made of my personal life. I collected the printout and handed it to Hannah. She looked like she wanted to say something more to me, and then thought otherwise. Without another word she turned around and walked away, leaving me reeling with the empty reality that I had created for myself. Suddenly my passion for work disappeared, my enthusiasm to stretch myself vanished in the midst of the realisation that I had been the sole architect of my own miserable loneliness. I opened up the email and looked at the date. More than three months had passed since he had sent it to me. Futures were worth fighting for; that was what Bibi was doing. At that moment, an email arrived from Mia and I opened it.

I know you're about to email him, but I want you to do one thing before you make contact, and that's to ask yourself, what if your gut instinct was right about the text? Mia xx.

I switched back to the empty message I had opened to reply to Sam. I didn't know where to start. The white screen left me bereft of words. I looked at the time. It was mid-afternoon, and I promised myself I would compose an email on the way home. Amidst the chaos of self-doubt and deep loneliness, it took a good friend to remind you that you had indeed made the right decision. But nothing compared to the one thought that rang through me: what if I had been wrong?

For the first time since I started at Namhar Capital, I left work on time. Intent on scripting that reply to Sam, I dispensed with my rollerblading evening in Hyde Park and headed straight home to a quiet house where I could carefully compose my thoughts.

'You're home!' Rita *bhabhi*'s announcement told me that that was the very last thing I would be able to do as I walked into the living room to find Jamal *bhai* and Chachijhi.

'Oh thank God you're home!' Chachijhi cried out as she grabbed me into a giant hug.

I looked over her shoulder at Jamal, who rolled his eyes.

'Is everything OK?' I asked as Chachijhi stemmed her sobs and pulled me down to sit next to her. She dabbed at the corner of her eyes before looking at me.

'It's my Meena,' she whispered, trying hard not to break down into a crying fit. As she took her time to compose her words, I looked to Jamal again and he shook his head. 'She's . . . she's . . . oh my God above, she's brought a *rishta* home.'

'Really?' I feigned excitement despite feeling my despair deepen at being the sole remaining singleton in the family. 'Well that's fantastic! We can have another wedding along with Maya's—'

'I can't, I can't, I can't do it!' Chachijhi cried as Rita *bhabhi* walked over and hugged her.

'I . . . I don't understand. Isn't this good news?' I asked in confusion. I saw Jamal mouth something but I frowned in confusion. He mouthed it again; I shook my head.

'He's black!' Chachijhi wailed it out before breaking down in body-shuddering sobs. I stared in stunned silence at *bhai* before turning to Chachijhi. 'What will everyone say?' She wept. 'My baby wants to marry a black man!' Then she grabbed my arm and leaned close to me so that I could feel her paan-scented breath. 'You have to stop her.'

'W . . . what . . .'

'You have to stop her. You're the only single girl left in the family; you can explain that being single doesn't mean you have to date a black man.'

'Chachijhi, if she's happy . . .'

'Happy? She can't be happy when I'm close to dying from shame? You're single; teach her she doesn't need to go to these desperate measures to find a man.'

'Have you met him?'

'Are you *pagul*? Have you really lost your mind!' she demanded in outrage. 'Her father would disown her if he knew!'

'How determined is Meena?'

'I am not eating a single thing until she stops this madness; I'm fasting until it kills me.' Chachijhi declared melodramatically as she beat her ample chest with a clenched fist.

'You don't need to give up food . . .'

'How could she? How could she do this to me?' I looked to Jamal, but Chachijhi grabbed my chin, forcing me to look back at her. 'Only you can stop her. Please talk to her, make her understand why marrying a Bengali boy is the only way for us. Please, please, please make her see sense.'

Rita *bhabhi* pulled my distraught aunt into her arms and held her as Jamal indicated for me to join him in the kitchen.

'When did this happen?' I asked quietly as he closed the door behind me.

'Meena told her on Sunday.'

'Man-eater Meena? She's always been quite wild, but this . . .'

'Well, it looks like Man-eater Meena's found God and wants to marry a black Muslim convert.'

'No!' I whispered, taking off my navy Burberry princess-line trench coat as Jamal perched on a stool.

'Seriously, she's in hijab, prays five times a day and now she wants to marry this guy.'

'How long has this been going on?' I switched on the kettle to make some refreshments.

'For six months, apparently.' I stopped and turned round to look at my brother. 'No one had a clue, and apparently Leila refuses to have a word with her.'

'As the older sister, she needs to.'

'Leila's met the guy, she likes him and she refuses to stop Meena,' Jamal told me.

'I can't tell her to stop seeing a guy just because he's black.' I stopped at Jamal's stern look, then quickly carried on. 'I know it's not our way, but would Chachijhi rather have someone like that idiot Malik?'

'No one's married out in our family, Yasmin . . .'

'But if he's a decent, educated, employed man who's God-fearing and most importantly considerate of Meena, why would you want to stop it? I can't do that. She'll have to find someone from Maya's family,' I told Jamal *bhai* determinedly.

'We're family,' Jamal corrected. 'Chachijhi's spoken to them, but they're too caught up trying to keep her wedding on track and say that this kind of scandal could derail it.'

'What is it with our people making life impossible for each other?'

'Yasmin, it's hard to change our ways.'

'Is it so bad that Meena's finally sorted herself out and found a decent guy she wants to settle down with?' I asked *bhai*, who stared at me. 'There are only a few Bengali guys out there, but our ways tell us that even the bad apples are still better than marrying a black man.'

'It's our ways, Yasmin. Don't undermine that.' I paused at his firm words.

'Muslims can marry Muslims of different races. Meena's not technically doing anything wrong.'

'She wants to marry out of the community, Yasmin. That makes her an outsider, and it places us, her family, at the centre of community speculation and ridicule,' Jamal pointed out.

'So it doesn't matter if he's a doctor or a lawyer or a multi-millionaire; it just matters that he's black.'

'Correction, it matters that he's not Bengali.'

'I can't do it,' I stated as I switched off the kettle and folded my arms around me.

'Can't?' Jamal asked me with contained anger.

'OK, won't. I won't do it.'

'I don't know what this job is doing to you, but you've changed and it's not for the better.'

'Leave my job out of this, *bhai*.'

'Meena's not the only one who needs to settle down within the community.'

The comment stole my breath from me and, hurt, I stared at my brother.

'Don't look at me like that,' he said.

'Like what?' I asked quietly, feeling the sting of tears.

'Like you can't see that you're carrying on as if you're a single white female, throwing money away on designer labels, not caring about where you work, what you expose yourself to, and with no consideration for where your life is going.'

'It's because I care about my work.'

'And what would the community say if someone had spotted you walking into one of those stores?'

I stopped and stared at my brother and shook my head.

'Do you know that in Syria, mothers and aunties go lingerie shopping for their daughters to ease their transition into womanhood and to celebrate their entrance into marriage?'

'You don't live in Syria.'

'Oohhh, you're so stubborn!' I cried out as I slammed my hand against the counter.

'Because you're my baby sister and it's my job to see you right.'

I shook my head again and looked at Jamal.

'I am not a child, and if you think that I don't know the difference between right and wrong, then trust me, it's too late to start teaching me it now.'

I left *bhai* sitting on the stool and walked out of the kitchen. I entered the passage and stopped at the sound of Chachijhi lamenting the loss of Meena's innocence. Shaking my head at the melodrama, I walked into the study, locked the door and switched on my computer. I logged on to Hotmail, clicked through my folders and opened up Sam's last email to me. As I read his message, I realised I had nothing to say that wouldn't unleash another drama, and I didn't have the perseverance to entertain that. I thought of calling Mia, but rejected the idea at the thought of explaining myself yet again. I couldn't think straight for all the advice that was thrown at me. Mia, Jamal, Bibi, my auntie, everyone seemed to have an opinion. And the only thing I wanted more than anything was space. Space to know what I wanted, to know what I didn't want, but most importantly to be myself, on my terms. I couldn't do that whilst I was fighting everybody.

Dubai. Zach's suggestion came to mind. I looked it up on the internet and read through the many ex-pat message boards and forums. I knew I was running away from a life that was going nowhere fast. But maybe, just maybe, Dubai would enable me to run towards a life on my terms alone. Whether or not it did was irrelevant; what mattered was that I gave myself that second chance.

Lesson Eight:
Taking the smallest step can make
the biggest difference to your life

Every woman knows that the secret to feeling sexy is naughty lingerie. It's immaterial whether its barely there sheer kiss-and-tell lace, or suggestive silk. What matters is that it caresses the skin in a way that makes you feel like you would be the best present for any man to unwrap slowly. So I donned my latest indulgence – the sheerest, smallest, smoothest nude tone set I had bought from Victoria's Secret as a celebration of my regained confidence. Every girl needs to feel special. At least that's what I needed to believe to attend my firm's annual party as a singleton. Whilst this pointed to an unenviable question-packed reunion with my old team, it also afforded me the opportunity to convince Hannah to consider me for the Dubai project. So I slipped into my second indulgence, the towering four-inch nude tone peeptoe Louboutins. I teetered upright, giggling and wobbling at the elevated height, until I found my balance. By any measure my toned, supple body with ample curves was one to celebrate, so I switched on my radio and danced around my bedroom in just my underwear and heels. The height was impossible to manage and when Cyndi Lauper's 'Girls Just Want to Have Fun' blared out, I shimmied and spun around without a care until I fell on to my bed laughing. I gasped for breath and wondered what madness had driven me to buy the insanely high heels. Instantly I regretted the thought as I recalled how the very expensive spending spree had done little to prove Jamal *bhai* wrong.

'Yasmin, Mia's here.'

'Wait, wait, wait.' I screamed to stop Kamal from entering my room. Grabbing the duvet to cover my near nudity, I stared at the door that was held ajar. 'Don't come in. Tell Mia I'll be ready in five minutes,' I added as I slipped off my heels. I pulled on my black curve-hugging skinny jeans and then a tiny silk teddy before slipping on the sheer butt-skimming skin-tone chiffon Grecian dress. I returned to my dresser whilst looping the leather strings several times high around my waist. Once there, I pulled my hair back into a slick low pony, clipped on a pair of big round hoops and pulled on a pair of extra wide gold bangles. Then I looked at my reflection. I forced myself to acknowledge the pretty woman who stared back, to notice the delicate features, the almond-shaped eyes, thick lashes and full red lips. Taking a deep breath, I upended my make-up bag, grabbed the best of Bobbi Brown and gave myself smoky exotic eyes, bronzed cheeks and glossed natural lips. I looked down and counted to ten as the sharp fear of seeing Zach and being overlooked hit home.

'Hey,' Mia said as she knocked before entering my room.

'You look amazing.' She ignored my compliment. She had caught my sadness before I could bury it and came to crouch before me.

'You look beautiful,' she said as she cupped my face and forced me to meet her eyes.

'You look stunning,' I repeated with a mischievous smile.

'No, you look fantastic,' Mia returned as she stood up to give me a twirl in her emerald-green shift dress and killer heels.

'No, you look divine!'

'Lady, you look fabulous!' Mia threw back whilst pointing at me.

'Wait, you haven't seen me in the Louboutins!' I laughed as I raced over and slipped them on. I stood up unsteadily and took minutes correcting myself. Mia watched dubiously, and we burst out laughing as I struck various poses whilst trying to stay upright.

'God help you, but I can't wait to see you pull your moves on the dance floor!'

I grabbed a pillow and threw it at her. The effort made me lose my balance and I fell back on to my bed. Mia doubled over laughing and I followed suit. We laughed until we sobered and looked at each other.

'You ready to go to the ball, Cinders?' Mia asked, holding out my black tube purse to me.

I nodded, and grabbed her arm to stand up. I took the purse from her and threw a black shawl around myself. It was time to make an entrance.

Isis, the Lebanese restaurant in Green Park, was buzzing as the perfectly groomed, designer-adorned employees of Namhar Capital mingled against the backdrop of free-flowing champagne and never-ending trays of nibbles. Mia and I entered the opulent bar having descended down the candlelit brass stairs.

'Hello, hello.' I froze as Randy Raj appeared before us. I gripped Mia's arm. 'You look too stunning. You want to dance?'

'Yasmin, you should go dance!' Mia encouraged as I glared at her.

'Listen to your friend, Yasmin, let's go boogie on the dancing floor.' Raj had a tendency to talk loud, very loud, and with the music in the background, he felt he needed to shout in my face. I stared at him, our wannabe Shah Rukh Khan, and asked God, quite simply: why me? Even in the darkened restaurant he stood out like a sore thumb in his bling-encrusted Gucci shades, tight tan leather trousers and see-through white cotton shirt that had one too many buttons undone. 'Come on yar, the music is pumppppinnnngggg!'

I jumped at his order and glanced at Mia.

'I . . . uh, I need to go to the bathroom.'

'No waaaaayyyy, man! Rihanna is singing "Don't Stop the Music"; we can do some mambo in the ending of the song.'

The thought of doing the mambo in four-inch heels whilst Raj busted out some Bollywood moves put the fear of God into me.

'I really really need to go pee . . .'

'Wowowo . . . OK, lady, no need to dish the dirt. Raj does not need to be knowing if you want to do a number one or two, OK? I'll be back when you finished your lady business.'

I nodded very quickly as Raj jived back towards the dance floor. In silent horror, we watched as he threw out some pulsating Bollywood pelvic moves whilst jiving like an Indian John Travolta.

'Promise to kill me before he comes back for me?' I muttered to Mia, unable to tear my eyes away from a grinning Raj

'I'll pay just to see him get you on to that dance floor.'

Raj looked over to find us watching and gave us a thumbs-up sign.

'God help me if that happens,' I said as I waved back before dragging Mia away.

'Aah, give the guy a break . . .'

'More like stop the guy from breaking my neck!' I returned laughing as we walked around the dance floor to move between the soft chiffon drapings that segmented the low-seated lounge area from the shisha smoking area and the self-service buffet area.

'Yasmin! You look amazing!'

Mia and I turned at Selina's over-the-top shriek. She was as ever the office achiever. Every workplace had one; these were the extra-driven women who always turned up in the latest fashion, immaculate make-up, nails and hair, and who would without a shadow of a doubt stab the nearest colleague in the back to get further than any of their peers.

'You look fantastic! Is it a man? It has got to be a man. Who is he? Is it someone from the company? That's naughty, oh so naughty. Where is he? Go on, point him out, I promise not to tell!' The queries came thick and fast. 'And you should know that your knock-off Prada makes you look sexy as hell.'

I raised a brow at Selina's back-handed compliment and caught Mia's exasperated sigh as she walked away to peruse the treasure trove of nibbles.

'Selina, are you wearing any of the lingerie Hannah sent you home with?' Selina's eyes frosted over as we exchanged air kisses. 'Falafel?' I offered with a wide white smile whilst holding up the Lebanese dish.

'I heard that Zachary Khan once had you personally removed from the team?'

I put the serving tray down to buy myself time.

'Be very careful how you respond.' The deep rich tone was firm and made us all turn in surprise.

'Oh Zachary! Speak of the devil!' Selina laughed sexily as she reddened at being caught gossiping.

A slow smile crept on to my face as we looked at the

very handsome Zach Khan dressed in a tuxedo. He looked me over slowly and paused when he realised I had caught him looking. I felt my cheeks burn, but refused to break the eye contact.

'It's good to see you, Yasmin,' he said before leaning forward to give me a kiss on the cheek. My eyes widened at his familiarity, but not as wide as those of Selina, who looked lost for words at being overlooked. I cleared my throat and stood back as I read the assumptions she was silently jumping to. 'Selina, as always, your reputation precedes you,' Zach added. She laughed too excitedly and looked at me with widened eyes at the acknowledgement.

'Oh, and what reputation would that be?' I bit my lip at her obvious flirting.

'The reputation for requesting the most, uh . . . products for review.'

A little glimmer of mischief faded in Selina's eyes but she continued smiling.

'Excuse me, ladies.' Zach walked off with nothing more than a short smile. I needed to talk to him about the secondment but didn't want Selina to intrude.

'First-name basis with Hannah's protégé; how did you manage that?' Selina asked, watching Zach. A slow presumptive smile crept on to her face. 'Or need I ask?'

'Selina, not every woman walks around knicker-free in short skirts just in case a chance for promotion comes knocking.'

'OK, the DJ's banging out Timbaland and we're hitting the dance floor,' Mia announced as she grabbed my arm and led me away from the astounded Selina. 'You are on fire tonight. What has gotten into you, girl? Three months ago you'd have laughed that off and accommodated Selina.'

'I don't want to be Ms Nice and Walk All Over Me, Mia. That Yasmin's hit the road, sister!' I announced as we started doing John Travolta's jive walk in our march towards the music. Mia innovated the steps and I followed suit laughing all the way.

'Yasmin.' I spun around as Zach called out my name and took hold of my arm. I froze, mortified that he had seen our embarrassing dance routine.

'I want to introduce you to Rania Jayachand, daughter of Arun Jayachand and new MD of Baby O.'

I looked at the simple, unassuming young woman and did a double take.

'You're . . . we met . . . you're the lady from Covent—'

'We met at Baby O,' Rania finished as she reached out to shake my hand. 'I liked your honesty and integrity, Yasmin.'

I looked to Zach and then back at Rania.

'Zach tells me you're on the turnaround team?'

I nodded and shifted from foot to foot, knowing that this was my chance to get myself on to the Dubai team. Only with Zach so close by, I couldn't think of a single intelligent thing to say, so I just kept smiling. Rania looked a little put off by my grinning silence and glanced at Zach. He frowned and watched me until I cleared my throat.

'So, so . . . are you enjoying Baby O? The store in Covent Garden . . .' I trailed off, as Zach spotted Hannah and wandered off. I took a deep breath, looked back at Rania and laughed. 'I get intimidated easily,' I confessed and watched her laugh along with me.

'I do too. But trust me, this is nothing compared to being handed a failing boutique to turn around!' She was very down to earth and I felt comfortable around her.

'Do you mind if I ask you why you took this challenge? I'm new to private equity, but I have a team, a manager, a director to learn from. You've jumped in at the deep end.'

'Do you know why Baby O was created?' Rania asked

as she took a flute of champagne and overlooked my lack of what should've been basic knowledge. 'I'm the youngest of seven girls. Papa launched Baby O for Oshanti to give us the best range of silk, lace and satin lingerie available. He was worried that we had to go to these bawdy or sleazy boutiques and couldn't reconcile that with his conscience.'

'Oh my God . . . that's just so touching.' I breathed out as Rania's smiled dropped.

'My mother ran it until she passed away five years ago, and it's hardly been looked at since. This seemed like a good opportunity to keep my father's hope for young women alive.'

Rania wasn't your cosmopolitan partying jet-setting girl; she was a decent homely woman with traditional values. Baby O suddenly felt alive, valuable, and I cared that it continued.

'You've got a tough challenge keeping it from being stripped and sold off in bits,' I advised.

'Yes, that's true. The world of financial geniuses is a different world to mine and I struggle to keep up.' Rania had been protected from the world of business and now had jumped in at the deep end to rescue some of her father's assets. 'But my mother, who had no business acumen, made it a success. So I know I can do it. I have the same, if not more, passion to make it a success.'

'I hear that the UAE's a good business option for lingerie.' Rania paused at my comment. 'Did you know that seventy-seven per cent of European lingerie exports to the Middle East is accounted for by UAE and Saudi Arabia?' I repeated Zach's fact and watched her interest pique.

'You've done your strategy homework, Yasmin,' she commended as I smiled.

'Private equity isn't only about asset stripping; it is

about reviving brands, and I love the idea of reviving Baby O.'

I heard Zach clear his throat to mark his return and to reel me back from saying too much.

'Me too! We share the same passion.' Rania's Indian enthusiasm was charming. 'I want to revive Baby O's roots and turn it into an international boutique label. You know, like an exotic Victoria's Secret.'

'Oh, I love Victoria's Secret.'

'So do I!' Rania squealed. 'I really love the Sexy Little Things range.' We paused as those around us stopped to look at Rania. She wilted beneath the stares and turned to me for help.

'La Perla's Fairoz range is to die for,' I offered in the silence. Rania looked at me with total seriousness in her eyes.

'Do you think that it is possible to turn Baby O into the next Victoria's Secret or La Perla?'

The quiet, honest question couldn't have come at a worse time. Zach was standing nearby with Hannah and they both looked at me with piercing judgement. I avoided Zach's eyes to smile at Hannah. But she didn't smile back. So I took a deep breath before nodding at Rania, whilst ignoring the silent wrath of Hannah's disapproval. The Ice Queen wore an age-appropriate blush-pink Versace dress, and despite being half her age, I felt insignificant in comparison.

'Remind me again who you used to work for,' Hannah asked in that tone that crushed you into nothingness.

'I was . . . I worked with the . . .' She intimidated me so much that I could hardly get the words out. 'I was a senior analyst for Jason Lewis's team.'

'Oh, you really were one of the data miners. Well, that's marvellous! We always need a runaround girl on the team.'

Smarting at the flippant comment, I stared at her and wondered if she would support me in my bid to go to Dubai.

'I'm . . . I'm happy to run . . . to be the runaround girl in Dubai.' Hannah's icy blue eyes darted across to Zach. 'I hear . . . if I'm not mistaken, that is, if there's still opportunities . . .'

I stopped as the awkward silence became prolonged and everyone turned to Rania for a response. When she looked confused and the silence became deafening, I decided to accept it as my response.

'I . . . I'm going to go dance . . . uh, excuse me,' I said before walking fast towards the dance floor looking for Mia and Ella. It was then that I spotted Randy Raj bopping his way towards me with an overeager smile. Fear coursed through me at the thought of reliving a Bollywood blockbuster in front of my managers, and worst of all, in front of Zach. I moved to the right to indicate my intent not to dance. Raj shifted likewise. I shifted to the left and he followed suit, and then he stepped forward still grinning from ear to ear. There was no escaping him. Without another thought, I turned around and grabbed Zach's arm.

'Would you dance with me, please?' I pleaded. Everyone looked surprised at my forwardness. 'Excuse us,' I added whilst watching Randy Raj's smile drop at my rejection.

Without a word, Zach took my hand to lead me on to the dance floor. I continued watching, as Raj asked Ella to dance. It was then I realised that Zach and I were swaying to the slow sultry voice of Taio Cruz. I hesitated to place my hands on him as he moved against me. I settled on putting them on his chest and caught Mia's look of sheer amusement. I mouthed, 'Help!' but she winked and turned away. I could feel every part of Zach against me and stiffened as I felt his hand slip down to my lower back. My heart raced, my senses spun and I did what all thirty-something singletons would do, I stumbled. I stumbled and trod on his toes hard enough for him to grunt in pain.

'I . . . I'm sorry, I didn't mean to hurt you,' I whispered in humiliation. 'You should know that there's a queue of girls waiting to dance with you . . .' But Zach pulled me close and we started dancing again.

'I know.' His arrogance forced me to look up at him.

'You know?' I asked.

'So you thought you'd push in front of them all and get in first?' he teased.

'Not that I want to dent your ego, but I was trying to escape Randy Raj.'

'Randy Raj?' He looked at me dubiously.

'Due diligence, corporate finance, Indian secondee who's just joined our team?' Zach spotted Raj the same time as I did. 'He seems to think that just because we're the only buds in the firm, we're meant to be together.'

'Buds?' He looked surprised at my non-PC reference.

'OK, I mean we're the only Asians in the firm.'

'I know what the reference means,' Zach returned. 'And you're wrong.'

'It may be hard for you to accept that you're not the only admired person in the room. He has been chasing me all evening and the only reason I pulled you on to the dance floor was to avoid him . . .'

'I mean you're not the only buds in the firm.' I paused at what sounded like a reluctant admission and looked up at him. 'I'm part Bengali.'

'Sure you are!' I laughed in disbelief.

'I am part Bengali,' Zach repeated.

'You're as Bengali as Elton John is straight,' I joked until I looked up at him and realised he was serious. We stood still as Taio continued singing and people danced around us. I cleared my throat as we started dancing again.

'But you're more gora than you are a bud. I mean, we act bud-British, but you don't. Nothing about you is bud-British. I mean, I thought you had bud in you, but you act white, so you're not really a proper bud . . .' I stopped talking as I realised just how wrong I sounded.

'Do you have any more opinions you want to share?' I shook my head and slowly peeked up at him. He had a glimmer in his eyes.

'It's nice to see you have a sense of humour, part-Bengali Zachary Khan.' He laughed at my comment and swirled me around before pulling me back to him. 'I want to be on the Dubai team,' I stated as he stared at me to assess my determination. 'I'll be the runaround girl, I'll take notes, I'll arrange meetings, book flights. I'll do whatever needs to be done, but please allow me to be on the team.'

'It's not my call, Yasmin. Hannah's directing the project,' Zach reminded me.

'Hannah respects your opinion, and if that opinion suggested that I would be an asset . . .'

'Rania doesn't need a yes girl; she has no need for a PA either,' Zach told me.

'I know the lingerie market, I know the designers, the supply chain, the movers and shakers; that's all I've been learning for months. I have opinions; I believe Baby O can be revived . . .' I lost my breath as he spun me and brought me to a sudden stop against him.

'Rania's asked to have you on the team.' I stared into his eyes, trying to read whether he was playing me, but he was serious. Slowly I smiled and he nodded to assure me.

'I'm going to Dubai?' I whispered, and he grinned and burst out laughing as I wrapped my arms around his neck and hugged him with delight. 'Thank you, thank you, thank you!'

'Yasmin.' Zach's call brought me to my senses, because at that moment I realised that we were being watched by those around us. Slowly I unwound my arms and stepped back from him. He looked embarrassed and I bit my lip to stop myself from screaming with excitement.

'You're serious?' I asked, unable to believe what he had just implied.

'Rania asked for you after you chatted with her in the store. So she's serious,' Zach clarified. I couldn't stop smiling. I looked around, feeling free already, restless to see the world, excited to discover it on my terms. I looked back at Zach and found him smiling at me.

'Thank you,' I mouthed, as I backed away from him and quickly turned to seek out Mia.

'Yasmin! There you are!' My search was short-lived as I walked straight into Randy Raj. 'I've been waiting for you all night. But all is well now I've found you and we can dance till the sun coming up, no?' I didn't have a choice. Raj grabbed my arm and led me past dancing couples and groups until we stood in the middle of the dance floor.

'Raj, I need to find Mia . . .'

'Oh my lordy God goodness, it's John Legend's "Green Light"! I love this song. Follow my lead.'

I wanted to tell John Legend not to ask for the green light, not to let Raj throw himself into the uncoordinated hip-hop Bollywood dance style that cleared the space around us. But John sang and he sang loud.

'Dance! I tell you dance!'

I jumped at Raj's bark and shuffled from foot to foot as I dodged his arms and avoided his grinding moves. I ignored everyone who watched us and counted the seconds as Raj obliviously bumped and bounced along to a tune that had no connection to the one that was playing. I stopped when the pelvic thrusts started, but he grabbed my hand and pulled me back to him. I was all hair and heels as I tumbled against his chest.

'Hello, hello.' He smiled as he held me close. Then I screamed as he threw me into a spin and grabbed my hands to make me dance circles until my head reeled and I fell back against him. Some people whooped around us, others laughed, but I gasped for breath, wanting to die as the song came to an end. 'We make good couple, eh?' I smiled up at Raj and groaned when Usher's club anthem started.

'This one's mine!' Mia shouted, racing forward to grab my hand. 'This is our anthem,' she told Raj as she whisked me away.

'Next one's mine,' he promised, blowing me an air kiss.

'I'm going to Dubai,' I whispered, trying to catch my breath. 'Zach's just told me I'm on the team. I'm going to Dubai!'

'Dubai?'

'Yes, I'm on the international team.' I stopped to let it settle in. 'I'm going to Dubai!'

'Is Raj going too?' Mia asked laughing as the thought wiped the smile off my face.

'Did you see how he grabbed me to demonstrate the best of Bollywood's dance glory?'

'I watched you relive your *Saturday Night Fever* dreams!' She laughed as Usher's anthem pulsated to life.

'He danced bad, didn't he?' I asked reluctantly. Mia hesitated. 'He did, right? And I looked like a div, didn't I?' she nodded slowly. 'Right.' I accepted, taking a deep breath. 'Well, there's only one way to rectify that, isn't there? Let's show everyone what I'm really made of!'

Mia read my cheeky expression and we started

dancing. Mia and I loved dancing together, and now we brought Usher's video to life. Our colleagues circled us, only this time they clapped and cheered us on as we took control of the floor. I laughed as I swerved, swayed and spun until all I heard and felt was the music. I felt someone behind me and turned to find Ella dancing. Before long, several others took our lead, and it wasn't long before everyone had followed suit. I laughed in a way I hadn't felt like laughing in a long time. It felt good to feel free. It felt good to make life happen. It felt good to know that sometimes, taking the smallest step could make the biggest difference to your life.

Lesson Nine:
Everyone deserves a second chance

Of course, making the biggest change happen in your life never comes easy. That's especially true as a single, Asian Muslim girl. Wanting the norm is normally unmentionable; wanting anything different from that is unthinkable. Yet here I sat thinking that distance from the norm was the only thing that was right for me. In short, I craved space from my life. And yet my duties as a daughter, sister, ex-girlfriend and friend made me doubt my very decision to go to Dubai. Restless to talk to my father, the dilemma caused me to leave the party early. At home in my kitchen I rustled up Daddy's favourite chocolate butter cake topped with berries and cream and set it out with tea ready to serve. I stared at the clock in front of me and knew that Daddy would be home at any moment. So I waited. With all my hopes and fears, I waited for Daddy to hear me and give me his blessing.

'Yaya?' The sound of his arrival made me jump.

'Hi, Daddy,' I replied, walking around the island to take his coat from him to hang back in the hallway. 'Was it a busy evening at the restaurant?' I found him at the counter cutting into the cake.

'Should I be worried?' he asked.

I perched on the stool next to him to pour him a cup of tea.

'You always worry, Daddy,' I told him as I stared at the cake longingly.

'Have some,' Daddy suggested, cutting me a slice.

'Oh no, I have worked for months to get toned, I can't afford to eat cake at two a.m.!'

'Have some,' he insisted, holding out a big spoon of moist cake.

'Daddy . . .'

'Open.' I did as he said and spent the next few minutes enjoying every single calorie that bite had cost me. 'Talk. What's worrying you?'

I watched him tuck into the cake and felt nerves consume me. I pulled my shawl around me and took a deep breath.

'I've got an opportunity to go to Dubai with work.' I was too nervous to look at my father directly, but I noticed how he put his spoon down and paused in thought.

'Why?' Of all the questions I thought he'd ask, this wasn't one of them. I couldn't meet his eyes, I didn't know where to begin without seeming ungrateful for the life he had given me. 'What's in Dubai that you don't have here?' And instead of having an adult conversation, I did what every child did. Argued like a child.

'It's only for two weeks, and it's part of my job.'

'No, no, no . . .' Daddy said, shaking a finger at me. 'Jamal told me he wasn't happy with your job.'

'This has nothing to do with Jamal *bhai*!' I pointed out. 'Daddy, it'll be good for me. The company will take care of everything, cars, hotels, flights . . . you wouldn't have to worry about anything.'

'Yaya, you'll be in a foreign country alone!' he stated as if I had missed that fact. 'What if something happens to you? I can't come find you, I can't ask your brothers to check on you . . .'

'Nothing will happen to me!'

'What if you get lost, or hurt or caught up in an accident?'

'I won't, and if I do, I'll have colleagues there to make sure I'm OK.'

'Colleagues, Yasmin; not family, but colleagues!' he shouted out in disgust. 'You sound like Meena, only caring about what she wants.'

'Daddy, I'm thirty years old.'

'You are still my responsibility.'

'Responsibility?' I breathed out in disbelief. 'Or burden, Daddy? A burden you want to palm off on another man.'

'How dare you?' The quiet question embarrassed me.

'I'm sorry, I didn't mean that,' I said, taking his hand, but he pulled it away. 'I'm asking you to allow me to go to Dubai for two weeks.'

'What if it turns into three weeks, maybe four, even six months?' he asked.

'It's two weeks, Daddy, in a safe country where there are loads of Asian girls working.'

'Girls whose parents don't care if they're married or have a husband to look after them,' he pointed out. 'I am a better parent, Yaya, I encourage you to remember that I am your father.'

'And I'm asking you to remember that I am your daughter,' I reminded him, and he looked at me with eyes that told me he was worried.

'I promised your mother I'd look after you every day until you had settled with a good man,' he whispered, and tears stung my eyes. 'I can't . . . I can't look after you if you are not here with me, Yaya.'

'Please let me go,' I whispered as tears dri

my lashes at the pain I was causing him.

'Why? Why is this so important to you?' he asked as he wiped the tears from my face.

I shook my head to clear the confusion that the past few months had created. When I composed myself, I looked up to meet my father's eyes.

'Because I'm scared that if I don't go, I'll stop caring,' I told him.

'What . . . what do you mean, Yaya?'

'I'm scared I'll go along with life without caring because it'll make everyone happy.'

'Yaya . . .'

'I'm thirty years old. I know I have to get married; I want to get married.'

'So, why are you running away?'

I couldn't stop crying. 'Because I still remember how Mum's eyes lit up when you walked into a room. She glowed, Daddy, she glowed with happiness, and she was strong for it. Till her very last minute, she glowed,' I whispered. 'I thought I'd found that, Daddy. I thought I had, but I was wrong. I was so wrong, and I'm scared that I'll never know how to trust myself again.'

'Yaya, when did this happen?'

I looked at my father and decided it was time to be his daughter. And so I began. I told him about Sam, about my hopes and my crushed dreams. I told him about work and how the last rishta had left me without friends. I talked to him until he saw that I needed space and that only space would give me the peace that I sought.

When I'd finished, he sat quietly and cut himself another slice of cake.

'You need to go,' he accepted.

I felt my heart swell with love and I burst out crying. Leaning over, I hugged my father until he pulled me into a strong warm bear hug. I cried harder, and he held me until I had no more tears to cry. And when that moment came, he cupped my face and smiled at me. 'You have your mother's strength and your mother's lust for life, my Yaya, don't you ever forget that.'

Two weeks later, Daddy dropped me off at Heathrow. He stood by me amidst the disapproval of my brothers and the despair of Chachijhi Fauzia. My mobile buzzed with enquiries from Ella and Helen, but I held on to Daddy, refusing to cry and unable to let go.

'Yaya, I'll see you in two weeks.' I nodded at what now seemed like an eternity. 'You need to go check in.' Once again I nodded. 'Make sure you call me every day, make sure you eat well and don't forget to take your multivitamin tablet each morning.'

'I promise,' I muttered against his shoulder as he pulled back and cupped my face.

'Do what you have to do, but come back to me glowing.'

I smiled at his words and closed my eyes as he kissed me on the forehead and patted the top of my head.

'Asalaamalaikum,' I whispered as he walked away. I dabbed away the tears that trailed down my face and watched him until I could no longer see him.

'Yasmin?' I turned around at the loud call and spotted Ella dragging a huge suitcase behind her. Dressed in a floor-length maxi dress and oversized hoops, she looked like she was heading out for a holiday as she carried several bags, a laptop and a handbag along with the compulsory oversized sunglasses, glossy fashion magazines and the *FT*. 'There you are. I've been looking for you everywhere!'

'I was just seeing my dad off.' Ella stopped at my comment and frowned at the idea. 'I'm close to him.'

'I look like I'm dressed for St-Tropez, don't I?' she

whispered, taking in my fitted jeans, pumps and crisp white shirt topped off with a fitted black blazer.

'You look like you're going to be comfortable on the flight,' I assured her.

'I'm so excited. I can't believe Hannah chose us to go.'

'I don't think she did; it was Rania who made the call,' I corrected as we headed towards Virgin Airline's check-in counter. 'Have you seen Helen?'

'Hey, ladies!' We both stopped at the hyper-happy call. 'So are we ready?' Helen piped up as she strolled towards us with her perfectly matched Samsonite cases. She was dressed in a cream pencil skirt and black silk top that matched her patent black killer heels.

'She's going to get the upgrade,' Ella whispered just before Helen joined us.

'How exciting is this?' Helen asked with a wide white smile. 'I can't believe I'm not going to see my fiancé for two weeks, but I'm not going to talk about him. I've decided that's the only way I can manage without him.'

I ignored Ella's groan and patted Helen's arm.

'Hey, pretty ladies!' Randy Raj's arrival was loud and over the top.

'Hello, Raj,' we chimed back as he stopped before us and put his hands on his hips.

'So, we ready to party!' he asked, holding his hand up for a high-five.

'Bring it on!' Ella returned as I rolled my eyes before turning around and heading for the counter. The others followed close behind.

'Come on, Yasmin, Dubai is capital city for non-stop partying! All the Bollywood actors party there all year long: Shah Rukh, Amir, Saif Ali, Preity, Rani . . . Oh my God, you name them, they all party there,' Raj announced.

'I want to dance Bollywood style,' Ella stated as we queued up.

'It's no problem, I'll show you. It's easy as—'

'Do you think we'll get an upgrade?' Helen asked as she surveyed the Virgin counter assistants. 'We could if we checked in separately,' she whispered with an arched brow.

'I don't mind sitting as a group,' I returned as we were called to check in.

'I have a club card,' Helen stated as we all rolled up to the counter.

'I'll book you in separately,' the perfectly groomed assistant returned as she flicked a glance over in our direction, obviously deeming us unworthy of an upgrade. I looked at Ella as she glared at the oblivious Helen.

'Have you seen Rania?' Raj asked, looking around.

'She's in first class,' Ella returned as we handed our passports to the assistant.

'Could you provide us with seats as close to business class as possible, preferably with a window?' The assistant looked at me and smiled. I knew I could have blagged that upgrade with Helen, but I couldn't sell out on kooky Ella and Randy Raj.

'Shopping,' Ella stated with barely contained excitement. 'Dubai duty-free's a shopper's paradise, Yasmin, and the malls . . . there are so many.'

'I've earmarked them, along with the evenings that I'm hitting them,' Helen stated.

'I think I have enough suntan lotion. I got buy-one-get-two-free at the pound shop,' Raj announced, as I wondered why a brown man would need it. 'I made an agenda of clubs I want to go dancing at,' he threw in.

'Guys, somewhere amidst all this we've got to fit in work!' I reminded them.

'Morning, geeks.' We heard Selina's cold greeting and

found her checking in to business class dressed as if she was ready to walk straight into a boardroom. 'Cattle class is pretty good on Virgin. Do pop up and say hello,' she added.

'She's coming?' I whispered to Ella, who nodded reluctantly. 'Why?'

'Does anyone know if gorgeous Zach is coming to Dubai?' Helen asked with wide-eyed excitement. 'Can you imagine going on a desert safari with him all dressed up like Lawrence of Arabia!'

'You're engaged!' Ella and I reminded her at the same time. Her smile dropped, and we took our tickets and headed for our flight.

We landed in Dubai amongst women dressed in long black luxurious abayas. The full-length gowns billowed around them as they walked behind tall broad men in dish-dash and gowns, ex-pats heading for meetings and holidaymakers eager to shop as hard as they planned to party. The large opulent air-conditioned terminal did little to prepare us for the heatwave we walked into as we exited and waited for our driver to pick us up. Two minutes later, we watched Selina walk out with an escort who carried her bags. A black Mercedes waited for her but she stopped to look at us.

'You really need to learn how to stop looking like backpackers and more like business executives,' she stated with half a smile. 'I'm happy to give one of you a lift.' Ella pinched Helen to stop her from volunteering. 'Don't say I didn't offer.' We watched as she folded herself into the cool Mercedes.

'I love Dubai,' Helen muttered. To hide her disappointment she pulled on a slim black pair of Gucci shades and held a mini fan before her. 'I wish my fiancé was with me . . .'

'We've got a packed itinerary. You're here to work,' Ella told her drily.

'You wouldn't know what it's like, would you?' Helen returned with a hard stare.

'Why did you come if you're going to whine about leaving him behind?'

'If you two are going to bicker throughout our stay, I'm sharing with Raj,' I threatened.

'Really?' he cried out with excited anticipation.

'No, because you two are going to stop bickering, right?' Raj's excitement faded at my direct answer as I looked to Helen and Ella. Reluctantly they nodded as our driver arrived in a huge white Land Rover. 'Roll on the good times!' I laughed as we whooped in excitement and jumped in.

The chauffeur eased his way into Dubai's traffic, crossing the floating bridge before joining Sheikh Zayid road. The three of us sat in awed silence as we weaved past the twin towers, Emirates Mall and the towering Burj Dubai.

'Hannah's PA has just emailed through our meetings,' Ella stated as she looked at her iPhone. 'I barely have time to check in before I have to head straight back out.'

'What meetings have we got?' Helen asked as we all brought out our iPhones.

'We're meeting the accountants at the designers' boutique,' Raj said.

'Crap, I've been doubled up with Selina,' Ella complained.

'What are you doing, Yasmin?' Helen asked.

I stared down at my schedule and groaned silently. Then I cleared my throat and looked up with a smile.

'I'm supporting Rania Jayachand,' I said as we weaved on Jumeirah Road.

'What?' Helen queried with distaste as Ella glared at her.

'I'm supporting Rania,' I repeated as I stared at the magnificent Burj Al Arab.

'That's great, Yasmin, you get to work with the MD,' Ella said, pointing out the positive of being Rania's unofficial PA.

'Oh . . . my . . . God! We're going to Mumbai in the second week!' Helen cried out.

'No!' I breathed out, turning around to face Raj and Helen. I checked my iPhone and realised that I wasn't included.

'Yes, yes, yes!' Helen shouted in excitement. 'We're going to Mumbai. I am so going to blag tickets to Zamil Hussain's fashion show out there!'

I stared down at my itinerary again in case I had missed that fact. I hadn't, I was the runaround girl, the girl who took notes, arranged meetings and grabbed the right coffee. I saw Ella watching me with a sorry smile.

'You get glorified PA responsibilities and I get to be a glorified subordinate to the mighty Selina,' she said as we pulled into the drive of the Arjaan Rotana, our hotel.

'But we're in glamorous Dubai, Ella, so let's make the most of it!' Helen laughed as she gave her a quick hug before stepping out of the Land Rover.

'It could be worse, Yasmin, we could have been partnered with Ms Perma-Perky!'

I bit my lip at Ella's comment and accepted that it could've been worse.

I took a cab to the sublimely subtle One and Only Royal Mirage to meet with Rania. Dressed in white linen trousers, red silk blouse and navy heels, I felt elegant and chic as I wandered through the cool corridors.

'The Eau Restaurant?' I asked at reception and

followed the petite Filipino assistant who led me out via a water footpath into the famous restaurant. 'I'm here to join Rania Jayachand.' The maître d' escorted me through to the decking which looked out on to Jumeirah Beach.

'Yasmin.' Spotting Rania, I thanked the maître d' and waved at her.

'Wow, this is amazing!' I said as I pushed my shades on top of my head and exchanged air kisses.

'Welcome to Dubai,' Rania announced as we sat down. 'You look fantastic, that's a great look.' I smiled at the compliment and ordered a sparkling water.

'Rania, thank you for selecting me to come out here.'

'Not at all. I have my father's advisers, my legal team, my banking team, my accountants, Namhar Capital. I don't need another adviser, Yasmin. I need someone who can tell me what works from gut instinct, and I like your spirit.'

'Spirit?' Confused, I looked at Rania for an explanation.

'You're not a sheep, you're not just another doer at Namhar Capital and you're prepared to think beyond the fastest way to profitability.'

I bit my lip at Rania's conclusion. 'It may be because I don't know the fastest way to profitability.'

'Sh, sh, sh.' I stopped as Rania waved a finger before me. 'Never doubt your gut instinct, Yasmin. Business is not just about making profit; it's about how you keep on making profit. That's something those Namhar Capital sheep do not understand.'

I took a long swig of my drink and prayed she wasn't overestimating my abilities.

'So . . . where do I start?' At my question, she handed me a folder.

'I've read your profiles on the four prospective

Emirate partners I'm meeting. Yes, they're big retailers but I don't get a feel for their lingerie or retail interests specifically.'

'We weren't able to obtain the company statistics in time.'

'The accountants will get those. I want you to go see the companies, visit all the malls, watch the clientele, get the vibe and feel of the stores.'

'You want me to do field research?'

'And I want you to get me details on who the manufacturers are for these shops. Look at Nayomi, find out who they source from, call them and get me volume/value figures.' The maître d' arrived to inform Rania that the first of the prospects had arrived. 'Oh, get me retail space figures for all the malls in Dubai. The credit crunch has hit Dubai hard, so we have to try and see how much flexibility there is in those figures.'

'I can get those from our research team in London.'

'I want the figures sourced from here and I want them to go to my accountant.' Her request jarred with me. She read me quickly. 'I'm trying to save my company, Yasmin, I need to know how.' Rania was in her element away from the party scene; she had transformed from the shy quiet girl into a sharp determined businesswoman.

I nodded and watched the waiter lead in a tall man dressed in a long white dish-dash and black head robe, a sign of royalty in Dubai. He looked like a handsome Arabian prince.

'Rania.' He greeted her warmly before turning to me.

'Asalaamalaikum,' I said instinctively without waiting for an introduction and saw his startled but pleased reaction.

'Walikumasalaam.' I smiled at the rich warm greeting.

'Waleed, how are you?' Rania said with a wide smile. 'This is Yasmin Yusuf; she's with Namhar Capital.'

I didn't know if he would be insulted if I held out my hand, so I smiled.

'Pleasure to meet you, Yasmin Yusuf.' My heart skipped a beat at his tone and I felt like sighing as I noted how thickly lashed his grey eyes were.

'Yasmin, this is Waleed Umar Ibn Haktoum, of Haktoum . . .'

'. . . Incorporated,' I finished as I watched him take a seat. He definitely had royal blood and I had never felt happier to be the unofficial PA. 'Nice to meet you.'

'Yasmin.' I heard Rania call me, but I couldn't tear my eyes away. 'Yasmin, I'll see you tomorrow.' I turned to face her as her words sank in. I had been dismissed so I composed myself.

'Thanks, yes, yes of course,' I said, picking up my bag and folder. I caught Waleed's eyes and paused to smile.

'Thanks, Yasmin,' Rania said. Clearing my throat, I nodded at her.

'It was nice meeting you,' I said again to Waleed with a lingering smile. Hearing Rania's cough, I dragged myself away and headed back into the Royal Mirage.

Lesson Ten:
It's about being brave, doing the unexpected, trying things that no one else has the courage to do

'I fell in love today,' I announced to Ella when I let myself into the apartment and found her surrounded by paperwork at the dining table where she had set up her laptop.

'Well that's a productive day!' she muttered, taking off her spectacles to look at me.

'Seriously, I did, and I think he's an Emirate prince,' I added as I took my heels off in the hall and dropped the many bags of shopping I had bought whilst officially working.

'Great, which number wife will you be?' Ella asked as I fell on to the couch. I looked at her and raised an eyebrow. 'OK, OK, I take it back. But whilst you were busy falling in love, Selina sent me off on a wild goose chase to somewhere called DIFC. It took me an hour to find out that that meant the Dubai International Financial Centre, and when I got there she left me with the notes and recalculations to work out.'

'If it helps, I spent the day traipsing around Ibn Batutta Mall and checking out lingerie stores like some kind of addict,' I said, letting Helen in before walking into the kitchen to pour myself an orange juice.

'Was this before or after you met the prince?' Ella asked.

'Oh . . . my . . . God! Check out the size of your apartment!' Helen said as she wandered around before joining us at the dining table. 'I wish I hadn't taken the single room; you have en suite bathrooms, balconies, dressing rooms . . . This is great.'

'Where are you off to?' Ella asked as we looked with envy at Helen's black sequinned bustier, skinny jeans and five-inch peeptoe heels.

'I thought we could go hit some of the clubs.'

'Pass, I'm exhausted,' Ella said, as she rifled through her papers.

Helen looked to me.

'Me too, I need my sleep,' I added as I curled up on the couch.

'Thank God. I came prepared just in case you were going to go without me.' Helen breathed out as she took off her heels and joined me on the couch. 'Raj crashed out ages ago. The heat's really gotten to him.'

'We wouldn't go without you,' I lied, avoiding Ella's eyes but catching her smile.

'I wasted an entire day waiting on the local team here. There's no urgency to get anything done.' Helen pinned her hair back into a bun, then checked her buzzing phone and ignored it.

'Everything OK?' Ella asked, putting aside her work to join us on the couch.

'My fiancé keeps calling.' I frowned at Helen's answer and looked to Ella. 'I mean, what's with the harassment? He's going to join me in Mumbai to do the wedding shopping anyway!' she said petulantly.

'And that's a bad thing because?' I asked as she shook her head and hesitated.

'I'm having doubts about marrying him,' she finally answered. 'I feel bad even admitting it.'

'W . . . Why?' Ella asked, surprised at Ms Perfect's not so perfect state of affairs.

'I don't know if I love him.'

'But he adores you, right?' My query made her look at me as if I was stupid. 'How long have you been together?'

'Over a year, but it feels like it's been too long,' Helen told me as she shook her head. 'I just don't know if I can spend forever with him.'

'There's always divorce,' Ella suggested unhelpfully.

'I just want space from him.'

'I totally understand.' I breathed out and found both of them staring at me.

'Are you getting space from your man too?' Helen asked.

'No, I'm getting space from being the unmarried Asian girl everyone worries about,' I corrected with half a smile.

'Are you getting pressure?' Helen asked. I could read the pity in her eyes. Singletons hate that. It's the reason why we avoid attached people.

'I could do with an arranged marriage,' Ella said as she twirled her hair. 'I'd try anything to find Mr Right.'

'That's just it, there isn't a Mr Right,' Helen stated. 'He's just the guy you make fit you.'

'But everyone has a Mr Right,' Ella stated with determination.

'If that's true, how do you explain falling in love more than once?'

I looked at Helen and frowned at her question.

'Maybe you need to go through a few Mr Wrongs to find Mr Right.'

'So how do you know Mr Right is Mr Right and not just the guy you make fit you?'

I stared at Helen, saddened by her attitude.

'Maybe Mr Right isn't the objective; maybe it's just falling in love with someone who loves you back,' Ella concluded, looking to me for support.

'All I know is that whatever it is, whatever label we put on it, we keep on looking for it until we find it, so it must exist, right?' I pointed out.

Helen's phone buzzed to life again, and we all stared at it until she answered it. I didn't know whether or not to feel happy for her. What I did know was that Helen knew he wasn't the one. Ella returned to her work as Helen wandered to the kitchen to chat. I headed for my bed, feeling good knowing that my search wasn't over. In fact, I felt good that my search had just begun.

The following days raced past in a blur. Contrary to our aim to hit Dubai's party life, we were locked behind closed doors researching interested parties, informing deals, projecting scenarios and reporting figures. Rania and I stepped out at the Habtoor Grand and headed for Al-Diyafa, the international restaurant where we were scheduled to meet with Amira Fahani, female entrepreneur of the year for three consecutive years.

Exhausted by the hectic schedule, mounting workload and never-ending deliverables, I tried to keep up with Rania as she interrogated me about the data I had given her on retail space in Dubai malls and lingerie manufacturers.

'Why is Selina talking to acquirers and sovereign wealth funds?' Rania's question surprised me as we headed for the restaurant. She stopped to stare at me as I hesitated. 'Yasmin?'

'The economy's plummeting; Namhar's looking at all its options,' I concocted.

'So why is Baby O unique?' I heard the vulnerability in her voice and shook off my tiredness.

'Its history, Rania; the reason why Baby O was created in the first place.' My explanation failed to convince her, so I continued. 'Right now, only branding differentiates the boutiques, otherwise they all sell the same thing.'

'Baby O does the same thing; it sells bras and panties.'

'But we know the clientele for La Perla isn't the same as those who frequent La Senza or Coco de Mer.'

'They have different price points and range type,' Rania clarified.

'What's missing now is a coming-of-age destination point for ladies. Every teenager turns into a lady; these ladies need to celebrate their coming of age. If Baby O became Lady O, you'd have yourself a unique proposition.'

'The teenager isn't after designer lingerie.'

'In Syria, it's customary for the mother or aunts to prepare a treasure chest of lingerie for new brides. We can create the same concept for the teen market and build loyalty so that when they become ladies we're the automatic wedding lingerie treasure chest providers.'

'Keep talking,' she said as we walked into the restaurant and were led to our booked table.

'If Lady O catered for the different stages of womanhood instead of the male fantasies of women, then it would become unique.'

Rania nodded eagerly as she took off her Versace shades and ordered a drink.

'You mean brand the celebration of womanhood?'

I nodded with a smile. 'Celebrate with treasure chests.' My concept made her laugh excitedly. 'With exclusively priced items, the return on investment is a no-brainer.'

'Have you done the return on investment figures?' I paused at her question and hesitated. 'Yasmin?'

'I . . . I'm not a qualified accountant; my figures . . . I haven't run the scenario permutations . . .'

'Don't worry, get Raj to work you through the figures,' Rania said as she looked at her watch before meeting my eyes. 'I can't let them sink Baby O, Yasmin, I can't sit by and allow that to happen.' The quiet admission was candid and filled with fear.

'Excuse me, Ms Amira Fahani has arrived.'

Rania and I stood up to greet Amira, who despite being dressed in an elegant black abaya and headdress turned heads as she glided confidently across to our table. 'Asalaamalaikum,' she announced as we kissed cheeks before taking our seats. I couldn't stop staring at her immaculate eye make-up, noting the thick black kohl and smoky brown shadow that sculpted her green eyes.

'Amira, this is Yasmin Yusuf from Namhar Capital.' I smiled at the stunning woman and noted her look of surprise. 'She's not gone over to the dark side . . . yet!' she added as Amira laughed.

'Nice to meet you, pure one.' Amira's accented drawl was slow and controlled.

'Rest assured, I have no intention of joining the dark side!' I replied. She didn't smile at my attempt at humour.

'Rania, I think what you're doing is brave, very brave,' Amira said after ordering her lunch in Arabic. I ordered a chicken Caesar salad and listened to them discuss the details for a joint venture. Quietly I admired Amira, who represented a new breed of Muslim women who worked hard but refused to compromise their identity.

'I have spent the last five years trying to get a simple handbag and accessories line to be taken seriously. I still have executives who talk to my male accountant or lawyer before addressing me.'

'You've come a long way, and there are more women following your lead,' Rania said as our lunch arrived.

'Right now you have to concentrate on reviving your label, getting the right designer on board to create your first range. Without that, how will you know if you're making the right partnership?' Amira's advice deflated Rania. '*Habibi*, if you don't do that, how will you broker the best deal? I can make a joint venture with you, but if I pay you next to nothing, it's no good for you.'

'Amira, those conversations are taking place. We have a concept revival, we're in negotiations with Zamil Hussain.'

'*Habibi, habibi, habibi!*' Amira's sweet reference to her beloved friend was marked as she placed a hand on Rania's.

'Amira, please don't talk to me as a friend.'

'I'm talking as a sister in business!' she corrected before turning to me. 'Women do business differently, you know that?' I nodded even though I had no entrepreneurial experience. 'We're emotional creatures, we care for more than the profit line because it's our reputation, our womanly integrity on the line.'

'I guess Rania's trying to do that.'

'Sh, sh, sh.' Amira tutted and waved a finger at me. 'Rania and I grew up together, we went to the same school, we studied at London Business School together. I—'

'Amira . . .'

'Let me finish, *habibi!*' Amira told Rania with a caring smile. 'Rania is trying to do business like a man, thinking profit, profit, profit. That's the problem with you women in the West: you try to be men, so how can you ever be as good? Look at me: you see only my face and my hands, but I run the third largest Middle Eastern retail brand with my brain.'

'Business is business, Amira, you still care about profit,' Rania pointed out.

'For sure I do, but I am a woman, I listen to my instinct, I listen with my heart and my head. Yes, I am emotional: some days I want to scream for the sake of screaming, and I do. And all the men respect me for screaming because they shout when they want to.'

'Oh Amira, being emotional doesn't help.'

'Listen to me, *habibi*, if there's no emotion involved, don't go into business, because it is all about emotion: it is about being brave, doing the unexpected, trying things that no one else has the courage to do. If you choose not to be emotional, go and be a trust-fund baby. Why try to save the company? Why care, no?' Amira pointed out elegantly.

'To be fair, Rania cares. I think that there's so many people running the show that it's difficult to get emotional about it.'

'Stupid girl!' I balked at the insult she threw at me. My reaction was lost on her but Rania had seen it.

'They're desert people, Yasmin, they have thick skins and think everyone else does too,' she excused before turning back to her friend. 'I'm overwhelmed and I'm very close to losing control.'

'I promise you, *habibi*, you come to me if you run out of time and I'll partner you as a last resort. I give you my word. But before then, my advice to you is to fight like a woman, not a man. If you believe in Baby O's success, fight, because you will lose yourself if you don't.'

I looked at the hard-nosed woman, still smarting from her insult. She saw me.

'You're a good adviser, naive, but good for Rania,' she said. Once again, she thought nothing of insulting me.

I leaned forward with half a smile.

'Excuse me, I'd politely like to . . . um, disagree. I'm not naive.'

'Disagree all you like, but until you build a three-hundred-million-pound retail business, you're naive.'

'I . . . I can see how you come to that conclusion, but you'll find that you're mistaken. Men who knew all about billion-dollar deals and investments have brought the global financial market to its knees; men who have run conglomerates spanning the globe should've known better, but they didn't. I'm not naive; I'm learning, and with all due respect, I want to point out that there's a big difference.'

Amira stared at me, and I refused to waver beneath the wilting look. Then she broke into delightful laughter.

'You are precious,' she said before turning to Rania. 'Hold on to her, Rania; this one has fight. She's deceiving to the eye, but she has spirit.'

Rania tried to stop herself from laughing, but couldn't stop. I smiled at Amira's nature. She was strong, feisty and an unapologetic, savvy businesswoman who was unafraid to speak her mind. Finally I gave into the laughter and joined in. My alarm came to life and I checked my iPhone to realise that I was running late.

'I have to leave,' I told Rania as I searched in my bag to rout out my shades. When I found them, I turned to Amira. 'It's nice meeting you.'

'Darling, it was a pleasure meeting you,' she chimed, grabbing my face to kiss my cheeks.

'Oh Yasmin, could you pick up my outfit for the gala dinner tonight and help get ready?' Rania asked as I dropped my napkin on the table and stood up. 'I hope you don't mind.'

'Not at all. Just email me where you're getting ready and I'll get there for six p.m.,' I said with a smile. Excusing myself from the meeting, I turned and headed out. There are plenty of stories about how the mail-room boy ended up heading a multinational company by learning from the bottom up. It was no effort to pick up a dress; in fact, I had accepted that if I was to become a success, learning the ropes from the bottom was the only way forward.

By the time I left DIFC, I was running late. Nervously I waited for the taxi to pull into the Mall of Emirates and jumped out to find the Armani store. I took off my Nine West three-inch slingbacks and raced up to the information point where two Emirate teens sat talking to each other.

'Excuse me,' I said, as if me standing there wasn't enough to attract their interest. I waited until one of the scarved teenagers paused and rolled her eyes over to look at me. Worldwide, teen attitude was the same. 'Could you direct me to the Armani store?'

She looked to the shoes I clutched against me, and then turned to speak Arabic to her colleague. They looked at me and laughed before continuing to chat. I knocked on the desk and turned to the colleague.

'Is she stupid or does she not understand English?' I demanded in the style of Amira. The shocked, offended silence continued as I stared at both girls. 'Where is the Armani store?'

'Yes, ma'am, the Armani store is right here,' the friend answered, grabbing a map to point out the location to me. 'Please go straight, turn right and up . . .'

'Thanks,' I threw over my shoulder as I grabbed the map and raced past couples, families and groups of teenagers to seek out the store. Finding it exactly where the assistant had directed, I ran in and came to a sharp stop at the patronising glare of the assistant. Suddenly I felt like Julia Roberts in *Pretty Woman*, when she was judged to be unworthy of being in a designer store.

'I need to pick up Rania Jayachand's outfit,' I explained, still holding on to my heels.

'Yes, of course, please wait.' The tall modelesque Eastern European assistant looked me up and down long enough to make me feel out of place in the store with its shiny black ceramic floor and walls that were made of large silver and black glass panels. Without a word, she sashayed into the back room.

I leaned on the counter to catch my breath, and noticed the two large video walls projecting recent collections. They illuminated the store and brought the clothes to life. I was too tired to browse, knowing that everything would be out of my league, so I avoided tempting fate and slipped my heels back on. As I checked my iPhone, an Emirate family walked in, trailed by a Filipino minder who struggled to control the four young children. Intrigued, I watched as the fully concealed wife walked around the store and pointed out a dozen outfits for her maid to pick out. A second assistant rushed up, forcing the husband to usher her away as he played with his mobile. In the meantime, the wife continued to pick out accessories as if she was picking up sweets.

'Here it is.' I turned back to my assistant and watched her return with the blush-pink delicate gown. She laid it out on the counter for me and I looked at the price tag and tried not to look shocked. 'Do you like it?'

I nodded, my heart actually skipped a beat and my knees went weak at the price tag, so I looked up at the assistant and smiled nervously. Silently I prayed I wouldn't do anything clumsy like trip on it and tear it or sully it with dirt.

The assistant put the dress into a long protective cover and packed it away. I signed for it and took it from her. But before I left I paused and stared back at the wife, smiling, as she looked like she was far from finished. She would've have spent my annual salary in one shopping spree. In any other country that would've been crazy, but in Dubai it was normal. It was ironic: my world pitied these women for being locked behind the purdah. Yet I stood here and realised that the women in my world worked day and night dreaming to have the kind of financial freedom she had. My phone buzzed to life and brought me out of my thoughts.

'Yasmin, where are you?' Hearing Rania, I checked my watch and rushed out of the store.

'I'm on my way,' I lied, racing through the mall to find an exit with a taxi rank. 'I've just picked up the dress and I'm about to jump into a cab, so I'll get there as soon as possible.'

'You'll find me at Burj Al Arab. Ask for Victor; he's been informed of your arrival and will show you to my room.'

I stopped at the mention of the most luxurious iconic seven-star hotel in the world.

'Burj Al Arab,' I mouthed as Rania hung up. 'I'm going to the Burj Al Arab,' I shouted when Ella answered her phone.

'Burj Al Arab?'

I spotted an exit and rushed towards it whilst balancing the outfit, my bag and my phone.

'Yes, yes, yes . . . I'm going to see Rania at the Burj Al Arab!' I shouted as I jumped the queue at the taxi stand and stepped into the nearest one available, ignoring the protesting tourists who knocked on the window. 'Burj Al Arab,' I told the driver.

'That beats snowboarding at Ski Dubai,' Ella stated and my smile dropped.

'Oh, Ella, I'm sorry. I'll come find you guys, OK?' I promised.

Ella laughed and told me to have a good time, so I sat back and looked out towards Jumeirah. I had had the most amazing day and I felt that it was far from over. The long balmy breezy days of Dubai were a million miles away from the hectic, frenetic pace of life in London. One offered glamour and luxury against sultry sunny climates, whilst the other offered a chic fast-paced life that left you more exhausted than exhilarated.

The stunning sail of the Burj Al Arab grew bigger as we drew closer to it, as did my smile. I was falling in love with Dubai, its promises and its freedom to actually live life. It was a new, vibrant, alluring city that made you believe that anything, truly anything, was possible. Its leaders were pioneers, visionaries and strategists who had crafted a global cosmopolitan state-of-the-art city with stunning skyscrapers on a coastline where once only sand had resided. That resonated with me. Dubai made you believe that anything was possible, that something could be built on nothing, that ultimately you shaped your own future with visions, dreams and intelligence. I liked this city. I liked it a lot.

Lesson Eleven:
Afford yourself respect by
not compromising

The tall sail of the Burj Al Arab can be seen from miles away, and the closer we got, the more I felt breathless with excitement. I couldn't stop smiling and when the cab pulled up at the security post, I opened the window. There were tourists hovering at the post, taking pictures of the breathtaking structure, unable to pay the prohibitive price of using the hotel's facilities.

'I'm here to see Rania Jayachand. Victor's expecting me.'

The young Indian guard checked his guest list.

'Yasmin Yusuf,' He stated. I smiled and nodded.

I felt like I had arrived when the guard pressed a button. The mechanical barrier rose and he waved us through. We pulled up on the bridge that led to the towering building, and I leaned out of the window laughing out loud as we approached the hotel. The driver laughed at my antics, and when he parked outside the entrance I paid him and, with a huge smile, stepped out with the dress in hand. I took a deep breath and nodded at the many doormen before I walked in through the revolving door. The grand opulent lobby with its huge water feature and stunning aquarium stole my breath away and I stood transfixed.

'Date, ma'am?'

I looked at the attendant who stood at the entrance holding a silver platter of dates. Smiling, I took one and thanked him.

'Can I help you?'

I turned at the enquiry and looked at the short Nigerian attendant with the kind face.

'Could you direct me to Victor?' I stopped at his short laughter. 'I'm here to see Rania Jayachand. My name's . . .'

'. . . Yasmin Yusuf,' he finished. 'I'm Victor, I'm the front-of-house manager. We've been expecting you. If you follow me, I'll take you up to Ms Jayachand's suite.' The warm hospitality was beyond anything I had experienced.

Victor headed for the escalators and I rushed behind him and screamed when I skidded on the marble floor. The lobby area came to a standstill as Victor spun around and grabbed my arm to steady me.

'Are you OK?' he asked as I pushed my hair back and cleared my throat.

'Yes,' I breathed, stepping on to the escalator as humiliation filled every cell within me.

'This is your first visit to Burj Al Arab?'

I nodded at Victor before watching a shark swim past in the aquarium beside the escalator.

'It is breathtaking,' I told him.

We stepped off the escalator and into a foyer that gave a spectacular view of the 180-metre-high atrium. I spun around looking at the huge fountain, the Al Iwan traditional restaurant and the Sahn Eddar lounge area that was bathed with live soothing classical music played by a small orchestra. Victor had walked ahead, and I rushed to catch up with him at the glass elevators.

'If you give me Rania's room number and what floor she's on, I can save you the trouble,' I told him as we waited for the glass lifts to arrive.

'Ma'am, the Burj Al Arab never leaves a guest unattended,' Victor explained. 'And we don't have rooms here at the Burj; we only have suites. Ms Jayachand has a club suite.'

I stopped listening to Victor as the elevator lifted us on the outside edge of the building up into the Dubai skies. I caught my breath as I looked out on to the bright blue sea and then turned to look at the Dubai landscape.

'It's breathtaking,' I repeated. 'I'm here to see my boss so this is a perk for me,' I explained.

Victor nodded with a small smile. 'Well, it's a very worthwhile perk.'

I laughed at his comment and followed him out on to the seventh floor.

'Each floor has a designated concierge desk, so if you need anything and you can't find me, then ask here.' I nodded at Victor's direction but paused to look over the balcony and down the magnificent atrium to the water fountain in the foyer.

'Ma'am.' Turning around, I saw Victor waiting for my childish enthusiasm to abate before he introduced himself on the intercom. 'Have a good day, Ms Yusuf,' he said as a butler opened the door to let me in. Victor announced my arrival and with a curt bow departed.

'Victor,' I called out, making him turn. 'Thank you,' I said with a wide smile before I stepped into the glorious suite.

'There you are!' Rania announced, walking out in a stunning emerald fitted dress.

'You . . . you're dressed. I'm sorry I got held up. You

still have time to change into this gown,' I said as I dropped my bag on the desk in the office space before walking into the living room. The view of the sea distracted me. 'This is gorgeous!' I breathed as I walked to the glass wall and stared out at the orange sky. Everything in the suite was unmatched in luxury, space and opulence.

'Yasmin . . .'

'I'm so sorry for being late. By the way, you look amazing, but this dress is something else. I didn't even touch it, but it's exquisite, so if we rush, I can help you get changed into it.'

'Yasmin . . .'

'Honestly, I didn't mean to screw up, I really didn't. I just got caught up at our office . . .' I stopped when Rania cupped my face with her hands to silence me.

'You like the dress?' she asked. I raised my brows as if anything else could be true.

'It's . . . breathtaking,' I answered and watched her smile.

'Good,' she said, walking away to grab her purse. 'You have fifteen minutes to get changed and get to the gala. Use the second bedroom suite. My maid, Princess, will help you change and my butler will direct you to the gala.'

'Wait, wait, wait . . .' I called out, running after Rania to stop her at the door. 'Wh . . . what . . . what do you mean?' I asked in stunned confusion.

'I want you at the private bankers' gala.'

'The gala . . . but the dress . . . I can't afford it . . . it's a third of my annual salary . . .'

'You don't have to,' Rania said. Then she paused and took my hands. 'Yasmin, we have to save Baby O. There are financiers here with connections to the right people, so I need you to network your ass off tonight.' She smiled warmly when I released a deep and long-pent-up breath.

'Smile, you're going to the ball, Cinderella!'

I laughed nervously, and then threw my arms around Rania.

'Thank you,' I whispered, squeezing my eyes shut to stop the tears from falling. 'Thank you for believing in me.' Rania patted my back before stepping away.

'You're creasing my dress!' She said. I jerked back from her and then laughed as I realised she was joking. 'I'll see you at the Al Falak ballroom, Cinders.'

I watched Rania walk out and then clasped my hands and squealed with excitement.

'When you're finished, shall we get you ready?'

I turned to the elderly Indian lady and froze with embarrassment. This must be Princess, Rania's maid. I ran and picked up the gown to follow her up the circular staircase to the second suite. I tried hard to look unimpressed, but the living quarters that led to the sumptuous bedroom were too much.

'Strip.' I spun round at Princess's command and looked at the petite woman dressed in a white sari and sandals. 'Shower. Condition. Moisturise. Then I'll get you ready, OK?'

I nodded at her order, watched her leave and then stared in amazement at the world I had entered. With a whoop, I raced and jumped on the bed until I fell on to it breathless. Lying back, I stared up at the gilded mirror on the ceiling. I pinched myself and winced. This was happening, I was living this dream.

'Ms Yasmin, you have thirteen minutes to get to the gala.'

Jerking upright at Princess's reminder, I blushed at my childish behaviour. I cleared my throat, and shuffled off the bed. Without another word, I walked into the bathroom.

*

Fifteen minutes later, Princess, along with a hairdresser and make-up artist, stepped back from me. Nervously I stepped forward and looked in the mirror.

'Wow,' I whispered, shocked by the woman who looked back. 'Wow,' I repeated, forcing myself not to smile in case I ruined the make-up. Somehow they had managed to tame my unruly curly hair into a sleek high 1960s bun. I twisted in the blush-pink floor-length Grecian dress with a circular bejewelled collar that left my arms and shoulders bare. I swished the train around me and spun around until the hairdresser and stylist clapped.

'You're late,' Princess advised as I leaned close to the mirror to inspect the immaculate barely there make-up that left me with smoky black eyes, sculpted cheekbones and natural full lips. 'And you look beautiful.'

'Will you take a picture on my phone? I won't believe this is happening unless I have a picture.' The butler complied and the four of us posed for many pictures until Princess ushered me towards the stairs. I stopped and held her hands. 'My belongings, I've left them behind . . .'

'We'll have them delivered to your hotel,' she assured me as she escorted me to the door. 'Now, rush; don't run, but rush, my little flower.'

I smiled at Princess before enveloping her in a hug. Then, without a word and with the sheer chiffon billowing behind me, I skipped down the corridor in Rania's Swarovski crystal-encrusted four-inch heels. I stepped into the elevator and smiled as guests stared at me. Somehow I had been transferred into a parallel world where the once dowdy, unconfident, self-doubting Yasmin faded into a distant memory. I was so far beyond excited that I could barely breathe.

When the doors parted at the conference hall, I stepped out and into the patron-filled foyer. Taking a deep breath, I walked towards the ballroom, noticing the admiring looks. Nervously I allowed myself to enjoy the attention as I entered the palatial two-tiered Al Falak ballroom. I stared at its golden dome, and then looked over the balcony to the glamorous dinner gala below. I spotted Rania at one of the round tables, and an empty seat beside her. Turning around, I froze when I saw Zach standing before me.

'Yasmin?'

I smiled tentatively at his surprised expression, but struggled to think of anything to say to break the silence. He cocked a brow at my appearance and I swirled around to allow him a full inspection. I laughed with delight when he chuckled. My laughter died when he stepped close. My heart skipped a beat and I stared up at him.

'Yasmin.' He took my hand to swirl me around again. 'You are stunning,' he announced as he thoroughly looked me over, before meeting my gaze. 'Yes, you are.'

'Thank you, Zach.' My breath caught at his perusal so I laughed nervously. 'I'm surprised to see you here.'

'We're at a private bankers' gala, and I'm a private banker, but you're surprised to see me here?' he asked calmly, as his eyes sparkled with mischief.

'Point noted, Mr Khan,' I said as he took my hand, placed it on his arm and led me down the stairs.

As we descended, Zach stopped on a number of occasions to greet peers, and on each occasion he was mindful of introducing me. I watched, noting his fine handsome face, wide smile and charming eyes. He caught me looking and I smiled when he did. He lost track of the conversation and had to remind himself of what he was saying. With a small smile I extracted my arm, and gently gathered the skirt of my dress.

'Excuse me,' I whispered, leaving him to find Rania. I was stopped several times by bankers making an introduction. I accommodated politely, and made strategic replies to gauge their relevance for Baby O. By the time I reached Rania I had bagged several business cards and blushed with the effort involved.

'You look amazing,' Rania cried out as we hugged and then looked at each other.

'Thank you.'

'You're turning many heads, Yasmin,' she said as the compère announced the beginning of the ceremony.

'Given that there's a male to female ratio of ten to one, we could've worn potato sacks and still turned heads!' I returned, making Rania laugh.

'You've certainly caught Zachary Khan's attention. He's looked over in your direction no less than half a dozen times since you left him on the stairs.'

I curbed a smile at Rania's comment as we took our seats. I stopped myself looking to find out where he was sitting.

'I don't want to be another notch on his bedpost,' I whispered to Rania, who smiled in understanding.

'It's good that you're going to make him work,' she said with approval.

I spotted Zach walking to his table to take a seat between a portly German banker in a pinstriped suit and red braces and what looked like a senior Emirate. I didn't take my eyes off him, but turned to Rania.

'Who . . .'

'He's being courted,' Rania answered before I could finish.

The first course of the seven-course meal arrived and I tucked into the soup and let the delicate flavour caress my taste buds.

'By the royal family's bank,' she added. I nearly choked at her statement and took a long swig of water to clear my throat.

'Did I hear you right?' I rasped as I put down the glass of water.

'He's going on to bigger and better things and he'll do well to move away from London,' Rania said as she indicated for her plate to be taken away. 'It's all under wraps, Yasmin, so you mustn't say a word to anyone.'

I looked at Zach and found him in deep conversation with the Emirate. It upset me to hear that the man who had involuntarily become my rock might be leaving. I struggled to maintain my smile, and thanked God when the lights were dimmed for the award ceremony to start.

'Is Zach up for an award?' I asked, and stopped when I found Rania watching me. She had seen my response, and placed a hand over mine. I smiled sadly and realised that all this was temporary, that this wasn't my life or anything close to it. Determined to enjoy the here and now, I parked away any romantic notions about Zach and tucked into the second course.

The evening was filled with laughter, conversation and smooth effortless networking. Rania and I worked the tables discreetly and confidently until we made the right contacts. Awards were handed out, acceptance speeches were cut short and winners were cheered on by supporting colleagues. When Zach won, Rania and I stood up and whooped loudly enough to make everyone laugh. I beamed with delight as he accepted his award with charm and humility. As he walked back to his table, he passed by, stopping to give Rania a peck on the cheek. I caught his eye and smiled until my heart raced so fast I thought my knees would buckle.

'Rania, would you excuse me if I steal Yasmin away from you?'

I looked to Rania, who winked at me as Zach reached

out to take my hand. He weaved around the tables and guests to lead me out of the dimmed ballroom.

'Zach, is everything . . .'

'I need some air,' he explained as we stepped into the elevator. 'You can only stomach so much of the back-slapping.' He held out the heavy silver and gold award to me and I took it from him to look at it closely. I leaned against the glass and looked out on to the lit-up skyline.

'It's very impressive, Mr Khan, but why have you dragged me out with you?' I sensed Zach was standing close behind me, close enough to feel his warmth.

'Because . . . because you're normal and you don't have an agenda,' Zach answered.

I smiled sadly at his response. I wore an Armani dress worth thousands of dollars, crystal-encrusted heels and diamonds worth thousands more. I had been preened and prepped until I felt like I could grace the red carpet at the Oscars. But to Zach, I was normal. Just normal. His hesitant reply told me he was as unsure of me as I was scared by the attraction between us. I hid my disappointment and gasped when he pulled me around to face him. When he leaned in, I closed my eyes and felt his gentle lips against mine. When the doors glided open to let two Emirate women step in, I pulled back. They stared at us, catching my startled reaction as I turned to stand with my back to him.

'She's in Bollywood,' one whispered. 'I'm telling you, it's that Priyanka Chopra.'

'No, it's the other one, the new girl, I can't pronounce her name.' I caught Zach's eyes and read the mischief.

'She's carrying an award. It is Priyanka,' they continued as the elevator arrived at the grand arrivals floor. 'Is that Saif? No, he's seeing Kareena . . . Quickly, use your phone, take a picture . . .'

'Come on, Priyanka, let's go party!' Zach said with a

heavy Indian accent as the doors opened up. The two women stared at us in awe and parted to allow us to stride past them. When they regained their wits, they told each other off for being slow and scrambled to get their mobiles out. Laughing at their antics, I clasped Zach's arm and walked past the fountain to take the escalators down to the lobby. There, Zach asked for his car to be brought round to him.

'Ms Yusuf, you're a vision,' Victor complimented as he spotted me.

'You think?' I asked, never tiring of swirling around in my pink Grecian dress.

'I don't think, ma'am, I know.'

Zach took my arm to lead me out as I waved to Victor. I saw a waiting Rolls-Royce and turned to Zach confused.

'I've instructed the driver to drop you off at your hotel.'

I closed my eyes at his words. 'You're sending me away . . .'

'This is not you,' Zach told me. 'This is not you . . .'

'I know I'm not the Armani-wearing jet-setter who drops in at the Burj Al Arab . . .'

'I don't want to turn you into my type, Yasmin.' I paused at his statement and looked down. 'You deserve more than that.'

'You don't do attachments,' I whispered with realisation, feeling my wonderful magical evening come to an end.

'I can't be with you, Yasmin,' Zach said as he raised my chin to make me look up at him. A short while passed until I allowed myself to look into his eyes.

'Yes you can,' I told him and watched him fight himself to believe me.

'What do you want?' he asked as if to remind me of myself. With a small smile, I pulled away from his touch.

'I want the package. I want the Bengali engagement, my father's blessing, the grand ostentatious marriage, two boys and one girl and a promised future of happiness. I want the package, Zach,' I told him.

Zach watched me for what felt like an eternity, but I didn't waver beneath the weight of his stare. I needed him to believe it was possible, but when he shook his head, I knew it was time for me to leave. As I turned to go, he grabbed my arm.

'Yasmin . . .'

'Good night, Zach.' I waited until he released my arm. He opened the door of the Rolls-Royce for me to step in. I opened the window to look at him.

'Good night, Yasmin.'

I smiled at him before turning to stare straight ahead, scared that if I moved, I'd race back to Zach and make good with however little he was prepared to give. So I sat frozen, until we drove down the bridge, joined Jumeirah Road and finally pulled up in front of the Arjaan.

Sometimes there were no words to explain the perfect moment. But now I knew what my mother felt when she saw Daddy. Zach made me feel precious, he made me feel alive. More than anything he made me glow, and that was more than I could ever have dreamt of. This felt so different, so much more than what I had with Sam. I didn't despair that Zach wanted to get rid of me, or that I wasn't good enough for him. I didn't feel insignificant, replaceable or somehow lacking. None of the debilitating insecurities that Sam had stirred in me appeared. With Sam, I'd feared a future of never being enough. And I realised I had changed. This was real, this was hope-based and so much more worthy for that fact. I felt empowered by Zach. This, whatever it was, made me long for a future on my terms where I was more than enough. I guess that's what we women do: we crucify ourselves with all the things we don't have. Instead I looked at my magical night and felt blessed with the respect I had afforded myself by not compromising. I wanted the package; nothing less would do. I was proud of my unwavering conviction, and because of that, I knew I was glowing.

Lesson Twelve:
Refuse to allow yourself to have
unrealistic expectations of a man

Back at the Arjaan hotel, Ella opened the door to our apartment and I glided past her.

'Holy lord, the Emirate prince has done a *Pretty Woman* on you,' she gasped as I leaned against the wall dreamily. 'That's beautiful, how much did it cost?'

'About twenty grand . . .'

'What?' Ella cried out as I leaned down to slip off the heels. 'And those?' she whispered, pointing to the shoes I held in my hands.

'It doesn't matter,' I sighed as we walked into the living room and fell on to the couch. 'I was kissed.' I breathed out and leaned back on the sofa. 'I'm in love.'

'Oh my God, you're going to be one of those women who marry into Arab royalty and you're going to live in luxury all your life and we're going to read about you in *Hello!* magazine . . .'

'Ella!' I laughed at her assumption as she leaned forward.

'You waltz in a few days ago saying you've fallen in love with a prince and today you turn up in haute couture, the original and not the knock-off polyester version, looking like you've stepped out of the editorial pages of *Vogue*, and you think I'm insane?' Ella threw at me as I covered my face with my arm. I wondered if I could trust her or not, but I had to tell someone.

'I had the most beautiful evening, Ella, the most perfect magical night ever . . .'

'Who is he?' she asked, hugging her knees to her chest as she curled up on the couch. I stared at her and bit my lip. 'Yasmin Yusuf, who is he?'

'I can't . . .'

'Oh my God, he's married.'

'No! I'm single, quite possibly desperate, but not immoral!' I pointed out with a laugh.

'So tell me!' Ella demanded as I leaned forward close to her.

'He kissed me,' I whispered and smiled as her eyes widened.

'Woman, who kissed you?'

'Zachary Khan.'

Ella stared at me in silence and I nodded to assure her I had spoken the right name. She shook her head and once again I nodded.

'Zachary Khan?' She breathed out as if she didn't recognise the name. I took the opportunity to go and pour myself an ice-filled glass of mango juice.

'I'm ordering a pizza,' I stated as I called the concierge and asked for a chicken jalapeno feast. 'For some reason, I can never eat properly at these events, no matter how good the food is.'

'What event . . . what food . . . why are you talking about pizza when you've just told me that you kissed Zachary Khan?' Ella demanded in utter confusion.

'Unzip me,' I asked her as I returned to stand with my back to her. When she complied, I walked into my bedroom, slipped off the magical dress and stared down at it. It was the most beautiful fragile material in the world. It was at that point that I realised how sheer it had been. Covering my boobs, I raced over to my dressing room and threw on my nightshirt. I pulled my hair free from the bun, and tousled it until it fell unruly around my shoulders. Quickly I popped into the bathroom, grabbed several cleansing tissues and then walked back into the living room wiping the make-up off my face.

'So you tell me you kissed Zachary Khan, the hottest, richest bachelor in our world, and keep me hanging on for details for fifteen minutes,' Ella stated as I sat on the couch facing her. 'Are you insane or do you want to kill me out of sheer curiosity?'

'But that's all that happened . . .'

'What?' Confused, Ella groaned and threw a cushion at me.

'Rania invited me to the event, bought that beautiful dress for me and got me ready for the evening . . .'

'Get to the kissing bit!'

I laughed at Ella's impatience and finished off my juice. 'When I arrived at the ballroom, Zach was there and we connected . . .'

'Connected? Do you mean that your eyes met, or he brushed past you?'

'I don't know, we connected!' I told her. 'He stood there in his tuxedo . . .'

'Tuxedo? Oh my lord, he must have given you hot flushes with one look!'

I nodded. 'I couldn't stop staring at him, Ella. He was so handsome, he made my heart race.'

'You're in love with Zachary Khan? Do you realise what you're saying?'

I stared at Ella and nodded again.

'I fell in love with him tonight,' I stated knowing it to be true. 'He escorted me around arm in arm. After he won an award, he came up to me and took my hand to whisk me away.'

I stopped, and knew that at this point he had decided otherwise.

'And?' Ella prompted, just as the doorbell rang. Screaming out in frustration, she went to open it for the waiter to bring through my pizza. 'On the coffee table, thanks,' she directed. I didn't wait for her to show him out and picked up a large slice.

'He kissed me as we descended in the elevator.'

'You made out in an elevator? That's like an Aerosmith music video.'

'Ella, it was barely a kiss; it was the briefest but most perfect kiss in the world.' I breathed out with half a smile.

'And then?'

My smile died as I looked up at her.

'He put me in a Rolls-Royce and bid me good night,' I finished.

'What?' Ella demanded, stunned by the sudden end. 'What do you mean, good night?'

'Just that . . .'

'But what plans did you make? When are you going to meet next?' she asked, picking up a slice of pizza.

'That's just it, we're not going to meet.' Ella's smiled dropped. 'I want the package, Ella. I'm at that stage in my life where I don't want to mess around without any direction.'

'You told him that, didn't you?' she asked with total dread. I nodded and she cringed.

'I told him I want the whole shebang: engagement, marriage and kids.'

'And what did he say?'

I smiled and shook my head. 'Like I said, he put me in a Roller back here.'

'But you don't think he's worth testing out?'

'He is not a second-hand car that needs to be road-tested, Ella!'

She stared at me until I couldn't hold her gaze.

'So, that's just it, you're not going to do anything else?'

I shook my head and Ella snorted in derision.

'Seriously, there's nothing I can do unless he's willing to go the whole hog.'

'Yasmin, I think you need to think this through properly,' Ella advised without a hint of humour.

I shook my head and smiled at her. 'I don't need to think it through. I refuse to be another company one-night stand and I refuse to allow myself to have expectations of a man who won't ever live up to them,' I told her bluntly. 'I would only have myself to blame when things ended badly, and they would. I've been there, done that and I don't want to do it again.'

'But you love him.'

I nodded and smiled at Ella's confusion. 'But he doesn't know that, and he's not going to know it . . .' I held up my hand to stop her from pushing any further. 'I won't fool myself by having unrealistic expectations of Zach. I can't do that to myself again.'

Ella stared at me until she looked away shaking her head. She handed me another slice of pizza. I took it and bit into it. I avoided her eyes and smiled softly. The truth was that no matter how many times I told myself I would not consider any future with Zach, I couldn't stop my heart from racing each time I thought about him.

Friday morning was the first time the four of us actually met for breakfast. Helen and Raj arrived at our apartment carrying a huge bouquet of roses.

'Someone's been keeping the teacher very happy,' Helen announced as she placed them in the centre of the dining table and held out the sealed envelope. I rushed up to her and took it from her. 'Yasmin, what have you been up to, woman?'

I opened up the small envelope and turned it around to keep it out of her eyesight.

Yasmin, no offence was intended by crossing the line with you. Z

He was apologising for kissing me. Irritated, I stared at the flowers, wanting to return them.

'Who's the secret admirer?' Helen insisted as Ella walked into the living room and stopped at the sight of the stunning display. Turning to me, she raised a brow.

'Unrealistic expectations, eh?' she asked sarcastically.

'Who is this guy who is moving ahead of me in the wooing race?' All three of us turned to stare at Raj, who was checking out the flowers.

'Raj, I am not in a race, nor are you wooing me.'

He looked at me and laughed as he glanced at Ella warmly. I studied the two of them, but then shook my head telling myself that I had imagined the intimate exchange between them.

'And the mystery man is?' Helen pushed as I leaned close to the flowers, smiling at the gentle fragrance.

'OK, OK, who cares, yar!' Raj muttered, clapping his hands. 'We got a busy day. First, breakfast, then shopping at Ibn Batutta, then lunch and then the great desert safari.'

'I'm going to Jumeirah Mosque for Friday prayers, so I'll join you guys after lunch,' I said.

'Oooohhh!' Helen chimed in with a wide smile and a cheeky wink. 'Or are you going to meet Mystery Man?'

'No, Helen, it's Friday prayers. Will you be joining me?'

She hesitated at the question and looked uncomfortable. 'Uh, I'd rather hit the malls.'

I rolled my eyes and shook my head.

'Breakfast!' Ella shouted as she ushered everyone out. We headed for the lifts.

'I should thank him for the flowers,' I said to her as we watched Helen preen herself in the large mirrors. Ella stifled a smile and nodded. 'What?' I asked as the lift arrived and we stepped in.

'Nothing,' she quipped.

'You're smirking.'

'I'm not smirking,' Ella returned as Helen and Raj looked at her.

'Isn't she smirking?' I asked them.

'Why is she smirking?' Raj asked, confused by the exchange.

Ella looked at me, waiting for me to explain. When I glared at her, she smirked.

'Now I'm smirking!' she stated.

The opening doors marked our arrival in the breakfast area. I shook my head and led the way. Raj avoided the table and headed straight for the self-service breakfast buffet area. Ella followed him.

'Raj and I have switched off our iPhones to make ourselves totally unavailable today,' Helen said as we sat down. She watched me log on to my mail using my phone. I'd decided to respond to Zach, otherwise he'd think that I was offended or too immature to handle what had happened. 'Yasmin!' Helen called, making me look up apologetically.

'I'm just emailing my brothers,' I lied as she ordered a green tea before heading off to get breakfast. I bit my lip and hesitated, doubting my decision, and then scripted a reply.

No offence taken! The flowers were breathtaking. I'm

going to Jumeirah Mosque for Friday prayers. Why don't
you let me buy you lunch for understanding? Yasmin

'Hey, you working through breakfast?' Raj's appearance made me jump and press the send button. Instantly
I wanted to recall it, but the pile of food on Raj's plate
distracted me.

'That's breakfast?' The plate had everything, from
turkey sausages, beef bacon, eggs, beans, toast and
pancakes, to hummus, tabbouleh, naan and olives.

'We're going on a desert safari, Yasmin. We need to
prepare in case we get lost.'

I stared at Raj as if he was deluded.

'You're not a camel, Raj . . .'

He held up his hand as if to stop me from speaking.

'Yasmin, you should never get between a man and his
food. Please. Go.'

I balked at his instruction and went to speak. But he
shook his head and waved his hand as if to usher me away.
Frowning, I shook my head and headed off to the buffet.

'Raj is stocking up for months,' I told Ella, who was
making herself toast.

'Aww, leave him. It's endearing to see him enjoy his
food.' Ella's soft tone caught my attention. I looked at her
and saw her watching Raj with a small smile.

'Your toast is burning.' Ella jumped and turned to her
toast only to realise that I had caught her watching Raj.

'No!' I whispered as she blushed.

'What?' she demanded, buttering the toast before
pouring honey on it.

'That's about a thousand calories,' Helen piped up,
holding her carb-free, fruit-filled plate.

'But *I'm* eating those calories,' Ella told her pointedly.

'I'm just saying . . .'

'Don't', Ella continued as I helped myself to turkey
sausages, eggs and beans.

'So . . .' I asked after Helen marched off to join Raj. Ella refused to look at me. I waited until she couldn't busy herself and in silence until she finally looked at me.

'OK, we made out . . .'

'WHAT?' My shout made those around us drop their cutlery and cups. Instinctively we both pointed at Helen and tutted disapprovingly to divert attention. When the confused looks moved away from us to Helen, I stepped in front of Ella and stared at her. 'You made out with Raj? Randy wannabe John Travolta Raj?' I whispered as Ella closed her eyes. 'You did!' I announced as she placed her hands on her hips and stared at me.

'Whilst you were snogging Zachary . . .'

'Ssshhhh!' I hissed as we stepped away from the table to give another diner access to toast.

'OK, whilst you were otherwise *engaged*, we hit DesiDNA at Indonica. And we were slow-dancing, and it happened . . .'

'What happened?' I asked, taking a bite of sausage, stunned with disbelief.

'We . . . well, you know . . .'

'No! Not all the way?' Ella glared at me. 'OK, I take it back. How far?'

'Well that's just it, he was such a gentleman about it.' I frowned at the description of Raj and turned to look at the rookie Indian export. Helen sat in silence with her fruit, watching with distaste as Raj resolutely worked through his pile. 'We made out, that's all. And then he brought me back here and we spoke for hours. He left just before you arrived . . .'

'And you didn't say anything?' I demanded as Ella smiled at me.

'You were literally floating on air, Yasmin, it was nice to see you so alive.'

'How . . . how did you leave it?' I asked, distracting

myself from thoughts of Zach. 'Are you officially on?'

'Well that's just it. He's not been out with an English woman, so we want to keep it low-key.'

We both turned away when Raj appeared for a top-up.

'You haven't eaten yet. Come before your toast gets cold,' Raj said as he touched Ella's back. The considerate gesture made me smile.

'You're going for another round?' I asked as he smiled and nodded.

'You know what they say, Yasmin?' I shook my head and watched his smile falter. 'A man with big appetite has other big appetites!'

Ella laughed at his words and I smiled as he looked warmly at her, just as my phone buzzed with the arrival of a message.

'I'll see you back at the table.' Leaving them to it, I took a few steps before checking my phone.

Food sounds good. I'm heading out to the mosque myself, I'll pick you up at twelve. Z

Frowing at the message, I sat down and reread it.

'What's wrong?' Helen asked grumpily. 'Has Mystery Man gone into hiding?'

'Do you think Zach's Muslim?' I regretted asking her the question the instant I spoke.

'Why? What difference does it make?' she asked with confusion.

'None, I was just wondering . . .'

'Trust me, if he was Muslim, I'd become single just for him,' Helen told me matter-of-factly.

'Really,' I muttered, questioning the logic of asking him to join us for lunch. I looked at Helen properly, with her perfect mane of hair, immaculate make-up and pretty face. I couldn't help but feel insecure about Zach meeting her socially. She frowned at my inspection, and I wished I hadn't emailed him in the first place.

There was no need to get friendly with him, not when he could be distracted by the younger woman.

'What?' Helen demanded, breaking into my thoughts. 'All right, so it's not the nicest thing to hear from an engaged woman, but I can't help it. I've been here for five days and I can honestly say that I've enjoyed being single.' I wished she would stop talking; she was making my insecurities worse. 'That's terrible, isn't it?' she asked.

I didn't want to advise her so I smiled and pushed my breakfast away, having lost my appetite. I looked around for Ella and found her laughing with Raj by the breakfast bar.

'Do you know, they left me alone for ages at the club last night?' I looked back at Helen. 'They just disappeared. I looked for them everywhere but couldn't find them.'

'Really?' I asked, keeping Ella's confidence as I asked for a top-up of coffee.

'They had a blast. Look at them, they can't stop talking about last night,' Helen said. 'I've got to say, Dubai has an amazing club scene and the *bicharas* are hot, the men here . . .' She whooped and fanned herself before smiling a slow wide white smile. 'The men are smoking hot.' She breathed out.

'So, you did have company!' I guessed and caught her naughty smile. 'Helen?'

'It was harmless!' she defended. 'Everyone's having the time of their life here, so it's only fair I have some fun.'

'You're engaged!'

'But he was hot, I'm talking H.O.T. Only the Nando's spicy range, the top of the range, very, very hot.' I stared at her, truly disappointed at her lack of faithfulness. 'We danced, that was all. All right, slow-danced. He was packed solid. He took my number . . .'

'You're engaged,' I repeated, refusing to mirror her sense of amusement.

'Yes, engaged, not dead from the neck down, or incarcerated in my hotel room.'

'You know, whatever!' I breathed out with a derisive laugh. 'It's your life, but I'll say one last thing. Karma is a bitch, and she will come back and bite you in the ass.'

'What is your problem?' Helen demanded of me, frowning at my irritated tone.

'What's going on?' Ella asked, returning to hear the last of our exchange.

'People like you are my problem. You should know better, you should value faithfulness and you should treasure what you have instead of chasing cheap thrills,' I threw at Helen, as Raj and Ella stood there stunned by my outburst.

'You've been cheated on, haven't you?' Helen asked, contrite.

I stopped and controlled my anger. To refuse to reply would seem childish, so I looked at her.

'Yes,' I admitted. 'Yes, I have, so I know what it feels like. You're a lady, but if you want to be a respectable one, grow up and get decent.'

Helen stared at me open-mouthed, as did Raj and Ella. I tossed my napkin on to the table and stood up to leave.

'Yasmin . . .'

'You guys go ahead to the malls, I'll hook up with you for lunch,' I told Ella with a warm smile.

'Come with us,' Ella said, grabbing my arm.

'Let me get some air, and I promise I'll find you guys for lunch,' I said, waiting until she nodded and then released my arm.

By twelve, I had worked out my anger at Helen in the gym, showered and changed. In fact, uncertain of what to wear, I had changed several times. I veered from the cosmopolitan-chic St-Tropez look to a casual-smart shalwaar kameez to the boho hippy-chick style to the sporty sun option. Using the mosque as my point of influence, I returned to my first outfit, white linen flares with a navy twinset and roman sandals, set off with big Chanel shades. I threw my ruby-red pashmina into my tote bag and headed down to reception. Taking a deep breath, I whispered, *He's just a friend* over and over again until the elevator doors slid open.

'Hi, Zach!' I greeted as I spotted him by reception.

'Yasmin.' Two voices called simultaneously. I didn't know where to look.

Turning to the entrance, I found Helen staring at Zach and then at me. Moments passed with neither of us knowing who to look at.

'Zach, this is Helen Choudhury. She's one of the accountants on Baby O,' I introduced as we both walked towards Helen. 'Helen, this is Zachary Khan.' I looked away as they greeted each other, not wanting to see the spark of attraction in their eyes.

'I didn't know you ... that you had company ...' Helen stuttered, unable to hide her shock.

'I don't,' I corrected to stop her making rash assumptions. 'Zach and I are going to the mosque. We were planning on joining you guys for lunch.' I stopped talking as it was too quick and too nervous.

'I thought we could go to the mosque together,' Helen told me reluctantly as she showed me her scarf. 'You made a lot of sense this morning. I could do with praying, but I can go another time ...'

'Helen,' I called out to stop her from leaving. 'Come with us,' I said despite myself, and regretted it when I saw her wide white smile appear.

'Really? I'm not intruding or anything? Not that you have to tell me ...'

'By all means join us.' I heard Zach's invitation and felt a stab of jealousy. I took a deep breath and reminded myself of my convictions.

'Oh! That's why you asked if I thought Zach was Muslim this morning! You thought he wasn't . . . how funny!' Helen chimed as I closed my eyes and avoided Zach's look. 'The roses!' Helen shut her mouth quickly as she read the situation and stared at us wide-eyed. I looked to Zach, whose patience seemed to be wearing thin.

'Let's go to the mosque,' I stated, pushing between Helen and Zach to lead the way before she had the chance to open her mouth again.

The journey to the mosque was an ordeal. I sat next to Zach as he drove his hired Porsche in silence. Helen squeezed in at the back, but chose to lean forward between us and talk non-stop in her hyper-happy often giggly tone. She flirted and teased shamelessly, laughing huskily close to Zach until I felt like I was invisible. I zoned out of the conversation, which become a drone set on a continuous helium loop, and enjoyed the chilled drive down Jumeirah Road.

'We're here,' Zach stated as he touched my arm to break me out of my thoughts. He had pulled into an adjacent street and parked up close to the stunning mosque.

I wrapped the thin pashmina deftly around my head to cover my hair and shoulders and then stepped out of the car. Helen followed suit and sidestepped to allow the many pilgrims to rush past to the mosque.

'There's a separate ladies' entrance round the back. I'll meet you both back here afterwards,' Zach told me. I nodded and watched him disappear among the many men heading in the same direction.

'Are you and Zach . . .' Helen raised a brow when I glared at her.

'Helen, we are in front of Allah's house,' I told her patronisingly. Shaking my head, I tutted and headed for the mosque with Helen trying to keep up with me in her high luminous yellow wedges.

'I'm just asking, you know, because if you're not . . . well, I'm trying to decide if I love my fiancé enough, and—'

'You can't break up with your fiancé just because you fancy Zach,' I told her.

'Why not?' Helen asked, and I struggled to give her an answer because there really was no justifiable reason why she couldn't. 'If Zach is the one for me, I don't want you to get hurt.'

'Are you saying he'd choose you over me if he had the choice?' I demanded.

'No!' Helen answered as she grabbed me to a stop to make me face her. 'Zach is Mr Right, Yasmin, and he could be Mr Right for me. He's successful, rich, powerful; he's everything I've ever wanted.'

'You have a crush, Helen,' I told her, frowning as I started walking again.

'I'll leave Zach be if you're interested in him.' I halted at her words and turned around to find her still where we had stopped. I walked back to her and saw the confusion in her eyes. 'I'm trying to do the decent thing, Yasmin, and I'm asking you to help me.'

I didn't know what to say. The right thing would be to give her my blessing, but I couldn't. I couldn't because I didn't want to let Zach go.

'Let's pray,' I told her as the mu'alim sang the ikama call to prayer. It resonated all around us as I led the way to the ladies' section and found a spot for us.

I sat through the Arabic sermon conscious of the

dilemma I was in. I prayed for guidance and the strength to do the honourable thing. When everyone stood for the prayers, I followed suit as the imam led us through the jummah ritual. Jummah passed far too quickly for me, and as those around us rushed to get back to their daily business, I sat and prayed. Helen sat patiently and silently next to me, waiting until I completed my supplementary prayers.

'Why don't you go and wait with Zach?' I offered. Helen stared at me, surprised by the blessing I had given her. I nodded but couldn't bring myself to smile. 'I haven't finished here, so why don't you go ahead and wait with him?'

'Are you sure, Yasmin?' she asked as she went to stand up. I couldn't hold her look, but I nodded.

Helen left without another word. I raised my palms and stared at them through tear-filled eyes. I told myself it was the right thing to do, the best way to protect myself and my hopes, but no matter how hard I tried to convince myself of that, it hurt. It hurt to give up on hope.

'Hey, there's our St Yasmin!' Helen chimed out with a false laugh. I smiled at her infectious charm and looked to Zach.

'You ready?' he asked as I avoided his eyes and unwound my pashmina and tousled my curly hair free.

'We're going to Chili's Steak House; it's a five-minute drive from here,' Helen informed me. 'Zach recommended it. Raj and Ella are going to grab a cab there. Oh, and guess what? Zach's agreed to join us for the desert safari. Isn't that great!'

I looked at Zach and failed to muster any enthusiasm. Helen held the passenger door open and indicated for me to get into the back with a cheeky wink.

'Great,' I muttered before stepping into the low, hard

back seat of the Porsche. Zach and Helen climbed into the front, and I sat quietly as Zach eased on to the main road.

'Did you know that Zach's half Bengali, Yasmin?' Helen asked as she twisted in her seat to look back at me and to give Zach a great view of her ample curves.

'Really?' I muttered uninterested before looking out of the window.

'But he's never visited Bangladesh because he never knew his father.' I closed my eyes at Helen's lack of tact. 'That's really sad, really really sad.' I rolled my eyes at her baby-doll voice and saw Zach shift uncomfortably at the conversation. 'Have you ever thought about finding him—'

'The mosque's beautifully understated,' I cut in to change the topic. 'I expected it to be much grander and opulent, like the mosques in Istanbul, but I loved its simplicity.'

'Yes, but it was a bit plain, wasn't it?' Helen added, struggling to voice a sincere opinion.

'Is this the first time you've attended?' I asked Zach, refusing to meet his eyes in the rear-view mirror.

'Only when you're in Dubai, though.' Helen stated the obvious and we sat in silence cringing at her answer.

'You're surprised I even know what a mosque is, right?' Zach asked me with a smile.

'I'm not. Any idiot knows what a mosque is,' Helen answered eagerly.

'Why thank you, Helen.' Zach's dry tone made me smile.

'Oh, you're very very welcome.' I bit my lip at Helen's breathless answer and saw Zach's attention veer to her chest as she arched her back in a fake stretch. My smile died at the fickle stupidity of men.

'I'm totally surprised that you not only know what a

mosque is but that you actually attend one,' I threw in, ignoring Helen, who spun round to glare at me for insulting Zach.

'Why is that, Yasmin?' Zach asked as Helen mouthed, *be careful* to me.

'Because you're known on the jet-set party scene, you drink and you swap hot totty like boys swap football cards, so it doesn't take a rocket scientist to figure out that you're not the most godly of people,' I answered as Helen balked at my reply.

'You party quite well yourself, Yasmin.'

'But I don't drink, and I have no problem with people knowing what my faith is.'

'So, I keep my faith private.'

'Until you're here, where it's more profitable to be seen to be praying, right?'

'Yasmin!' Helen breathed out in shocked outrage.

'What difference does it make to you whether I pray or not?' Zach asked as he pulled up in front of Chili's.

'None,' I answered, following Helen out of the car.

I walked on ahead as she waited for Zach. I entered the steak house and was led to a booth for five on the first floor. I dumped my bag on the seat and sat down. Minutes later, I saw Helen arrive on her own. Frowning, I looked to see where Zach was as she sat down opposite me.

'Did you have to be so rude—'

Before she could finish, I raced down the stairs and slammed out of Chili's to find him driving off.

'Zach!' I called out, stepping forward with the hope that he'd see me. He didn't.

'Yasmin?' I turned round at Ella's call and saw Raj paying the taxi driver.

'Thank God you're here,' I breathed as she stood before me.

'What's happened?'

'Zach and I planned to go to the mosque together, Helen decided she wanted to talk to God and tagged along, and then she decides to make a play for him, so I back off and spend the rest of the time insulting him, and now he's driven off,' I explained as Ella's eyes widened at the detail I provided.

'Hi, Yasmin,' Raj said, pausing to look at us. 'I hear that boss man is joining us.'

'No, boss man isn't joining us, Raj.' I breathed out. 'Helen's inside on the first floor,' I told him as Ella encouraged him to go ahead without us.

'Yasmin, what's going on with you?' Ella asked as we found shade from the fierce heat of the midday sun.

'I really like him, Ella. I can't act on it, but I like him,' I told her with frustration. 'I know I should be gracious and step back, but she has everything, and . . . and . . . he kissed me.'

'He just drove off?' Ella asked, frowning as I nodded.

'Ella, he kissed me, and it meant something to me, it was special. As stupid as it is to believe he won't ever make another girl feel like that, I know he will, but I don't want to see it, I don't want to hear about it . . .'

'Call him,' Ella advised, bringing my tearful rant to a stop. 'Call him, apologise, make amends and then let things be.'

'But she's . . .'

Ella shushed me into silence. 'Call him.' She brought her phone out, found Zach's work number and dialled it for me. Handing me the phone, she smiled before walking on into Chili's.

'Zachary Khan.' I closed my eyes at the sound of his voice. 'Hello?'

'Z . . . Zach . . .' I was so nervous, my throat dried and I could barely whisper.

'Hello?'

I cleared my throat. 'Zach, it's Yasmin. I . . . wanted to say . . .' I paused and rubbed the back of my neck. 'I was out of order just now, it was wrong . . . Please join us today.'

'I plan to. I need to tie up my diary, get changed for the desert safari and then I'll meet you guys back at the Arjaan.'

'Y . . . you're coming back?' I asked breathlessly.

'Yeah, I told Helen that,' he said as my heart raced.

'Good,' I said, and smiled. 'I'll see you later, then.'

'Yasmin . . .'

'Yeah?' I cringed as I answered too quickly. I held on to the phone and listened to the silence.

'That was the most reluctant apology I've ever heard!' I burst out laughing at his comment. 'Next time, make it more heartfelt.'

'Zach?'

'Yeah?' He answered too quickly as well, and I couldn't stop smiling.

'There won't be a next time.' I hung up before he could come back with a retort. He didn't call back, but I knew I was seeing him later. Sometimes instincts failed to listen to logic. In this case, my heart refused to listen to my brain. Whilst the two fought it over, I was happy to enjoy Zach for now. Time had a way of sorting messes out, so I decided to stop thinking about the mess and to start living.

Lesson Thirteen:
Enjoy being you: not a wannabe younger or innocent you; enjoy being you now

Shades donned, Bollywood music blaring and Land Rover cruising, the five of us headed out to our late afternoon desert safari. Our guide spoke Arabic to Zach, who sat in the passenger seat whilst Helen tried to involve herself with the conversation. Raj, Ella and I sang along melodramatically to tracks as we coasted towards Fujairah.

'Everything OK?' Ella asked me as Raj sang to his heart's content.

'I want him.'

Ella looked stupefied by my statement.

'Yasmin, he's replaced his bedposts several times over because there's no more space for notches. Do you know what you're letting yourself in for?'

'What am I meant to do?' I asked as I leaned on the back rest to look round at her.

'Ignore him,' she told me.

'What?'

'Ignore him. No man, especially one with a big ego, likes to be ignored.'

'I left the playground a long time ago.'

'You might have, but men never do,' Ella whispered. 'Look at him.' We turned to Raj and watched him singing like a kid who'd had too many sweets. 'And him.' We looked to Zach, who was trying to take control of the steering like a boy who had to have every toy. We then looked to the driver, who was attempting to maintain control like a meek schoolboy.

'Ignore him?' I whispered and watched Ella nod.

'Ignore him, but order him around.'

'You're now the font of love advice?'

'Who is?' Helen asked at my dry comment. 'I thought we figured out who Yasmin's secret admirer was . . . Oh, you're talking about the gorgeous prince? Has he contacted you?'

'Prince?' Above the blaring music and Raj's singing, somehow Zach had heard Helen.

'Yasmin met this prince on Monday and she fell for him!' Helen explained all too helpfully. 'And it looks like he's still chasing her!' I went to correct her but yelped at the fierce pinch Ella dealt.

'What happened?' Raj asked, pausing only to see me glare at Ella.

'Nothing,' I muttered as I looked away from Ella to a confused Helen.

'So who's this prince, Yasmin?' Zach asked as he turned the volume down.

'Helen's exaggerating . . .'

'Oh no I am not. Monday night you walked into your apartment and declared that you had fallen in love.' I looked from Helen to a watching Zach, searching for a mitigating answer. 'Did you or did you not say you had fallen in love?'

'I meant it . . .'

'So, who is this prince?' Zach asked again, leaning on the headrest to look back at us.

'She met him at a meeting. He's been pestering her for dinner but Yasmin's not budging,' Ella stated as if her arm was being twisted. I looked at her, silently begging her to restrain her overactive imagination, but she winked at me and continued, 'He sent her this softest, thinnest red pashmina because she loves her shawls.'

'The one you wore today at the mosque?' Helen connected with excitement. 'When did he send that?'

I couldn't look at Zach, so I stared at Ella, who looked as sincere as sin. She looked at me and encouraged me silently to join her little charade.

'Tuesday. Tuesday morning . . .' I stuttered.

'He sent her the pashmina wrapped in silk with the loveliest little sonnet dedicated to her,' Ella elaborated.

'Sonnet?' Zach threw out with disgust. 'Who writes sonnets these days?'

'Tell me, what did it say? Yasmin, that is so romantic!' Helen sighed out.

'Sonnet?' Zach repeated as if he had never heard of them.

Ella struggled to think of a sonnet and nodded at me to come up with something.

'Yasmin, was it a saucy sonnet?' Helen giggled as she looked at Zach. 'Come on, tell, share the details.'

Ella leaned forward and I shook my head at her to stop her.

'Didn't it begin with: *The sunrays grow bolder, the raindrops are pearlised* . . . What did it go on to say?' She looked at me to continue and I searched for inspiration as both Helen and Zach looked at me.

'*The sunrays grow bolder, the raindrops become pearlised* . . .' I repeated. '*If only you submitted, my dreams would be realised*,' I rhymed as Ella nodded with a cheeky smile. '*Roses, lilies and sunflowers, fragrance abound, yet without you my heart cannot be found. Come to me, my beauty red, let's make this world our glorious bed.'* Raj, Ella and Helen applauded excitedly as I cupped my face, blushing with sheer embarrassment.

'That's beautiful!' Helen breathed out. 'Oh my God, it's moved me to tears.'

'Fantastic, this man, he is a poetic genius,' Raj announced. 'Genius.'

'And he sent that with a scarf?'

'Pashmina,' Ella corrected as Zach shook his head.

'He's got too much time on his hands. What business is he in?'

I looked to Ella for creative answers.

'Oil,' I told him after she mouthed it. 'He's in oil, but you know, I'm not interested.' I caught Ella's glare to not cave in now, so I continued. 'But he is so handsome.'

'I want to meet him!' Helen chimed as Zach turned the volume back up.

The driver pulled into a stopover to have the air reduced on the tyres, and we all stepped out to stretch our legs, with the exception of Helen, who raced into the gift shop to buy all types of tourist tat.

'Are you going to have that dinner?' I turned around and pushed my shades on top of my head to look at Zach.

'I haven't decided,' I told him, unable to meet his eyes. 'I've got another week here, unlike Helen, who's heading out to Mumbai tomorrow night. It's so sweet: her fiancé's joining her there so that they can shop for their wedding.'

'You should go to Mumbai too,' he stated, ignoring my subtle reference to Helen's fiancé. 'They're meeting the manufacturers.'

'Helen's going to have a marvellous time in India with her fiancé, so it'd be a shame not to be taken for a glamorous dinner with a prince,' I said, catching his eye and holding my nerve.

'Why aren't you going to India?' Zach muttered as he brought his phone out.

'I think Rania needs me to finish the mall data.'

'Our local team here can finish that.'

'W . . . what are you doing?'

He pointed at me as if to stop me from talking. 'You should go to India,' he stated before walking off.

Turning around, I joined Ella and Raj in front of the gift shop.

'He's arranging for me to go to India!' I said, holding in a smile.

'You're coming with us?' Ella whispered with dancing eyes.

'I think so!' I squealed, trying not to jump with excitement.

'Look at what I've got!' Helen called out, clattering out in her wedges and coming to a stop before us. Opening up her carrier bags, she brought out all kinds of Dubai memorabilia. 'You all missed a shopping treat!' she trilled with delight.

'We're heading for the desert,' the guide shouted, causing us to all head back to the jeep. Within a few minutes, the vehicle shot into the steep, unending sun-baked sand dunes of Dubai. We cheered as the guide pushed it to its limit, taking it up near-vertical dunes against screams and shouts of sheer fear. Zach roared as he leaned out of the window, Helen screamed non-stop and the rest of us laughed as our guide pushed the jeep to its limits.

He stopped at a summit, and we rushed out on to the sand. The setting sun brought the inner child out in all of us. Without any inhibitions, we raced down the dune with the wind rushing past us, the crisp hot sand cascading beneath us, and laughter resonating through the barren desert. We ran around, chasing and fleeing and climbing and rolling down until we could laugh no more. Pictures were taken randomly, in groups, singles, from all angles. I waved up at Ella as she took a picture and froze as I saw Zach storming down a steep dune, too fast to control the momentum. 'Yasmin!' he shouted when I didn't move in time, and he grabbed me and took me racing down with him. I screamed and screamed until we tumbled down to the base of the dune, where he landed on top of me with a thud. I grimaced and held my reeling head.

'Yasmin, are you OK?' I looked up at him, unable to focus as the sun behind him blinded me. Zach cupped my cheeks and looked into my eyes. 'Yasmin?'

'Hi,' I mumbled with half a smile. He grinned back. 'I think you need to get off me,' I told him, squinting to meet his eyes.

'Is that right?' Zach asked. I nodded but neither of us moved.

'Zach, oh my God, are you OK?' Helen's high-pitched screech could be heard from the summit of the dune, from where she had refused to budge in case sand got into her hair. 'Talk to me, say anything, say something!' she called.

'You better say something . . .' I trailed off with a laugh that died when I caught his eyes.

'You say something,' he mumbled.

'I'm coming to save you,' Helen screeched as she stuttered down the dune. 'Oh God, oh God, oh God . . .'

Zach leaned back in exasperation. I grabbed two fistfuls of sand and threw them at him.

'No, you don't get away that easy,' he shouted when I scrambled away, grabbing my legs and pulling me back beneath him. I struggled, laughing with him as we tussled in the sand.

'What are you doing?' Helen demanded, looking down at us as we fell on to the sand exhausted. 'You've got sand everywhere.'

I looked at Zach and he looked at me. He was covered with sand and I rubbed a little off his shoulder.

'Don't start.'

'I was helping you tidy—'

'Don't even think it . . .' Before he could finish, we were back tussling and laughing.

'I don't know what's going on, but this is not funny. You!' Helen called out to the driver and beckoned him. 'I can't climb this in my heels, they'll get ruined. Come, come and help me up! Hey . . . hey!' she cried in outrage when the man walked around to the driver's seat and jumped in behind the wheel. 'He's going!' Helen cried out as he started the engine.

Zach and I stopped and stared at each other. Without another word we stood up and raced up the dune to catch the jeep in time. We followed Raj and Ella and laughed breathlessly as Helen clambered up to the top, flustered and bedraggled.

'Drive,' she ordered, unamused, as she stepped in, patted her hair into place and slammed the door shut behind her.

Zach looked back at me and held up a bottle of water. Helen took the bottle he held out as I shook my head and stifled a laugh. I stared out of the window, glowing like the setting sun, unable to stop smiling.

Our guide somehow managed to find the highway and drove across more desert to a huge gated campsite. The site was lit up with several floodlights, where a few hundred other visitors decided between camel rides, quad-biking, sandboarding, henna art and shisha smoking pipes.

'Sandboarding!' Raj announced as we filed out of the jeep and headed into the open-air camp for a cold drink.

'No thank you, I pass,' Helen stated princess-like. 'I'm going to have henna applied; anyone want to join me?' She looked at Zach, who passed and followed Raj. She turned to Ella and myself and raised her eyebrows.

'Sandboarding,' we said together, albeit reluctantly, but feeling like we should try it.

'I'll come find you straight after,' I promised, but Helen had disappeared before I could finish.

We raced after the guys and caught up with them at the base of the dune. We queued up, clutching our boards, until our turn came. Raj and Zach climbed up the dune first and we waited until they got to the top before we started our climb. I stopped to watch Zach masterfully board down the dune and then laughed when Raj cried out in fear as he stuttered down.

'Come on!' Ella called and I sped up to join her at the top. 'So we just strap our feet in and slide down?' I nodded and did as instructed.

'On three we go?' I shouted as my heart raced with adrenalin. 'One, two . . .'

'Go!' Ella screamed as we bent our knees and leaned forward. I joined in with the screaming as I mastered balancing and weaved down the dune. Everything flashed by and suddenly I realised I didn't know how to stop.

'Ella!' I screamed, looking around for her. 'I can't stop, I can't stop!'

The base of the pit was getting closer. I spotted Zach. I flailed my arms to get some control, and looked away when he laughed and pointed up at me. 'No, no, no, I can't stop!' I screamed as I crashed straight into a stranger and landed with a heavy thud in a heap of limbs and equipment.

I tapped the stranger and looked down at him. 'Are you OK? I am so sorry.' The stranger wasn't impressed and we scrambled to separate. The sand board proved tough to control, and I fell back flat and stared up at the sky, humiliated beyond belief. Zach had seen every single embarrassing moment of my ungraceful, uncontrolled descent.

'Yasmin, you OK?' I looked over at Ella and saw the laughter in her eyes.

'Did he see everything?' I asked. She nodded and I groaned with laughter.

'He's coming over.'

Once again, I scrambled to get up and fell back on my butt, laughing at the effort.

'Is that the way it's done?' Zach asked as I looked across at him and nodded. 'You having another go?'

'Will you break my fall this time?' He shook his head as I laughed. 'Then I'm going to pass!'

Zach helped get me to my feet and crouched down to unlock the foot restraints. Ella caught the gesture and winked at me as I smiled naughtily.

'Thanks,' I said as Raj called out for Zach and Ella to join him near the top. 'I'll go find Helen,' I told him with a smile as he nodded.

Heading back to the camp, I looked for Helen. I found her at a low table, sitting back on cushions replicating an Arabian setting in the middle of the camp.

'Look at what I got.' I stared at the three handbags she held up. 'They're the best fakes I've seen. I've got Gucci, Prada and Versace!' she spelled out with excitement. I shook my head and sat down next to her.

'You're brilliant,' I said as I poured myself some water.

'He doesn't like me,' Helen stated, and I felt guilty for enjoying Zach. 'He's totally uninterested and I've never experienced that.'

'Maybe you're being too hard on yourself,' I said before I took a long swig.

'No, a woman knows when a man is interested.' I put my water down and looked at her. 'I called my fiancé, I really miss him.'

I frowned. 'You miss him because Zach didn't give you attention?' Helen nodded and smiled. My point was completely lost on her, so I shook my head and smiled. 'Let's go get henna.'

Beneath the stars, we worked around the camp. I got henna whilst the guys chilled out with sheesha. Then I convinced Helen to join me for a camel ride, whilst Ella, Raj and Zach went quad-biking. We were exhausted by the time dinner was served. Silently we queued and I chose a medley of grilled meats, hummus and flat bread before joining everyone back at the table. We passed the evening talking, teasing and laughing until the lights were dimmed and loud Arabic music filled the evening. Men around the stage whooped and cheered as a belly dancer took centre stage. Raj stood up and clapped, as Helen and Ella whistled. I looked to Zach and found him watching me.

'I'm shattered,' he muttered and lay back on the mat to stare up at the stars in the dark, dark night.

I looked at the show and found everyone captivated by the woman who was living up to every male fantasy. I lay down beside Zach.

'I'm shattered too,' I said, keeping my gaze fixed on the stars. I felt his eyes on me and I smiled. 'Don't say a word,' I told him. He obliged and looked back up at the star-lit sky.

It was the most serene night I had ever experienced. Its simplicity was spellbinding. Nature was forceful, and being natural inherited that force. I enjoyed being me, not a wannabe Helen, or even a younger, innocent me. By all accounts Zach too enjoyed me, enough to lie by me living our moment in silence. Silence spoke volumes, and for now it was the only sound I wanted to hear.

Lesson Fourteen:
The only thing self-help books fail
to tell you is how to be you

We arrived in Mumbai late on Saturday. Despite being only a few hours from Dubai, we could've been on another planet. Where Dubai was organised and spacious, Mumbai was chaotic and congested. I grabbed a bottle of water from a vendor and felt the heat get to me straightaway. We wheeled our trolleys through customs to arrivals, where we tried to spot our driver amidst the hundreds of faces waiting to greet their loved ones.

'Ms Choudhury? Ms Yusuf?' Above the manic calls, we heard our names being shouted out and found our driver. He led us through the congested airport to a seven-seater people carrier. I jumped in at the back and switched on my iPhone. I tabbed through to my messages and smiled when I received one from Zach.

Enjoy Mumbai. Stay away from rajas or ranas or any other regal bachelor. I'm meeting the Jayachands there, but diary is fully booked. See you back in London. Z

I stared out of the window, but registered nothing as I recalled how Zach had carried me half-asleep back to my apartment on the night of the safari and how we had been in constant contact ever since.

'We're never going to make the show,' Helen muttered. 'It's the only international lingerie show we're attending, and it doesn't look like we're going to make it.'

'Could you put the air-conditioning on?' I asked the driver, irritated by heat and humidity.

'It's broken,' Ella told me, making me groan and take a swig of the bottled water.

'If we put our make-up on en route, all we have to do is get changed and head out,' Helen suggested.

'You want us to do our make-up in the car?' Ella asked in disbelief.

'I might give it a miss. I need a shower and a sleep.'

'Come on, Yasmin, lingerie shows are new in Mumbai; the vibe's going to be electric.'

I looked at Helen, who had already started on her make-up, and admired her dedication.

'I need half an hour to shower, change and get ready,' I offered, and smiled when she stopped to wink at me.

'Half an hour, otherwise we head off without you,' she returned, making us all laugh.

I nodded and watched the street vendors who moved amongst the traffic to sell their goods. Spotting a puchka seller, I opened the window and beckoned him over.

'Don't have street food, Yasmin, it'll make you ill.'

'Raj! I'm pretty much a local. I can handle a few puchkas,' I laughed as I dug out some change for the vendor.

'Even the locals avoid street food.'

'You are such a snob, Raj. These guys are just making a living,' I told him as I paid for six crisp puchkas packed with chickpeas, imli and potatoes.

'You're paying too much!' Raj pointed out.

'What's a few pounds to me?'

'I am not taking this girl shopping. She'll have a crowd of beggars following us everywhere taking us for every hard-earned penny,' he muttered angrily.

'Anyone want some?' I shrugged when the others passed, and bit into the snack.

'She's going to pay for this,' Raj told Ella knowingly.

'It'll be worth it. This is so good!' I breathed as I tucked into my second puchka with relish. 'You guys are missing out!'

'She's nuts, the lady is nuts,' Raj continued as Ella leaned forward.

'Don't wind him up,' she advised. 'Save me one!' she added with a wink.

'Ooooh you too!' Raj burst out with exasperation before turning to Helen. 'Are you going to go against my good advice too?'

'Ooooh, no way!' Helen answered as she stopped applying her mascara to wrinkle her pert nose. 'I would never touch street food. These people don't know anything about hygiene or cleanliness. Goodness knows how they prepare the food.'

'Exactly!' Raj finished as he pointed to Helen. 'You see, Helen has common sense. But you two, you two . . . you have too much Western bravado.'

'Oh Raj, chill out,' Ella said as she finally caved in, took a puchka and took a hefty bite from it. I looked at her and burst out laughing when Raj sat back, arms folded in a sulk.

Later in the afternoon we arrived at the grand Renaissance Mumbai that looked out on to the Powai Lake. As we were ushered through the majestic hotel, I caught my reflection in the many mirrors and smiled. Whilst Helen had opted for all-out evening glamour in a floor-length red halterneck dress, and Ella had chosen a navy-blue maxi dress, I'd gone for my oyster blush chiffon shalwaar kameez with towering open-toe Louboutin slingbacks, and felt like a million dollars. With dark red lips, thickly lined almond eyes and sixties-inspired slick bob, I felt like I belonged in front of the crew of cameras that we walked past. The show was hosted out in the gardens and we nodded at famous faces, socialites, designers and financiers as we were taken to our seats in the second row moments before the sounds of a sitar filled the evening.

'Oh my, there's Preity Zinta!' Helen whispered to Raj, who proceeded to subtly take pictures of Bollywood's celebrities instead of the show.

'Focus on the show. These guys are launching themselves so we need to know what works and what doesn't,' Ella reminded Raj, nudging him to behave himself as the stage was brought to life with a heart-stopping burst of fusion bhangra music. The tension heightened to mark the start of the show, and then the catwalk was bathed in the flashing lights of cameras as model after model sashayed down it in hand-crafted fragile retro-style corsetry and ultra-romantic lingerie. I made notes of everything: the range of models used, the size of the crowd, its make-up of celebrities, designers, media and money-makers. I jotted down illustrations of the setting, the sophisticated aesthetic mixed with sensual music, until I could write no more. Finally I committed the range to memory, the delicate, provocative but discreet sets that teased the observer with barely there sheer material so that when the show came to an end the audience stood up and applauded the new designer with much gusto.

'That was amazing!' Helen squealed out as we watched the designer take to the stage with the models. 'I want one of everything!'

'I do too, if I could fit into anything!' Ella added as we left our seats. 'I can't wait for Zamil Hussain's show. He's a seasoned designer, so his show's bound to be amazing.'

'Baby O is a million miles from this,' I murmured, feeling the first signs of doubt at its revival strategy. 'How are we going to get to this point?'

'That's not our business,' Helen reminded me as we headed to the Velvet Lounge for the after party. 'Look at all the media,' she breathed out as we passed stunning Bollywood stars giving press quotes about the show.

'Ma'am, how do you think the show went?' I stared at the mike that was shoved in front of me and then looked at the journalist, who grinned at me. 'Do you think Mumbai's glitterati welcome this?'

'I . . . I . . . I think this marks—'

'The show was breathtaking, simply breathtaking,' Helen said as she grabbed the mike and smiled into the camera with her flawless white smile. 'I loved it, it—'

'The show was awesome, man, awesome!' Raj laughed as he took the mike from her.

'Is this live?' Ella whispered to the journalist, who tried to rescue her mike back. 'Will it go out to England?'

'The show was great . . .'

'. . . fantastic, man, some of those models were . . . man . . .'

Ella punched Raj back into reality and I took the mike from Helen.

'I think the show was great, but look out for Baby O. The Oshanti range will be mind-blowing.'

'Really, Baby O?' the journalist asked with confusion.

'Yes, out at the end of this year, and we'll have a famous Bollywood face heading it up.'

The journalist's eyes almost popped out and I smiled as she threw half a dozen questions at me. Without another word I handed back the mike and escorted my colleagues towards the party.

'You can't announce something like that,' Ella told me quietly.

'Why not? If Baby O launches with a . . .'

'. . . a Bollywood face?' Raj laughed whilst shaking his head. 'Yasmin, you're lucky you're in Mumbai where no one knows any different.'

'Guys, look around. There are models everywhere and Bollywood stars from the small and the big screen, and we've got an opportunity to change things.'

'Do you guys have an off button?' Helen asked drily. 'We're at a glamorous celeb-packed party and you're still in business mode.' Without another word, she waltzed off. We followed and entered the packed, noisy bar that was thumping with the latest tracks.

'Oh my lord of God above, they're playing Masta Masta!' Raj shouted as he dragged Ella off to the dance floor.

Laughing I waved her off and then headed for the bar. Ordering a cold juice, I watched the evening unfold. Fashionable socialites and handsome hunks took to the floor, designers debated the show and media darlings networked for deals and business.

'Hey, darling.' Turning at the deep charming voice, I looked up at the long-haired hunk who grinned at me.

'Hi back,' I returned before looking back at the dance floor where Ella was being swung around by Raj.

'I'm Anil. Anil Sen.' The man beside me was somebody, but not somebody that I knew.

'Yasmin. Yasmin Yusuf,' I returned as we shook hands.

'You're new, but I feel I know your face. Are you . . . an actress?' I stopped myself from rolling my eyes and smiled at the compliment.

'Yes, yes I am.'

'I knew it!' He laughed as he snapped his fingers. 'I spotted you at the show and thought I have to meet you. I love your work, I think you're a fantastic actress.'

'Really?' I asked and watched him nod emphatically. 'Which show's your favourite?' He looked lost for words and I stared at him with a raised eyebrow. 'Nice meeting you,' I said and then walked away as he stared on speechless.

'Congratulations.' I stopped at the quiet compliment from a young cosmopolitan lady.

'Excuse me?'

The bespectacled woman was dressed in a black poloneck and high-waisted sailor trousers that told you that she was someone in the design industry.

'It takes a lot for a single woman to avoid falling for the charms of a gorgeous model.'

'Not when you value intellect,' I returned and watched her chuckle. 'I'm Yasmin Yusuf.'

She shook my hand and invited me to follow her.

'Sharmeen Kapoor,' she threw over her shoulder as I admired her towering burgundy Manolos that defied the laws of gravity. 'So what line of work are you in? Acting, modelling?'

'Oh no, I'm a private equity analyst.' Sharmeen looked stunned by my correction. 'We're working on a turnaround for an Indian lingerie label and looking to recruit a designer.'

'Brains *and* beauty. No wonder you put the airhead in his place.' Sharmeen laughed.

'And you? Are you a designer?' I asked as I followed her into the VIP zone.

'She's with me,' Sharmeen told the security guard, who stepped back.

Taking a seat in the lounge area, I tried not to look star-struck as I recognised faces from the Bollywood world. 'Close your mouth, they're just people,' Sharmeen instructed. Snapping my mouth shut, I looked at her with a guilty smile.

'Sure they are,' I returned, and shook my head when she offered me a glass of Cristal.

'You think the range today was any good?'

Stopping at the question, I looked at Sharmeen.

'Tell me you're not on the design team?'

Sharmeen laughed at my question and then pointed to a table where the design team celebrated raucously.

'It was lukewarm, right?' I nodded and watched Sharmeen smile. 'Talk freely. I sit as lingerie and sports-wear director on the board of the Indian Fashion Industry Council. I'm the harshest critic around, so you'd have to go to some length to offend me.'

I couldn't believe my luck. I looked around for Zach to see if he had somehow orchestrated the introduction, but reminded myself that he had already told me he would be too busy to make time for me in Mumbai. So I looked back at Sharmeen and smiled.

'I was impressed. But the show lacked originality or inspiration,' I said and watched her nod. 'The craftsmanship of the corsets was outstanding, but there was nothing new.'

'So, this Indian lingerie label, who is it?' Sharmeen asked as she pushed her heavy fringe back from her eyes. 'Whoever it is, they have some serious international competition.' I nodded in agreement and ordered a juice from a passing waiter.

'My favourite right now is Aubade, I've not yet seen anyone who does provocative in an elegant, delicate and naughty way like they do.'

'We're looking for an Indian label to have that kind of reputation. I like Jolidon, they do lingerie for the couture buyer. They've just launched five charming collections, all reaching out to an emotion a woman relates to, like "Lovely Feeling" or "Romantic Rose"; you know, it's saying something about what is really just flimsy bits of material that cover our privates!'

I laughed in agreement and turned around as I heard Helen's surprised call. Sharmeen indicated for the guard to let her through and she laughed with delight as she met Sharmeen. I cringed as she barely listened to the introduction, instead focusing on the celebrities partying in the cordoned-off area.

'Sharmeen's a director on the Indian Fashion Industry Council,' I stated, shaking my head when Helen nodded before wandering off. 'I'm sorry, she's . . . she's a little . . .'

'I'm in the fashion industry, Yasmin, I know fickle very well,' Sharmeen told me with a laugh. She beckoned to some colleagues who were standing nearby and introduced me.

'Sharmeen, are Bollywood actresses interested in lingerie endorsements?' I asked as her colleagues laughed at my question. 'So, what's so funny?'

'B-list Bollywood actresses will endorse anything: we mean *anything*, darling.' I smiled at the colourful man with the very camp Indian accent. 'The only thing it won't buy you is credibility.'

'There must be some marketing weight that small-screen actresses can bring . . .'

'Name me three such actresses that you like and I'll tell you their marketing power.'

I stared at the man, knowing that I would struggle to name three Bollywood actresses.

'I'm from England . . .'

'I tell you, my dear, that no one with international marketing power will be on anything but the big screen,' he finished off, offering me a glass of champagne. Shaking my head again, I looked round at the celebrities partying riotously.

'The problem is this, Yasmin. India is still a conservative country with traditional values. Lingerie modelling is new and clashes with the ideals.'

'But the films are so forward these days. Half the time the actresses are walking around in mini itsy-bitsy items in the films.'

'I didn't say that India wasn't without contradictions. If you want a face for lingerie, it has to be an established model who is willing to shock and build her brand value through lingerie,' Sharmeen finished as she ordered another bottle of Cristal.

'Someone like Bipasha, who I see as being sexy and sensual without being sluttish.' I refused to join in with the muted laughter around the table.

'Yes, someone like her.' The man laughed as he patted me on the back.

'Would you happen to know anyone who would be willing to do that?' The laughter around the table told me that I was naive about the world of fashion and celebrity. I caught Sharmeen's eyes and knew that that naivety was admired and encouraged. I joined in with the laughter and called out to Raj and Ella to join us.

'She's tenacious,' Sharmeen told them.

'Tell me about it; there's no off switch on Yasmin,' Ella returned, making everyone laugh. I refuted the statement animatedly and laughed when the whole group joined in.

The evening stretched into the early hours, and it didn't matter that the invisible barriers between the designers, celebrities and media world remained. What did matter was the number of business cards that I crammed into my clutch bag, knowing that at some point they would come handy in the revival of Baby O. I had been given the opportunity to be more than just a runaround girl; Rania had given me that chance. As I looked around the packed VIP section, I smiled. This was my moment to prove myself, to make a difference to the outcome of this project, and I was determined to do just that.

The following morning we woke late, skipped breakfast, and headed out to see the most of Mumbai. It was fantastic to have Raj with us. He spoke Hindi and Urdu and made sure we were given the service we deserved. We went to Chor Bazaar and rummaged through jostling crowds and chaotic streets, picking up bangles and trinkets along the way. We walked around in the midday heat, enjoying the vibrant, busy stalls. Having missed dinner and passed on breakfast, I couldn't resist the street vendors selling puchkas and, in spite of Raj's warning, helped myself to two servings. In a bid to get away from street vendors, Raj whisked us away to The Courtyard near the Fariyas Hotel at Colaba. There we moved from one designer store to the next and stopped at Suraya's, where we stood in silent wonder at the gorgeous saris and shalwaar kameezes on display.

'The prices here are painful, girls. I'm just warning you,' Raj added quickly when we glared at him for breaking our reverie. The store attendant offered us courtesy drinks, which we accepted, and I ordered another serving of puchkas. I picked up two saris for my sisters-in-law and one for Chachijhi Fauzia. I then found a sheer blood-red chiffon sari with tiny black beading along the edges that was exquisitely simple. Without a second thought I smiled cheekily and bought it, before turning with relish to the puchkas.

'God this is good!' I said as I started on my fourth one.

'Yasmin!' Raj cried out, taking the plate from me. 'They buy this from street vendors! You can't take the risk of eating food from street vendors.' I stared as he carried the plate to the bin. He looked at me for permission, and reluctantly I nodded.

'What do you think?' Turning around, we saw Ella step out of the dressing room garbed in a sky-blue sari. I ran across to her to adjust the asol and then clapped with delight as she walked before Raj.

'You look beautiful,' he told her as Helen joined us and complimented Ella. 'Buy it.'

Ella nodded and he asked the attendant to cash up. Helen failed to notice Raj paying for the sari, but I saw Ella's eyes shine with happiness.

'Let's go eat,' she suggested as Helen grabbed my arm.

'My fiancé's arrived; he wants to meet me back at the hotel. Do you guys mind if I head back?' She didn't wait for an answer. Instead, she gave us all a quick hug and departed.

Raj and I waited for Ella to change and then got our driver to take us to 5 Spice. He weaved at a snail's pace through the traffic, pedestrians and cattle as we sweltered in the vehicle.

'How are you set for tomorrow?' I asked Ella, who was fanning herself with a piece of paper.

'Helen and I are meeting with Zamil Hussain. Helen's going to try and blag us some tickets.'

'That's what I want to do!' I muttered to Raj. 'I'm going with Ella for her first meeting and then meeting one of Rania's advisers in the afternoon.' I saw Raj shake his head. 'What's wrong?' I asked.

'Ms Jayachand is working so hard to save her company, but we know they're going to cut it up into bits and sell its core assets.'

'They can't do that,' I argued. 'Rania still has a stake in the company and we don't want to lose the Jayachands as private clients.'

'True, but reviving a retail brand in the current economy . . . no, it's not profitable.'

'Nor is selling it off at dirt-cheap prices. Why shoot yourself in the foot if you have the liquidity to ride out the recession?' I asked as the driver turned sharply and then came to a sudden stop. I felt queasy and steadied myself until the feeling passed.

'What if we don't have the liquidity but could find it?'

I paused and looked at Raj. He knew something. The driver opened the door and we stepped out and headed into the cool, dimly lit Chinese restaurant.

'Selina?' I asked, and he nodded. 'She's found a buyer to run a hostile takeover with?'

'I'm not saying anything,' Raj said, following the waiter to a table for three.

'So this is all for nothing, all this research and these fact-finding exercises?' I said, making a note to call Rania as soon as possible.

'Experience is never for nothing,' Ella said sagely as we sat down and inspected the menu.

My stomach rumbled and then cramped painfully. Suddenly I felt nauseous and light-headed. Drinking a little more water, I excused myself to seek out the ladies'. I made it in time, but I felt weak and doubled over at the pain.

Ten minutes later I walked back out into the restaurant, trembling and faint. I fell into my seat and finished off the water.

'Are you OK?' Ella asked, looking at me closely. 'You look really peaky . . .'

Before she could finish, I turned around and threw up on to the seat beside me.

'It's the puchkas, she's paying for the street food,' Raj stated and Ella walked around and patted my back.

Waiters rushed forward and handed me several bags before taking away the chair.

'I want to get back to the hotel, I feel awful,' I gasped.

'Let's go,' Ella agreed as she helped me back towards the car.

I didn't make it. I raced back to the ladies' and cried out in pain. Breathing deeply, I winced until there was nothing left in me to dispose of. By the time I rejoined Ella at the entrance, I was fighting to stay upright. I grabbed her arm, but all I could see was the fast-rising floor.

I woke up in my room, and looked around to find Ella slumped in a chair beside me.

'Ella.' I spoke, but the raspy voice wasn't mine. 'Ella!' I waited until she roused and slowly looked up at me. 'What day is it?'

'Monday.'

'No . . .'

'You had severe food poisoning. That street stuff at Chor Bazaar was really bad,' she told me as she stretched in front of me. 'We took you to a hospital straight away. Once the doctors diagnosed you, we had you brought back here. You have a nurse on twenty-four-hour call.'

'Thank you,' I whispered as she smiled and patted my arm.

'Hannah wants you to get the first flight back to London.' I looked at Ella in surprise. 'I also spoke to your oldest brother.'

'No, tell me you didn't.' My throat was parched and it hurt to talk.

'I think he was booking tickets to come out here as we spoke.' I turned to Ella with horror. 'But I convinced him that we're going to get you home as soon as possible.'

'God, this is so unfair!' I breathed out. 'I'm in

Mumbai, the fashion here is unreal, and I won't get to see any of it!' I covered my face and instantly regretted the movement as the room swirled around me. I grabbed the bowl in front of me, turned on my side and threw up with such force it left me panting for breath.

'I haven't eaten anything; how can I possibly have anything to throw up?' I whispered as the nurse took away the bowl and gave me water to gargle with.

'As soon as you're strong enough, we'll have you on a plane home,' Ella assured me, making me tear up with the idea of being back at home.

'My meetings . . .'

'. . . have been rescheduled or cancelled.'

'Raj . . .'

'. . . is out visiting some distant family and friends, and Helen is shopping with her fiancé.'

I struggled to keep my eyes open. I fought for a while, knowing that I wasn't making any sense. I promised to close my eyes for one minute whilst I listened to Ella. It was the longest minute's sleep I ever knew.

When I opened my eyes again I saw Zach. I saw his striking lashed eyes, his stubborn sculpted cheeks and his brow furrowed in concern. I could sense him; he was close enough that I could smell him. Sighing, I smiled and closed my eyes, enjoying my dream. When I opened my eyes, there he was again. I didn't know if I was dreaming or not. Eyes closed, I reached out and gasped when I touched his face.

'It's you,' I whispered as I opened my eyes. He smiled. I froze and then yanked the blanket over me.

'Yasmin . . .'

'You can't see me like this,' I said from beneath the blanket. I cringed at the idea that he had seen me make-up-free, pale, unkempt and ungroomed.

'Yasmin . . .'

'No, I've been in bed for nearly two days. I'm not fit to be seen.' Zach's patience ran out, and he yanked the blanket from my grasp. I looked at him as he neatly folded the blanket up to my shoulders. 'What are you doing here?'

'Ella told me you were unwell, so I cut down my time with the Jayachands.'

'But you can't just walk into my bedroom . . .'

'It's too late for that,' he told me with an amused glint in his eyes. 'Your dad's worried out of his mind.'

'You spoke to Daddy?' I asked and watched him smile at my reference.

'Ella informed your brother, and your father's called several times since.'

Tears blurred my vision. I missed my father immensely and the thought that he was worried left me upset.

'You OK?'

I nodded, cleared my eyes and looked at my room. Zach's cases were in the corner, and my table was covered with his documents, laptop and coffee cups. He had thrown his jacket and tie on the sofa, and set up an office in my room. I frowned and looked back at him.

'How long have you been here?' I asked, noticing the stubble before meeting his eyes.

'Since yesterday evening.'

I didn't need to ask him if he'd stayed with me the whole time.

'You haven't slept.'

Zach ignored my statement but I knew it to be true.

'You must be starving,' he said. He frowned as I shook my head. The thought of hurling up in front of Zach killed my appetite. 'You're not hungry?' My stomach rumbled just in time to turn me into a fraud. 'You're hungry.'

'I'm starving!' I announced and watched him look at the in-house menu. 'I just want some plain chicken soup, Zach,' I told him. He called room service and ordered a breakfast for himself and a chicken soup with toast for me.

'Your meetings and commitments . . .'

'. . . are being dealt with,' Zach told me as he folded into a chair beside my bed.

'I've missed all my meetings.'

'Everyone knows you weren't pulling a sickie, so you have nothing to worry about.'

'But Baby O needs rescuing and Rania needs all the help she can get.'

'You like her,' Zach noted as I nodded.

'I admire her,' I informed him. 'I admire people who step up to their responsibilities in tough times.'

'It has nothing to do with the fact that you're both new to your professions and scared witless about delivering?' The amused question made me chuckle.

'That may've contributed to our mutual respect for each other,' I accepted and turned to the loud knock on the door. Zach went to answer it.

'Zach! What are you doing here?' I heard Helen's shocked question and prayed he wouldn't let her in to see me at my worst.

'What are *you* doing here?' Zach's unamused question made me smile as I could hear Helen struggling to answer.

'This is my fiancé . . .'

I didn't hear any more as my mobile buzzed. It was a struggle to turn and reach for it, and the dizziness caused by the movement scared me. I fell back on my pillows, light-headed with the effort.

'. . . she tires easily so keep it short,' Zach was directing.

'Honey, why don't you wait here with Zach, whilst I go see Yasmin?'

I tried to tidy my hair. No matter how ill I was, the thought of being seen by Ms Perky Perfect forced me to make the effort of self-improvement.

'Yasmin!' she whispered, shuffling towards me with her arms held wide open. 'Look at you.' She took my hand, sat on the bed beside me and looked down at me with pity. 'The good thing is that this illness has given you cheekbones.' My smile faltered as she studied me.

'I'm big on projectile vomiting, Helen, so I'd keep a healthy distance.'

Helen grimaced and naturally leaned back.

'You've missed so much!' Even at my lowest, she somehow found a way to make me feel worse.

'Really?' My ironic tone was lost on her.

'Totally. My fiancé's spoilt me rotten and maxed all his credit cards out for our wedding.'

'As long as you both found what you want . . .'

'Both?' she said, wrinkling her nose as if it was a foreign concept. 'I got everything I need for the wedding! As for work, we got some killer figures from the manufacturers' meetings, but the designers . . .' I really didn't want to hear it, but Helen was as always oblivious to the needs of others around her. 'We've been to fashion shows, after parties, I even bumped into Saif Ali Khan, but . . .' She paused, checked behind her and then leaned close to me. '. . . the best part is I wrangled some free designer lingerie from Zamil!' I forced myself to smile at her shriek of excitement.

'Which shows did you go to?' I asked, wishing Zach would appear and remove Ms Perma Perky.

'Don't worry, I took pictures so that you didn't feel like you missed out.'

I watched as she rustled out her mobile and then proceeded to show me a series of pictures profiling her in every shot with a commentary that always ended with 'Oh, that's me in the centre there.'

'I'm going to throw up,' I announced, acting like I was heaving. Helen shot up and scrambled around.

'Wait, wait, wait . . . let me get Zach,' she called out, racing out of the room.

I settled back down on the pillows, heard Helen depart with her fiancé and smiled when Zach rushed into the bedroom. He looked at my composure and frowned.

'I know it's wrong, but I had to get rid of her,' I explained and watched him break out into a smile. He walked over to the desk and dialled a number before coming over to me. 'I'm not apologising to her,' I said firmly.

'It's your father,' Zach told me as he held his mobile out to me. I stared at him as I took it from him.

'Asalaamalaikum.' Daddy sounded tired and I took a minute. 'Hello?'

'Daddy . . .' My whisper was barely audible. 'Daddy, it's me.'

'Yaya!' The worried call of my father brought tears to my eyes. 'Yaya, oh my Yaya, how are you?'

'I'm doing much better, Daddy.'

'Tell me the truth, Yaya, I don't want you to lie to make me worry less,' he told me.

'I promise, Daddy, I'm feeling better,' I assured him and heard him thank God.

'We've been so worried about you. Your brothers were going to fly out, but your manager told us he was keeping an eye on you. Since your mother passed, I've never been so terrified; without your manager to speak to, Yaya, I would've lost my mind.'

I listened to my father speak, knowing that the smallest word from me gave him the comfort he sought. I looked at Zach. He was staring down at his paperwork, fighting sleep and lost in thought.

'Your brothers call your manager every half-hour and he takes every call. He's a good man, Yaya, a good man. Please thank him for me.'

'I'll thank him, Daddy, I'll tell him the family think he's wonderful.'

Zach turned at my words and I beckoned him over, patting the bed beside me. He stared at me, but I took his hand and encouraged him. He slipped his shoes off before lying down beside me on top of the covers, keeping space between us. I carried on talking to my father, hearing accounts of Maya's upcoming henna and Meena's marital mess, and chuckling at stories of Chachijhi Fauzia's never-ending emotional meltdowns. I turned to look at Zach to find that he had drifted off. With a small smile, I returned to my conversation with my father.

I watched Zach as he stirred from sleep. My nurse had closed the curtains and left my bedside table lamp on. Shrouded in darkness, I committed every detail of his face to memory. I worried. I worried that I was in far too deep, far too quickly. He opened his eyes and caught me looking. I smiled gently.

'I nodded off,' he stated quietly. I nodded.

'I'm scared,' I told him, and he understood. 'I don't want to be another notch, Zach.'

'Is that what you think I'm doing here?'

'No,' I corrected instantly. 'No, I don't. But I don't know why you *are* here.'

'I'm looking after you.'

'For how long?' Zach stopped at my question and we fought our silent battles. 'I'm scared because I'm in deep,' I said, and closed my eyes at the silence that followed.

Every self-help book would tell me not to put my cards on the table, not to ask for direction, not to be who I am. They would tell me to be bold, coy, worth fighting for. The only thing those books don't tell you is how to be you.

'Good.' I frowned at his answer and opened my eyes.

'Good?'

'Good, because for a minute I thought some Arab royalty was going to whisk you away.'

'He's my rebound guy.' Zach laughed, and I looked at him to see the laughter fade from his eyes. I bit my lip and knew that Ella would reprimand me, but I had to tell him. 'The prince kinda didn't exist,' I admitted as he cocked a brow. 'Well he did, but he was more a figment of our collective imaginations.' I stopped as I caught the glimmer of amusement in his eyes. 'Just know that I'm in no danger of being whisked away!' I finished as he chuckled before looking at me with a serious expression.

'Your family . . .' he began but stopped. 'I'm not the perfect candidate.' His words made me gasp in shock.

'You want to meet my family?' I whispered in disbelief.

'You don't want me to meet them?'

'No . . . yes . . . I just . . . when did you decide . . .' I struggled to find the words, so when he cupped my face and looked at me, I simply stared at him.

'I'm not going to waste time with you if . . .'

'I don't want to waste time either,' I told him without any hesitation.

'. . . if your family refuse to accept me. I'll do right by you and your family, but if they won't allow that to happen . . .' I reached out and took his hand. 'You don't think they'll accept me, right? That I'm not good enough . . .' I placed my fingers against his lips to silence him.

'I'm in bed, dressed in the same pyjamas that I wore

three days ago, make-up-free, washed-out and at my worst, and you ask me if I don't think you're good enough for me?' He laughed at my words. I entwined our fingers and took a deep breath. 'Tell me about *your* family.' I couldn't meet his eyes as the silence prolonged itself. I sensed he was struggling to bring up his past, so I forced him to meet my eyes. 'Please,' I asked. He held my gaze for what felt like an eternity, and just when I was about to give up, he began.

'My father was a labourer from Bangladesh; my mother tells me he was from Komila, but I don't know how true that is. They met when he worked in the factories in the East End and lived together. She tells me they were devoted to each other; she's white, he a non-white, so I imagine back in those days you'd have to be.' I watched Zach as he spoke factually. 'They got news that his father was seriously ill and that he wanted his son to wed before he passed away. And that was it. He left and never came back. She knew she was pregnant before he left, but she didn't tell him; she believed he would come back, and when he didn't, she accepted it.'

'She sounds like a very strong woman.'

'She had no choice. She dedicated the rest of her life to making something of herself and to bringing me up.'

Zach's neat summary left me unsatisfied.

'She never married or had any more children . . .' I trailed off as he shook his head. 'But you . . . you seem fine . . . why aren't you angry?' He laughed softly at my question.

'My mother gave me the best childhood, Yasmin, I've nothing to be angry about.'

'But your father, you know nothing about that side of you.'

'My mother took me to Bengali after-school classes

and I remember her fighting to get me accepted into the mosque because I was a mixed-race child born out of wedlock.'

'That must've been tough.'

'For my mother. I learnt everything about tenacity, bullishness and ambition from her.' He looked at me closely, cupped my cheeks and smiled. 'I didn't miss him, Yasmin. My mother and I were stronger for it; our life was and still is filled with laughter.'

I paused and held his hands.

'What if she doesn't like me because I'm Bengali?' He stared at me and then burst out laughing. 'I'm serious, what if she doesn't!'

We spoke quietly and gently for the rest of the evening into the early hours of the morning. I told him about my mother's passing, my father's devotion and my crazy aunt. He told me about the possible move to Dubai and we talked about how it would affect my father if I joined him there. There was so much to talk about that we debated, disagreed and laughed until sleep took over.

'Yasmin!' I opened my eyes and heard Ella running through the hall. I was entangled with Zach and pushed at him to get free before she arrived. 'Yasmin . . .' I gave up when she came to a stop at the end of the bed.

'Morning, Ella,' Zach muttered despite looking like he was still asleep.

'I . . . I can come . . . back,' she murmured as she looked at me with wide-eyed wonder.

'That'd be good,' Zach said.

I looked from Ella to Zach and back again.

'No, don't go,' I called out when she turned to leave. Pushing Zach's heavy arm from around me, I heaved myself upright 'Ella, it's not what you think . . .'

'It's exactly what you think,' Zach cut in, still refusing to open his eyes and wake up.

'It's not what you think . . . doesn't matter, but it's not,' I told Ella, who grinned. 'No, it's not.' She winked at me and I shook my head. 'Seriously, he's fully dressed, we were just talking.'

'OK, drop the details. I'm here to tell you that in less than a couple of hours we need to be at the airport. Namhar managed to secure us last-minute flights, so we need to get packing.'

I looked round at Zach and found him watching me. Our time was being cut short.

'Shall I leave you to it?' he asked.

'No,' I said, giving him a soft smile, before turning to Ella. 'I don't have much to pack, but I could do with a hand . . .'

'I'll sort that out,' Zach said, sitting up and rubbing the back of his neck.

'Is Raj coming back with us?' Ella shook her head. 'Thanks for coming with me, Ella—'

'Shut up, I wouldn't dream of letting you go home alone. I'll be back in fifteen minutes, OK?'

I nodded and smiled. Ella had become more than a work colleague. I beckoned her over and pulled her into a hug.

'It's the drugs that are making me sentimental,' I whispered as she laughed and patted me on the back. 'Thank you for looking after me, Ella.'

'You're going to get me started!' she said as she pulled away and smiled. Pushing her oversized glasses up, she looked at Zach and put her hands on her hips. 'I know you're my boss, or at least very close to my boss, but don't be an idiot and hurt Yasmin.'

'Ella . . .'

'No, Yasmin, let me speak.' I covered my mouth

and looked to Zach, who leaned back on the headboard with half a grin. 'I'm serious, Zach, she deserves forever, and if you can't give her forever—'

'Our families are meeting as soon as we can arrange it.'

Ella looked stunned at Zach's words and turned to me, unsure if she heard right or not. I nodded and she gripped her hands together before turning back to Zach.

'I'm glad to hear it, Mr Khan.' I knew she wanted to scream with joy for me, but she just winked and then turned around to leave.

'Ella?' She spun around at Zach's call.

'You're a good analyst.' She smiled at the recognition. 'But you're a better friend, and you'll do good to call me Zach from here on.' I smiled at him, warmed by his words.

'Good, good,' Ella said before leaving.

'You ready to go home?' Zach asked. My smile faltered at his question, but I nodded.

'Daddy told me to go back glowing,' I told him as I turned to face him with a wide smile. 'I feel like I'm glowing,' I whispered.

Zach and Raj took us to the airport to see us off, cutting it fine as they both had meetings to race off to. Once we checked in, we waved them off and went to our departure gate silently. No hugs, no kisses; no romantic farewells were given, and yet we sat in silence as if we were leaving our hearts behind.

'I miss him,' Ella stated. 'It's been five minutes and I miss him.'

I took her hand. 'He's flying back tomorrow,' I told her as she shook her head.

'It's insane, but I can't remember my life as a singleton,' she said with a smile.

'I can. You moaned incessantly about it.'

'What, all the time?'

I nodded at her incredulous question. 'We both did.'

'And we're both going back attached!' I laughed with Ella. 'What will your family say?' she asked. My smile faltered and I looked down.

'I don't know, I don't want to think about it.'

The reality of what I was doing was terrifying, but when Ella took my hand, I smiled.

'Raj is serious, Ella, he's not messing around,' I told her and watched her smile fondly.

'Zach cancelled some high-level meetings to be with you. He's not messing around either,' she confirmed as a little toddler caught my attention. We were giving each other confidence to believe that our luck was finally changing. 'I knew it the night of the safari. You were zonked out, and he carried you like the most precious thing all the way back to the hotel.'

I left Ella and walked towards the toddler, who was heading for the balcony which had a pane of glass missing. The toddler ran to the cord across the gap as a scream pierced the hall. I bolted towards the child and grabbed him as he lurched forward.

'*Mere jaan, mere jaan, mere jaan!*' the mother cried as she took her son from me and wrapped him into a bear hug. 'My love, are you OK? Are you fine?' She put him on his feet and checked him over frenetically.

'He's fine, he's fine,' I told her as she wiped away her tears and pulled her son back into a hug.

'Thank you. God bless you, thank you. He's my life, he's everything I have, thank you.'

I looked at the beautiful model-like woman and smiled.

'It's fine . . .'

Before I could finish, she pulled me into a hug and cried into my shoulder. An entourage of helpers and minders raced forward to comfort her, and I realised she was a woman of importance.

'Thank you, you saved Khan Sahib and Sharmila's only son, what can we do for you?' a mature suited gentleman asked. I stepped back and looked at the toddler who giggled at all the attention.

'Yes, yes, what can we do?' the young woman asked as she brought her purse out.

'Nothing, really, I'm just glad he's fine,' I said as they paused to stare at me.

'Ma'am, I believe I'm indebted to you for saving my son's life.' I stared at the woman as she took my hand and put it on top of her head. 'Please tell me how I can repay the debt.' I tried to pull my hand away. 'Take my card. If there's anything you need, please call me.' To appease her, I took her business card before once again being enveloped into a bear hug.

'Take care of him,' I said before walking back to Ella, leaving the entourage confused and befuddled by my response.

'Good going, Superwoman,' Ella murmured as I sat down next to her and gave her the card.

'All in a day's work!' I laughed, stopping when Ella grabbed my hand and gripped it. 'What?'

'Don't say anything. Just act normal, don't look around, look at me, keep looking at me and act like we're just talking normally.'

I unlocked Ella's grip and looked at her.

'You're not acting normally.' I pointed out.

Ella forced a smile but refused to look in my direction.

'Because I don't want to be star-struck,' she said.

Our flight was called for boarding and we stood up to join the queue. I looked back at the group and saw the young woman talking animatedly on her mobile as she carried her son with her.

'Who is she?' I asked of Ella, who stole a look in the woman's direction.

'Sharmila Aurora.'

I took a double look at Ella. 'How the hell do you know that?' I didn't expect her to know more about Bollywood than I did.

'Raj took me to the movies. She's in the latest block-buster, supporting role, but she's making a comeback.'

My mouth widened at her words. I stared back at the movie star and saw her son wave at me. I waved back and then looked at Ella.

'I *am* Superwoman!' I breathed as I looked down at the business card and thought of Rania's revival campaign. Ella handed the air stewardess our seat stubs. The stern stewardess stared at us.

'Will you follow me,' she said as we looked at each other with concern. 'Ladies, you've been upgraded to first class. Enjoy your flight.' Looking at each other, we burst out screaming and hugged each other. 'Ladies.' At the stern call, we stopped, ignored the disapproving stares and all too happily took to our seats for the flight back home.

Good things did happen when you least expected them. It seemed impossible to relate back to that girl who was lost, confused and broken. I wanted to hold her and tell her that everything would be better than she could ever imagine. Seeing Ella lie back into her seat, I laughed and leaned back likewise. That's what dreams are for, making reality better than you could ever imagine.

15

Lesson Fifteen:
Invitations aren't always welcoming

Every member of my family and Chachijhi Fauzia was there to greet me at Heathrow. I was enveloped into what was a giant group hug. Somewhere in the middle was Ella, and I laughed as I hugged everyone like I hadn't seen them for years. Then before I knew it, Jamal *bhai* and Daddy whisked me off straight to the hospital for a thorough check-up. Once I was discharged with a course of antibiotics, they took me back to a home that was filled with all my cousins and friends with a feast ready to feed the whole of Africa.

'Here she is! Here she is!' Chachijhi Fauzia cried out, pushing past everyone to grab my arm as if I was incapable of walking unaided. 'Move, move, move!' she shouted, shoving young teenagers out of the way as she led me to the living room.

'Yasmin!' I spotted Mia and Gemma and smiled at them.

'Get up!' Chachijhi Fauzia barked at the youngsters on the sofa.

'Really, I'm fine . . .'

'Sit!' I sat and lifted my arms as she placed a blanket around me. Instantly I was inundated with questions and comments. I spotted Ella with a mug of coffee sitting with Gemma and caught her smile.

'You people will make my Yaya ill again with all these questions,' Daddy said as he came and sat next to me. I leaned back against him, wanting to tell him everything about Zach.

'It's good to have you home, Yasmin,' Kamal *bhai* said as he squeezed on to the sofa next to me. 'We missed you.'

'More like he missed your desserts!' Rita *bhabi* corrected, starting another round of jokes and mickey-taking.

'Has Daddy been well?'

'Well apart from you giving him sleepless nights, he's been fantastic!' I punched Kamal for his sarcasm. 'He stayed with Jamal *bhai*, he loved the gardening.'

'Could you pass my bag?' I asked my cousin Maya, who dug out my mobile, somehow knowing what I wanted, and handed it to me. 'How did you . . .' I stopped and took the phone from her. I'd said more than I should've done and she smiled.

'We'll catch up later,' she promised with a cheeky wink. 'You're coming to my *cinipaan* engagement party on Sunday, right?'

'Sunday?' I stared at her. Zach flew in on Sunday.

'Your brother's going to pick you up, so remember the colour scheme is emerald green.'

I smiled and nodded before checking my phone. I had a couple of missed call from Zach. Squashed between my brother and father, I put it on silent mode and bit my lip, wondering when I'd get any time or space to call Zach.

'Eat,' Chachijhi Fauzia stated as she handed me a plate piled with biriyani, lamb bhouna and raita. 'You've turned into a skeleton.'

'I thought she was dying. Look at her, she looks stunning,' Cousin Leila said as she walked into the room. 'Is what you have contagious, because I'll have some of that!' The girl was shameless and we all stared at her as she laughed and then perched on the armrest next to Maya.

'You need whatever she's had,' Kamal threw back, causing everyone to jump in with an opinion about Leila's recent weight gain.

I stared at my beautiful family and smiled. But it was bittersweet. Zach was missing and I felt he had a place here. I wondered if those around me would accept him, I looked at my father and saw that he was watching me. I smiled with hope.

'You're glowing, Yaya,' he said as he kissed my forehead. 'You've come home glowing.'

Several hours later, I hid away from the family in the kitchen under the pretext of making a big pan of masala tea, Bengali style. Zach and I had been texting each other throughout the afternoon. Staring down at his question, I agonised over how to break the news about us to my family.

'You want to talk about it?' Turning at Maya's question, I hid my phone quickly. 'I see you're still in denial.' Grinning at my pretty cousin, I stared at her until she laughed and held up her hands.

'You're trouble,' I told her, smiling at her down-to-earth nature.

'Are you going to propose to him like I proposed to Jhanghir?' she asked as I stirred the tea. 'I'd be more than happy for you to become the queen of community gossip.'

'Oh no no no! You more than deserve that crown. I have no plans to steal it from you,' I stated as Maya placed the mugs on a tray.

'So?' she asked, turning to face me with a cheeky smile.

'Does Jhanghir know what he's letting himself in for?'

I asked, watching her laugh with that innocence of never feeling heartbreak.

'Yasmin, I know it's not easy being single, so you let me know if I can help, OK?' Her offer touched me and I paused stirring to look at her.

'Promise me you won't say a word,' I said. She held her right hand up as if she was making a Brownie promise. 'There's a guy . . .' I paused at Maya's laugh of joy and waited until she looked at me composed. 'I met him at work, and he's serious about wanting to meet the family.'

'So what's the problem?' Maya asked with a frown.

'He's half Bengali and half English.'

'So his Bengali parent can talk to your dad, right?'

I shook my head at Maya's question before pouring milk into the masala tea.

'He doesn't know who his father is. He was abandoned as a child and his mother brought him up alone. He doesn't know the language, and he just about knows enough to pray.'

'Well that's more than most Muslims,' Maya muttered unhelpfully. 'Seriously, your dad's really down to earth. Talk to him, Yasmin. He's bound to understand.' She stopped at my look of disbelief but continued. 'His only worry right now is not finding you someone suitable to settle down with, so if you take him a decent guy, he's bound to welcome him with open arms.'

'You serious?' I asked, surprised by the conviction in Maya's advice.

'It beats asking him to marry you in a fit of desperation in front of your entire family!' I laughed at her quip and smiled when she gave me a quick hug. 'Invite him to my *cinipaan*, Yasmin. Let me meet him.'

'No way.'

'Come on, it'll be a great way for your family to see he is Bengali.'

'You want me to have a heart attack?'

'Listen to me, Yasmin, I'll say he's a friend of Jhanghir's. Jhangir won't be at the *cinipaan* as it's not protocol for him to be there, so he won't be able to verify who is or isn't his friend,' Maya suggested with a cheeky smile. 'Wouldn't it be a great way to get your family to meet him without the pressure of an arranged introduction?'

'Whose arranged introduction?' Spinning round at the question, Maya and I watched Mia walk into the kitchen.

'My . . . my introduction,' Maya said quickly.

'But I thought you're getting married.'

'She is. Maya was telling me how she never had a conventional arranged introduction,' I told Mia, but I knew she didn't believe a word of it. Maya smiled at me before taking a tray filled with tea, biscuits and sweet desserts through to the living room.

'Gemma and I are making a move,' Mia said as Gemma appeared at the entrance of the kitchen. There was still a tense awkwardness hanging between us. 'It's good to see you home, Yasmin.'

'Mia,' I called out, stopping them both from leaving. 'Thank you for coming to see me. I missed you guys.

They smiled as they pulled on their jackets.

'I have to run, but we'll catch up over the weekend, right?' Mia asked. I nodded. 'Good, because I know you just lied to me and I want to know everything about him.'

'Mia!' I breathed out with mock exasperation. We laughed at the good-natured banter and then paused to look at each other. 'Is Bibi OK?' I finally asked, seeing Mia look down.

'She's avoiding good advice, she's avoiding us and living with the futile hope that that jerk's going to propose to her,' Gemma answered as she shook her head.

'There's a difference between being a hopeless

romantic and being hopeless,' Mia stated as I showed
them out.

'If she asks, will you tell her I have her favourite
blueberry muffin waiting for her any time she's craving
one?'

Both of them nodded at my request and I laughed as
they pulled me into a huddle. It was time to let old
grudges go, if only to delay the chance of premature
wrinkling. I smiled as they waved goodbye. It felt good to
be back.

The following morning I made breakfast for Daddy and
waited for him to join me at the breakfast bar, knowing
that at some point I would have to speak with him. Zach
had insisted on making the introduction first, but I
needed Daddy to give Zach his blessing.

'Yasmin!'

I started at the call and walked around the work island
to find him at the door. I spotted Mia and Gemma and
stopped, realising that I had lost the chance to talk to my
father. They stood nervously, watching me and hoping
our differences were in the past.

'Good timing, I've just put breakfast on!' I gave each
of them a quick hug as they filed into the kitchen. 'Daddy,
where are you going?' I asked as he put on his white cap
and coat.

'Your brother needs help with the garden,' he said
hesitantly. 'But if you need me to . . .'

'Go, Daddy,' I told him with a smile as he patted me
on the cheek.

'You look healthy, skinny but healthy, and your
brother, he asked me to help, he doesn't know anything
about the garden . . .'

I smiled and stopped him from feeling guilty about
leaving me.

'I know he doesn't, Daddy, and he's lucky to have you to help him.'

Assured that I was OK, he nodded and left. Smiling, I closed the door behind him and returned to the kitchen.

'You're baking and it's not even ten a.m.!' Mia noticed in awe. 'What's wrong?'

'Nothing!' I answered with a bright smile. Laying out their plates, I offered them fresh pancakes with blueberries and honey.

'What's with the Stepford Wife attitude?' Mia pursued, narrowing her eyes. 'What's happened?'

'Nothing,' I repeated as I offered single cream. She hesitated, but relented when I hovered it above her pancake. 'Oh, I've got your gifts here,' I remembered.

'Wo wo wo wo . . . Stop, stop, stop,' Mia ordered, making both of us freeze. 'Something's not adding up here,' she added as she stared at me.

'Mia, presents!' Gemma rasped before looking at me with expectant eyes.

'We part on a bad note – I mean Bibi isn't here – and that doesn't bother you. You go away for two weeks, and in that time you don't say boo, and then we find out that you've collapsed from extreme food poisoning. And we turn up today, you're baking for all of west London and you have gifts for us and you're smiling, you're genuinely smiling . . .'

Gemma's smile faltered at Mia's detective routine.

'I'm happy,' I said with a frown.

'Happy?' Mia repeated as if it was a foreign concept. 'We're women, we're programmed to be unhappy. Why are you happy . . . ah!' She gasped and covered her mouth with both hands. 'You're not happy.'

'I'm happy,' I stated, knowing that she had clocked on.

'You're not happy,' she said, shaking her head.

'I'm happy, I tell you, I'm very very happy.'

'She's happy, she says she's happy,' Gemma supported, frowning at Mia.

'She's not happy!' Mia stated forcefully, whilst pointing a finger in my direction.

'Stop pointing.'

'When did it happen?'

'It's rude to point,' I added as Mia stifled a smile.

'Who is he?' she asked slowly and confidently.

'Who?' Gemma asked, totally lost with our exchange.

'Well?' Mia pushed.

'Who is who?' Gemma demanded, so I topped up her pancake with more cream.

'Yasmin Yusuf, who is he?'

'OK, that's it!' Gemma shouted in frustration. 'Yasmin, for the love of God, if there is a he, who we don't know to be a he, who is the who that Mia is talking about, please just tell us.'

We stared at Gemma's plea and then burst out laughing.

'It's good to have you back, Yasmin,' Mia said as she leaned over the counter and hugged me.

'It's good to be back,' I accepted as I perched myself up on the counter.

'So who is he?' Mia asked as Gemma groaned and we descended into laughter again.

That afternoon I headed to my offices to update myself on the project. I spotted Steve, the extra-cautious security guard, and waved at him to let me in.

'No bags,' I promised as I held up my hands. He stared at me unimpressed and held out the log employees had to sign on the weekend. 'Thanks.' He nodded but remained silent. I smiled and headed for the elevator.

Stepping out on my floor, I headed for my desk and

paused when I spotted Hannah, Selina and the suits talking animatedly in her office. I started up my computer and looked back again, only to catch Hannah's eye. She watched me carefully, and I nervously looked away and sat down before my screen. Logging into my email, I scanned all the updates and communications, and noted down the three most urgent requests I had to deliver.

1. Prepare monthly investor presentation for retail sector.
2. Quarterly portfolio committee meeting: circulate minutes and distribute agenda/documents to committee members.
3. Prepare a two-page review of all the current portfolio companies in retail sector to be given to investors. Talk to deal teams and reference due diligence materials and quarterly reports.

'Yasmin.'

I jumped at Hannah's unexpected call. Holding my chest to support my racing heart, I turned round to face her.

'Hi, Ms Gibbs-Smythson.' My breathless answer made her frown at me. 'You scared me . . . surprised me!' I corrected as I pushed my hair back nervously.

'I'm sorry to hear that you were unwell in Mumbai. How are you feeling?'

I stared at Hannah, unsure whether or not to believe her concern. Then I realised she was waiting for a response.

'I'm much better, a lot better, thank you,' I said with a nervous laugh.

'Good. I'm glad to hear it.' She smiled and then went to return to her office. Breathing out a sigh of relief, I held my head in my hands. 'Yasmin.' Shooting up straight, I turned to face her.

'Yes, Hannah?'

She looked to her office and then back at me.

'The minutes need to be taken for this meeting.'

Whilst it wasn't a request to be refused, I felt she was inviting me for the purpose of including me. And I was all too glad to find out what was going on. Without a second thought, I picked up a notebook and followed her back to her office. Selina looked appalled at my involvement, but remained silent under Hannah's cold powerful control.

'Carry on!' she ordered, making a suit jump up and do as she asked.

I took the minutes, trying hard not to react to the discussions about the hostile takeover plans that Selina had pushed forward in Dubai. Selina talked at length about the transfer of control from Rania to another group of shareholders that was led by none other than Waleed Umar Ibn Haktoum. I gasped at the mention of Rania's stunning Arab friend who I had met at the Royal Mirage. He knew the bid would be against the wishes of Rania, and yet it appeared that he was financing the bid to gain control of Baby O's Covent Garden site to enable the introduction of his label into the UK. I remained quiet as the team debated the merits of the bid and the values involved.

'Deals like this in the retail sector aren't happening; the fact that we're this far into negotiations is an achievement,' Hannah stated as she left her desk.

'The sector is consolidating, boutique labels are disappearing, but those that hold on will benefit most from the upturn,' one of the suits offered as Hannah shook her head.

'Baby O's losses are too significant; we have no option but to make this deal happen.'

'Namhar Capital's gain will be one and a half times what it invested,' added another suit as he flipped through his spreadsheets.

Hannah leaned forward to make her point. 'If Namhar Capital sold its stake along with ICIC Bank, which is looking to offload its minority stake to Waleed's investment firm, a hostile bid is inevitable,' she summarised. 'Legal have green-lit the plan.'

'The management board are aware that this bid will be tabled. They're running around trying to pull together a counter-strategy, but our figures are too solid,' Selina cut in as she stabbed at her notes to drive through her point. 'They haven't got anything guaranteed but a half-hearted plan of maybes and what ifs.' She laughed, and the suits joined in. Hannah's stern expression turned the amusement into uncomfortable silence.

'What about compliance?' she asked as she paced up and down the office, her enthusiasm reflected only by the way she rubbed her hands.

'Compliance has made positive noises. They'll notify us formally on Monday.'

'Who's in touch with the banks? Do we have it on record that they're on board?' Hannah queried as she took a document that one of the suits held out to her. 'They're on board,' she read with half a smile. 'A deal like this will help make our bottom-line margins look pretty unbeatable,' Hannah stated as she looked at me with narrowed eyes.

'What about Rania? She's still intent on reviving Baby O,' I asked. 'She's getting all the right backers; all she needs is time.'

'Thank you, Yasmin,' Hannah said with a smile that failed to reach her eyes.

'You're discounting too deep on Baby O's property portfolio. All you have to do is give Rania time, and she'll give you a bigger return under a five-year turnaround strategy.'

'Yasmin, have you finished?'

'Needless to say, we'd lose the wealth management business from the Jayachand family.'

'Thank you, Yasmin,' Hannah said with a finality that made me stop short. 'Shall we continue?' She looked to Selina and I shook my head as the discussions started up again around me.

The suit next to me handed me a note to read.

Jayachand family's assets have been frozen.

I groaned aloud and froze when I realised everyone had heard and stopped to stare at me. Hannah raised an enquiring brow.

'You're carving up the company because Rania has no bargaining power,' I stated. 'She needs you most now, and instead of helping her, which will help us in the long run, you're ousting her to carve Baby O into pieces.'

'Welcome to the world of private equity, Yasmin,' Selina stated sarcastically.

I looked to Hannah, but she didn't display an ounce of remorse as I searched her eyes for some sign of compassion.

'You need to look at the ROI on the five-year turnaround strategy,' I persisted when I found none.

'What?'

It was obvious that she wouldn't take well to being told what to do. But I held on to my courage as Selina and the suits gasped at my forwardness.

'You need to look at the alternative option. We've got all the data, all the necessary parties, the strategy . . .'

'Bring the details to me on Tuesday,' Hannah accepted. The surprise breakthrough I had made left me gasping along with Selina and the suits. 'I want to see the figures.' I tried not to smile at her, but I couldn't help it.

I nodded and looked down at my notepad, convinced that once she saw the data, Selina's strategy would naturally be overruled. 'If there's nothing else, shall we continue?'

A suit stood up and started talking, but I wasn't interested, I was already planning Baby O's strategy.

I went straight home to pull the information together for Hannah. I mapped out the deal-brokers, the designers, the required conditions and the revival strategy. I invited Raj and Ella around to my house to work on the financial model. I kept an ample supply of food and dessert at hand to ensure that no one flagged. We debated, challenged, argued, shouted and then agreed next steps non-stop. By midnight, my living room was covered in paperwork, data sheets, diagrams and images and the loved-up couple were huddled on the sofa. I heard Daddy arrive home and froze when he walked into the living room.

'What . . .'

'Sshhhh!' I whispered and pointed to Ella and Raj. Dropping my notes, I followed him into the kitchen and leaned on the counter and rubbed my face.

'This isn't good, Yaya.'

I parted my hands and looked at my tired father.

'I'm sorry,' I said, immediately pulling his dinner together.

'No, no, no. Stop,' he said. I turned and saw him patting the seat next to him. 'I was at your brother's, I've eaten with him.'

I looked at him with surprise.

'Daddy, I always make your dinner.'

'I know, Yaya, I know,' he said as he patted my cheek. 'When you went away, I went to stay with your brother. I enjoy being with my sons. They live on the same street, I feel secure with them.'

I tried not to look hurt, but failed.

'Daddy . . .'

'I can't work any more, Yaya, my joints hurt too much, I don't have the energy.'

'You don't have to. I can look after you.' I stopped as he chuckled.

'Look at you, Yaya, you're working on a Saturday . . . excuse me, it's now Sunday.' I felt guilty for neglecting him. 'You came back glowing, but you came back changed, and I'm a simple man. I enjoy my family. I need to be around my family.'

I took his hands and shook my head.

'I haven't changed, Daddy, I've just grown up.' I stopped him from speaking and smiled at him. 'There's a girl I'm working for. She's fighting to save what her father left her. Fighting, doing whatever she can to save it. She doesn't know if it's the right thing or not, but she's working like her life depended on it. And my company, they want to take it away from her and sell it for a cheap profit. And I am doing everything I can to help her save her company. It's a daughter thing, Daddy; she's doing it for her father. I may lose my career over this, but I wouldn't be able to live with my conscience if I didn't do everything to help her.'

Daddy smiled and cupped my cheeks to kiss my forehead. He nodded and stepped off the stool. Slowly he started to make his way to his bedroom.

'You have your mother's heart, Yaya. Yes, you're your mother's daughter.'

I smiled at his parting words and made myself a mug of coffee. Taking a blanket from the airing cupboard, I covered Raj and Ella before sitting in front of the laptop. I emailed Rania asking her to call me urgently, and then called Zach. He didn't answer his phone so I left him a message. Baby O had come to mean more to me than I had realised. Amira was right. It wasn't just about profits. It was about creating something that grew, that built opportunities, jobs and trends. That was what women did: we created and we nurtured. Our only obstacle was our fear of fighting.

Lesson Sixteen:
Mixing business with pleasure
is not for the weak

When Jamal *bhai* came to pick us up for Maya's *cinipaan* engagement party, I was still in my pyjamas and plugging away at the financial models.

'You have thirty seconds to move, otherwise I am setting fire to every single piece of paper in this room.'

Without another word, I closed down my laptop and raced up to my room. I showered, pulled on my emerald-green chooridar shalwaaar kameez, straightened my hair into a neat shoulder-length bob and applied enough make-up to show that I cared where I was going. I grabbed my green kusis and pulled on my Indian sequinned slippers before racing down the stairs. At the base, I slipped on my thick antique gold bangles.

'We're in the car,' I heard Jamal shout out as I raced around the rooms to make sure everything was closed and switched off. I came to a sudden stop to check my phone. Zach hadn't called. He was meant to have landed but there was still no message. We had agreed he would attend Maya's *cinipaan* as one of Maya's fiancé's friends. But he still hadn't confirmed he would land in time to make it. 'Yasmin!' Jumping at Jamal's yell, I put my phone away before racing out to the car.

We got to Mehdis in Hammersmith in time to see Maya arrive with the Malik family. She looked stunning as she glided through the room in her mint-green sari and jewels. I smiled when she gave me a quick wink as she passed me to go and sit on the main table. I stemmed a laugh when Maya's mother cried uncontrollably into Chachijhi Fauzia's arms as if she had already lost her daughter. My smile faltered as I realised I missed my own mother. Reaching out, I sought my father's hand. He held it and gently tapped it, understanding the tears that stung my eyes.

'Oh no,' Jamal *bhai* breathed when the whole restaurant went silent. 'It's Meena and her fiancé.'

We watched Meena lead her man in to stand by Leila. Even Leila looked uncomfortable and turned to talk to Rita *bhabhi* on the pretext of not noticing her own sister. I admired Meena's gutsiness, and when I caught her nervous look, I gave her a cheeky wink of support. She looked pleased by it and gave me a short smile before turning back to her fiancé. They made a cute couple, and I smiled knowing that times were changing our old ways. The whispers made their way to Chachijhi Fauzia at the main table. Everyone knew when she heard them, as a Bollywood-inspired reaction was delivered.

'Hai Allah!' she cried out, in case anyone hadn't noticed the unravelling drama.

I covered my mouth when she grabbed her chest and then fell on Maya's mother, sobbing as if she was mourning the loss of her daughter too. The two aunties seemed to get into a competition as to who could cry the loudest and longest, until Maya looked completely at a loss.

'Meena!' she called out as her sisters tried to shush her. 'Meena!' she repeated as she beckoned her to the main table. 'Come and sit here, bring your fiancé.' My jaw dropped at Maya's courage and I smiled as Meena looked relieved.

'Now my niece is turning on me. Death must be better,' Chachijhi Fauzia cried melodramatically as she pulled away from Maya's mother.

'They're practically married and it's religiously acceptable, so would you control her!' Maya whispered. 'Jhanghir's family are here!'

'And they've all heard you,' her sister told her.

'I disown this event,' Chachijhi Fauzia shouted. 'I don't mean any rudeness to you,' she told Maya's in-laws-to-be, 'but my soul is broken. My ungrateful, disobedient and unloving daughter no longer recognises her mother and I can't—'

'Would you please cut with the drama!' Meena asked impatiently. Chachijhi turned away and rushed from the main table.

'Chachijhi!' I called out, opening my arms to hug her. I took her to the front section of the restaurant, away from the crowds, and sat down with her.

'They . . . they don't care any more,' she sobbed, picking up my chiffon una and using the scarf to wipe her face. 'Why?'

The doors chimed open and I looked up to find Zach at the entrance. He went to greet me but I shook my head to stop him just as Chachijhi spotted him. Suddenly my nerves kicked in.

'Who are you?' Chachijhi asked, also surprised by his sudden appearance as she continued to use my una to wipe her face.

'Zachary Khan.'

'Whose son are you?'

'He must be one of the groom's friends,' I said quickly as Zach looked to me. Chachijhi blew her nose, wiped her face and then walked up to him. She took his left hand and smiled when she discovered that he was without a wedding ring.

'Allah has answered my prayers. Maybe I have time to change Meena's mind,' she said to me in Bengali, all the while smiling sweetly at the very confused Zach. 'Come, *bhetha*, let me take you in.'

I stopped myself from laughing as Chachijhi hijacked Zach through to the main section. I followed after them and froze when I saw her heading towards the groom's side. I held my breath as she made introductions, watching as they surveyed each other nervously until Zach broke the ice and had everyone laughing. Breathing a sigh of relief, I joined my father and Rita *bhabi* at our table as the meal began to be served. My stomach was a mass of knots as I tried to concentrate on the conversation and not seek out Zach.

'He's gorgeous,' Rita said as she caught me staring at Zach.

'I wasn't looking . . .'

'I'm married and I'm looking.' She laughed as I smiled nervously. 'Every single and married woman in this restaurant noticed him when he walked in. Who is he?'

'I . . . I . . . why would I . . .' I stopped and took a long sip of my drink. 'He's a friend of Jhanghir's, Maya said.'

Rita *bhabi* looked at me and frowned at my behaviour.

'Do you want some more chicken tikka?' I asked her.

'Yasmin . . .'

'The lamb cutlets are fantastic.'

'Yasmin, you have five seconds before I call your brother over here,' Rita blackmailed me.

'He's the manager who made sure I was OK in India.

I thought it would be a good idea for the family to thank him.'

'You know him!' Rita *bhabi* asked, and I smacked her hand to get her to lower her voice. 'Jamal!' I stared at my sister-in-law and cursed myself for telling her, knowing that she was a law unto herself. 'Jamal!' she called until my brother was beckoned to the table. She pulled him down close to her. 'That's the manager who looked after Yasmin in India. She invited him so we could thank him personally!' She had that look that told Jamal *bhai* to go find out Zach's credentials. My plan to get Zach known in the Bengali community was drastically backfiring. And when I saw Jamal head for Daddy, I wanted to curl up and die. I watched as my brother whispered what Rita had told him and froze as Daddy headed straight for Zach. Daddy enveloped Zach into a big bear hug and held him as everyone else looked on in surprise. I sank into my seat and covered my face at the drama.

'Yasmin!' I heard my father's call, and quickly checked my mobile, pretending that a text had just come through. 'Yasmin!'

'Yes, Daddy?' I asked, looking up from my mobile to stand as if I had just heard him.

'Why didn't you tell us that you invited your manager?' Daddy asked as he kept a friendly arm around Zach. I avoided Zach's cocked eyebrow and looked at all the expectant expressions on my family's faces.

'You said he was on the groom's side!' Chachijhi pointed out and I squirmed.

'He is, he's a friend of Jhanghir's too,' Maya said from the main table, even though Jhanghir's family looked at Zach with confusion.

'You work with him?' Chachijhi asked me with narrowed eyes.

'*You* work with *him*?' Rita *bhabi* repeated, working

through the confusion to stare at me with half a smile. I looked away from her, trying not to get unnerved, and nodded.

'*For* him. He's very senior, and now we're on different teams, actually different companies . . .'

'So what was he doing in India?' Chachijhi pursued.

My brain froze at the inquisition; my throat dried up as I searched around for a half-decent convincing reply.

'Well, he's overlooking . . . the project . . . and um, he flew in and, uh . . .'

'I manage the private wealth client Yasmin's working with,' Zach supplied, thoroughly in control. I refused to look at him, or anyone, for longer than two seconds. All I was thinking about was stopping my knees from giving way in front of my entire family.

'Well thank you for coming, Mr Khan. I'll see you on Monday,' I said stiltedly, before turning away to go and sit down before I passed out. At the table, I poured myself a long glass of water and gulped it down.

'Yasmin! Zachary's not eaten; pull a plate of food together for him!' Daddy told me as I looked at them whilst still drinking my water. Only I drank too fast and coughed ungracefully to clear my throat. Chachijhi rushed over to slap my back with enough force to cure a chain-smoker's cough for life.

'Thank you,' I rasped when she finished. I pushed my hair back from my face to look up at my unimpressed audience.

'He's Bengali! Why didn't you introduce him to Meena?' Chachijhi whispered. 'He might have a problem with your age, but my Meena could still be saved.'

I looked over at Meena and smiled as she spoke warmly to her fiancé.

'I don't know, Chachijhi, Meena doesn't look like she wants to be saved,' I said, respecting Meena for her dignified strength and composure. Chachijhi stopped and glared at me. 'Every single girl has been gawping at Zach since he walked in, but not once did Meena look at him. Why do you think that—'

Before I could finish, my aunt stormed away. Daddy coughed at our not-so-hushed exchange and I placed a plate of koobideh, taouk and naan before Zach. The grilled meat dish looked succulent and inviting.

'Don't be shy, please help yourself,' Daddy said, encouraging Zach to sit down between himself and Jamal. 'I can't repay you enough for looking after my Yaya. She's my heart, Mr Khan, my heart.'

Zach looked overwhelmed by my family's consideration.

'I can't eat alone,' he said, handing Daddy and Jamal each a fork. 'Please join me.' It was an age-old Arab tradition that built bonds.

Daddy looked at me, impressed by the gesture. He shared the same tradition and thought well of people eating from the same plate. My heart melted at Zach's invitation and I wished they knew.

'Join us,' Zach invited, but I shook my head and watched him turn to Rita *bhabi*. 'Surely you'll join us.' She giggled at his invitation.

'I've eaten, Mr Khan. We women have to be careful what we eat.' She laughed, and I bit my lip when I caught Jamal *bhai* rolling his eyes at his wife's behaviour.

'I promise you, you don't have any such thing to worry about.' Zach's reply made Rita look to Jamal with a stern look.

'Do you see, that's called chivalry, that is called a compliment, just in case you—'

'Woman, please don't start.'

'Don't woman me, Jamal Yusuf. We may have been married for five years, but a woman needs to know—'

'Rita, my son adores you!' Daddy said, coming to Jamal *bhai*'s defence as we all stopped ourselves from laughing at the married couple's playful exchange. 'Otherwise why would he put up with you for five years!' At Daddy's teasing finish, we all looked at Rita's outraged expression before bursting out in laughter. Even Rita *bhabi* joined in when Daddy patted her hand warmly. I caught Zach's laughing eyes and smiled. He fitted in so easily.

'Asalaamalaikum, *bhaya*.' My smile faltered as we all turned to an aunt from the community. She had with her a perfectly preened stunning daughter, and she was eagerly sizing up Zach for her. 'I haven't seen you in a long time, but it's so nice to see you and your children.'

'It's good to see you. Is your husband here today?' Daddy asked as I spotted Rita standing in front of the girl to obscure her from Zach's view.

'Oh, he's at work. You know our restaurant life gives our men no time for socialising,' the aunt said as she positioned her daughter in Zach's direct view before smiling at him too keenly. 'I'm so lucky, though, I have my wonderful daughter who takes me anywhere I need to go! She passed her driving test first time, first time I tell you, and she's my absolute lifeline to social engagements.'

Daddy clocked on and raised a brow.

'Well you must hold on to her as long as possible, then!' he returned as the aunt struggled to retain her composure.

'Yes, quite,' she agreed before trying again. 'She's working in a law firm now, corporate law. She can talk!' I saw Jamal nudge Zach and they both muttered something, which they clearly found funny. I wasn't so amused. 'Talk! Say something!' she barked at her daughter. I stared at the shameless mother and then at the poor girl who was being paraded without any dignity.

'My name's Sonia,' she said meekly before breaking out into a wide practice-perfected smile.

'Oh lord, save me the humiliation,' I muttered.

'Yaya,' Daddy warned before looking to the mother. 'You should come around for dinner one day,' he said, ignoring the woman's intent to be introduced to Zach.

'*Bhaya*, this surely isn't one of your sons?' Instead she chose to push for an introduction. I rolled my eyes and caught Zach's amused look.

'No, he isn't. Well you know Jamal.' My brother salaamed her on cue. 'Kamal and his wife have their own home now, they all live quite close to each other. He's doing well in accounting. And you know Zamal's also in corporate law, that's the same line as your daughter.'

'Oh, that's your hot-tempered son, right?' she asked nervously. 'Is he still very religious? I mean, he's pretty orthodox, isn't he?' By the way my father sat up straight, I knew she had offended him. But he was too decent to put her right.

'Yes, that's right, he's very learned and successful,' Daddy returned.

'I take it your son's adjusting well out of rehab?' The aunt's face froze at my question.

'Yaya!' Daddy chided as she grabbed her daughter's arm and marched her away.

'I assume Yasmin didn't compliment her?' Zach asked as he continued eating. I looked at Jamal and Rita *bhabi*, who seemed equally unimpressed.

'She shouldn't have insulted my brother,' I said defensively.

'You know better,' Daddy said as he clapped Zach on the back, enjoying the fact that he had a good appetite. 'Yaya, give Mr Khan more food.' Zach smirked enjoying the fact that I had to serve him.

'I'm sure Mr Khan can help himself, and Daddy, we need to talk about work—'

'No,' Daddy cut in as he shook his head. 'No. No work today. No disrespect to you,' he said to Zach, 'but Yaya landed on Friday, and worked all day yesterday, all night and through to the early morning. No, no business, I won't allow it.'

'Zach.' I looked to Zach for support, but he looked at Daddy and nodded.

'I agree with your father. You need to switch off.' I stared at him aghast, and then turned on the spot ready to stride away. 'In any case, I can't stop for much longer, as I have footie to catch on TV.'

I cringed at the comment. I looked back to watch Zach talking football with Jamal and my father. And no matter how much I tried to extract him or them, they sat intent on winning the Liverpool vs Manchester United debate. Normally I'd join in with the argument, but they were just being rude.

Everyone else cheered at Jhanghir's unexpected and unconventional appearance at the *cinipaan* to surprise Maya. It provided a natural pause in conversation as Daddy, along with Jamal *bhai*, instantly left the debate to welcome him. I scooted on to the seat next to Zach and watched the rowdy raucous welcome.

'You have a wonderful family,' Zach said and paused when he read my unimpressed expression. 'We were talking football, we were bonding . . .'

'Bonding?'

'Bonding!' Zach insisted before laughing at my expression. 'Listen, I've got to run. I need to go see my mother.'

'You like my family.' I smiled as I watched how Jhanghir teased Maya. 'My family liked you, but Zach, I need to talk to you about Baby O. There's a hostile takeover strategy—'

'Yasmin, stop,' Zach stated.

'I just want you to hear me out. I have a successful strategy, but no one's listening to me.'

'We're not talking about work, Yasmin.'

'Rania's getting stitched up—'

'Stop. Your father said no work; I want you to respect his wishes.'

I stared at him. 'So now you're my father's best friend?'

He nodded with a grin and stood up. 'Don't bother calling me tonight if it's going to be about work,' he told me before heading out. He paused briefly to talk to my father and brother, and then with a quick handshake he departed.

Daddy returned to the table to sit next to me, and I smiled at him.

'That's odd,' he said, looking at me.

'What, Daddy?'

Confused, he looked to Maya and Jhanghir and then back to me.

'He left without congratulating his friend.'

My smile vanished and I stood up quickly. 'I'll get you a tea,' I said before disappearing.

It had gone better than expected. The subtle introduction had proceeded without any major dramas or family feuds breaking out. I smiled, knowing that hope overcame fears. Patience delivered hope, and this Deshi girl's designs for success were beginning to pay off. Now all we had to do was wait for our families to take the next step.

Lesson Seventeen:
Women should do emotions like
they do business

Only my family didn't take a next step. They didn't mention Zach at all beyond saying what a nice accomplished man he was. When Daddy continued the Liverpool vs Manchester United debate on the way back from Maya's *cinipaan*, I nearly cried out in frustration. When Jamal *bhai* dropped us off in Shepherd's Bush without coming in to have that all-important let's-find-out-more conversation, I slammed the door shut behind me without even a goodbye. And when Daddy yawned and called in an early night, I grabbed a blueberry muffin and a huge mug of cocoa before falling asleep in exhaustion.

'So?' I looked up with a start when Ella rolled her chair over to my desk.

'So what?' I asked, turning away from the turnaround scenario excel sheet to stare at her.

'Have you told your family?' she asked with wide excited eyes. I shook my head. 'Why?'

'They loved him. I nearly had a heart attack when he turned up at Maya's *cinipaan*, but they loved him. They just weren't interested in him for me,' I told her in exasperation.

'Why can't he come forward himself? Oh, nice heels!' she noted, looking at my new pair of brogue heels. I stuck my leg out and modelled the shoes, laughing when she tried to steal them from me.

'He's going to at some point, but it's just easier if they seek him out, because he doesn't have an elder to come forward on his behalf.'

'Yasmin!' The bark from Hannah's office made me jump.

'I wish she would stop doing that!' I whispered to Ella as I took my shoe back to slip on. Grabbing my notepad, I rushed to Hannah's room.

'Where's the turnaround model?'

I stopped at the sharp demand. Hannah walked around her desk, put her hands in her pockets and leaned back on the desk. Nervously I looked back at my notes to make sure I had heard right.

'The deadline was set for Tuesday . . .'

'No, I need to see the figures today,' Hannah told me quietly.

I looked down at my pad and sought out the deadline I had noted in the minutes for Saturday's meeting.

'But you asked . . . you said for it tomorrow . . . I wrote it down in my notepad,' I said holding it out for her to see.

'I want it today. Can you get it for me today?' She sounded like she was going to explode if I said anything but yes.

'Yes,' I lied as she pierced me with her ice-blue eyes. I wondered why she was so mad and whether it was just me she hated.

'So why are you still standing in my office?'

Jumping at her question, I rushed out and headed back to my desk.

'What did she want?' Ella asked.

'Is she still looking out of her office?' I whispered, pretending to stare at my screen.

'No.'

Instantly I rolled across to Ella's desk.

'She wants the model today, but Rania's not approved it yet. She's in another time zone and I only emailed it to her this morning in draft format. She needs her risk, compliance and legal team to review it first, so I can't let Hannah see it in raw form,' I whispered in explanation.

'Call Zach, get him to have a word with Hannah.'

'I can't do that.'

'Get your boyfriend to look out for you.'

I refused to be drawn into Ella's playful debate.

'How credible am I going to look if Zach bales me out each time I come up against an obstacle?' I asked as I stared back at Hannah.

'You can't take Hannah Gibbs-Smythson on,' Ella whispered nervously. 'You give her raw information and she will have you out of here so fast—'

'I'll give her the draft version and make sure she knows that the figures aren't confirmed,' I told Ella, who rubbed the back of my neck.

'Yasmin, Baby O is not your fight; it's not worth your career.'

'Maybe I don't want a career unless I care about it,' I told her quietly, plagued with the dilemma of what to do.

'Yasmin!'

We both jumped at Hannah's bark. Scrambling back to my desk, I opened up the draft version and hit the print button. I grabbed the copy from the printer, ensured it had the draft watermark and rushed to Hannah's office. She was on a call, so I waited to point out that they were unconfirmed figures in case she missed the watermark.

She beckoned me to hand her the printout, but she didn't pause in her conversation. I held my hand up to get her attention.

Leave, she mouthed. I pointed at the printout, but she wasn't interested. She glared at me until I swirled around and closed the door behind me.

'She's going to kill me, she's going to kill me,' I told Ella, who peeked over at me. 'She didn't let me tell her they were provisional figures.' When Ella's eyes widened, I nodded and looked back at my screen.

'Hey, guys!' Helen had the unbelievable knack of turning up at the wrong time. 'What's new?' Neither Ella or I stopped staring at our screens. 'Fine, I'm sorry I didn't check in to see how you were doing, Yasmin, and I'm sorry that I didn't take you to any of the fashion shows in Mumbai, Ella, but my fiancé was there and I was trying to get us back on track.'

'We get it, Helen,' Ella mumbled.

'Good! Now that we're talking, here's an invitation.' She giggled and handed us pink cards with sexy kittens sprawled across them. 'It's my fiancé's birthday and we're having a private party at Mint Leaf, and you're both invited,' she announced with pent-up excitement.

'I'll check with Raj to see if we have anything planned.'

'But if you don't know, surely that means you're free,' Helen pointed out.

'Then we have to decide whether we want to be busy on our free night,' Ella said drily before looking back at her screen.

Helen stared at her with impatience and then turned to me with a bright white smile.

'I'll have to get back to you too.'

Helen's smile turned into a grin and she winked at me. 'You're more than welcome to bring lover boy along!'

The fleeting sense of pity I felt for her disappeared, and I stared at her unamused.

'As I said, I'll get back to you.'

Helen's smirk disappeared, and in a huff, she spun on her heel and stormed away. I ignored her playground antics and returned to the matter in hand. Looking up Rania's number, I called her to get the confirmed figures. But she didn't answer her phone, leaving me with no option but to chase her via email.

To: Rania@Jayachand.com
From: Yasmin.Y@namhar.com
Subject: Urgent Update

Dear Rania,
Hannah has the first set of provisional figures for the turnaround strategy. If there are any risk/compliance/legal issues, please forward those on to me. Otherwise, I need urgent confirmation of financial model asap.
Rgds,
Yasmin

I watched the email fold into a little envelope and disappear into cyberspace. I knew there was little else I could do. As I tidied up the papers on my table, I found Amira and Sharmila Aurora's business cards. I debated whether or not to reach out to them. There was a fine line between chasing success professionally and clutching on to long shots desperately. I was the underdog, the naive novice with sharp instincts that no one yet trusted. I was more than a pretty, accommodating Deshi girl and I wanted more than a permission-based career. But at the same time I wanted a career, not a fast-track exit from one. Tapping a finger on the cards, I stared at them and then shook my head to file them away. I also put the lingerie market report away and opened up another project, trying to concentrate on preparing the monthly investor presentation for the retail sector. I pulled out the statistics, liaised with different teams and looked through the deals database. The diagrams, charts and commentary were rudimentary, and yet I struggled to focus.

I picked up the business cards again and stared at them. I shouldn't do it. I knew I shouldn't do it. Logic told me that it would be a mistake to contact them, a move that could end my career. I put the cards away again and left my desk to go to the coffee vending machine. A small group of analysts stood by, discussing the latest hostile takeover and mocking the crushed founder for fighting to save her company. They were disparaging of her, almost vicious and patronising of her desire to dream. I punched in 33 for an espresso and noted the group's sharp custom-made suits, designer accessories and expensive jewellery. They were my peers and yet I couldn't relate to them; or more importantly, I didn't want to.

'You're working on Baby O, aren't you?' I heard the question and turned to look at the young suited accountant with the geeky glasses and designer ruffled haircut. I nodded. 'Is it true that the dragon's preparing for a vicious, bloodthirsty hostile takeover?' Word had gotten out, and I wondered how far our turnaround strategy could counter the hostile takeover.

'You know I can't talk about projects outside of the team,' I told him as I picked up my cup of coffee. 'Though Selina's really outdone herself this time,' I added, giving the young accountant a teasing smile, interested in finding out exactly how much he knew.

'Our colleague Blake has told us everything. His uncle

heads up the biotech portfolio and is dating Selina, and he said that Selina is already negotiating her promotion package to partner for pulling this deal together.'

I held my smile, though my heart plummeted. I had only just submitted the turnaround strategy to Hannah, and Selina was on her way to a cute but hefty reward for signing off the end of Baby O.

'Well it takes a lot of balls to make deals when the economy's crashed,' I said.

'Come on! You know Selina's agreed the investment with the Arab wealth fund,' he told me with half a smile. I mimicked the act of zipping my lips and throwing away the key. 'Seriously, how close are we? Have we signed already?'

Even though my heart was racing, I gave him a naughty wink before returning to my desk. I fell into my seat and searched through my emails to see whether Rania had replied. She hadn't, so I held my head in my hands. Looking back at Hannah's office, I found her in deep conversation with Selina and her suits, poring over the data sheets I had given her.

'Hey, you look defeated,' Ella called across.

I turned to her and smiled.

'The bid for the hostile takeover, it's less profitable but I can't seem to make them believe me. They're sifting through my figures to discredit them.'

'Whatever plan you're concocting, don't do it,' she advised as I looked down at the two business cards I had filed away.

'I think I just found my conscience,' I murmured. I shut down my laptop, bagged it up, and collected my belongings. 'Ella, I'm not feeling well so I'm going to take the rest of the afternoon off.' I avoided her continuing advice as I put on my mac and slipped off my heels to pull on my trainers.

'I don't need to know, do I?' Ella said, accepting my decision.

I shook my head and looked back at Hannah's office. Hannah noticed my departure and narrowed her eyes. She continued staring, but I wasn't afraid of her any more. I smiled and nodded, before leaving the office.

I waited for Zach in the bar overlooking Broadgate Circus in Liverpool Street. It was only 3 p.m., but financiers, brokers, bankers and the rest were already drinking and mourning over the tough day they were having. Nervously I sat with my orange juice and waited. I needed advice, and as with everything in the past four months, Zach was my only steering point.

'Hey,' he said as he unbuttoned his suit jacket and sat opposite me. I looked at him, surprised by his lack of affection, and noticed his agitated demeanour. 'I don't have much time, Yasmin. What's up?' I stared at him, worried by the way he avoided my eyes and checked his Breitling.

'Is everything OK?' I asked as he looked at me, waiting for me to get to the point.

'Your family haven't said anything?'

'I've been heads down in this project.'

'Well then, let's get to your precious project.'

I stopped at his curt instruction and waited. He stared at me until I did as he asked.

'There's going to be a hostile takeover for Baby O,' I leaned forward to announce.

'If Hannah's decided that's the best strategy, you're not going to stop her . . .'

'You know Hannah well enough to influence her. Tell her to reconsider.'

'Stop,' Zach breathed. 'Stop,' he repeated when I went

to make my point. 'Hannah is an industry veteran; she was brokering deals before you were born.'

'Stop defending her like she's your idol.'

'Be careful, Yasmin. I've known Hannah a lot longer than I have you.' His words caught my attention. His blind allegiance and admiration for Hannah angered me.

'What are you saying? That you won't help me?'

'You have been in the industry five minutes and you're trying to prove a veteran wrong.'

'That's my point. She's dealing with this like she's some sort of chess guru, like she's moving a few pieces in the right direction until the opponent has no choice but to crumble.'

'Winning is the ultimate aim, Yasmin.'

I stared at Zach. Something had changed in him; he was acting like a stranger.

'There are different ways of winning . . .'

'Yasmin, I don't have time to debate semantics. You're an analyst in private equity; do as you're told, learn the game and then play it.'

I shook my head and stared at him until he looked at me directly.

'This isn't a game, Zach. This is about Rania and her family business.'

'Listen, if they were doing their jobs, they wouldn't be in this position.'

'She's only been in her job a few months. She needs more time,' I told him.

'Why do you care so much?' Zach asked me, barely containing his anger.

'Because I know how important it is to have that one person believe in you to change the course of your life.' Zach paused at my words and finally looked at me. 'She can do this, Zach. I know the turnaround strategy inside out and I've judged all the variables. She will dispose of non-core assets, locations and stock to revive the label. She's got a rebranding concept and sales strategy, she's got all the players, the designer, the manufacturer, the store layout manager . . .' I paused as Zach rubbed his jaw and shook his head. 'We've got a five-year financial model that generates Namhar Capital three and a half times the profit the alternative strategy provides.'

That fact caught his attention. For a while he debated whether or not to get involved. Finally he looked at me.

'Are you sure about the figures?' I nodded. 'Has Hannah seen these figures? If your facts stand up, I know that she wouldn't choose the alternative.'

'She has, but she just doesn't believe in a five-year turnaround strategy. She wants an exit strategy now,' I told him as he finished my drink for me.

'Get Raj to go over every number with a fine-tooth comb for both strategies. Make sure the business case for the turnaround is strong, watertight and more profitable for Namhar Capital.' I nodded at him, biting my lip to hold back a smile. 'Get that done before the takeover meeting next Monday. Richard Haverford is chairing that meeting. As founder, he chairs all hostile meetings. If Hannah doesn't change her mind, make sure Rania's armed with the strategy, data and facts. If the facts speak for themselves, Richard Haverford will act in the best interests of the firm.'

'Thank you, Zach,' I said.

He stared at me, nodded and then left. I knew he felt disloyal to Hannah, and I knew he wasn't happy about what he was doing. I didn't know anything about the past they shared, and for now it didn't matter, because I was the new woman in his life and today he had chosen me over her.

*

I went home and switched on my laptop straight away. Rania had sent me through the latest approved strategy and data. I laughed when I saw that she had further negotiated down the manufacturing costs, increased the number of store disposals from sixteen to twenty, and secured Zamil Hussain for four seasons. Moreover, the model showed that the turnaround strategy could be accomplished in four years and not five. Digging out the business cards from my pocket, I noted Amira's email and jotted down what I had to do.

To: Amira@Fahani.com, *Rania@Jayachand.com*
From: YasminYusuf7@hotmail.co.uk
Subject: Women in Business

Asalaamalaikum Amira,
My name's Yasmin Yusuf, better known as the 'stupid girl' during the lunch you had with Rania Jayachand at the Habtoor Grand in Dubai. You said to Rania to get in touch with you if she was close to running out of time, so I'm here to tell you she has less than a week to save Baby O.
I am writing to you without counsel and as a woman listening to her instinct, knowing in my heart that giving Baby O the chance to be is the right thing to do. Being able to cite your Fahani Inc. as an investor may just allow that to happen.
Having integrity isn't just about giving advice, it's about living up to it too. I hope that the data attached with this email will convince you that this indeed is a profitable venture for you not just to save but to continue the success that you have already started to gain.
Regards,
Yasmin Yusuf

As soon as I sent that email off, I began my next one.

To: Sharmila.Aurora@managementinc.com
From: YasminYusuf7@hotmail.co.uk
Subject: Airport Incident

Dear Sharmila,
My name's Yasmin Yusuf, I'm the lady who caught your son as he raced towards that dangerous balcony in the airport last week. I'm sure this email may come as a bit of a surprise, but you asked me to get in touch with you if there was anything you could do for me.
There is.
I'm an analyst for Namhar Capital in London and working on a turnaround strategy for a boutique lingerie label. The founder is Rania Jayachand, of the Jayachand dynasty. We have a make-or-break meeting next Monday morning to prove this lingerie label is worth saving. I believe it is, as Zamil Hussain has agreed to design its range. It dawned on me that we would have a stronger business case if you agreed to be the face and body endorsing this label. Please agree to help me.
Yasmin

The odds were stacked against me but I was prepared to take them on, if only to tell myself that I did everything I could to win. I smiled at that thought. Maybe I wasn't cut out for private equity, maybe I was doing business as an emotional woman; either way it didn't matter. What mattered was that I was in control of the doing.

*

I didn't pass on the new data to Hannah. The following days I went in and worked diligently to get through my workload, to buy me time to keep plugging away at Baby O. Zach arrived for a meeting with Hannah. When that meeting turned into a raging argument, no one in the office was left in any doubt that Baby O was at the heart of it. The office had never felt more tense. Hannah, Selina and the suits rushed off to never-ending closed-door meetings with lawyers, bankers and accountants, whilst the rest of us waited to see what hand would be dealt. Ella, Raj and I kept a low profile to avoid getting pulled into the firing line, but Hannah's eagle eye left us in no doubt that we were being watched.

I raced after Zach and caught up with him at the elevators.

'Don't,' he warned me as I stopped before him.

'What happened?' I asked, pausing when he jerked away from my touch.

'Yasmin, I've done my bit for you. When are you going to do your bit for us? Or is there an us?'

'Of course there's an us.'

'Really?' I froze at his demand. 'From where I'm standing, the only time I'm of interest to you is when I can sort your career out.'

'That's not true.'

'Tell it to someone who thinks different.'

I stared at him as he stepped into the elevator and disappeared. Reeling from the argument, I headed back to my desk. I pulled out my mobile and texted him.

You're the man who makes my dreams come true. If I'm to design my success, you have to believe in me. You have to believe that that success means a lifetime with you. So please, believe in me.

I didn't hear from Zach, but prayed that he would

believe me, because I couldn't stop. Not now, not when I had so much to prove.

I checked my emails regularly and tried not to feel despondent that I hadn't heard from either Amira or Sharmila. Regardless, every day I went home to continue polishing the turnaround strategy proposal. At last, the early hours of Friday morning, I smiled as I found an email from Amira.

To: YasminYusuf7@hotmail.co.uk,
Rania©Jayachand.com
From: Amira@Fahani.com
Subject: Women in Business

My dear Yasmin,
A mere runaround girl with the passion of a lioness to save the business of my sister Rania humbles me. Having reviewed the business case and forecasted returns, I have spoken at length with Rania and agreed to establish a joint venture.
Thank you for making this decision easy for the head and the heart.
WaSalaam,
Amira Fahani

Whilst there was no reply from Sharmila, I couldn't stop dancing around the room. Then I realised that the strategy prospectus needed to reflect that news. I sat down and opened up the document, then called Rania with the changes for her to approve instantly. There was a lunchtime deadline if we were to get the prospectus printed by close of business. Taking a long swig of my coffee, I smiled. It was going to be a long day.

Lesson Eighteen:
The past always catches up with you

'It's done, it's done, it's done!' I celebrated come Friday evening as Ella, Raj and I headed down to Helen's fiancé's birthday bash. 'I'm shattered, but I haven't felt more invigorated by work in my life! How do I look?' I asked, nervous about seeing Zach for the first time since our argument. I stopped beside a Pizza Express to look at my reflection. I had on my Reiss perfect black trouser suit over a crisp white bespoke shirt, making me look tall, slim and cosmopolitan. I had left my hair free and curly around my shoulders and applied barely there make-up. I felt natural, healthy and glowing.

'Do you think you've done the right thing?' Ella asked just as I stopped to answer my mobile. Zach told me that he was parking in front of Mint Leaf and I agreed to find him before we entered.

'I've no regrets,' I told her definitely. 'If I hadn't done it, I'd be a clone like Selina, and I have more spirit than that.'

Ella laughed and shook her head.

'All I am saying is that I do not want to be accountable should Hannah find out,' Raj said.

'Oh Raj, she's not going to find out,' Ella said as she looked towards me nervously.

'I've given you my word, if she finds out, it'll be only my name she hears, OK?'

'OK, OK, that's fine. My heart is not beating that fast now,' Raj accepted, making us all laugh.

I spotted Zach at the end of the road and felt that nervous excitement as our eyes met.

'You good?' he asked, looking me over before greeting Ella and Raj.

'It's done. Rania's got the prospectus,' I told him with a wide smile. 'We're not stopping long. I skipped lunch, so let's say hi and bye quickly and go spend time on us, OK?'

'You sure?' I nodded and frowned at his comment. 'I mean, we could skip dinner and go rescue another business, or rope your friends into giving up their lives to help you . . .'

'You're not funny!' I stated as Ella and Raj laughed at Zach's teasing nature.

'She's the most dogged person I know,' Ella told Zach as we entered Mint Leaf and walked down to the bar. We handed our coats and bags in at reception and then walked into the darkly lit Asian fusion bar.

'Thank you for coming!' I whispered to Zach as he put an arm around my back.

'For future reference, I refuse to find you another job no matter how much you cry!' he said before we all burst out laughing.

'Yasmin!' Turning at Helen's perky call, we saw her rush over to us. 'Oh my God, oh my God, oh my God, you made it!' she said as she hugged me excitedly before she spotted Zach. She froze, stepped back and looked at me with a wide grin.

'You're welcome,' Ella muttered as she handed over

a paltry box of Quality Street to Helen. 'Happy birthday.'

I bit my lip at Ella's attitude and looked to Zach, who grinned at the look of disdain on Helen's face.

'So where is the birthday boy!' Raj asked excitedly.

'Let me take you over to meet him,' Helen suggested, as she wove her arm through Zach's to lead the way. I looked at Ella and rolled my eyes. 'Honey, I want to introduce my work colleagues to you,' Helen said as she patted her fiancé's back. 'Sam, you met Zachary Khan, private banker at Namhar, in Mumbai . . .'

I didn't register anything more. I froze as I looked at Sam, the man who had broken my heart. He recognised me in the same instant. My heart raced and my knees weakened, and I looked to Helen, who was staring at me. She had been his fiancée for the past year. I was his ex-girlfriend from several months ago. She was H from *that* text. I was the girl he was never going to marry. I was the one who was the bit on the side, not the other way around. Unable to deal with that truth, I listened to Helen talk excitedly as I felt unable to look away from Sam.

'Yasmin!' Turning to Zach's call, I realised that our silent exchange had been noted.

'You guys know each other?' Helen asked reluctantly.

'No,' we answered together.

'You look like you need a drink,' Helen told me as she took what looked like orange juice from Sam to hand to me. I accepted it to avoid a scene and to calm the fury welling in me. I was so angry that I was shaking. Shaking inside, outside, until I couldn't comprehend any feeling apart from the one telling me to get away.

'Excuse me, I need the ladies',' I whispered before walking away from the group.

I rushed towards the reception and headed for the

ladies'. Slamming into a cubicle, I locked the door behind me and threw back the drink until there was nothing left. When I put the glass down, I gasped for breath. I opened the top buttons of my shirt and leaned down to stop the explosion of emotions taking over. I shook my head wondering how I had missed it, how in all the conversations I had had with Helen, I hadn't pieced it together. And then it dawned on me. Helen didn't know. She had no idea that her fiancé had been cheating on her. She was so lost in the world of Helen that she was oblivious to his darker side. Not knowing what to do, I cried out in frustration.

'Yasmin?' It was Ella. I couldn't bring myself to talk, so I slowly opened the door and looked at my friend. 'It doesn't matter who he is, Yasmin, you're here with Zach.' I closed my eyes to stop the tears, but I nodded. She waited until I could look her in the eyes. 'Let's go,' she said when I had regained my composure.

I walked out with Ella and joined Raj. Leaving them chatting, I wondered off to find Zach, and spotted him engaged in conversation with people he appeared to know. I wanted to leave Mint Leaf with Zach so that there was no connection to my past. I stopped to make small talk with colleagues from Namhar Capital, all the while watching Zach move from one group to the next, wishing he would join me.

'Yasmin.' Closing my eyes, I heard Sam behind me. 'Yasmin, I'm sorry . . .'

'Don't,' I whispered. He jerked me around to face him, and I pulled my arm away.

'Look at me.' The voice brought tears to my eyes. I didn't want him to see he had any effect on me. 'You look beautiful, you've become stunningly beautiful.' Tears dropped over my lashes and down my cheeks. He had lied all the time we were together; it had been one big lie. Even after he was caught he had lied. And he was lying now. I couldn't separate what was worse, the confirmed deceit or the realisation that I had always been the other woman. All the pain he had caused welled up within me, and I wanted to cry for the girl who had pinned all her dreams on him. I turned my face away from him as he reached out to wipe my tears.

'Don't . . .' I said again.

'It should've been you,' Sam told me quietly. In that instant, the pain turned into anger.

'Don't you dare! I shouldn't have wasted a minute with you.'

'It wasn't meant to turn out like this . . .'

I took the drink from his hand and laughed a little too wildly.

'Yasmin . . .'

'Don't you dare,' I warned him before upending the drink in one go. I stopped a passing waitress. 'I want another one of this birthday boy's drinks.'

'Zach's watching our exchange. I suggest you smile when you talk to me.'

I turned around subtly and indeed found Zach watching. I smiled softly at him, wishing he would wander over and whisk me away. But he nodded and carried on talking. I felt cold without him, and in that moment I knew Sam was nothing. Meant nothing. I looked at him and grinned.

'Happy Birthday, Sam.'

'Don't go . . .'

'We have nothing to say to each other.'

'I miss you . . .'

'My heart bleeds,' I returned as I took the drink from the waitress and threw it back before she left. 'Another one,' I ordered.

'You cut me out of your life without a chance to explain myself.'

'It was the best decision I made.'

He reached out to take my arm, but I held out a hand to warn him to stay away.

'Because you have your filthy rich banker, I'm not good enough any more? What do you think he'll do if he finds out about us?' Sam asked, his grin failing to hide the expression of contained anger.

'Why don't you tell him?' I tested.

'You're bluffing!' he mocked, sneering at me.

'Am I?' I taunted with a raised brow, ignoring the light-headed feeling that filled me with a confidence I didn't know I had. 'Let's face it, Sam, he's a better man than you. He's more successful than you, he's way richer than you, and guess what, he doesn't have a secret fiancée.'

'You think I won't do it?' Sam asked with a slow, controlled laugh.

I took the drink the waitress returned with, and waited until his laugh slowly died.

'Let's!' I agreed, nodding emphatically. 'In fact, why don't you tell Helen too? Whilst you're at it, why not tell everyone what a skanky, cheating, gutless wonder of a man you are?'

His grin faded fast and he glared at me.

'You think you can treat me like shit because you got some fancy banker wrapped around your finger.'

'No, Sam, I can treat you like shit because you deserve to be treated like shit,' I corrected, holding his eyes until he realised that I was serious. He shoved past me. I was shaking from the exchange and I finished off my drink. Placing the empty glass down on a nearby counter, I took a backward glance at Zach and then left to get some air.

*

I didn't know whether it was hunger or the fresh air, but I was woozy and buzzing. The exhilaration of escaping Sam's shadow and putting him in his place left me light-headed. Feeling overcome with emotion, I waited until I stopped shaking, and put the giggly giddiness down to high spirits. Taking a deep breath, I returned to the party, spotted Zach, and walked over to him.

'Hey, baby,' I said as I hugged him, looking at him closely. 'I'm glad you're with me,' I told him with a wide smile.

'You OK?'

I stared at his mouth to register what he said and then looked up at him before nodding. Holding the hand he placed on my hip, I turned to look at the cosmopolitan couple he was with. I felt giggly but I tried hard to remain composed.

'I'm Yasmin.' I stuck my hand out and waited for them to shake it. 'Nice to meet you.' My head felt fuzzy, so I kept smiling whilst the conversation continued around me. I watched them carefully, trying hard to keep up with the topic, but I couldn't focus.

'I love this song!' I shouted as I heard the Sugababes' anthem 'Here Come the Girls'.

'Yasmin . . .'

'Don't you like this song?' I asked, leaning towards the young blonde. She looked like she didn't understand me, so I repeated myself louder. 'Isn't this song by the Sugababes called . . .' I waited for the chorus and sang with it, *'here come the girls* brilliant?' She nodded and said something that didn't make sense. 'Huh?'

'I'm not a big fan of pop.'

I raised an eyebrow at the condescending tone and looked round at Zach to lean close to his ear.

'She's a bit ooh la la,' I told him honestly.

'Yasmin . . .'

'Don't tell me off. She's the one with the attitude,' I defended, pointing at the blonde woman.

'Excuse me,' Zach muttered. I stared at him as he took my arm and led me away.

'What?' I asked, trying hard to walk steadily next to him, but I couldn't.

'Did you have something to drink?' He seemed angry and I pulled my arm away to stare at him.

'I don't want you to buy me alcohol. I'm a Muslim,' I reminded him, annoyed by the suggestion. I pulled back but he grabbed my chin to look at me closely.

'What have you drunk?'

I burst out laughing at the closeness of his face. Only he didn't find it funny, so I suppressed my laughter and looked at him seriously.

'Zach, you know I'm a Muslim, why ask me for a drink?' I said, bending over because I couldn't stop laughing. The movement made the world turn upside down, so I shot up straight. 'Oh, my head is spinning,' I mumbled, holding it to steady myself.

Zach grabbed my arm, and dragged me behind him. I tried hard to keep up with him but I couldn't avoid bumping into him when he came to a sudden stop. 'Sorry, I didn't mean to . . .' I moved around him to look him in the eye. 'I didn't see you stop,' I told him, intent on making him believe me. But he wouldn't meet my eyes, so I cupped his cheeks to make him look at me. 'I promise you I didn't.'

'What did you give her?'

I frowned. 'I didn't give anyone anything,' I told him, trying to make him look at me.

He took my hands and turned me around with such force my head reeled. I heard angry words around me but all I could do was try and stop my brain from spinning. I opened my eyes and saw Sam and Helen standing with Ella and Raj. I beckoned Helen over to whisper in her ear.

'He's not a good man,' I told her, frowning when she jerked back.

'You're shouting,' Zach barked before turning to Sam. 'What did you give her?'

'He didn't give me anything . . . Zach, that's the point,' I told him, trying to stop him from getting angry.

'She took my drink from me,' Sam told him as Helen looked on in confusion.

'Ella, tell him. Tell Zach I didn't get my Schl . . . Schlumberger Tiff . . . Tiffany ring. I didn't get my marriage proposal. I didn't get nothing from him.'

The silence around me was confusing, and I covered my mouth, knowing I had said too much. I looked at Sam and gasped. It was him, he was breaking me up all over again. I shook my head to clear the cloudiness, but it didn't help. I didn't want to hurt any more, so I looked up at Sam.

'He lied. He lied to me . . . He's a liar!' I shouted, and I slapped him so hard the force of the impact made those around us gasp.

'Yasmin!' Helen screamed as Zach pulled me back. Sam held the side of his cheek and gritted his jaw. 'What's wrong with . . . Why did you . . .' Helen stopped suddenly and stared at Sam. She shook her head when he reached out to her.

'She's drunk . . . she's out of her head,' Sam told her before he turned to Zach. 'You need to control your woman . . .'

Helen screamed again when Zach hit Sam with such force that he fell to the ground. He struggled up to take Zach on, but Raj held him back.

'It's him, isn't it?' Helen asked quietly. I heard her

despite the confusion. Shaking, I dragged my arm free from Zach's grip to leave. 'Don't walk away from me. It was Sam, wasn't it? He's the guy who cheated on—'

'Helen, she's pissed out of her head. I rejected her advances and she's . . .' Sam pleaded.

'Shut up! Shut up! Shut up!' Helen screamed at him. 'Yasmin, please, tell me.'

I didn't want to have any part in what was unravelling in front of me, so I turned to Zach.

'I don't feel well. I want to go home . . .'

Turning to Helen, I held my head, trying to stop it from spinning. I pointed at Sam. My heart was racing and I felt hot and clammy and unsteady.

'He's not the one for you, Helen. Your fiancé is not a faithful man.'

'Don't do this,' Sam breathed, trying to get free from Raj.

'I thought he was the one for me,' I told her as I frowned at the pain he had caused.

'Yasmin . . .'

I held my hand up to a nervous Ella to silence her.

'He was my world and he broke my heart with . . . with . . . with empty promises and lies about a future.' I laughed as I remembered that text. I waited until the manic laughter passed. Taking a deep breath, I looked at Zach. 'I thought that I had caught him cheating with a bit on the side, but tonight . . . and here's the irony, everyone . . . tonight I realise that I was his bit on the side. Helen, he was cheating on you with me, and he's still trying to get you to marry him.'

My laughter died in the silence that faced me. Helen stared at me until she burst into tears and raced away. Sam broke free of Raj's grip and raced after her. I stood there, brow raised, waiting for someone to say something as everything started spinning around me.

'I'm going to be sick,' I whispered before racing off to the ladies', where I fell to my knees over the pan and emptied my stomach until I leaned exhausted against the cubicle wall.

'Yasmin?'

My head pounded and I turned to the door and found Zach watching over me.

'You're in the ladies',' I told him as I wiped my mouth. He was disappointed and tears stung my eyes. I looked away and held my hair back from my face. 'I forgot, he mixes his juice with vodka. I forgot,' I whispered as I dashed away the tears.

'I'll get you home.'

The sombre words made me close my eyes. I was exhausted. Tapped out. Spent. I nodded and walked over to the sink. I leaned over and washed my face with freezing cold water. He took a hand towel, soaked it in cold water and held it against my head. I closed my eyes at the cold compress and leaned against his shoulder.

'I'm still broken, Zach,' I said before exhaustion swept over me.

Lesson Nineteen:
Dreams once broken may stay broken

My head hurt the instant I opened my eyes. I shut them tightly and groaned, trying to remember how I got back home. I found I was in my room and still dressed in yesterday's clothes. I fell back on my pillow and held my head, quelling the nauseous feeling.

'Helen knows . . .' I whispered as bursts of memories flashed through my mind. I tried to remember everything I had said, but couldn't piece the memories together. And then the image of Daddy shouting blue murder made me shoot up in bed. I suppressed the nausea, ignored the sandpaper taste in my mouth and changed into my pyjamas, then raced downstairs and stopped as I found my brothers sitting in the kitchen with Daddy. No one acknowledged me. I couldn't remember what was said or done, and heart-racing, I hesitated at the entrance.

'Yaya, go have a shower.'

'Daddy, it wasn't my fault.'

'Go have a shower and then join us.'

The disappointment in his voice broke my heart. I waited for one of my brothers to talk to me, but the silence was damning. Turning away, I went upstairs. Something was wrong. My instinct told me something was very badly, drastically wrong. I called Zach and closed my eyes when it went into voicemail.

'What did I do?' I whispered when Ella answered her phone.

'Have you heard from Zach?' she asked. I was worried by the concern in her voice.

'Why? What happened?' My heart started racing with Ella's silence.

'Maybe you should call him . . .'

'I've tried, but he's not answering,' I told her as I stood by my door and peeked out through the crack to ensure no one could hear me. 'Ella, please.'

'Sam mixes his juices with alcohol, but you forgot that when you took his drink. You told everyone about Sam; actually, you slapped him so hard, diners at the end of the restaurant could hear.'

'Please, tell me what happened with Zach. What did I say to him?' I whispered with dread.

'It's not what you said, Yasmin. Zach took you home, your dad went ballistic, and he lost it when he saw the state you were in. Raj and I were in the car; we could hear everything.'

'Oh God no, they blamed him . . .'

'Your brothers were there too. They physically threw him out, they said all kinds of things, things about his parents, his mixed race . . .'

'Oh no!' I cried as tears stung my eyes.

'They told him that if he had a single ounce of decency in him, he'd leave you alone.'

I couldn't listen to any more. I told Ella I'd call her later and hung up. I redialled Zach's number, and dashed away tears when it went into voicemail again. Hanging up, I leaned my head on the door, if only to stop the queasiness I felt. Taking a deep breath, I forced myself to move. I did as Daddy asked. Showered, changed and then walked downstairs slowly. I entered the kitchen and took a seat at the round table. The silence was haunting but I waited. I waited and watched as Daddy placed dry toast in front of me and then poured me a cup of coffee. I caught his eye briefly, but he turned away and offered coffee to my brothers. None accepted.

'I'm disappointed in you, Yasmin.' Daddy spoke calmly, with the composure of a learned wise man. A tear tripped over my lash at his words. 'I thought you knew better.'

'It wasn't my fault . . .'

'Shut up, Yasmin,' Zamal muttered, barely containing his anger.

I looked at them, and my heart raced with fear. I shook my head. I had to put it right with Zach, I had to make them understand what they had done.

'You turn up drunk . . . drunk, Yasmin. A woman like you, from the family you come from, with the lessons we imparted to you, you turn up drunk . . . Do you know how shameful that is?' I went to speak, but one look from Daddy made me reconsider. 'But you go one step further. You get that man to carry you home.' I frowned at their misunderstanding and shook my head. 'How dare you?'

I jumped at the force with which he struck the table with his palm. I closed my eyes, I wanted to make them understand but I didn't know where to start.

'Dad wants you to move in with us.'

I turned to Jamal and shook my head. He refused to look at me, so I turned back to my father.

'W . . . why?' I whispered. 'You don't understand . . .'

'Why do you bloody well think?'

I started at Zamal's furious shout and tried to calm my racing heart.

'Zamal!' Daddy commanded before he looked down at

his clasped hands. 'I'm not capable of looking after you, Yasmin. I don't recognise you.'

'I'm me. I don't need to move home. If you'd just listen to me . . .'

'Listen to you? Are you stupid? You shamed the family, Yasmin!' Zamal shouted, jerking back from his chair to pace the kitchen.

'You're wrong!' I breathed.

'So you didn't get your boyfriend to drop you home drunk last night?'

'You've misunderstood . . .'

'He's a bastard child.'

'Don't call him that!'

'You're defending him? We don't know who you are any more!' Daddy shouted, making us stop. 'Pack up.'

'I'm not leaving . . .'

'What's happened to you?' Jamal asked quietly, frowning at me.

'Nothing, and I'm not leaving.'

'You peddle smut, traipse around the world, bring men to family events, and turn up drunk. What's happened to you?' Kamal said with disgust.

'My drink was mixed,' I whispered, looking down at my clenched hands.

'If you think you're ever seeing him again . . .'

'My drink was mixed . . .'

'We'll disown you if you ever see him again.'

'My drink was mixed!' I shouted and breathed raggedly as they stared at me. My father frowned and shook his head. 'The guy I told you about, Daddy, the one who messed me about . . .'

'What guy?' Zamal demanded, but Daddy raised his hand to quell his question.

'He was there. I forgot he mixed his drinks with alcohol. I took it from him but I forgot it was mixed. It didn't smell, it was like a fancy sparkling juice. I drank one after the other, not realising,' I explained. 'Zach realised straight away and went to sort him out.'

I paused and gritted my teeth. Zamal rubbed the back of his neck and Jamal cursed. Daddy looked at my brothers as I shook my head at what must have happened.

'It wasn't Zach's fault, Daddy. He looked out for me, he cleaned me up, and he brought me home.'

The silence that followed my words was deafening.

'Who's this man?' Zamal asked as he looked at me with regret. 'Yasmin, who is he?'

'He's a nobody,' I said.

'I want to know who he is.'

'Why? You've already done enough damage!' I shouted at my brother before stifling my tears.

Daddy looked at me intently, and then the realisation dawned on him.

'I owe Zachary an apology,' he muttered with his head held low.

I closed my eyes and felt the tears leave a trail down my cheeks. Pushing back my chair, I stood up to leave.

'Yaya . . .'

I shook my head at my father's call and left the kitchen to curl up into bed.

Throughout the day, I called Zach, left umpteen messages and sent even more emails. Daddy came and went, my brothers in turn came up to check on me; even my sisters-in-law appeared with varying desserts to cheer me up. I listened to the small talk, and then when I couldn't bear the dread of losing Zach, I asked to be left alone.

Time stood still, and each second that passed amplified the fear that I had lost him. Zach had given me hope when everything else failed. I recollected our evening together at the Burj Al Arab, the desert safari, and how we had spent the night talking in Mumbai. But by nightfall I had heard nothing, and I knew I had lost him. Tears seeped down my face and nothing I did stopped them.

'Hey, sweetie.' I heard Mia arrive and turned to look at her when she came and sat on the floor before me. 'You look like crap.'

Her comment made me smile, but my eyes filled up with tears and I couldn't stop crying. Mia leaned up and hugged me. She stroked my hair back until I had no more tears to cry.

'Your dad called me. He's beside himself, Yasmin,' Mia said. 'He's asked me to stay whilst he's at work. He told me what happened and he's so very sorry.'

I nodded but kept my eyes closed.

'I'm not mad at him,' I whispered, wiping away the tears. 'I should've left the minute I saw Sam . . . None of this would've happened if I had left.'

'None of this would've happened if you hadn't drunk his drinks.'

I listened to Mia's words, but it didn't make it OK. It didn't bring Zach back or undo the scars dealt by my family. I started crying again, from deep within the core of my being, until I curled up into a ball and held myself.

'He's not dead, Yasmin.' Mia's odd comment caught my attention. 'He's not dead.'

'But I'm dead to him,' I told her as I looked across at her.

'Did he tell you that?'

'I've called, and texted, and left voicemails and emails . . .'

'OK, I get it. He's mad at you, he's mad at your family, and he has every right to be,' Mia told me. 'But he's back in the office on Monday; at worst you can find him there. Sweetie, we'll get you to see him one way or another.'

'You think?' Mia nodded and her confidence made me sit up. 'You don't think it sounds a little stalkerish?' I asked in a dry raspy whisper.

'Yeah, well let's not think about that right now,' Mia said as I smiled. 'Oh my God, she remembers how to smile. No, no, no . . . don't lose it.'

'Mia, they said some unforgivable things to him,' I whispered as tears stung my eyes.

'And when Zach calms down, he'll understand.'

'You think?' I asked again.

Mia smiled slowly, and then stood up.

'Shift up,' she said. I made some room on the bed and she lay down facing me. 'Aren't you hungry?' I shook my head and smiled at her.

'I fell in love with him in Dubai, Mia. I wore the most beautiful Armani gown.'

'Girl, when did you start earning the kind of money needed to wear an Armani gown!' I laughed at her words. 'OK, OK, I won't interrupt.'

And so I began telling Mia about our time together in Dubai and Mumbai. I told her every detail, every stolen glance and loaded moment. We spoke late into the evening, and when Mia drifted off, I rose and slowly made wudu, ablutions for prayer. When I returned to my room, I laid out my prayer mat and stood on it. I had nothing left to lose and everything to gain. Allah gives and he takes, that's what we believe. In my short life I had lost a lot, felt a lot of pain, but I never turned my back on Allah, so now I prayed for him to be fair. I asked him to answer my prayers, to give me the strength and patience to win Zach back.

*

On Sunday I woke up early, checked my phone and found there were no messages. I covered Mia with my blanket, changed into my tracks and headed down into the kitchen. I looked in the storage cupboard and brought out my assortment of cleaning products and tools. I switched on the radio, where Lady Gaga sang 'Just Dance', so I pulled on a pair of Marigolds and threw myself into it. I started in the kitchen. There was a method to my cleaning: dusting preceded wiping, which was followed by scrubbing and cleaning, that was then finished up by sweeping and mopping. Only when the room was gleaming with everything back in its place did I move on to the office. I applied the same principle there and then to every room, until all there was left to do was plump the cushions and place them neatly on the leather sofas.

For fear of waking Mia and my father, I left the stairs and the first floor. Instead I put my materials away, washed up and then concocted a feast for breakfast. Fresh pancakes with cream, blueberries and honey, muffins, cheese toasts, scrambled eggs with beans were all laid out in covered dishes ready for breakfast, when Daddy would inevitably be joined by my brothers. A shower seemed like heaven, so I stood beneath the power shower until I felt alive. I changed into a pair of jeans and a white shirt with black pumps, then, grabbing my work bag, I scribbled a short note for my father and headed out to the office.

Steve allowed me in without any hesitation and I headed up to my desk. I busied myself with tasks that need completing and searched the internet. Silently I prayed that Zach would appear like he had done previously, but deep down I knew he wouldn't. I stared at my phone, looked at Zach's number and then called him at work. My heart raced when it was answered, but I felt like an idiot when it went through to voicemail. Replacing the receiver, I looked back at my computer and opened up Baby O. I promised myself I wouldn't get involved, but I needed to keep myself busy. I called Rania and she wished me long life, telling me that she had just been talking about me with her advisers. I smiled at her down-to-earth nature, and agreed when she invited me to join her advisers' meeting via a conference call to prepare for the big showdown with Hannah tomorrow morning. Before long I was switching between documents, forecasts, projections and facts. I challenged and was challenged, I proposed and counter-proposed and outlined key strategy benefits until I felt I knew Baby O better than the founder herself. When I hung I up, I felt exhausted. Steve wandered up and told me that the office was going to be closed, and I realised that I hadn't eaten. I switched off my computer, grabbed my bag and made my way down. I walked past Steve and then paused to look back at him.

'Did Zachary Khan pop in today?' I was positive his eyes softened at my quiet question, but he shook his head and I smiled at him. 'Have a good evening.'

The house was empty when I returned home. Daddy had left a note telling me he was going round to Jamal *bhai*'s house to give me space. I dropped the note and walked through to the kitchen. He had cooked my favourite dish, chicken korma with sticky rice, and laid it out for me. I dropped my bag and took the plate to the island, where I perched on a stool. The house was unnervingly quiet. Pushing the plate away, I wandered through to the living room and switched on the TV. *Pretty Woman* was on ITV2, and I smiled as Julia Roberts appeared in that red bustier dress that made Richard Gere lose his breath. I closed my eyes. I was too tired to cry. So I kept them closed until I succumbed to sleep.

Lesson Twenty:
When that unimaginable, bewildering, wonderful thing does happen, you feel alive

Everyone arrived extra early on Monday morning. Dressed in sleek flared black trousers and a fitted pink shirt, I sat at my desk watching Selina and the suits race between offices in preparation for the meeting. Helen appeared make-up-free, hair pulled back in a tight bun, and devoid of any expression. She avoided any interaction, headed straight for her desk and silently got to work.

'You OK?' Ella asked and I nodded. Nervously I tapped my pen against the desk as I watched Rania arrive with her team and head for the conference room. She stopped at my desk and leaned down.

'Thank you for everything. We'll speak after the meeting,' she said and whisked off before I could reply.

'You, in my office.'

I didn't have time to look at Hannah as she stormed past my desk with her PA racing to keep up with her. I knew she would be mad as hell when she discovered the new data. I expected to be fired, but I didn't expect it to happen before the meeting.

'Close the door,' she instructed when I entered the office. Shutting the door behind me, I took a seat before her. 'How dare you?'

'The figures were provisional. I tried to warn you but you wouldn't let me speak. But it was noted on the sheets . . .'

'How dare you judge my son?'

I paused, wondering whether the pace of the private equity deal had gone to her head. Frowning, I looked around to see if there was anyone else in the room.

'Ms Gibbs-Smythson, I think you have the wrong person . . .'

'How dare your family throw my son out like some third-class citizen?' I covered my mouth, balking at the realisation that she was Zach's mother. I shook my head, unable to accept the implications of her words. 'People like you walk around like victims of racism; you use that badge to every advantage, wave the flag until the PC police turn up . . .' For the first time, I saw Hannah upset. She was close to tears but she refused to look away as she took a deep breath and composed herself. 'You had no right to judge him.'

'Hannah . . .'

'You want to know what real racism is? What it does?'

'Please, give me a chance to explain . . .'

'Zachary's father left me in a one-bedroom flat in Shadwell. I was sixteen, with a family that disowned me for falling in love with a Bengali man. He told me he was coming back, so I waited for him to come back. But he didn't.'

'Please, I didn't mean for—'

'I brought Zach up single-handedly. I studied when he slept and taught him what I learnt. Coutts gave me a part-time secretarial job and I grafted until I was taken seriously so that no one would ever think I was insignificant, that my son was insignificant.'

'You don't understand,' I pleaded as she walked around her desk to face me.

'I understand that he was thrown out on to the street and called a mongrel.'

'Please . . .'

'I told him to stay away from your lot, I warned him.'

'You're mistaken . . .'

'Your time here is limited, Yasmin. Start looking for another job,' she told me as she grabbed a tissue to dab at her eyes.

'You can't do that,' I whispered, and she laughed in a way that failed to reach her eyes.

'Blows can be dealt in many ways, Yasmin. You think I'm unaware how you've been more loyal to Rania than to Namhar Capital? How you and your little friends gave her the financial models, scenarios and data?'

I froze at her comment.

'I want to make it right with Zach . . .'

'Oh, you're too late, darling,' Hannah said as she pressed her intercom. 'Get my files together for the meeting,' she ordered, and then paused, surprised to see me still looking at her.

'Why . . . why do you say that I'm too late?'

'Reality bites, Yasmin. There are no second chances in life,' she told me before walking past me to head off to the showdown meeting.

'Wait!' I called out after her. 'Please let me know why you—'

'Stay away from him, Yasmin. You and your family have done enough damage.'

Stunned by the cold warning, I stepped back and watched her leave. I was too late. I frowned, wondering what she meant. Shaking my head, I refused to accept her word. I raced to my desk and grabbed my bag and jacket.

'Yasmin!' Ella called out to stop me.

'I'm going to find Zach,' I said. And then I raced straight into Sharmila Aurora.

'Yasmin, I've been trying to find you all morning.' The entire office came to a standstill at the sight of the Indian superstar.

'You came,' I whispered as I looked back at the conference room.

'I couldn't not come!'

I laughed nervously at her comment, knowing that every second that ticked past meant I was closer to losing Zach.

'Yasmin, the meeting . . .' Ella whispered as she sidled up with a pen and paper for Sharmila to sign. I stared at her in exasperation when she handed me her mobile to take a picture with the star. When I refused, she pinched me until I relented. Then I grabbed Sharmila's hand and raced her through to the conference room. Before we entered, I stopped and looked at her.

'What's the size of your fan base?' I asked.

She frowned and looked at me. Then she took my hand and smiled.

'Yasmin, I earn fifty million pounds annually in endorsements for one territory alone. Trust me when I tell you I can help Rania sell Baby O.' I looked at her and frowned. 'I'm wearing Zamil Hussain underneath. I'm sure the male decision-makers will appreciate the new product line if they can see it with their own eyes.'

I stared at her in silent admiration before we both squealed and jumped with excitement. 'We have to go in!' she breathed as we stopped and composed ourselves. With a quick nod, I knocked and walked into the middle of Selina's introduction.

'Excuse me, I'm sorry to interrupt, but Ms Sharmila

Aurora, Bollywood superstar, supermodel, and business-woman extraordinaire, has arrived to join Ms Jayachand's team.' I caught Rania's shocked expression as Sharmila entered with a confidence that belied her knowledge of what she was getting into. 'She's agreed to be the international face and body of Lady O.'

The gasps around the room were only mitigated by Hannah's ice-cold indifference. She refused to acknow-ledge me, and I knew I had to go and put things right with Zach. With a quick smile at Rania, I turned to leave.

'Hold on a minute . . .'

I paused and peeked my head back around the door.

'Hello!' I breathed out in surprise as I stared at the man who had helped me at Southwark Bridge the day after I discovered Sam's infidelity.

'Broken heel lady! How on earth are you!' He laughed as I walked in to shake his hand. 'You work here?'

'Yes, yes I do. I'm in Hannah's team . . . I'm Yasmin, Yasmin Yusuf.'

'Yasmin, Hannah's runaround girl? I take it it was you who took the initiative to get this lovely actress involved too?' I nodded. 'And it was you who pulled the turnaround strategy document together. And I see you still insist on wearing ridiculous heels?' I laughed as he shook his head when I raised my trouser leg to show off my four-inch court heels. 'It's an impressive strategy, Yasmin. I look forward to hearing the case for it.'

I looked round at Rania and smiled broadly.

'Thank you . . .'

'This is Richard Haverford—'

'*The* Richard Haverford?' I breathed, cutting into Selina's irritated introduction. I smiled as he nodded. 'What are the chances that you saved me at the bridge and now you could quite possibly save the first turnaround project I have had the privilege to work on?'

Richard chuckled at my comment and then jumped at the thud of the files Hannah dropped on the conference table.

'Are there any more stunts you want to pull, or shall we just cancel the meeting now whilst you two have a friendly catch-up?' she demanded.

'I should leave,' I whispered to Richard as I backed towards the door. 'It was nice meeting you,' I said before turning around.

'Wait.' Once again I froze and turned around. 'Since you worked on much of the strategy, it's only fitting that you sit in on this meeting.'

I heard Hannah's frustrated mutter, and Selina's irritated huff. I needed to go find Zach, but I considered the opportunity Richard was offering me. I would never work again in private equity if I refused. I looked at Hannah nervously, then nodded with a smile.

'If it's OK with everyone, I'd be delighted to.' Rania, Sharmila and the team all beamed to confirm their approval. 'I'll just get my folder.' Excusing myself, I rushed across to Ella's desk.

'Richard Haverford's invited me to the meeting.'

'Yeah, sure,' she muttered.

'Ella, I'm serious.' I waited until she looked up from her screen.

'You're serious!' I nodded and watched her scream with delight. 'I wish I could see Hannah's reaction!' she laughed.

'Hannah's Zach's mother.' She stopped laughing as I nodded again. 'Don't tell anyone, but she hates me. In fact, after the meeting I don't think I'll have a job.'

'She's Zach's mother!' Ella mouthed in disbelief.

'I'm diverting my phone calls to you. If it's Zach, please come and drag me out of the meeting. This is my password; check my emails and let me know if he contacts me,' I told her as I scribbled down my user log-in details. Then, grabbing my notebook, phone and strategy documents, I hurried back to the meeting.

Quietly I took a seat next to Sharmila and listened to Selina. From the get-go the meeting was intense. Notes, questions, challenges, interrogation of figures, forecasts and valuations left everybody exhausted. I caught Hanna's eyes many times; she gave nothing away, and I wished things were different. When Rania stood up to introduce the pitch for the turnaround strategy, she faltered and Selina's suits smirked with laughter. I glared at them before watching as she looked around the table and continued to stutter nervously.

'Potty break?' I called out, whilst raising my hand. Everyone including Richard looked at me like I had lost my mind. 'Nature break? Time to wash hands . . . Can we have a five-minute break?'

Richard looked amused at my behaviour and chuckled.

'Well timed,' he accepted.

As members of both teams filed out to take a break, I walked upto Rania and took her aside.

'I can't do this,' she whispered as I shielded her from the icy wilting stares of Hannah and Selina. 'Yasmin, you have done more for this project, you should do the presentation. I . . . I can't . . .'

'Rania, look at me.' I waited for her to stop hyper-ventilating. When she looked at me, I stared at her without warmth. 'This is not about you, about how well you speak, your accent or what they think about your apparent lack of experience. This is about your family, about their reputation, their worth. Remember that vision you had for Baby O?' She nodded. 'That's all you have to talk about. Don't worry about the rest. Talk about the vision.'

She stared at me until my words sank in. Then she looked at me as if a light had been switched on.

'Thank you, Yasmin,' she whispered before she walked to the head of the table and stared down at her notes. Putting them aside, she waited for everyone to return. And when they did, she began.

She captivated everyone with her first words, and a small smile played on my lips. I watched with bated breath as she dealt with challenges, questions and criticisms with the poise of a grand visionary. Where we could, we pitched in, but Rania ran the show and it felt great to believe in the vision she spelt out. The attendees burst into laughter when she presented Sharmila Aurora, but the laughter soon transformed into stares of admiration as the actress paraded Zamil Hussain's product. Sharmila refused to be mere eye candy, and when she spoke with confidence about her influence and reach, Rania beamed with pride. She knew her vision was close to becoming realised.

Girlfriend, you had better answer your phone right now, and I mean right now.

I froze and along with everyone else looked down at my phone. It was Mia. She must have news about Zach. I caught Hannah's worried expression and prayed it was good news.

'You had better answer that,' Richard advised with a glint in his eyes. Grabbing the phone, I looked at Rania, who mouthed, *Thank you*, and then left the grand room.

'Mia, Zach's in his office, isn't he? I'm on my way,' I said as I raced towards my desk.

'No.'

I came to a stop at her quiet answer.

'Mia?' My heart thudded slowly and I frowned. 'Mia, tell me?'

'He's taken the job in Dubai, Yasmin. His android of

an agent told me that he's sealed the deal to move out there. She refused to comment on whether he's already gone, but since his calendar's been locked, it looks like he has,' Mia said as I leaned back against my desk. 'I'm so sorry, sweetie.'

'That's OK.'

'Yasmin, I'll come round tonight.'

'No, I'll be working late. Stupid Cupid, what was I thinking, right?' I said, laughing at myself even though I wanted to cry. I cleared my throat and stood up. 'OK, Mia, thanks for letting me know. I gotta jump back into a meeting.'

I hung up and folded my arms around me. Then, taking a deep breath, I headed back to the conference room.

Early evening we finished up, and left Richard Haverford and his committee with all the strategy documentation, forecasts and presentations to consider. I saw Hannah storm out of the room closely followed by Selina and the suits. I trailed behind them despite the strong presentation that the Baby O team had pulled off.

'Yasmin.' I stopped and looked to Richard. 'I was very impressed by your performance today.' His comment made me smile. 'It's not often that a mere runaround girl amounts to so much.'

I shook my head. 'You should have given me more credit, Richard,' I told him with half a smile. 'Hannah Gibbs-Smythson was the original runaround girl. I'm learning from the best.'

Richard laughed heartily, whilst pointing at me. Shaking his head, he struggled to find words and then said, 'Hannah considered you to be a liability, but I'm holding on to you, young lady.'

'If you release Yasmin, I want her to head up Baby O's transformation into Lady O in Dubai,' Rania stated. I stared at her, then at Richard. 'I'm serious. Whatever it takes, Yasmin, I want you heading it up.'

'Rania, you've had one tough fight today saving Baby O; you're going to have one hell of a fight stealing Yasmin from under our noses!'

I stared at the two leaders and left them to it as I went in search of Hannah. I stood by her office and watched her lose it with her team. When I refused to be ignored any longer, I knocked on the door and stepped in.

'I need a word with you, Hannah,' I said. Selina and the suits gawped at my courage.

'I'm busy.' The smirks caused by Hannah's response didn't put me off.

'Get out,' I told them as I held the door open.

'Who the hell . . .'

'I'm the person who's already lost her job, Selina, so get out before I throw you out!' I shouted and watched them hurry out.

'You've got some nerve.' Hannah's calm collected words made me smile.

'Then we have another thing in common.' I closed the door and took a seat before her desk.

'I have nothing in common with you.'

'We have Zach in common,' I corrected and caught her attention. 'I love him and I can't lose him. You have every right to be mad, angry, hateful of me, but equally you have to accept that I love him and I want to spend my life with him.'

'Your family . . . what about your family?'

'You think I'm going to repeat your experience with Zach, that I'm going to abandon him like his father abandoned you?'

'He's the only thing I have in this world.' The quiet admission brought tears to my eyes.

'Daddy wants to apologise. What he said was

inexcusable, but he said it as an angry father who believed Zach had taken advantage of his baby. He knows that he made a huge mistake; my entire family do.' Hannah sat down and switched on her computer. 'We're not all the same, Ms Gibbs-Smythson, we're not all racist, narrow-minded people. Ask yourself this: if you stand in my way today, how different are you from people like that?'

Hannah paused and looked at me for a second. Then she looked back at the screen and made notes. Crying out in frustration, I spun around to leave.

'Yasmin. Zach's flying out late tonight. You can find him here.' I turned back to her and saw her holding out a note to me. 'Don't hurt him like his father hurt me.'

Nodding quickly, I nervously stepped forward and took the note from her. I wanted to hug her, but I knew she still needed time to accept the very thing she feared most. So I smiled at her thankfully before I turned around to leave.

'Yasmin?' Once again I looked back at her. 'Well done on Baby O. Your instincts are impressive. In fact you remind me of me when I started out.' She managed something that resembled a smile, then without another word she stared back at her screen.

Turning around, I raced over to my desk, and froze when I saw Daddy and Mia talking to Ella.

'What's going on?' I asked, causing them to turn and face me. 'Daddy?' I whispered when he held out my coat and bag for me.

'We don't have any time, Yaya, we need to go now.'

Frowning, I looked to Mia, who rushed over to grab my arm to make me hurry up.

'Zach has an evening flight to Dubai. He's at an inauguration reception at the Gherkin; you have less than forty-five minutes to get there before he leaves.'

'What . . . what . . .'

'Stop waffling. We're going to put this right once and for all,' Mia told me as she took my files and dropped them on my desk.

'Daddy . . .'

'We have a cab waiting downstairs for you, Yaya. We have to hurry otherwise it'll get moved on.'

Throwing myself into Daddy's arms, I laughed with joy.

'We have to go,' Mia shouted, pulling me away as we rushed towards the elevator.

'How . . . how did you find out?' I asked Daddy as the elevator took its time arriving.

'Mia told me about the unhelpful secretary Zach has, and I went to visit her.'

'You visited his office?'

'Mia showed me in,' Daddy confirmed with a proud smile. 'I had a gentle word with the young lady, explained to her the situation and she was more than helpful.'

'You're amazing,' I breathed as Mia seconded that. 'Daddy, Zach's mother is that lady over there,' I said, pointing towards Hannah's office to find her staring at us.

The elevator arrived and chimed open behind us.

'You're not coming with me,' I whispered, and he nodded before searching his pockets. He extracted a ring and placed it in my right hand.

'This is the ring your mother gave me. I want you to give it to Zachary. Tell him this is my apology and my blessing.' Tears slipped down my cheeks at my father's humility. He brushed them away before pulling me into a hug. 'Let me go make my peace with his mother, Yaya. You go and find Zach, and know in your heart that he makes you glow.'

I hugged him again, lost for words and overcome with emotion.

'Go put it right now, Yaya!' Daddy laughed. 'You're going now!'

'Cry any more and you will miss Zach,' Mia said as she dragged me into the elevator. I watched the doors close and looked at her. 'We're going to put this right,' she promised.

'I'm not dressed, Mia.'

'Of all the things you want to worry about . . .'

'I'm going to try and get Zach to believe in me, and I look like—'

'Yasmin, you do not have time for a makeover,' Mia told me as she cupped my face to smile at me. 'Trust me, you look beautiful.'

I nodded at her comforting words and then breathed deeply until the doors chimed open. We rushed to the exit where a black executive car waited for us. Mia jumped in and I followed.

'I'm really going to do this,' I whispered.

'You're going to do this,' Mia confirmed as I gripped her hand.

I looked at my dearest friend and nodded with the most nervous smile. She nodded too and I looked out of the window as we headed towards the iconic Gherkin. As adults we programme ourselves to fear pain, to fear rejection, to fear fear. We become so paralysed with that fear that we forget that sometimes the unimaginable, the bewildering, the wonderful can happen. The truth is that when that unimaginable, bewildering, wonderful thing does happen, you feel alive. Right now, I felt wonderfully alive.

Lesson Twenty-One:
Happy-ever-after only comes
if you chase it

We arrived at 30 St Mary Axe with fifteen minutes to spare. Slamming out of the car, we raced into the Gherkin's impressive reception lobby. Spotting the marketing team, we rushed across and found Zach's secretary, Ingrid. I avoided her steely stare, and waited as Mia spent five minutes convincing her to give me access to the reception deck. I heard the clatter of stilettos and found the android had come to stand before me.

'I'm giving you my access card; do not lose it,' Ingrid stated as she handed me a plastic card. 'Head for the thirty-ninth floor and then take the stairs up to the bar. You'll find Mr Khan there.'

I looked at her in surprise, and though she didn't smile at me, she nodded towards the turnstiles to encourage me to go find Zach.

'Go!' Mia shouted as if to bring me to life, and with that I raced through the turnstiles towards the lifts.

Stepping into the elevator, I pressed for the thirty-ninth floor and watched the doors close. Then I scrambled through my bag to reapply my eyeliner, lip balm and blusher. I brushed my hair into glossy order, thanking God that I had straightened it into a flowing bob that morning. Clearing my throat, I neatened myself up, wishing I had chosen a hundred other different tops or styles to work.

Feeling my nerves reach breaking point, I gasped when the elevator came to a sudden stop. When the doors slid open, I stepped out hesitantly and looked around slowly. I circled the dining area and became concerned when I was unable to spot Zach. I took the circular stairs up to the bar. Excusing my way through groups in conversation, I spun around, worried that I was unable to see him anywhere. I kept scanning the space with its breathtaking views of London at night, until someone called me.

'Yasmin Yusuf?' Turning at the call, I recognised one of the suave bankers that Zach had introduced me to at the gala dinner in Dubai. 'Am I mistaken?'

'No!' I laughed. 'Not at all. It's good to see you again, albeit in less glamorous attire,' I said as I shook his hand.

'Are you meant to be here?' I paused at the question and shook my head as he chuckled in amusement. 'I'm sorry, you look . . .'

'. . . out of place,' I finished as I looked over his shoulder to see if I could spot Zach. I looked back at the banker and smiled. 'I'm not actually an invitee, I'm here to find Zachary Khan,' I explained, shaking my head as he offered me a drink.

'He's over there.'

Looking across in the direction he pointed, I found Zach in conversation heading towards to the exit. Even from a distance he turned heads, dressed in a tux, fully poised and groomed. I looked back at the banker and smiled.

'I'm sorry, but I have to . . .'

'It was nice seeing you.'

Nodding at his understanding, I headed off, weaving around the patrons until I reached the stairs. My heart pounded as I tried to keep Zach in my line of sight. Taking the stairs down, I perched up on the tips of my toes to ensure I was heading in the right direction.

'Excuse me,' I whispered as I knocked a drink out of a stunning model's hand. 'I'm so sorry,' I added before moving on. I lost sight of Zach and looked back at the stairs, wondering if I had the guts to call out to him. Shaking my head, I moved in the direction that he had been heading, rushing around people to find him. In that moment I became caught between two large groups that had arrived. Edging through them took some effort, and when it became impossible, I turned around and sought an alternative route. Feeling increasingly anxious, I rushed towards the exit and heard the chimes of lifts. Pushing past people, I stopped when I spotted Zach enter one of the elevators.

'Zach!' I called out, and froze when he turned around. I noticed his gorgeous companion, and looked back at him. He looked stunned at my presence and I lost my ability to speak. I frowned at the woman beside him and watched as the doors slid shut. 'Wait!' I shouted, running towards them. The steels doors closed as I came to a stop in front of them. I felt the stares and heard the hushed whispers and speculation around me. Leaning my head on the steel doors, I closed my eyes and shook my head. Then Alicia Keys' song 'A Woman's Worth' came to mind. And in that moment I knew that I had more to give than Zach realised. I refused to believe, to accept, that I had lost him.

Pressing the button, I waited for another lift to arrive, wanting to catch him in the lobby. Racing into the elevator, I pressed for the lobby floor. I stared down at my clenched hand and slowly opened it. The ring sparkled up at me. Closing my fist tight, I anxiously paced around the small space until I arrived at reception. Racing out, I spotted Mia.

'Have you seen Zach? He came down.'

'What are you talking about?'

'Did you see Zach?' I demanded as I searched the lobby area. Mia shook her head. 'I saw him just as the lift doors closed. He should've come down by now.'

'He probably got off at the next floor and headed back up to find you.'

'He was with another woman,' I told Mia across the turnstiles.

'A blonde woman with an Audrey Hepburn dress and stilettos?' Ingrid asked as she came over to see what all the fuss was about. I nodded at her question. 'That's his new PR agent. She's here to personally invite the best financial players to Zach's inauguration party in Dubai.'

'He's gone back up, Yasmin, and that's where you need to be heading.' Mia pointed to the lifts.

'This is . . .'

'Stop talking and go seal the deal, woman!'

Laughing at Mia's orders, I turned around and raced back to the elevators. When one arrived, I stepped in and headed back up to the thirty-ninth floor. The climb back up felt like it took forever, and I thought I was going to lose my mind. When the bell chimed the lift's arrival, I took a deep breath and watched the doors slip open. Slowly I raised my eyes and found Zach waiting. My heart pounded so loud that I thought he would be able to hear it. I took a deep breath and stepped forward until I stood before him. We stood there for what seemed like a lifetime. I hadn't prepared anything to say, so I wasn't ready for his question.

'What do you want?' The stern tone told me I had a

tiny opportunity to get him to listen. Only my brain felt like it had chosen the worst possible time to go on strike. I stared at him, struggling to find the right answer. Eventually he lost his patience, shook his head and turned away.

'I'm not here for work,' I told him to stop him from leaving. He looked back at me. 'This, me being here, it has nothing to do with work.'

'Ladies and gentlemen, if you take your seats, the evening will formally begin,' the compère announced. I waited as those around us hustled fast to get to the dining area.

'I have a cab to catch to the airport, so are you going to tell me what you're doing here?' he asked again, drawing my attention back to him. I didn't know what to say to undo the hurt and humiliation that I had caused him.

'Zach,' I whispered, frowning as I clenched my hands, and causing Zach to stare at me in confusion.

'Is it the deal?'

I shook my head.

'Will you be joining the inauguration ceremony?'

'No,' we both snapped at the assistant who disappeared quick smart. This wasn't what I had imagined. Making amends shouldn't be this difficult, but I was lost for words. The elevator opened behind us to allow in latecomers who raced to make the start on time.

'Goodbye, Yasmin.' He left me standing and walked into the elevator. I shook my head and breathed out before racing in behind him. He looked at me with a mixture of anger, confusion and pain. The doors slid shut behind me and I stared at him as he came to a stop before me. I didn't know what to say, so I held out my hand.

'What is it?'

I smiled nervously and opened my hand. He looked at

the ring and then back up at me with narrowed eyes.

'My dad gave it to me to give to you.'

'Your father banned me—'

'It's his ring,' I explained as he stared at it. 'He gave it to me to prove to you that he is so very sorry and to show you that he's given us his blessing.'

'He's sorry?' I nodded at Zach's question and heard the anger in his tone. 'Do you know what he said to me, what he said of my birthright?'

'Zach . . .' I stopped when he shook his head and stepped back away from me.

'You don't know, do you?' he demanded.

I held his eyes and then shook my head.

'He can't take back what he said, but he can ask for you to forgive him.'

'That's why you're here, to apologise for your father?'

'No, Zach. I'm here for you.' The admission stunned him as it did me, and I saw what it meant for him to hear those words. 'My mother gave this ring to Daddy when they got married,' I told him as he looked at the ring for a few minutes before meeting my eyes. 'He's ashamed of his behaviour, Zach. He went to your office when Mia told him that you could be flying out to Dubai; he badgered your secretary into telling him where you were. Forgive him,' I asked as I leaned forward to cup his cheeks. 'Please believe me.'

'My mother . . .'

'My father's with her now. I left him to make peace with her.' I smiled tentatively when Zach nodded in consideration.

We arrived at reception and the doors chimed open to a gathering of late guests.

'This lift's occupied,' Zach told them and pressed for the doors to close before hitting the emergency stop button. I looked at him and smiled.

'Your father's given his blessing?' he asked. I nodded.

'He says you make me glow and that's enough for him,' I told him, willing him to forgive us.

'And Sam, the guy who failed to give you the Schlumberger . . .'

'Ssshhh,' I whispered, placing my finger on his lips. 'He means nothing to me.'

'He really left you hurt . . .'

'Yes, he did,' I agreed and stared at him directly with a smile. 'If he hadn't, I wouldn't be here now. And I would go through it a hundred times over if it meant I could be with you.'

Zach narrowed his eyes as if to assess my sincerity.

'Forgive us, Zach, forgive me.' When he remained silent, I knew he needed more. So I stepped back and took a deep breath. 'Be with me,' I asked with every dream, hope and prayer beaming from within me. I paused when I saw the sparkle of amusement appear in his eyes.

'Are you proposing to me, Ms Yusuf?' Zach finally asked.

I smiled, but shook my head and watched his grin fade.

'I want the package, Zach, that's the only thing I'm proposing,' I corrected.

'So you are proposing to me,' he persisted. When I looked at him he was serious. 'I can do the package, Yasmin. I want the package.'

Nodding, I closed my eyes and nervously took a deep breath.

'Then I'm asking you to be with me for ever, always, for infinity,' I told him.

His silence worried me and I watched him until he took my hand and opened it up to look at the ring.

'I suggest you put this on then,' he said.

I contained a smile and took his hand. Holding the ring, I slipped it on to his engagement finger and stared down at it.

'It's written, Zachary Khan, we were meant to be,' I told him smiling when he looked down at the broad matt ring.

'You still want the Schlumberger, don't you?'

I laughed at his question and wrapped my arms around him as he pulled me into a bear hug. The doors buzzed before sliding open, and we looked around at the security guards who had prised it open, along with Mia, Ingrid and the marketing team. A chorus of giggles and clapping erupted. I looked at Mia with a wide smile, and at all those from the marketing team who cheered us on. Then I looked back at Zach.

'You think it's time that we gave up this lift?' I asked, and smiled when he shook his head.

'This one's all mine,' he stated as he reached out to hit the button. I laughed as everyone whooped cheekily when the doors slid shut. 'You good with that?'

'Zach, I'm the Deshi girl living the dream,' I whispered as he spun me in his arms until we laughed with joy.

There's a saying that all good things come to those who wait. I waited a long time and yet I think differently. I say better things come to those who choose to live, who choose to fight and who choose to laugh. There's never a better time for doing that than when you're single. It's a given that there'll be a happy end for the Deshi girl who dares to dream. I dared, I dreamt and I fought for that dream, and it gives me great pleasure to announce that I have now arrived at my happy-ever-after.

little black dress

brings you fantastic new books like these
every month - find out more at
www.littleblackdressbooks.com

Why not link up with other devoted Little Black
Dress fans on our Facebook group? Simply type
Little Black Dress Books into Facebook to join up.

And if you want to be the first
to hear the latest news on all things
Little Black Dress, just send the details below to
littleblackdressmarketing@headline.co.uk
and we'll sign you up to our lovely email
newsletter (and we promise that we won't share
your information with anybody else!).*

Name: _____

Email Address: _____

Date of Birth: _____

Region/Country: _____

What's your favourite Little Black Dress book?

_____

How many Little Black Dress books have you read?_____

*You can be removed from the mailing list at any time

Pick up a *little black dress* – it's a girl thing.

978 0 7553 4334 8

IT SHOULD HAVE BEEN ME
Phillipa Ashley
PBO £5.99

When Carrie Brownhill's fiancé Huw calls off their wedding, running away from it all in a VW camper-van seems an excellent idea to her. But when Huw's old friend Matt takes the driver's seat, could fate be taking Carrie on a different journey?

'Fulfils all the best fantasies, including a gorgeous, humanitarian hero and a camper van!' Katie Fforde

TODAY'S SPECIAL
A.M. Goldsher
PBO £4.99

When chef Anna Rowan and boyfriend Byron Smith are asked to star in a reality-TV show about their restaurant, TART, they find themselves – and their relationship – under the hot glare of the TV cameras. Do they have the right recipe for love?

A.M. Goldsher serves up another deliciously quirky and original romance.

978 0 7553 3996 9

Pick up a *little black dress* – it's a girl thing.

978 0 7553 4743 8

ITALIAN FOR BEGINNERS
Kristin Harmel
PBO £5.99

Despairing of finding love, Cat Connelly takes up an invitation to go to Italy, where an unexpected friendship, a whirlwind tour of the Eternal City and a surprise encounter show her that the best things in life (and love) are always unexpected . . .

Say *'arrivederci*, lonely hearts' with another fabulous page-turner from Kristin Harmel.

THE GIRL MOST LIKELY TO . . .
Susan Donovan
PBO £5.99

Years after walking out of her small town in West Virginia, Kat Cavanaugh's back and looking for apologies – especially from Riley Bohland, the man who broke her heart. But soon Kat's questioning everything she thought she knew about her past . . . and about her future.

A red-hot tale of getting mad, getting even – and getting everything you want!

978 0 7553 5144 2

You can buy any of these other
Little Black Dress titles from your
bookshop or *direct from the publisher*.

FREE P&P AND UK DELIVERY
(Overseas and Ireland £3.50 per book)

TO ORDER SIMPLY CALL THIS NUMBER

01235 400 414

or visit our website: www.headline.co.uk

Prices and availability subject to change without notice.